$HORT CHANGED

Dream Weaver Press
P.O. Box 3402
Annapolis, MD   21403
www.dreamweaverpress.net

ISBN 0-9746847-1-6

Printed in the United States of America

Cover model: Fitz
Doublefitness@aol.com

Photography: Earl Anderson
Africanheart71@yahoo.com

$hort Changed

A *novel by*

Andrea Blackstone

DREAM WEAVER PRESS

ACKNOWLEDGEMENTS

Thanks be to the Creator, once again, for allowing me to write another novel. What God has for me cannot be erased from my destiny. I pray that I can reach people with my words and thoughts, for an ultimate good, regardless of genre.

To my family:

Mom, I miss you so very much. I know you are in Heaven looking down on me. To the very end you encouraged me and defined love and goodness. I'll never forget you and I carry you in my heart every day. Had it not been for you I never could have completed either book. Your inspirational book is coming, I promise it's next on my list! You're still my best friend and always will be. Dad, thanks for doing everything you can in your power to help me to shine. I'm crossing my fingers that I'll make you very proud someday. I appreciate all of your love and support. Thanks for encouraging me to hang in there with my goals this year. Dana, thanks for being a good cousin.

To my friends:

Ivy, you have no idea how much I appreciate your help. You're one sharp sister! Thank you so very much for encouraging, supporting me, and checking in on my mom. Special thanks go out to Mr. Trotter for still being a great mentor to me, and Ericka for rushing over to comfort me when I needed a friend. To B.C., thanks for being a special friend to me this year and talking me through the hard times. Les, you're my favorite Q Dog! Thanks for your friendship and support. Nneka, you reached out to me and I appreciate it greatly! Taurus, thank you for helping out immensely. To my small circle of friends who are like my family, I cherish each one of you and I hope you know it.

To my writing network:

Special thanks go out to Arazel, the Evans family at Expressions in Baltimore, Lee at Karibu Books, Emlyn at Mejah Books, and of course, Earl Cox. Thanks to Tee Royal for her encouragement, and Gary at Black Men in America. Thanks to all of the readers who supported me by purchasing their own copy of *Schemin': Confessions of a Gold Digger,* and those that took the time to email me to let me know they enjoyed Jalita's crazy, jacked-up world. Fitz, you're an awesome cover model. Thank you for bringing Malik's likeness to life. Earl, you know your stuff! I appreciate the dedication of those who helped me to put this together. Lastly, thanks go out to those who contributed letters for this project. I'm honored that each of you allowed me to share your thoughts with others.

This novel is dedicated to my beloved mother who passed away while I was working on this sequel.

1

IF A WOMAN'S FED UP

Malik

"Wake up, boo, we're here. Are you ready to gamble?" my girlfriend Diamond asks.

"Hell yeah," I answer groggily. "It's been a minute since I've been to Atlantic City." I stretch my arms and yearn to stretch my legs after that three-hour car ride, but I still feel too lazy to peel myself up from the cracked, tan leather bucket seat.

"Well I'm glad I picked somewhere you think is worth going," she says, smiling. Today I was thinking—Malik and I need to talk, chill out and just act like lovers. What we need is an entire uninterrupted weekend of dinner, dancing, gambling, and walking along the boardwalk. We need this *us* time. So I hope this road trip I've planned is something my baby will never forget."

"Damn, Diamond! I don't know what's gotten into you but I like it." I smile and lean my freshly shaven baldhead back on the headrest which is covered by a clear, plastic hair-conditioning cap to keep it clean—how ghetto is that?

"It's called returning what's been given to you. Now hurry up and get it together. We're on a schedule tonight and the weekend will fly by if we let it," she says excitedly.

"Ok, ma," I reply, unlocking the door and finally raising my arms toward the darkening sky. Diamond gets out too.

"I have reservations for *Bally's* on the Boardwalk. Planet Hollywood is only one block from there, an outlet shopping mall is two blocks away, and they have four casinos. Count 'em—four! I've never been to Atlantic City so this is going to be the shit!"

"Well that all sounds good, but if memory serves me correctly the cross street is Park Place and you just turned on Marin Boulevard. Diamond, what are you doing, boo? Do you know where you are? You say you've never been here before so I think you're slightly off on your directions." I chuckle heartily. "You know your ass can't drive or follow a map anyway."

"Nigga, didn't I tell you I've got this under control?" she says playfully. "We're going to the Sandbar first. We can sip on a few drinks, and then get something to eat in the restaurant. Now let's go in and enjoy that Manhattan skyline I've heard so much about. I came all the way from Southeast, D.C. to get a good look at my man under the backdrop of a prime nighttime view. Everyone's talking about the Casbah but I hear everyone gets lined up and waits to get their ID checked before they can even get inside. I didn't want you to have to wait in a line 'cause I know that's not your style." She pauses. "Look at me going on and on. I'm sorry for rambling. It's just that I want to make up for all the times we argued, and when you put up with my kids crawling in bed with us when we were trying to be alone. If I have my way tonight I'll make all the wrongs right. Over the last few days I've realized how much I love you, and I've been thinking maybe I don't show you enough."

I walk over to Diamond, hug her warmly and rub her shoulders.

"Damn, Diamond. Don't worry so much. You need a break too. You can come back fully refreshed and able to take on life in the hood on Sunday."

"You're right," she agrees with a smile.

I release her from my embrace. When I look into her eyes I'm reminded she isn't fine enough to deserve my undivided attention. She's one of those chicks that look good from afar or with a face full of makeup, definitely not deserving of my chocolate sexiness. After all, I'm 6'2", a solid, muscular 240 pounds, and look much better than my fraternal twin who thinks he's a certifiable bitch magnet. But thoughtful shit like this makes me forget about Diamond's beauty deficit, and the meat that jiggles under her arm long after she's stopped moving. I wish someone would suggest plastic surgery and a personal trainer, but I'm not the one because she'd be looking at me to pay for it. I look at her raggedy kinky twists and the expression on her face.

"Shit!" Diamond exclaims.

"What is it?"

"There's only room to leave one bag in the trunk of the car because Twan's car seat and the Playmate Cooler is taking up the room on the backseat. One of us is going to have to take our bag inside. I can't chance nobody breaking into my shit," she explains.

"No one's gonna break into no car with age on it. Believe that. They have much better rides to break into if they're gonna do it. Don't be paranoid," I say to assure her.

"Maybe, maybe not, but where I'm from you don't assume. We're down to one set of wheels so taking that sort of chance wouldn't be wise, now would it?"

"If it will make you feel better I'll carry my bag in, ok?"

"Thanks, boo. It'll make me feel so much better."

Diamond kisses me on the cheek then licks me on the neck. Tingles run through my body, and I suddenly feel the vibe of being in Jersey with a freaky hood rat that apparently will treat my ass like a king just to save our makeshift relationship.

After lugging the suitcase inside, we are seated in one of the Sandbar's lounges listening to a tune I don't recognize. Moments later we are placing an order for two glasses of wine, which the bartender brings to us quickly. Diamond raises her glass.

"A toast to me and my man," she says. "Sometimes you gotta live it up 'cause you can't take it with you when you go!"

"Here, here!"

We clink our glasses to officially mark our journey in Jersey, and flirt with each other like we did the day we met. Right now I'm looking forward to letting the hang over I'm going to earn wear off, and getting my dick sucked in the process. This outing is truly a step up from the usual—Diamond standing over the stove in some run over scuffs that should've been thrown away last year sometime, serving me greasy eggs and fatty bacon that she never bothers to drain. Naturally she serves me first, making her kids eat after I get served and eat my seconds. And then we do the same shit all over again until it's time for her to go out, earn my money, and bring it home to daddy. What a dumb, *dumb* bitch! When

God was giving out brains I have no idea where Diamond was, but thank God for naïve women! Every man needs at least one woman who will always be there despite the obvious disrespect that he dishes out. Without women we can take for granted, the game would be too hard to play and women would put an end to our trifling game plan. But that day will never come. Most women deny reality. They'll keep and claim us until we give them gray hair, another baby, a disease, or a wake-up call—like another woman calling home explaining where we've been and how long. Even with all of this women have a hard time cutting us loose when they know they should. Now whose fault is that? Not Malik's.

Diamond's voice snaps me out of my trance. "What are you thinking so hard about? Let me in on the big secret, Malik. Don't be selfish with your thoughts."

"I'm thinking about how lucky I am to have a woman who knows how to treat a man. Someone I can count on holding shit down. You know—a ride or die chick. I like that in you, Diamond."

After we finish our wine we walk into the restaurant area. The waiter walks up and asks what we'd like to order.

"Prime rib for me and he'll have lobster. We'll start with the shrimp cocktail with some of that nice red sauce on the side, if you have it."

I sit there and don't say a word. I have no idea why a struggling, single mother would order the most expensive shit on the menu and continue to run up a tab, but it's not my business since she has the money to pay for our feast.

Three appetizers, five drinks, and two entrees later, Diamond gets up from the table.

"Where are you going," I ask, looking up at her.

"The wine and those virgin daiquiris have me needing to pee. Be right back, boo. Finish your food." She winks and switches away in her tight, dark blue jeans.

I pat my stomach because I'm full to the brim. "I can't eat one more bite. Hurry up so we can check into our room," I call after her.

Diamond stops and turns around. "I hope your jaws aren't too tired. You know I'm not a fan of niggas who refuse to go downtown. When we check in you better give it up after I treated you to first class shit."

I laugh when she walks away. I'm still chuckling and sipping on my liquor when my cell rings.

"Baby, I think I dropped something important from my purse when I got up. Can you look to see if it's on the floor or anywhere nearby?" Diamond asks sounding flustered. "Hurry up and look for it before someone else finds it—I had our hotel money in there. Damn, damn, damn! That was all of the cash I had on me!"

I place my drink on the table and start looking around. "I'm looking, I'm looking. You'd lose your head if it wasn't screwed on your neck. I see it. Everything's ok, Diamond."

She sighs. "Good looking out. Thank God. Goodbye. Now I can pee with peace of mind."

"Bye, fool." I begin to laugh again, enjoying the relaxing feeling that's taking over my body. I feel my shoulders loosen and the muscles in my neck limber up. When I end the phone call I discover that my name is written on the small envelope.

MALIK, OPEN THIS NOW!

I figure it's some kind of romantic game Diamond's playing to kick the evening into high gear, so I smile, pick up the envelope, and unfold the piece of paper inside.

Since I won't be able to put your needy and greedy ass on an income tax return I just wanted to let you know that I'm putting the brakes on you. I've already changed the locks to keep your ass away and keep your fingers off my glasses, plates, and Independence Food Card. Don't think I haven't noticed that you love to put in time making your way to the refrigerator, but you can't seem to put food in it. Your key to my place is of no more use to you, so you can take your shit elsewhere—like those that you betrayed me for. I've definitely hit the delete button and you won't ever have to run up in this piece ever again, put your greasy head and stinking feet up on my couch, clip your toenails on my rug, or live off me! You're a liability and you will not insult me inside the four walls where I pay rent, while you refuse to be a man and get a JOB. Why is it that the few months I been dating you, you managed to lay your ass up on my couch all day, eat up my kid's food, while steady

*telling that lie that you're going back to the NFL this season?
The season has already started...remember? I'm not tolerating
this off no nigga with no paycheck or respect for me and my
four kids. Have you ever thought about the fact that you're a
bad example for my son? He's got a little job now and pays the
phone bill, while you pay nothing! I'm trying to raise a man and
you're standing in the way of me being a good, strong mother.
You came to visit me one damn day and ended up moving bags
of dirty laundry in, bag by bag. Next thing I know you've got
your shit stacked in a closet from floor to ceiling, I'm washing
dishes three times a day, paying sky high electric bills, and
wishing your stale farts didn't smell like some animal crawled
up in you and died. I left you stranded out here in Atlantic City
to make sure you understand I'm serious as a heart attack about
the words in this letter. It took me all week to write it until I was
satisfied with every line, comma, and period. When you leave
my life, keep looking straight and don't turn back because no
nigga's pimping me. In fact, I pimp niggas! Malik—we're
through. In case you need me to spell it that's T-H-R-O-U-G-H.
Now pay attention to why you are about to find yourself stuck
with an expensive liquor and meal tab in Jersey.
Your ass busted up my Honda Accord and wouldn't even
change the oil, racking up mileage and shit. I'm surprised we
even made it to Atlantic City without breaking down. That was
all my ex left me and the kids before he went to prison when
his stupid ass was shot during that robbery attempt—you knew
that. Then you turn around yesterday and tell me you don't
have half your rent money, but I find out you're treating
unworthy bitches to dinner, clubbing like you deserve a break,
and tipping ashy ass strippers well. I can't even convince you to
put a bulb in the porch light, take the trash out to the curb, or
wipe your tail good enough so when I wash your drawers I
don't have to put up with pre-treating the skid marks with a
stain stick 'cause I'm sick of buying you new ones every other
week. What do I look like—an innkeeper, a bank, your
momma, your unpaid trick? You aren't on anybody's football
roster. I won't go into details but I know enough about you
being a broke down baller.*

If people in the housing office found out that your ass was laid up in my spot over night for as long as you've been, I'd lose my housing voucher. Then what? You don't give a shit if me and my kids turn up homeless. I'm tired of taking a gamble on you. Don't try to come around my neighborhood anymore because I've got people watching to make sure you stay out of dodge, and just remember that I have shady affiliates. Take your alcoholic ass and enjoy the Manhattan skyline while you wait for some unsuspecting gullible sucker in a skirt or low rider jeans to come to your rescue so you can start doing your damage elsewhere in someone else's life. In fact, maybe you can get a cell phone in "her" name and run it up to six hundred dollars like you did me. I guess you didn't stop to think whose cell phone I was using since mine was cut off because of you. Well it's my new man's, and you best believe I am coming up and will pass you this lifetime. I've got more shine that you'll ever know, so pick up your damn lip off the floor of the Sandbar and grow a plan to get your no-good, midnight black ass a ride back to D.C.

YOU NEED TO GROW UP AND BE A MAN. You won't be doing it on my time though, and that's the end of that. As for myself, I have a hair appointment, am getting my ass in Curves Gym, and am going to start saving money to go back to school. The next time you see me I'll be all that and a bag of chips again 'cause I'm getting me back! And to all my home girls around the globe, this shit was for you and me!

Diamond

P.S. You snore like a fucking bear! Now my kids and me can finally get a good night's rest. There's a disorder called sleep apnea. You might want to get checked to make sure that all that racquet you make is normal.

When I finally finish, I grab my suitcase, jump up from the table, and nearly trip on the tablecloth. I run to the parking lot to determine if this set-up was all a twisted trick to teach me a lesson for being a player. When I see the empty parking space where

Diamond's four-door burgundy car had been parked I know that it's no set-up.

"Shit! She's gone!" I yell into the night air.

"Hey, you've got a check here to pay. Where do you think you're going?" said a voice from behind me. "Catch that man—call the cops!"

I take off running. What am I supposed to say? I don't have the money today and some bitch put my ass in a sling? Since I don't have one dime in my pocket and that explanation won't fly, I figure that the best thing for me to do is run and puff, then puff and run, and hope the wait staff can't catch me. Small beads of sweat ball up on my forehead, and I'm thinking that if I only had my brother Wes's life I'd be straight.

2

BABY DADDY DRAMA

Wes

"Look, I'm going to warn your hardheaded ass one more time. Don't call me, don't two way me, and don't nose around to find out what city I'm in. When I dropped some dollars in your hand to get the abortion and take yourself on a shopping spree—that was it. If you don't stop stressing me out, by morning your husband will find out that you're a team whore who will do anything when you drink too much good liquor. Peace."

I hang up my cell phone hoping that one of my many side pieces will forget what my digits are. This is why I have two sets of cell phone numbers—none of the freaks like her will ever earn my respect enough to be taken seriously. They give it away then expect a baller like me to treat them like a lady. Who cares about that dick slurping principal's wife anyway? She's got one more time to piss me off, and it's on. If she doesn't leave me alone I'll mail that tape of my boys running a train on her and her sister to the school where she teaches kindergarten. The tape wasn't rolling when it was my turn, so who cares? What's wrong with her talking shit about wishing she hadn't aborted the baby? I found out she told all five of us she was pregnant, and of course we all dropped a few bills in her hand. We all knew better than to raw dog two whores, but we did it anyway. I don't know about what the others smelled, but that rotten fish odor should've told me that hitting that was a bad idea. You can find the worst sluts at any club—it never fails.

My addiction to pussy proves that some people shouldn't become fathers, and I'll be the first to admit to myself that Wes Montgomery is at the front of the line in that department. My raging hormones got the best of me in my teenage years, like those that belong to most illogical teenage boys that aren't interested in the consequences. I kept pushing the issue, pushing the issue, and pushing the issue to have sex until I got my girlfriend pregnant the very first time she agreed to open her pretty brown legs to experience the pleasure of adulthood with me or anyone else.

My scholarship was waiting for me, and I accepted the hook up I got from my guidance counselor at Dunbar High School with real appreciation. There was no I'll seize the opportunity next year. Had I stayed around playing daddy in the hood in Baltimore, I wouldn't have shit today—not a pot to piss in or a window to throw it out of. I can admit to myself that the way I left in that taxicab in the middle of the night was truly fucked up, but never to my ex's face. Marquita was in her last trimester of pregnancy, and had almost gotten kicked out of the house for her slip up. I promised that I'd come back for her and our baby after I made some critical moves, but I never made that call for her to come join me. Although I was less than an hour and a half away from a girl trying to be a woman and raise a baby without her mother's guidance, I didn't bother to call or visit. In fact, I never returned to Baltimore during those years fearing that someone we knew would see me and run their mouth about bumping into the missing person—me. Come to think of it I never even had the courtesy to let her know where I was living and how life on the basketball team was going. I just lost interest in my prior life. All I wanted to do was look ahead and dream of the smell of sweat funk, the sound of the buzzer, and fantasize over experiencing the roar of a cheering crowd that was shouting for an NBA team that I was a part of. Magic, Larry Bird, and Dr. J were all my idols. I had posters plastered on my dorm wall to prove it. I think I thought of them more than Marquita or the baby. In fact, I know I did.

Although I was "bribed" to attend the school of my choice, the sports car, spending allowance, special treatment, and tuition free education didn't go to my head. Basketball came first and school came second. Booty came third because I knew that if I made it to the NBA, there would be plenty of time to get laid and fuck around at my leisure. The way I laid out my life's map worked well for me; I stayed focused and met every goal. The problem is that since my ex reminded me on national TV that I've been missing in action most of my daughter's life, things haven't quite been the same in my world. Negative press began to surface on CNN, and then spread like wildfire to ESPN and every local channel around the country. The next thing I know I'm "that nigga" that's used as an example for all of the athletes who have children out of wedlock and experience an intentional memory loss when it comes to taking care of them. If I were a snitch I'd take all month naming names of players—white and black—who need to stop acting like they ain't hit something out there, ignoring what may be one of many child support obligations. If the truth be known, several of my boys and teammates have at least five illegitimate rugrats to claim. The thing is I'm not a snitch, so I'll take the heat and pay for my failure to do the right thing now that the public is all up in my business. Mistake duly noted.

I went from making eighteen points per game to nearly getting traded to Chicago. When coach called me to the back of the plane after the Blitzers were depending on me to whip some Detroit ass, the look in his eyes told me I'm was about to have a short shelf-life if I didn't get my shit together and represent rather quickly. I'm not out of the woods, but trying to face my daughter has helped me to focus a little bit more—enough to temporarily save my job, at least.

As I explained during the last press conference, I love my daughter, and it was never my intention to deprive her of the child support that she deserves and the law rightfully requires. To be honest, I never really thought about my daughter, as she got older. The NBA and kids just don't mix unless you force them to. Those two things are like oil and water—maybe that's why I lost the courage to desire them to coexist. I didn't appreciate what Marquita did by putting my business out in the street, but I can't help but respect her for having balls big enough to put me on the spot in front of the whole nation. My question to her is: How can I be a responsible parent when my father and mother set the tone for me to be a deadbeat dad?

My father ran off to be with a white woman who was married but still flirting. He also slept with half of Maryland on a regular basis. Who knows how many half siblings I have out there. I don't

19

even want to know. As for my mother, drugs crept into her life after my dad left, and within two months flat, she was a junkie—asking me to tie a rubber piece on her arm so she could shoot up in the living room and get high of off heroin. And that ain't the half of it. Eventually she gave up on being a parent all together and began parading her ass on Baltimore Street looking for any paying customer when she wasn't stripping and running around with a pimp who portrayed himself as an agent for entertainers. I don't know where she is today; come to think of it, I don't give a shit. My way to escape my fucked up dysfunctional family blues was to take it to the hoop. It was really the only way that I could cope and retain my sanity.

As if that isn't enough, life has been hectic for me these days. I try to get a piece of new ass in town and it turns out that my half sister was the one putting in overtime with me. I know that's nasty and bizarre, but the best way I dealt with it was to pretend it never happened and keep that secret in my front pocket. If the press ever got a hold of that, I could kiss my whole career goodbye. I'd never be able to restore my image, no matter what. About a month after that disaster and my crazy live-in nutcase trying to bust a cap in my ass for cheating, I went back to having sex, which I love. I can't give it up although I've tried, but so far it's only been something to pass the time. Even though many faces come and go, I finally came to realize that my baby's momma was the only woman I've ever loved and may ever love from now until I die. With each sunrise and sunset in each city I visit I crave my first love's touch, smile, and presence. Fuck that Marquita's married—I don't care. I'm going to prove to her, our daughter, and myself that the three of us were meant to build a home *without* her so-called janitor husband who is standing in the way of progress. I'm not scared of him or anyone else. They don't call me Wes, the best from the east to the west, for nothing. The nigga with the championship ring is about to remind Marquita of what's been missing.

After hearing two light taps on the door I look through the peephole and see Marquita waiting for me to open it. She's come to The Ritz Carlton in North West, D.C. to pick up our daughter. This was Dominique's first visit with me during game time and it's been quite an exhausting experience. How many times can a child ask the same questions? What difference does it make if the crusts are cut off of the bread on a sandwich—food is food! And then of course she won't go to sleep unless you leave a nightlight on because she's still afraid of the dark. They don't *have* nightlights in hotels—even five star ones. After the first night of meeting her list of demands I summoned twenty-four hour help to keep her entertained. No, I didn't take my daughter to see the Lincoln Memorial, the Washington Monument, or China Town, but the nanny *helped* me with that and did a bit more for me after Dom Dom went to sleep. I'm still deciding if it's true that blondes do it better 'cause that Spanish brunette, Soledad, is in a *league* all of her own. I said I was going to stop fucking the help but I just can't seem to break my bad habit. Maybe next time—maybe. It's just something about hitting it from the back while hearing Spanish sensually uttered with every stroke. I don't know what in the hell, "Te quiero papi. Te amo" means but all it did was give me the hard-on of a lifetime. I hear two more taps.

"Who is it?" I say just to fully annoy Marquita.

"Wes, open up. I know you can see me through the peephole. I heard you walking to the door. Stop playing games with me," she says impatiently.

I open the door to the suite slowly. Marquita looks me up and down like she's getting paid to inspect me thoroughly. I'm wearing my favorite diamond in my left ear, freshly showered and cologne fresh, donned in nothing but my boxers. I smile innocently, like I don't realize I'm half naked, showing my six pack abs and well-toned body—both compliments of several rigorous workout routines with a bossy, overpaid trainer that tells me what I already know from experience of training each season.

"Where's Dominique?" Marquita asks, crossing her arms defensively.

I smell her Dolce & Gabanna Light Blue perfume and lick my lips.

"Have you been beautiful all of your life or have I just forgotten how fine you are? I'm thinking the answer to that is yes. Damn, I just answered my own question." Marquita laughs and shows off

21

her nice smile. "What's funny? I meant what I said, beautiful," I reply.

Her smile quickly turns to an ice-cold expression.

"In case you haven't noticed, I'm not one of your groupies, Wes. Drop the act. I believe I came to pick up my daughter, not to have the displeasure of listening to one of your generic pick-up routines. One time was truly enough to last me for life."

"Hold on, she's okay. I need to talk to you for a minute though, parent to parent. This isn't about us, this is about her, so can I—I mean, may I, please have a word with you?"

I purposefully hold the door open wide enough so that she can notice the suite full of bunches of freshly cut red roses, hear the soothing, mellow 105.9 jazz spilling into the hallway, and observe the low, romantic lighting.

"Apparently, you're expecting female company. I can get out of here in no time if you go get my Dom Dom, Wes. Tell her mommy is here, *please*," she says, visibly annoyed.

"The only company I'm expecting is you, Marquita. Are you going to stand in the hall like we're strangers or are we going to make time to have the talk we should've had years ago?"

"I have a little time, but not much," she says, dropping her arms to her sides as she walks in.

When she passes me I smell her perfume lingering in the air and it makes me want to hold her close and inhale every inch of her brown skin. Instead of crossing the line I hand her a rose.

"What's *this* for?"

"Being you," I say sincerely. "Just being you, beautiful. There's a stack of clothes and gifts in boxes on the bed. Beautiful women deserve beautiful things."

"You want to talk to me so bad, so talk. Make it fast though because I have things to do. I want to get Dom Dom home and readjusted after our flight. I have a long day tomorrow. You may be on vacation, but I'm not. Some people have to work hard for a living without being rewarded with the big bucks."

Marquita looks over at the thirty boxes stacked in six piles on the bed, looks me up and down in disgust, then finds a trashcan and drops the rose inside like it's a crumpled up piece of paper.

She looks at me wide-eyed, crossing her arms again. I walk in a circle in the floor, and then stop and look at her, frustrated.

"You're making this hard for me. I'm trying to be nice to you. I'm really, really trying, Marquita."

"So what, Wes? Is that supposed to mean something to me? A whole lot of people, including a judge, some of the fans who were booing you coming out of the tunnel, and the media, agree with me that you deserve a hard time for the wrong you've done to an innocent child. You're a womanizer and I had to force you to stop being phony and revoke your free pass. Do you think I enjoyed having to put my face out there? Hell no!"

"Look, I was just trying to break the ice. I'm not a womanizer! I've been thinking about something after all of you pointed that out to me."

"Well what is it?" Marquita snaps, obviously annoyed.

I make a fist with my left hand and palm my right around it while puffing my cheeks with air. She's not making this easy.

"Last week I started thinking that I want—I—well, I want us—"

"Want *us* what?" Marquita remarks, her eyebrows raised.

I get up in Marquita's space and softly whisper in her ear. "I want us to be a family. I want you and Dom Dom to be in my life together, for real. I swear to you that I'll make my wrongs right if you give me a chance to do that. I promised myself that I'd try to do the right thing now that I'm trying to get to know my child. You were right, Marquita. She needs an identity and I want to give it to her the right way. Let's plan to get married and stop hurting each other. I don't like this one bit. I'm tired of us running from each, doing what we do. I admit now that I need you in my life, woman. You're the only woman I've ever met where the attraction is more than just physical."

Marquita steps back. "I hate to interrupt your speech but as you know, brain almighty, I'm married. If you loved me you never would have left me. This is about the chase for you, not the prize. You don't yearn for my love; you just want to put another notch on your crowded belt. Maybe in your world your baby's momma is the last one left because all of the hos don't make you work for the pussy or the relationship, or whatever it is when you sling your dick around and pay them for kissing your arrogant ass."

"You're out to make me the bad guy," I blurt out. "All you can do is blame and point fingers. I poured out my heart to you and admitted that I can't stop loving you, and this is what I get for it?"

"Look, Wes, it's good that you grew a conscience and everything, but this talk is I don't know how many years too late. I'm over the idea of having you around more than the time it takes to deliver or pick up my daughter for visitation. If I were you I'd check your facts regarding who took off and why before concocting this little agenda of yours. You really have a lot of nerve, don't you? You're so spoiled and caught up in the wrong world that you can't even see how ludicrous your offer is. Come up to my level and you can see things way more clearly."

"*Don't you hear me?* I'm thinking about us. I'm no stranger—it's me, Wes, and I'm talking about a family." I pat my chest twice then add, "This isn't a *little* agenda. I've got my head screwed on straight now. I'm ready to take you where you want to go. Get rid of your little weak-ass nigga. Divorce him and come home for real where you belong. What we share is deep. I need you, want you, and crave everything that you are. The way you think, the way you smell, the way you wear your hair. I'm talking about the total package. You won't have to work. Your job would be to look good when I come home from practice, give me good loving, and raise our child right. Look, we are meant to be together, and I feel it in my gut that the time is right for us to get this right and stop playing around. You're my first love and I'm yours. Tell me you don't want me. Tell me this attraction is one-sided, Marquita, and we will never have this conversation again," I say, pinning her against the wall and gently letting my weight press against her body. I finally am able to enjoy the smell of her perfume fully while rubbing up against her firm, round breasts. I can feel her nipples harden from my touch, her heart begin to pound, and the pace of the beating quicken. I know that she must enjoy it, so I continue pressing.

"All you have to do is say yes. I'll take care of everything. My legal people can get this done clean and fast. I'll even throw your husband a little something his way for his troubles," I say gently while tenderly caressing her face. Afterward, I run my fingers through her sweet smelling shoulder length hair, which accentuates her mocha colored cat eyes. I remember that always drove Marquita crazy and I miss igniting her raw passion.

"Stop," she says firmly, moving from side to side.

I don't move and ignore her protest. "Make me," I say seductively. "I know I'm turning you on so let's do something about the way we're both feeling. We can start with making another baby and going shopping for a ring in the morning, as a sign of true commitment. And you know the rock I put on your finger will be something special. Remember listening to your mom's old Earth, Wind & Fire records, me pulling your ponytail in Mr. Pearson's French class, and splitting vanilla milk shakes and Big Macs because we were too broke to have our own? A lot's changed, baby."

I run my hand over the middle of her slacks. I imagine the familiar feeling of her feminine silkiness, how wet she gets, and that makes me want to talk dirty and move beyond flirting. The next thing I know I'm sucking on her right nipple and cupping her left breast in my hand. My breathing becomes heavy and my heart begins to beat with excitement. My trance is broken when Marquita clears her throat.

"Contrary to your opinion I don't enjoy feeling your hot breath on my skin. I let you go far enough just so you can feel stupid when I reveal my true feelings for you, Wes. If you don't back up off of me in thirty seconds or less, my husband will gladly use one of his size twelve to jolt your memory and remind you that I'm a married woman. In fact, he's most likely about to walk in here any minute. All you did was get me ready for him tonight, so thank you, Wes. The day I sleep with you again will be the day Hell freezes over. One day you'll understand that it takes more than your ability to buy a closet full of shoes or clothes to turn a real woman's head. And for the record, I'd never be jealous if you ever married one of your hos because I know what a bum deal she's getting—there's not enough money in the whole world to compensate for that lifetime of misery. There are a million ways to please a real woman and you don't know the first one, so save your damn ring shopping trip speech and stop licking me like a dog in heat! Who knows what sort of germs you're infested with!"

She smirks like she knows I've been set up and I suddenly can't stand Marquita. I raise my head from her breast and push her away. "I don't know what I was thinking. You're the same big-mouthed bitch you were back in the day."

"Don't get mad because I'm a diva, and I'm not phased by cheap tactics like this. I do enjoy making love to my husband so it's not like I'm bitter against all men—I just don't want *you*. If he were here I'd fuck his brains out right in front of your eyes and show you how I can respond if I love someone. The more I think about him the more I want him to come and just pick up where you left off. Damn, I must admit, I've got the best loving a woman could hope for and I don't have to tolerate lies and games."

"No wonder I left your ass and didn't look back. Now I remember. I can't believe that you brought him here to pick up *our* daughter. I don't appreciate your disrespect—"

"If you were thinking about us you'd leave me the hell alone and be happy I moved on and found myself a good man who also loves Dom Dom," she says, cutting me off.

"What the fuck is that supposed to mean?" I ask, my nostrils flaring.

"What it means is that I can't believe that you haven't changed one bit for the sake of your daughter. You have no respect for me and obviously never will. The best part of you ran down your momma's legs when she was making you," Marquita says, pushing me back. Then she uses the palm of her hands to smooth her hair and straighten her tousled clothes.

"I'll tell you this, this is my last time trying to fuck with your stupid ass. Take your little broke-ass custodian husband, Mike, and continue living from paycheck to paycheck in your stank Section Eight dump. I don't need you. I can have whomever I want. I thought you'd like my offer and appreciate that I was trying to put some bling in your life—lace you like a diva so you could afford to rock more than a forty-seven dollar bottle of perfume. Now my last thought of you is official. This conversation is over and we'll never have it again. Bitches would kill for an offer like what I made you. This is your loss, not mine. You may have book smarts but you have absolutely no street sense in your ass. I can't stand you, Marquita! You truly know how to kill a nigga's desire to stand in the same damn room with you, let alone touch your frigid ass—you damn ice queen! You're good at killing erections, I'm sure."

Marquita chuckles for a moment and then stops. "In case you haven't noticed, your words don't faze me one bit, Wes. With that being said, just get my daughter right now so I can go home and shower your dog saliva off my breasts. And for the record I think I'll be taking my husband up on his offer to change my daughter's last name to his. I'll never insult you in front of Dom Dom, but I've raised her to be a smart girl. Soon she'll see for herself what a no-good sperm donor you are. In the meantime I suggest you prepare to spend your life a bitter, lonely man, with messed up knees and a bad attitude. No one wants *you;* they want *Wes the icon.* If you chose to not put on a big show you wouldn't have a friend to your name, or two dimes to jingle in your fucking pocket. You have no people skills, no personality, and chances are you're headed toward being cut by the team based on the way you've been fucking up on the court lately. Prepare to be a has-been and lose your spot in the NBA—your day is definitely coming! Your ass will self-destruct. Mark my words, Wes. Mark my words and remember who said it would come to pass on October 6th, 2004. Then we'll see who is smartest how."

"Don't play with me! Do you know who I am? I don't have to listen to your insults. Get the fuck out of my suite, whore!" I scream and point toward the door, feeling the veins pop out of my forehead.

Marquita slaps me with the force of a man. I grit my teeth, restraining myself from whipping her ass.

"Don't you ever call me out of my name or touch me in this lifetime ever again!" she hisses. "You got that? I don't care who you are, NBA player or not. You will respect Marquita Lewis Johnson from here on out! I'll never forgive you for leaving us when I needed you most. While you were the one acting like a male whore, enjoying yourself out in the world, I was home alone sterilizing baby bottles, and changing dirty diapers. I was the one who had to forgo attending Howard University because my mother said I would sleep in the hard bed I made when I became a teen mother. Since you took off I couldn't go to school. I had to work fulltime and give up my dream of being an engineer. You didn't even care if I had maternity clothes, or see to it that your child had milk to drink and pampers on her butt. You screwed me twice, you bastard! The hell if I'll give you the pleasure of doing it a third. I'm awake now. You caught me before when I was a green girl who was asleep."

"You could've worked and gone to school. Don't blame me for your decision to panic. People do it everyday, Marquita Lewis *Johnson.* I don't owe you a damn thing, including feeling sorry for you. I bet that taught you to keep your legs closed. And then when you all leave a baller and get with a piece of man with poor credit who can't lace you lovely, you resent the nigga you left who could. So really all this is about is anger. You can work your fingers to the bone and you'll never have shit going on so don't you dare hate on me for having the heart to chase my dream and do big things. I'm Wes, and all I see is a confident motherfucker who went for his and got it."

"Do you have a problem with my wife?" Mike asks, opening the suite door.

"Stay out of this, you broke-ass nigga! This is personal between Marquita and me."

"You should be thanking me for taking care of Dom Dom. Where were you when she needed a father to tuck her in, teach her how to ride a bike, or put her back to sleep after she had a nightmare? Nowhere to be found that's where. My wife and our child is definitely my business. From the look on my wife's face I can tell that she already reminded you that you were a sperm donor, not a father. Get it straight and stop hiding behind your fame and money."

"I didn't ask you to do shit for my child! You just did that to get in good with Marquita. I know that move—that's an old one from the player's handbook. Comfort a bitch when she's down and out, then work your way into her life while she can't think straight. Isn't that how you did it, Mike? She wouldn't have turned her head otherwise for a man like you. I'll bet you come home dirty, wearing a dingy school custodian's uniform, cleaning up pee from school floors. You ain't got shit going on, my man," I say in defense of myself.

"You know, I've been wanting to tell you what I think of you and the way you carried Marquita back in the day for a long time. The thing is that it would do no good. You're nothing more than a bad seed, a product of crazy-ass parents. I know all about your family. The apple never falls far from the tree so you may as well give up on putting on airs just because your ghetto-ass made it into the NBA. I know you've forgotten where you came from. Everyone's talking about what a screwed up individual you are, so what you said about me means absolutely nothing. *You* let Marquita go and now you can't stand the fact that the mother of your child goes home to a simple man like me every night. I may live paycheck to paycheck but I make her happy and feel like a real woman. Well get over it because that's how it is and how it will be."

I step toward that fool, my fists clenched, ready to whip his ass.

"If he swings, don't hit him, honey, he isn't worth it," Marquita says. "He'll get his someday. Let it go. What goes around comes around."

When Mike takes a few steps back I laugh at his weak ass. "Oh, that bossy bitch runs you, I see. What we have on our hands here is a pussy-whipped punk. I see who wears the pants in your house."

Out of nowhere, Dominique appears dragging a brown teddy bear by one arm. The argument stalls.

"What's all the noise out here? Daddy, that lady you left me with is smoking something that smells stinky and funny. It bothers my nose and makes me cough. I don't like her. Can I come in here with you tonight, pretty please?" she asks, looking up at me with an opened beer in her hand. When she sees Marquita and Mike she gets excited. "Mommy, daddy Mike! Is it time to go home?" She drops the bottle of suds and runs to them, hugging them both like she's been attention deprived.

Marquita doesn't utter a word. She takes our daughter's hand as Mike walks beside her toward the adjoining room where Dominique came from. She and her husband open the door and find Soledad puffing on a joint, watching an adult woman on woman movie on Pay Per View in her bra and panties. She's talking on the phone in her native language and doesn't even notice them.

On the other side of the room at least seven more people are sitting around talking in low tones. One is a well-known rapper who chills with me and my crew from time to time. With him is a chocolate hooker with a dried out blonde weave that I picked up on the corner of U Street. She's got a reputation for giving the best head in town, and those size triple whatever breasts stacked on her tiny size eight frame are a bonus too.

An assortment of liquor bottles line the table. Cocaine and weed are in plain view although my two burly bodyguards playing Spades are present as well. I really can't defend neglecting Dominique so I don't try to sugarcoat it.

Marquita and her husband don't bother to put shoes on Dominique's feet or remove her pink basketball nightgown and replace it with her street clothes. They head for the door.

"There are no words left to say except my husband told me so. He said I could only expect the worse from you and you just proved him right. Some people never learn that if you want respect you've got to live it, and if you want love you've got to give it. I knew you didn't have it all upstairs but what kind of parent are you, Wes? This will be your last unsupervised visit with Dominique on your turf. I just may see to it that she doesn't have to put up with you wrecking her life—permanently."

"Go to hell!" I snap.

"When you go to hell, you'll be at the front of the line to get in! I don't have time to argue with you—we have a long trip home, you hopeless sperm donor!"

I look across the room and gaze into an open space. My plan backfired and all I could do is move out of the way. I turn my head back toward my ex. Marquita gives me a look of death. I try to say goodbye to Dominique, but she cuts me off.

"You don't like me, do you Dad? I'm sorry you hate me." She begins to sniff and cry.

I was about to tell her that wasn't true, but I don't get very far because Marquita moves swiftly, pulling Dom Dom's little delicate arm. She almost had to run in her bare feet to keep up, tears flowing down her angelic face. Her mother slams the door of my motel suite so hard the room shakes like an earthquake hit it.

All of my friends look as if Marquita interrupted their flow of enjoying a serene high. I wonder if I've lost her for good this time. Since I can't figure it out I crawl in bed next to Soledad, grab the joint, and puff the memory of this nasty little scene away, wishing that Marquita hadn't forced me to own up to being my little girl's biological father. After that, the rapper, hooker, one of my teammates, and a woman I've never laid eyes on before, crawl in bed next to us.

When I feel my teammate's long brown hand touch my thigh, I knock it off assuming that he mistakenly put it there. A few minutes later I feel the same touch once again.

I give him a look. "Brother, save that for Soledad and the ho. You're on my side. Watch yourself!"

"Look at the TV, Wes," he replies.

When I turn my head toward the screen I see two men tonguing each while two women suck their dicks and caress their muscular thighs. The next thing I know the rapper and my teammate pair off, then the hooker and Soledad follow suit. Next I feel different pairs of hands groping at my body, but my mind drifts back to the one woman I can't seem to lure back into my life, no matter how hard I try. After that my teammate reaches to stroke me openly. "After a while you need more than women in boring hotel rooms, Wes. Join us," he says.

I smack his hand away from me again in disbelief. I can't believe my boy is going out like that. I'd heard rumors that he was also getting down with brothers but I'm stressed since I was the last to know. Needing an extra emotional crutch to get me through this fucked up night I get up, reach over to the side table and take a hit of cocaine. As the high begins to take effect I sit in a chair across the room and lay my head back with my eyes shut, remembering Marquita's lovely face. As I feel the burning sensation in my nostrils, I also feel a dangling nipple tease my lips. As I begin to instinctively suck it, I feel soft lips wrapped around my penis. After a while I lift my head and push Soledad away to look at who I assume to be the famous hooker, giving me the best head I've had in a long time. Instead, I find the rapper on his knees servicing me while my teammate beats his penis on his back. I drop my head back. Times like this I wonder if this empire I've built was all worth me losing the mother of my child—the one who I want to have a key to my door. What am I saying—I'm trippin'—of course it is. I'm still Wes, the best from east to west—the nigga with a championship ring. Believe that!

3

A HARDHEAD MAKES A SOFT ASS

Jalita

As I uncover my unlucky fortune under scratch off ticket after scratch off ticket, I find myself repeating, "Shit, give me another one. Shit, give me another one."

The female Ethiopian sales clerk with the sharp nose looks disgusted that I keep bothering her to ring up one ticket at a time, but I'm sure humoring me has something to do with the crazed look in my eyes. Forty-nine dollars later, gray paste that once covered the one and two-dollar scratch off tickets line the check out counter at 7-11 on 7th Street in Washington, D.C.

When I hit the fifty-dollar mark, I rub my hands together like I'm playing a crap game. "Come on now, Jalita needs a new pair of shoes." I bite my lip with great hope of winning something to help me win the portion of my rent money back, plus some. Upon discovering my measly one-dollar prize, I complain, "This shit is rigged!"

In disgust, I ball up the ticket and throw it behind the counter. With frustration, I walk over to the door and kick it open with my foot, warning everyone that they better stay out of my damn way because I have a bad attitude. That's what I get for bothering to gamble on the Maryland State Lottery. As I unlock my car I'm thinking that I need to revise my plan to pay my rent. A brainstorm turns up a viable solution. I can return a train ticket in my glove compartment to begin my fundraising efforts, and then finish them off with returning a few tagged items in the trunk.

When the ignition turns over I begin to think about the life circumstances that have my head twisted. My brother Wes is a jerk who doesn't see his rot is putting him on the fast track to fucking up his daughter's head. My old crush Seth has enough to deal with after getting an annulment and still trying to hold it down on the book tour circuit. I can't tell a man I could've loved that I just had a nervous breakdown, nor can I tell a therapist that was listening to me bitch for free that my whole loving myself proclamation was a false alarm that fell apart. I'm ashamed of myself and some things are better left a secret. This is one of them.

You can throw all the dirt you want to in life around but you will pay for slinging it at some point in time. Even if you think you've stopping paying, the debt may resurface and you may be forced to confront your collective rot again. Although I stopped using my body to get what I needed and wanted to survive by gold digging, paying the piper has just started. The screws are being twisted too tight on my butt in the karma department.

After three days of being held medical hostage on the psychiatric ward, being over drugged with antidepressants like Zoloft and an anti-panic attack medication called Paxil, I realized that my beat down by Charlene and her crew, my mother's letter explaining to me why I'd never be loved by her, me shooting a man, and even hooking up with a blood relative were unresolved issues that threw me into a huge slump. Even so, in the real world, there's no time to go crazy. Bills don't stop coming because you've grown a moral backbone or run out of steam because guilt sets in. As a former master of convincing others of things that aren't true, I was able to sit in front of three psychiatric nurses and one shrink and lie my way back home where my problems were waiting.

Shortly after I stop going to counseling, free of charge, I try going back to school. I run out of money and energy from working two jobs. Uncle Sam works extra fast, and the next thing I know I'm opening a letter from my student loan lender explaining that I'm in default. Then my entire exhaust system goes out on my Toyota. I don't have a dime to get it fixed, and the gas and electric company have disconnected me from the joys of modern conveniences such as heat and light. All the trip to the hospital did was add another bill to the pile, and keep me from harming myself so I can be responsible to pay it.

34

I'm not saying I don't want to act like I've learned my lesson about what happened in the past, but due to my circumstances I'm ready to go back to hell again if that's where I end up going. How else can I raise money for my rent and get back on point? Jalita's gotta do what Jalita's gotta do, and she's not going out like a weak punk. If I get out of this last little scrape, I'll never backslide again. This time I won't enjoy the game I'm about to run. The thing is I see no way out other than to put my PHD in whoring and scheming back to use. With that decision I turn on the radio and get into miss thang mode, bouncing my shoulders and singing Fifty Cent's *Candy Shop*. My store's been closed and hearing this song is the confirmation I need to temporarily open it back up.

$

Less than fifteen minutes later I'm smacking gum and collecting my parking ticket. I park in the garage at Union Station, in D.C. to turn in my train ticket for a trip I never took after I gave up my male sponsor habit. My boss turned sugar daddy told me I could pick any resort city in the country or Caribbean and go there for a week. He pampered, wined and dined me, treating me like a princess in exchange for the obvious, plus his *executive assistant* got a raise after taking a romp with him in the covers after a business trip up North. When I returned I felt guilty that I fell off the wagon—fucking around with a married white man with a secret brown sugar addiction. I told my therapist. I never saw him again but kept the ticket he sent me to meet him while he was on vacation. I'm sure I was replaced rather easily, and he found another twat to lick and stick. Hopes of a halfway decent salary went down the drain because I was fighting to stop collecting shit with my body and countless web of lies. That moment led to this moment and as a result I'm parking my heap of junk that is now spitting out toxic fumes from inside and out. I begin to regret that I voluntarily forfeited my Lexus to the buyer and returned to sitting on cloth bucket seats in this damn whooptie that is destined to show off at some point.

Andrea Blackstone

When I walk toward the escalators that lead into the main area, I hear R&B music blasting, just above the engine noise of a large tour bus with tinted windows.

"I like your hat," a man says.

My pace slows and the next thing I know I'm asking a question I already know the answer to, letting the man walk right into my deceptive web.

"Thanks. I hate to interrupt your concert and everything but where's Amtrak located?" I ask, thinking that he reminds me of Cousin It from *The Adams Family*.

"Straight ahead toward where you were walking, then turn right at the steps," he tells me.

I smile and cock my head to the side thinking of a scheme to wiggle into his pocket.

"Can I ask you a question in private?" I ask him.

"I'm not supposed to let you on here. I could get in trouble."

I smile, stare at his hanging bulldog jaws, and bat my eyelashes.

"Like I said, can I ask you *something* in private? No one's watching so no one can give trouble."

The next thing I know I'm stepping up into darkness on the bus. I wait for him to turn down the volume of the radio before I continue my scheme.

"It sure is dark in here. I bet someone with an active sexual appetite could take advantage of this." When he turns around to face me I add, "Have you ever—no never mind. I don't know you like that."

"What?" he asks, showing interest.

"Well, I'm not trying to give you the wrong idea, but I was just thinking about something that a bad girl would do. I'm not saying I'm a bad girl—I'm just saying."

"And what is it that you're saying?"

"Fifty dollars would inspire me to tell at least part of the story. I'd have to dig real deep to be inspired to bring out the freak in me in the presence of a complete stranger—especially since I'm not some professional who routinely comes on to men for cash."

The frumpy man pulls his wallet from his pocket and hands me two twenties and a ten like he really expects to get head for that small amount of money from a dime like me.

I up the ante.

"If you want me to show you the beginning, middle, and end of that story you have to do better than that. To tell you the truth my boyfriend and I just broke up and now would be a good time to have some fun *if* you were interested."

"This is all of the cash I have left. You better be worth it, sweetie," the man says, handing me an additional forty dollars. "This was my money to get something good to smoke after work."

"Come here. Of course I'm worth it. I made you look didn't I?" I slowly begin to motion with my finger.

"Wait a minute," he says.

He grabs a small bottle of Scope from somewhere, gargles, spits out his mouth's contents after opening a window near the driver's seat, and then brushes his hair. I watch dandruff pop off his scalp like popcorn jumping up and down in a pan of hot oil, and I nearly puke. After that, he turns to me like he just prepared to go out on a date or something.

"I'm ready. Now what?"

"Let's go to the back of the bus."

I cram the cash in my purse then pull his hand. I push him down in the very last seat. After I adjust it, I unbuckle his slacks. He smells like Cheez-Its, but the odor isn't coming from his mouth. I pretend not notice.

"Drop your pants to your ankles, unless you're shy. Let's see if you're packing, and I don't mean a nine," I say in a bossy tone.

After he does I moisten my palm with some saliva then begin stroking his penis while bumping up against his C cup sized breasts. He begins to breathe with relaxation, and I massage it until it's fully erect, which amounts to about four and a half inches. As I squeeze it and run my hand up and down the short length of it he begins to pant and moan.

"Tell me I can cum. Tell me. C'mon—say it," he begs two minutes later.

"No, not yet, baby," I calmly respond. "Keep your eyes closed. I'm shy and I don't want you to watch me suck it. All I want you to feel is a good jaw job."

I moisten my palm with saliva again, then whisper in his ear, "Keep your eyes shut. I'm taking off my clothes."

"Mmm," he moans. "I can't wait to see what you look like naked."

I continue talking dirty to him while walking backward, off the bus. When I approach the door I break out into a run. I reach the entrance of Union Station before I hear him yelling out behind me.

"Hey, you took my money!"

I quickly turn back and see the driver standing in from of the bus in striped boxer shorts. As I disappear into the crowd I hear people gasping and talking about a half naked man exposing himself in front of a bus. What's he complaining about? I gave him a half a hand job for his ninety-dollar *donation.* That would make up for the amount I lost in scratch off tickets, plus interest for getting my hand sticky after touching his sweaty, child-size, teeny weenie, with no girth or width. I'd rather suck on a lead pencil than put my mouth on that. It's not my concern that he didn't bust a nut in five minutes or less, and I have a no refund policy. Did he really think he was going to test drive my juicy lips or pussy that cheap? Come on now. Get with the program, Rufus—or whatever your name is.

$

"Is anyone paying by cash?" asks a customer service agent, walking up and down the line of the ticket counter.

"I want my money back for this ticket. Am I in the right place?" I ask.

"You won't get all of your money back," he says.

"Yeah, yeah. I know. They told me that already when I called the customer service number. Like I said, am I in the right place or not, fool?" I ask, lacing my voice with attitude.

He glares at me for insulting him. I was about to give him another dose when I hear another customer service agent.

"Next please."

I step up to terminal number sixteen and plunk down my roundtrip train ticket. When I look the man in the eye I hear the same dry explanation about me getting the cash, less ten percent, then he hands me a cash refund form. I fill in my name and address then he begins tapping the keyboard and talking to an agent next to him. After he hands me two hundred thirty nine dollars and forty cents, he requests that I sign where the x is, so I do.

"Hold on for your receipt. It looks like you're going to run away," he says.

I stuff the cash in my purse. "I don't need a receipt. The cash is what I was after."

Since he wants to flirt I bat my eyelashes and prepare to teach his ass a much-needed lesson. I smile deviously. "Could I shake your hand to thank you for your wonderful help?"

When he extends his arm I intentionally shake his hand with the pre-cum stained hand I used to begin jacking off the bus driver. I wink at him then he picks up my receipt. I wave goodbye and leave him holding the slip of paper out in the air.

I'm still addicted to dead presidents but I can't spend it on myself. I've got some more stops to make to get up funds to pay my rent although I long to crawl into my own bed. After being in the hospital and sharing a room with a woman who said she was seeing a witch at the end of her bed, and being awakened several times during the night to have my vitals checked for the last three days, I am more than ready to pass out. You would think you could rest in the hospital but that's not always the case.

When I turn the corner I see a policeman who's gossiping.

"Is there a post office in here?" I ask.

"Yeah, straight down there," he says, pointing.

He turns his head back toward the person he was conversing with and I walk past Sbarros Pizza wishing I could spend a few bucks on a large slice of pepperoni, but I can't. I'm short on my rent as it is and will have to bribe my landlord with some of the new items in my trunk to make up for my short funds. Time is passing and I figure I best not make any more stops and chance the rest of the day getting away from me. As my mouth waters, I see a small post office where ten people are standing in line. Just as I'm about to ask if they sell money orders I see a sign that says they don't. Since I waited this long I step up and ask anyway.

"We don't sell them here but we're working on it. You have to go to Massachusetts Avenue," says a light-complexioned, black woman with a round pie face.

"What kind of damn post office doesn't sell money orders? You people wouldn't get away with this if you were in Baltimore."

After venting I roll my eyes and turn to leave the post office. Since I'm already a few days late, I realize that I can't deposit the cash in my account because that will tack on another twenty-four hours to this process. I feel that the only viable solution is to head toward Massachusetts Avenue. So that's what I do although the only street I know well in D.C. is New York Avenue.

$

After being lost in D.C. for an hour I tire from going in circles and trying to figure out how to navigate past one-way streets and circles. I knew I should've stopped at the Lowest Price Gas Station on New York Avenue that I spotted on my way to Union Station, but I thought I could wait until leaving the city. As bad luck would have it I look at my gas needle and it's now below the empty mark. I gulp hard and pull over behind a parked white van with flashing blinkers. I put on my blinkers and search for someone to ask for directions. When I begin to cross the street a beat up car comes flying down the one-way street. Breaks squeal as I struggle to get out of the way, but I still end up falling on the hood of the car. The woman inside the car lays on her horn like I'm some evil pedestrian. At this point I notice that her windows are down and I point to the giant *Do Not Enter* sign as well as the one that says *Stop*. The woman continues to blow her horn and yell out her window.

"Move yo black ass, bitch! I'm in a damn hurry!"

I purposely take my merry old time, dusting myself off, slowly walking out of the middle of the street. She still insists on blowing the horn. When I look at her I spot a handful of her curved, three-inch acrylic nails, that someone with a name like Ling Ling must have applied in some nail shop, sparkling at me out her window.

I cuss at her careless ass as she pulls away, still trying to catch my breath. Before I can fully recover, a thirty-something, overweight black man that looks as if he's half-giant, half-human runs up with a machine that spits out parking tickets. I stop him before he has time to open his mouth or type in all of my tag information.

"Damn, I almost got hit! Did you see that? Look, I'm having an emergency. I'm out of gas. Can you tell me where I can find a gas station? So much is happening at one time."

He ignores me and replies, "You should've thought about that before you parked here."

"Can you hear? I wasn't trying to park here—I was stopping for an emergency. There's a difference. If you don't believe I'm almost out of gas you can look at my gas gauge."

"I'm still giving you this ticket," he replies. Shaking his head he adds, "I won't take it back."

"Put up your hood, baby girl," someone shouts from across the street.

"Pull into the alley," yells someone else. "He can't give you a ticket if you're off the street."

Confused by the conflicting advice, I put up my hood. When the man hands me a ticket anyway my eyebrows wrinkle. I'm fuming and can feel my ears grow Georgia hot. If anyone should've gotten a ticket it should've been the woman driving down a one-way street.

"Have a nice day," he says, smiling as he walks away.

My temper flares up and I grab the first weapon I can get my hands on—a half-rotten Sunkist orange. Before I think about what I'm about to do I throw the fruit in his direction. Somehow I hit my target and clock him in the back of his big watermelon head. The next thing I know I hear the whooping noise of a police siren and a crowd gathers on the sidewalk. I know I'm about to be hauled off to jail. Great, now my rent will be four days late and I didn't even get a chance to wash the bus driver's sweaty dick funk off my hands.

4

TWO GENERATIONS OF PIMPIN'

Malik

So why am I all fucked up anyway? Childhood, that's why. I've always had the ability to jump from ho to ho, and I never wanted to tell anyone every corner of the truth. I was introduced to dysfunctional relationships when I was six years old. My father used to take me all over Maryland with him when he visited one of his many mistresses. At the time, I didn't understand who was who, and can recall sitting on couch after couch, waiting on my father when he disappeared for blocks of time. When I'd ask him what he was doing he'd smile.

"Boy, just don't touch anything. I'll be right back," he'd say. "Turn the TV on and look at the boob tube until your old man finishes his errand."

My eyes stayed glued to Bugs Bunny, the Road Runner, Porky Pig or the Flintstones until I heard low moans escape from behind a door. Wondering if someone became ill, I'd tiptoe to the door, push it open slightly and scrunch up my nose as I watched my father squirming around on top of various women every Saturday. I didn't understand what he was doing but I knew it was something I wasn't supposed to watch. After spying a moment or so I'd ease the door shut, run back to the couch and pretend I'd never left my favorite cartoon characters. Sometimes I'd pretend to sleep to throw him off because I knew he'd believe I hadn't moved an inch, and had followed his explicit instructions to keep still and quiet.

On one particular trip with my father we were walking with one of my father's lady friends back toward her house. The three of us were on our way from Lexington Market when my mother's brother walked up to us.

"Todd, what brings you to this side of town?"

The tone of his voice was icy, and he wasn't playful with me like he usually was when I saw him. He appeared to be focused and cold towards my father and didn't even look in my direction. I felt attention deprived.

"Just Saturday morning errands, taking Malik to get some air, you know how that goes. The boy gets bored fast. He's not like Wes—he needs air like his old man."

"Right," he said. "Your wife happened to give me this shopping list, but since I ran into you I think you can handle it. Especially since it looks like you've been shopping once. You know bachelors hate grocery shopping, so I'm turning the duties over to you. One more trip should do the trick."

He handed my father the paper and then looked at his lady friend.

"And hello Ms. Jones. Me nor my sis were formally introduced but we feel as if we almost know you. I've heard you sing in the band and I've heard so much about you. That's a nice fox stole you have there. Very nice, in fact."

I watched my father's smile fall. "Well I'll be damned! Divorce papers. Stan, you're serving me papers?"

"Enjoy your day," he replied with a smile. "And forget about the groceries. It slipped my memory but I think I got my messages confused."

As my uncle disappeared down the street Ms. Jones hugged up on my father. "Well that's not the worst news in the world, is it? Now we can be together and you can make me an honest woman, Todd."

"Are you crazy?" my father snapped. "She'll get half of everything! And watch how you talk around my boy. I've got to go. Move out of our way."

My father grabbed my hand and tugged me along.

The woman dropped the two bags of groceries in the street, ran to my father and grabbed his arm. "Don't leave me! Don't leave me. Baby, come back! I need you. Don't do this to me!" she cried.

My father looked at her as cold as ice. "Shut up and go in the house!"

With those words I turned around and saw Ms. Jones on her knees in the street, crying so hard the mascara from her false eyelashes made messy black lines down her over powdered brown cheeks. Within a short time her hair looked as if she'd stuck it in a socket, and was sitting all over her head. Her fox stole lay on the dirty road like it was a piece of trash.

"If you leave me I'll lay down in this street and let a car run me over!" she screamed.

My father stopped in his tracks and turned around. He looked at her acting like a crazed madwoman, with her limbs stretched out in the middle of the street.

"Do what you want. I got me a white woman on the side that don't put me through all of these changes. It's over between us. By the way—a car's coming."

When my father turned around again and appeared unaffected by her tantrum, her wailing seemed to increase five octaves. A crowd began to assemble in the street. All of the sudden the woman hopped up and began throwing groceries at my father. We heard the thud of a pork roast, ham hocks, pork chops, and fruit fall but my father never turned around. He didn't even duck. He just shook his head and pulled me along.

"Son, zip up your coat. Before you know it your nose will be running like a faucet. And when your nose runs you're headed for a cold. And when you're headed for a cold that's medicine I've got to go in my pocket and buy. Why does your old man have to always remind you to put a hat on your head and zip up your coat? Listen boy, just listen. Would you?"

I don't recall anything about the trip home but when we made it back my mother was standing in front of the window. She lifted it up when we got closer.

"I guess you got my note."

"What in the hell are you doing?" my father answered.

"Giving you your walking papers to do as you please," she said. "Send my son inside."

"He's my son, too. You didn't have him by yourself," he said.

"I may as well have. Like I said, send my son inside," she insisted.

"No."

"Get in here, boy. That fool will get you in trouble."

I ran toward the door because my mother was the one who delivered spankings and any type of punishment for rebellion. The door opened and shut quickly. Someone I later discovered was my uncle pulls me inside like a vacuum. My father tried to follow, but the door had already been shut and locked in his face.

"Open my damn door," he yelled. "I'm coming in the house, one way or another, he said, trying his key.

"Like hell you are!" She placed her hands on her hips. "Go back to that ugly old bitch's house. You seem to like it there much better than your family's residence. You didn't want to be here before so leave and do what you do!"

"What have you and that brother of yours cooked up? I don't know what you're talking about," my father lied.

"I'll *bet*," Mom said sarcastically. She took a long breath then hollered, "Well I've got all the evidence I need. Playing late in your band? Bullshit! How stupid did you think I was? I take you back and you still can't represent properly. It's a shame you do like you do."

"I said I don't know what you're talking about," my father repeated. "If I'm looking up in your face twenty-four hours of the day I can't make money and be the sugar daddy that attracted you in the first place. You're a typical woman—never satisfied. I like 'em young like you, but all you younguns do is bitch, moan, complain and drive an older man crazy. Outside of the pussy, why in the hell should I look forward to coming home to you?"

"You don't even come home for that anymore. Look at these." My mother threw a pair of purple women's underwear out of the window. "Maybe if you stopped chasing women out in the street, coming home to me would be an easy thing to do, and I wouldn't have to complain about common sense things."

When I realized that my mother was going to stand her ground and may not let my father return home, I desired to look him in the eyes and remember every feature of his face. I craned my neck around my mother to get another look at him.

"Let me in. I know my rights. I pay the mortgage. You can't lock me out of my own house. Take the deadbolts, off. Do it or else!"

He picked up the underwear.

"Daddy, daddy!" I belted out after him.

"Shut up!" Wes said. "Stay out of grown folk's business, boy. Back up."

As my twin brother pushed me out of the room I could still hear my mother yelling at the top of her lungs.

"Everything you need for your move across town is in garbage bags under the porch. Scram nigga! I have nothing left to say to you unless it's through an attorney."

As my brother and I sat on the bottom bunk of our set of bunk beds my stomach began to burn when I heard my father yell back at her.

"You can't afford no attorney. Who you think you foolin'? I don't need you! One of my other women will be more than happy to have me."

"We don't need *you*! Fifteen years of marriage and this is the best you've got? I've lost count of how any times you've done this. This time it's a hussy in the band," Mom defended.

"You'll fall flat on your face without me, you crazy woman! You can't take care of those kids. Surely, you'll want this old man back. When I met you, you were a fifty-cent Go-Go dancer in a bar where my band was playing. I was the one that took you away from all that nonsense and showed you a better life. Now you think you have the right to act like you're the queen of Sheba or somebody."

I ran from the bunk bed in our room toward the kitchen window when I heard those frightening words. Before my brother could catch me, I watched as my father turned to grab the handle of his Cadillac. His mouth dropped open in shock when he discovered that it was sitting up on blocks. All four of the tires and radio had been stolen. I gulped and my eyes widened. My heart began to beating faster than I'd ever recalled.

"That's what you get," my mother taunted. "Call a cab, or the mistress you usually tongue down at the door in front of my children. And take this. Since it means nothing to you, it means nothing to me." She took her wedding ring from her finger and tossed it out of the window.

With those last words she slammed the window shut. Then she found Wes and me and dared us to shed one tear over my father's departure, or take one last peek at Todd Lester Harrison.

After my uncle left our row house the three of us inhaled the thick smoke of the unfiltered Camel cigarettes my mother puffed on. She sat down, crossed her legs, threw her head back, and played Billy Holiday songs, over and over again. Mom was much too pretty to cry, and much too young to know about the blues, yet she appeared to understand what it was and how you get it. When she wasn't looking I dipped my finger into the glass of alcohol and sucked the droplets of moisture from my lips. When my stomach was coated with warmth I decided that liquor was meant to mend wounds, and love is something borne from pain, not pleasure, as I listened to my mother repeat the same thing over and over.

"She can have your no good ass. She can have your noooooo good ass."

Before the night was over my mother fell asleep with her robe falling open, a bottle of liquor next to her, and an entire box of used Kleenex lining the floor. Wes and I fought all night long and that marked the beginning of me feeling as though he felt like he was my boss. He was first to be born and first to make me wish that I were an only child who could be who I wanted to be. It's not that I didn't try to succeed; it's more like my plan to live it up like Wes was foiled.

$

After being poked, prodded, and reexamined by many, the team doctor gave me two choices—go home and cut my losses for the season so I could get well, or keep playing and take a risk of doing permanent damage to my shoulder. Although I opted to push the envelope and play anyway luck wasn't on my side when I tore my rotator cuff. After countless steroid injections and physical therapy in the pool four times a week at a rehabilitation center, it became clear that my career was over. I went from being able to live large to living in my Escalade anywhere I could park it. I suddenly realized my whole life was falling apart faster than I could put it back together.

Watching my brother, Wes Montgomery, hoop it up, escaping street dreams in the hood, and getting everything that I wanted, jealousy began to consume me. Seeing him living lavish with his gated home and indoor pool in a spot in Mitchellville caused me to make a poor decision. I fucked his live-in girl, who definitely had more than one screw loose—not once, not twice, but over a long period of time. Now before I truly blame myself for the part I played in shooting some nut up in Tomi without a condom, I must say that she never would've gotten pregnant by me if my brother had shared with me. When life kicked me in the ass I asked him to look out for a brotha until I could gather my senses and start life over again. The day he kicked me out of his place in Mitchellville, revoked my key privilege, and told me I should've prepared for the day my football dream came to an end, was the day I realized that I didn't have any family in this world. Wes and I share no sacred bond. Technically, my twin is blood, but in reality, we're anything but family. If I keep it real, we're bitter rivals, archenemies at best. Enter the ugliness of sibling rivalry since the days of living in the ghetto back in Baltimore. At that point banging his girl in his custom-made bed when he was on the road hooping it up didn't sit all that badly with me. That was until I realized that Tomi was using me for spite—and that her agenda was to get pregnant by me or someone close to Wes. But as they say, God don't like ugly. She lost the baby and ended up getting locked down for pushing the envelope of Wes's lack of respect of their commitment a little too far. Better her than me, but the only problem is my ended cash flow left me needing a plan B. Plan B was part two of plan A.

Once you have NFL privileges and get used to people bowing and scraping for you, you can't just go back to being a *regular* person—that just won't do. When else would anyone lick a black man's boots and act as if rules don't apply to him? Never. But if you've got that NFL Player's card in your wallet, and belong to one of the most powerful organizations in the world, women automatically will concoct devious traps to try and have your babies. White folks automatically want to start shaking your hand, take pictures with you, and will even pay good money for one of your used shirts—happily bragging that they know you or saw you doing any trivial thing, including sitting at a stop light at an intersection. Imagine that—they're not scared of you and they want to befriend you. Having a little status is the only way the world will pay attention to a black man that's straight up from the ghetto and not from a privileged family. This is why most athletes, rappers, singers, and actors flaunt their bling, and remind the world that they are one of the select few who earns millions while mostly everyone else struggles to make thousands by honest means.

With all that I'm saying I never claimed to be blemish free. My drinking problem began as a private way to escape the disappointments of life—the disappointment of closed doors, and the reality of lost faith living within the spirit of a broken man. But with all of this, with all of the memories of being raised in the ghetto by absent parents, I had to get my shit together enough to act like it didn't hurt to give up millions of dollars. I had to pretend that it didn't matter that I wouldn't get the chance to run the ball at Fed Ex Field in Landover, or anywhere else around the country. Overnight, things changed. People were talking about me behind my back, white folks no longer wanted to shake my hand, and I was already grieving the loss of everything I worked hard to earn. But when Tomi planted seeds to deal with these things in a "different" way, I became a little less worried. I started drinking a little less, toned down to coolers and mixed drinks, cleaned up my ass, started shaving again, and looking the part of a nigga that still had it going on. Once I did all that I then began to feel as if I could stand on mountains, even though I had another baby's momma who was the cause of me not being able to live in my crib.

There was endless court case after court case, with her trying to steal my assets—using little Malik as a payday. Before long the facade of all of this crumbled. I had no money to back it up and no one to make it appear as though I felt strong from standing on someone's shoulders. The NFL Player's Association is in the business of looking out for players and their pensions but I needed more than that. I needed enough to make me feel like I was still cared about whether I was injured or not. Those secret weekly meetings with other guys in similar positions just didn't get me there. Why go back to bitch and complain in a circle with other people who are seated in the same kind of sinking boat as you are? I'm not a pussy; I'm a man with pride.

As a result I end up telling half-truths to any woman that will bend her trusting ear and listen, because a nigga needs a caretaker while his life is privately under reconstruction. I can't deal with not being a part of reading playbooks and getting my ass in the huddle. I started drinking like a fish again, and partying like I don't care if my liver shrivels up or stays in tact. I started screwing women who buy into the shortage of black men thing to get over on a daily basis. I'm what you call a con man, a player—whichever way you stack it, it adds up to the same pile of bull. I may be a shiftless nigga who has given up on himself, who doesn't have the balls enough to pick myself up and try again, but I'm not a broke baller. I will get my paper back. It's just a matter of when.

$

"Wake up. Wake up. Check out's at twelve. You were mumbling in your sleep. What are you talking about?"

I feel someone shake me. "Huh? Oh, shit!"

I awaken from my slumber and realize my mind drifted back to so much drama that happened in my life, including the day my parents broke up. I sit up in bed and look at who's been shaking me. I don't recognize the woman who is leaning over top of me.

"Who are you? How did I get here? Where am I?"

"We met last night at a bar, remember?"

"Not really," I admit.

"Well, I'm Monica. You fucked my brains out, and by the looks of you, you have one hell of a hangover."

"Yeah, I do. Where's Diamond?"

" *Who?* "

"My girl. We rode up here I think. Thick like mashed potatoes, brown, tight jeans."

"I don't know. What kind of name is *Diamond?* "

"Never mind."

"Who cares about her? If she was all that you wouldn't have told me you wanted to ride back to Maryland with me today, or done everything imaginable in bed. And don't worry, I paid your bar tab since you did me a favor by keeping some losers off my back."

"Thanks. I'll pay you back when you drop me off."

"That's not necessary. Look, I'm not trying to rush you or anything but you have two choices; be a one night stand, stay here and do whatever you'd like, or ride with me and my girls back to Maryland while you recover from your hangover."

"I'll take the ride as close as I can get to the city of taxation without representation."

"I thought so. Look, this is my first one night stand and I have no idea what got into me, but I think you doing your Q dance, drunk and barking, had something to do with it since I'm a Delta—plus I have a low tolerance of alcohol, and a situation that drove me to drink. I'm not exactly proud that I got down like this so could you please not mention to my sorors anything about us sleeping together? It's bad enough they'll want to pull my ass up for letting a strange man ride with us back home, but you being a brother will get me over. Better yet I'm going to lie and pretend I knew you and ran into you here. I'll tell them I asked you to stay so we could kick it in the casino last night and you rode up with your frat or something."

"That works for me. Mums the word, shortie."

"Unless you've got an extra day's hotel fee in your wallet I suggest you get a move on it. We've got ten minutes to check out and a sista has very limited funds."

"I'm right behind you."

"Good, that's where you belong. I don't know why but I think I want some more of what you gave me last night. You're one sexy chocolate man. Damn, so that's what people are talking about. I don't know what went on with your girlfriend but her loss may be my gain."

I pretend to still be in a daze as she rambles on. A plan begins to form in my head. "I'll reimburse you for everything. I feel like shit. I can't believe I cheated on Diamond. As soon as we get back to the Maryland line I've got some apologizing to do. No offense but that's my heart and whatever we did was a mistake."

"Humph. We'll see about that," she says.

We carry our luggage out of the room and close the door. I feel like I just hit the jackpot in Atlantic City because I just stumbled upon my new ride or die chick. She's light, bright, almost white, and has a body that makes Diamond's look like sloppy seconds. I think this high yellow bitch is going to enjoy the game I run on her. I'm already salivating over fresh meat that may not only replace Diamond but also prove to be the diamond in the ruff that I've been looking for.

5

TIED UP IN BONDAGE

Wes

"Yo, what up? Who dis'?" I say, picking up my cell phone without looking at the number on my caller ID. I press the mute button on the stereo and R Kelly suddenly stops singing *Big Chips,* which is being pumped through a crystal clear digital system.

"Daddy, where are you? Are you on your way to see me in The Nut Cracker? I thought you said you'd be here, Daddy," Dominique says with innocence in her voice.

I notice she sounds disappointed and I feel my heart flutter. I alter my tone of voice when I answer her.

"Oh, it's Dominique—daddy's girl. Daddy is just running a few minutes late but he'll be there to see his princess do her thing. I'm coming, sweetheart. I drove from Maryland all the way to Florida just to see you in that tutu of yours. Isn't that what they call those things that go around the middle of pretty ballerinas like you?"

"Yes. That's it, Daddy!" she giggles.

"What color is your little costume, Dom Dom?" I ask, in between puffing on a cigar laced with weed.

"Pink, it's all pink, Daddy," she replies. "I lost me another tooth, too. I'll show you when you get here and—"

"What are you doing on my cell phone? I told you not to ever touch it. It's not a toy."

I hear her mother in the background, sounding evil as always.

"But, Mommy, I just wanted to say hi to dad and ask him if—"

Her mother cuts her off. "Your teacher is calling you, Dominique. Join the others behind the stage before they get started without you. It's time for you to go and you should be concentrating on putting on your ballet slippers instead of sneaking to use my phone. Here. Hurry up and put them on."

"But I want to know if daddy's coming. He promised me," Dominique whines. Her voice begins to shake and crack.

"Look, I'm not playing with you Dom Dom," Marquita warns. "We've talked about this time and time again. Mommy and Mr. Mike are here, so be happy with us sitting in the audience. Now go on and prepare yourself for your performance. Your father has a history of breaking promises and he's probably sitting back in Maryland doing something he feels is more important. I was the one getting bubble gum out of your hair this morning, not him!"

I hear Marquita pick up the phone. "Sorry about that, Wes. The call placed to your black ass was an innocent mistake."

I inhale the smoke of the weed and exhale it slowly.

"Marquita, how could you say something like that? That was uncalled for. Why are you trying to poison my daughter's mind and teach her to hate me? Maybe if you would've let me stick my big dick up in you last time I saw you your ass wouldn't be so evil. You sound like a frustrated old bitch in need of a good all-night thrashing."

"Pleaase! You think you can stroll along and act like you can't tell motherfucking time? In time Dominique will hate you, without me giving my two cents. You left your daughter alone with a whole room of people getting high, watching porn, and let her get a hold of beer. Me, myself, I've got nothing to prove because over my dead body will I allow some shit like that to go down around my daughter again. You on the other hand don't even care about what you exposed her to because you're a treacherous nigga—a wolf in sheep's clothing that doesn't have at least one person fooled and that's me."

"There's no need to cuss at me, Marquita. I see your husband's influenced you for the worse. That's what happens when you hang with niggas with no class or cash. It never goes nowhere good, woman."

"Shut the fuck up! I'm tired of your trifling-ass bad habits and Lord knows I've tried my best to look the other way, but I'm to the point where I feel like cussing so damn it, I'll cuss. Talking about having no class, you ought to be ashamed to mess up with your

54

daughter again. You can't do right if you tried. Here she is in her first ballet recital and you can't even make up for your last let down by following through this time. I regret the day I fucked you, Wes! I wish my husband was her father and I never met your sorry-ass. I can't wait until Dom Dom turns eighteen so I can forget you ever existed. You have been a thorn in my side since the day I found out I was carrying your child. Apparently I'll pay for that mistake for the rest of my life."

I cough heartily a few times, and place the cigar in the ashtray.

"Give a nigga a break and get out of my crack, woman. I had a game yesterday and I have all kinds of pressures on my back. I know you heard about the brawl in Detroit, and I've got some heavy concerns as a result. And for your information, I'm in Florida and I'm not too far away. I said I'd be there and my ass will be sitting in the audience to see my baby girl rock the show like no one else. Now I'm tired of talking nice to your bitch-ass like you're a lady when you talk to me like I'm your little pussy-whipped nigga. I'm the fucking man so you better catch a case of respect for Wes Montgomery and stop yapping all of this bull in my ear. Get with the program, Marquita because my patience is wearing thin when it comes to you."

"Fine, so now you pay a little child support and you think you can act like you've been in Dom Dom's life all along?" Marquita replies. "You think you can insult a responsible black man like my husband who has been supportive of her and me from day one? Now that your business has been put out in the street you have an attitude because you have to contribute to your daughter's living expenses. Take care of your responsibilities, Wes. Come back to honesty and think about when our fathers weren't there for us in the projects. The least you can do is set a better standard for your daughter than how to be a world-class whore. You can take a nigga out of the ghetto but you can't take the ghetto out of the nigga. I'm not one of your stupid hos that you can tell anything to, Wes. I know you better than anyone, even better than you know yourself. You're not even close to Florida right now. And as far as the brawl situation, I told you, you're getting one step closer to self-destructing. Who threw a water cooler at a fan last year and got the athletes gone wild started? If you're implicated this time, so be it.

55

Before it's over with you'll be one of the players who make the league minimum, that can't afford to drive your Hummer since gas prices are so high. Prepare to trade it in like some of the others, Wes. SUV sales are down because so many of you niggas are going broke—haven't you heard? Your plastic worlds are falling apart, boo boo. The next step will be—"

"That's it. Two can play this game and I don't have time to argue with you. When I get there just be ready to take your little janitor husband and move on the other side of the auditorium far away from me. You try to act like you're such an uppity, classy bitch now. Don't make me have to remind you about your roots, Marquita. Neither one of us had shit up in the South Baltimore. The thing is you still ain't got shit and never will. You'll always be that girl from da hood who got her cherry busted, gripping the toilet in her mother's bathroom while she was cooking dinner on the other side of the wall. That makes you a ho for life, so who are you to judge me and how I run my shit? And just to prove a point, my H2 Hummer is equipped with so much custom shit from mink trim to four TV screens and twenty-eight inch wheels that my ride should've been in GM's first All-Car Showdown during the pre-game festivities for the NBA All-Star Game. Next year, it's on, Marquita. I will be crowned the king of bling."

"Listen to you. All you do is hide behind your fucking money, fool! What about other things besides money? I messed up and I sure as hell don't deny it, so what you say doesn't make or break me. You and I both know that you're not going to show up so why don't you do us all a favor and shrivel up and die as soon as possible. That's my Christmas wish."

The line goes dead and I'm stunned that my ex had the balls enough to wish me dead. Especially as I'm considering making a fifteen-hour trek just to watch a little girl jump around in pink tights.

As I'm driving, I feel my blood pressure rise. I don't know who Marquita thinks she is, carrying me like I'm some common hood nigga. As a matter of fact I need to pull my ass over on this highway and calm down before I kick my speed up to 120 and risk getting pulled over by the cops on 95 South. Who does my baby's bitch ass momma think she is? I'll be there when I get there. I'm not in Florida but I didn't forget about the recital and I'll make it up to my daughter. I'm a much better father than mine was—he didn't bother to make an effort to go to one basketball game or watch me swing a bat in little league. By my standards Dominique has it more than good. What am I saying? Maybe I need to admit it's time to talk to someone, but I'm not going to no shrink so the media can get wind of that shit. They have enough ammunition on me these days. I don't know if the weed has me too fucked up to reason, or if the ways of my father taught me to become a deadbeat dad, but it must be a sign that a steeple is in view, on the right hand side of the road. There are three sides to every story— my side, Marquita's side, and the truth. I'm feeling like I need a fourth opinion for the sake of my sanity.

$

"So what you're saying is my baby's momma is right for having a nigga that's been incarcerated up in her house, being a role model for my baby girl? I just can't see it. She should know better than that," I tell the minister.

He's about sixty, with a rotund gut, which tells me that the sisters in his church keep him well fed with Sunday dinners. He leans forward on the wooden pew.

"What was he incarcerated for? Do you know?"

"I know all right. A couple of days ago I found out that when this dude was in his late twenties he was a notorious drug dealer. Not only that but I also found out he's a recovering addict and still goes to Alcoholics Anonymous."

"There's still no right or wrong here, Wes," the preacher says. "If this man is going to A.A. to keep himself together, is employed, and has been taking care of the child before you stepped in, what right do you have to judge him? We all deserve a second chance so why doesn't he? Apparently, he did his time, got his life straight, and married you child's mother. But this isn't really about him or his prison record is it? You're bitter because the mother of your child moved on and married a man like her husband. Isn't that

57

more like what's bothering you? Another man is doing everything you ought to have done."

My eyes drift toward the red, blue, and green colors in the stained glass window. Then I turn back toward the reverend.

"I checked up on that nigga and I can't stand no drug dealers. Okay, so that was back in '85, but still. My little cousin got shot up because his brother was dealing. I'm past her, man. Believe that. How can he be better than me?" I sigh and rub the fabric of my blue jeans. "That chick's got issues—enough to make me pull over and take a chance that someone was up in this church. I felt like I could hurt somebody, and I can't be feeling like that 'cause I can afford to get her knocked off. I ain't trying to follow in Ray Carruth's footsteps."

The reverend grips his large burgundy Bible with both hands. "You say that you wish ill for this woman, but if that was the case you wouldn't have been talking about her for the past ten minutes. You're still in love with her and your hostility is a sign of that. Why are you running from the truth, Wes? It will do absolutely no good."

Out of nowhere I feel tears building up. I begin to sniff before breaking down in a constant flow of tears. I can't talk any longer and I feel my face growing hot as Arizona sand. The reverend stands. I can't bear to look him in the face so I concentrate on looking at his salt and pepper colored beard.

"Let's pray," he says. "Come to the altar and lay down your burdens. You need to confess your sins and make Jesus Christ a part of your life. If you do that it will simplify so much." He kneels and waits for me to do the same. "Do you not remember where your blessings come from?"

I stand and refuse to mimic him by kneeling. I feel angry with God and close my mind. "He is a part of my life. I don't need you to tell me I'm saved!" Tears fall from my eyes. I keep my head down so this man I barely know can't read the hidden hurt on my face.

"The fact that you can't kneel on the Lord's altar and give all of your sins and burdens to Him proves that you've been playing with God, and have fallen into the ways of the world. The ways of the world can lead people astray and you have been lead astray with materialism, sex, drugs, and fame. I see it in your eyes—you want to come home, Wes. Come home while there's still time for you to set the record straight with the one that truly matters. The Lord doesn't care about where you've been, just where you're going. Real men pray, so stop running from the importance of prayer."

"You don't know what it's like trying to be a father in the NBA," I say. "You can easily kneel on this altar telling me I'm so twisted, judging me and shit. You don't know what it's like out in those streets dodging people trying to get in your pocket, or trying to please coaches and fans. I'm no A.C. Greene. I'm not cut from that cloth—I've got a little too much bad boy in me. When I get up, then what? Where was God when I—"

"Why are you making excuses for yourself? You want to be a bad boy, so you are. Black men have an added responsibility to pass along a legacy of strength, not one of pain. Why are we making society happy by feeding into their madness, by keeping our families divided and perpetuating genocide? There comes a time when we all must move past what was and deal with what is by accepting personal responsibility. History teaches us you should be a father and a leader to set a standard for your progeny. These are things every black man should think on. Are you aware of your behavior becoming a Nubian? Have you forgotten that you are a hero to little boys who idolize you, and that what you do sticks in their minds? Come on now, son, our community is in crisis. Get caught up in the right life, and stay there."

"It's just not that simple. I was the first one in my family to make it out of the projects, the first to break the cycle of poverty—the first to make my paper the legit way. The rest you just don't understand. I need a sign so that I'll know God is here. I just need a sign that He knows my pain, my pressures, and my concerns. I'm a human being and just because I wear a jersey doesn't mean I don't have problems. I never asked to be anyone's hero, and I never asked one parent to lie to their child and claim that I am. How I make my money to put dinner on my table doesn't mean I don't need my privacy to live my life. I'm not a perfect man and I never claimed to be."

I walk in a circle in front of the altar, silently asking God for the will to kneel, but I still can't make my knees bend and fall.

Andrea Blackstone

"Why are you bitter with the Father? What has happened to you to harden your heart, son? Your words stay here—just let them go and God will catch them. Untie yourself from bondage."

"I just need some time to heal, ok?" I say, finally falling to my knees, clenching my hands in prayer as my mind flashes back to the eye of my storm. In my mind I hear my mother's harsh voice.

"Get over there and do what he asked of you, boy!"

I lay on my cot on the other side of the room. "He ain't my daddy— no! I won't do it!" I holler.

The gold rings that line the knuckles of my mother's pimp shine as he walks toward me like a cold thug would. I feel myself beginning to choke from fear and wish I could escape through the window, as I had done in the past. He throws my cover off of me and grips me by the neck.

"I told you to undress. Hurry the fuck up kid! You're damn right—I'm not your daddy. You can't get out of the window this time 'cause Snake done nailed it shut. In fact, every window in this dump is nailed shut. You need my permission to even breathe outside air, you got that shit?"

Tears stream down my face as the perverted man fondles me, and his penis lengthens. I squeeze my eyes shut wishing that my mother would save me. Instead she commands me to endure the pain and humiliation.

"I need a hit, and you need to eat. Man up, boy. Man up! Thank your father for this."

While I continue sniffling the pimp takes a strap and beats me until whelps and bruises form.

"Next time I don't want to hear a sound from you. If I call you over here, you obey me and come."

After I stand he kicks me across the room with his foot and I fall to the floor. I curl up into a ball and hide in the closet as I hear my junkie mother get a hit of crack in exchange for what she allowed this man do to me. When he finished with me he didn't want to have sex with my mother, so I knew that the rest of the night would consist of her turning tricks with multiple men. Sometimes Snake would wait outside of the bedroom door—other times he would kick me out of my bed while he watched and collected the money the second the dirt was done. I learned to

60

cope by staying in the darkness until my brother appeared from playing outdoors.

When my parents went their separate ways my mother, Malik, and I ended up in a one-bedroom apartment, and we all shared the same sleeping space. I'll never understand why my mother forced me to sleep with my nose toward the wall while Malik got to sleep on the couch in the living room, nor will I ever understand why I was molested and he wasn't, but it made me hate my twin Malik, even if he didn't know what I was going through.

The worse he endured was witnessing this man invade our space where we used to watch cartoons and fight over which channel we would watch. Occasionally he witnessed Snake watch one of the many porn tapes that lined the living room wall, or walking down the hall in the building to use the bathroom everyone shared because no one had one of their own. Me, I was the one who fetched beer, cigarettes, and drug paraphernalia for my mother. I was the one who lived in hell each time Snake molested me, robbing me of my ability to have my first sexual experience with a female. The first time he touched me it began as slaps across my face, supposedly to make me tough. I felt the sting as he dared me to cry, and his sinister smile and laugh became etched in my memory bank.

The reverend's voice snaps me out of revisiting these memories.

"I pray for your soul, young man. I pray for your soul. I don't know what is weighing heavily upon your heart but something is causing you to run from yourself. You can run all you want to but wherever you go you take yourself with you. Running never solves a thing." After he hands me a tissue, he adds, "I work with young men every day, out on these streets. People you wouldn't think have come to God in this house of the Lord—hustlers, pimps, prostitutes, drug addicts—some of everyone. Street life only goes so far then it will destroy you. If you want to play the game, you must be prepared to deal with the consequences of playing Russian roulette with your life. It's not a matter of judging anyone; it's one of personal responsibility—something that our culture has gotten away from. Something that the young have forgotten and the old are no longer around to teach them. I can't tell you what to do, but

I can deliver the message in my heart that God is telling me to share with you."

I don't answer, but I'm still listening.

"He's saying that you need to represent as a king. That you need to stop playing into the hands of the media and those that expect you and others like you to do the wrong thing, instead of being forced to do the right one. If you don't want to come to God right now, at least think about it and make your first step going to your daughter. Better late than never. Next time, be on time and consider that you should stop breaking your daughter's heart. She didn't ask to be here, but she is. This isn't about you or her mother—it's about her. Don't lose focus of the one who should be your focus. Go straight to your daughter, Wes. God has shown me that it is very important that you do so when you leave this house of the Lord."

Finally I've had enough. I rise from the altar and scream. "Don't preach to me about personal responsibility. Don't preach to me about taking care of kids. Don't preach to me about the black family. Don't preach to me about coming to God and seeking his face. I waited for God and He never came to save me! Both of my *fathers* left me. You don't walk in my shoes so don't talk about a life you have no idea I've led." I draw a deep breath, "You're right—I have been playing with God because *there is none*. I was playing with the image hanging on my wall. The white man with the blue eyes and blonde hair, that's not real. I don't know why I'm here—it's all a waste of time. Thanks for showing me the light. You've been a big help to me. I'm officially through with Todd Lester Harrison *and* the other one."

After various pieces of my life flash before me I tear my platinum gold cross from my neck and throw the sacred symbol onto the floor. I move swiftly toward the entrance of the church. As I inhale the night air, I feel a new anger fill my heart, while a foreboding sense of evil fills my spirit.

I hear an out of breath reverend tell me, "He was always there and still is right now. God looks like all of us, no one in particular. Take your words back, son. Don't give up on the one who can strengthen you!" He begins wheezing from being out of shape. "Please, son, do what I've told you. He's the answer to all your problems—take your problems to God! Reconsider your harsh words and stop living in sin! The good book says not to be conformed to the ways of the world, but be transformed by the renewing of your mind!"

As he heaves to catch his breath, I hit the stereo button, grab a joint, and pretend I can't hear the reverend, trying his best to reach a lost soul who feels like he's carrying the burdens of one thousand men. I pull away from the Baptist church in North East, D.C., and don't even give a shit about the cops when I open my window to blow out the smoke from the blunt. I feel invincible again because I remember that the NBA is my father and precious love. It created everything I am, opened up all kinds of doors in my life, and comforts me with the roar of the crowd, and by filling my bank account season after season. There is a God—and money is it!

6

A DAY IN THE LIFE OF DRAMA CENTRAL

Jalita

I really want to forget that I stood before a commissioner for assaulting a ticket cop with an orange, so I'll skip over rehashing the details of my night's stay in a D.C. jail. With all the lowdown street stuff going on in the city, they've got the nerve to lock me up for someone provoking me. The only good that came of it was that I raised the rest of my rent money after I was released, venturing to other stores to return merchandise and collect the much-needed cash.

Right now, I don't know what smells worse, the odors that floated past my nose in District Seventeen, or the perfume and funk combination that proves that some don't half wash their tits, hole and elbows. My landlord, Ms. Geraldine, is one of those types who never properly acquainted herself with soap—at least since I've known her. My eyes shift over her loud floral printed housecoat. A thick line of powder rests in between her droopy titties, which seem large enough to throw across her shoulders. As I look at her, I'm thinking I can't fathom that the queen of funk would toss me out on my ear in a mere seventy-two hours. Especially since her apartment building near Mondawin Mall is no palace.

"What do you mean, I've been evicted? I was in the hospital and you just took your rent money from me. I'm only three days late." I look at her in disbelief, as she tucks my five one hundred dollar bills into her bra.

"Look, I can't go around giving people free rides. I'm a landlord. In case you've forgotten, I've got to eat, too," she says.

"By no means am I asking for a free ride. Haven't you ever heard of landlord tenant law? You have to take me downtown. You can't just arbitrarily do this without following certain rules. And you just took this month's rent," I complain. I feel my temper heating up but I fight to keep it suppressed within the depths of my being.

"I didn't know if you were coming back. You could've called. Sorry," she shrugs, like she really just doesn't give a damn. "The place has been rented to someone else. And as far as this month's rent, you owed me for it because you broke the lease. You're lucky I'm not tacking on the late charge. Don't push it."

"What!" I explode. "I've been living in your apartment for the last six months and all you can manage to do is tell me sorry and stick my funds under your sweaty tit? I don't make any noise. I've never had one visitor. I helped fix up my apartment with my own money, and I've watched your grandkids for free. I put up with the hot water going out every other day in the middle of showers. I had to heat the place with the oven because the radiators don't half work, and I can't count how many times I've played tag with mice and roaches that I tried to catch with all kinds of traps. Now you mean to tell me this is what I get just coming out of the hospital? Look at this building. It's old and falling apart. You ought to be glad to have one tenant as sane as me."

"Well, I have six apartments and all six units are rented. You do the math. By my records not one of my tenants has any problem wanting to pay cheap rent. Where else can you go for five hundred dollars a month? Some of you are never satisfied. I try to give you a break and this is what I get for trying to be decent to my people."

"I need a place at the same price. Why are you doing this to me?" I ask, nervously cracking my knuckles.

"Look, business is business, Jalita. If you wanted to secure your place legally you should've had me type up a contract. You didn't even request it, so it's Ms. Geraldine's word against yours. Be my guest and go downtown and complain if you'd like but you don't have a leg to stand on with an oral leasing agreement. I'm telling you that right now. I don't know how long you've been renting places but I've been a landlord for thirty years," she says arrogantly.

Suddenly I hate Ms. Geraldine and wish I could snatch her whiskers off her chin. "I want my security deposit, this month's rent I just gave you, and my belongings. And for your information, with any lease under a year, I don't have to get it in writing. You're just going back on your word. I believed what you said. See, this is a prime example of why you can't trust people."

"You don't have any receipt or lease for anything. And what security deposit are you talking about?" she asks, placing her hands on her hips.

"I didn't damage anything and I'm due my deposit back. Don't play stupid with me. I gave you a month's rent up front. Come on now Ms. Geraldine. You know I'm telling the truth."

"Since you want to quote Maryland law, Maryland law states that I can evict you for non-payment of rent. I had the right to do so the day your rent due date passed. And if I did owe you a deposit back, which I don't, I'd have forty days to deliver it to you."

"Well what's the solution, here? I'm not going to keep standing in the doorway, arguing with you. Like I said, I was just released from the hospital and you have no idea what I went through to bring you your money. Give me a break, Ms. Geraldine."

"Where you go is not my problem. Some people don't want to spend nothing and still end up behind the eight ball," she says, clicking her dentures up and down in her mouth.

I want to whop her, or snatch back my money, but after just being released from jail I'm not trying to go right back for putting my hands on this old bat. Instead I begin to walk up the steps mumbling. "I've had enough of this shit. You try to talk to people with some respect and decency and you get carried. Don't think I didn't notice my new shoes on your feet, you trifling old thief! This shit happened to me my last year at school, now this. I must be cursed in life because wherever I go and however hard I try to do right drama finds me. I'm tired of life. I hate my life, I just hate it!"

When I reach the apartment at the top of the steps, I begin to stick the key in the door and the door opens.

"Is everything all right out there, shortie?"

"No in the hell it isn't," I say in a flustered voice. "And I'm sure you can tell that by the tone of my voice. The landlord gave my apartment to you and now I have no place to go. Can I get my stuff at least or are you going to try to run game, too?"

"I hate to be the one to tell you but the place was empty when I got here two days ago," the man answers. You can look around if you like. Shortie, I've got my own paper. I'm not interested in running game on you or no one else."

"No, I believe you. Shit, now what am I gonna do?" I feel tears beginning to form in my eyes. I shake my head wishing I could whip the landlord's ass and snatch my money back.

"Why don't you step inside and get yourself together," he says. "If you need to use the phone you can do that, too. I don't mind."

Since I know that my prepaid GoPhone is in the car with a dead battery, I walk inside, although I'm no longer down with getting close to strangers.

"I have a sister and I would want someone to do this for her. It's cool, shortie. I'm not going to bother you," he says after handing me the phone book I asked for.

I take a chance on his claim being true and smile slightly. I take the black cordless phone into my left hand and begin to thumb through the phone book. At this point I don't give a shit where I lay my head as long as I can rest without sexing someone for a spot. My hands begin to shake and I can't remember the alphabet well enough to make sense of the contents. I recall I was directed to fill some prescription for my nerves but I haven't been able to conquer that problem yet.

The man walks over to me. "I know this is stressful for you. Let's try a resource I know of. I can't remember exactly but it has something to do with a program for those who are evicted and left homeless. Let's call the Baltimore City's Department of Social Services and see what we come up with. Here's the number: 410-878-8650."

I reach for the paper, my hands still shaking.

"I'll do it. I got you," he says, taking the phone. After what seems like a long time, somebody answers. "Yes, I'd like to know what someone can do if they've been evicted and they're homeless." He pauses. "Yes, ok. Thank you." He hangs up and looks at me. "443-423-6000—the number to Homeless Emergency Environmental Services at 1920 North Broadway. Here we go again. Let's see what they've got to say." After he dials another set of numbers he repeats the same question. Then he asks me, "You're a city resident, right?"

"I *was* until Ms. Geraldine put an end to that," I reply sarcastically. I feel humiliated, getting tangled up with social services after running away when I was a ward of the state. I vowed never to return to the system, and now I'm listening to Angie Stone belt out some lyrics and wondering how far I'll need to go backward to move forward. I sigh loudly and continue to listen to one side of the conversation.

"Yes, she is," he says. After speaking with someone on the other end a bit longer he hangs up the phone. "This is the deal, ma," he explains, while scribbling some information on a piece of paper from a spiral notebook. "Go to this address, Monday through Friday between nine and four. Ask to speak to a case manager. That's all they'd tell me." He hands me the information and I can barely read his messy handwriting. Even so, I appreciate his effort. I stand, and when I do, I notice that my heart is pounding. I feel winded, and my concentration won't return.

"Thanks for your hospitality. I'll follow up on it. Sorry I came in here with a chip on my shoulder. It's just been a rough day for me."

"Don't worry about it. Are you okay? You don't look so good."

"I just got out of the hospital, but I'm straight," I tell him, sitting back down.

"Today is Saturday," he answers. "Do you have a place to go for a few days until you can get some answers?"

"I'm thankful my car wasn't towed while I was gone. I can sleep in there if I need to."

"Don't do that."

"Like I said, I'll be straight. It won't be the first or last time I've been in this situation."

"You're welcome to crash here for a few days."

"I can't do that," I explain.

"Well, I offered," he says nonchalantly.

"You did and I appreciate it."

"No problem. Take care of yourself."

As I get off from the couch I give the man I slight smile and leave. I walk to the car wondering what to do next. I'm broke as hell, thanks to my ghetto-ass landlord who's all about the money. I don't have time or energy to take her downtown, so I may as well swallow my lumps, make do, focus on getting out of dodge and hope that I'm stable enough to drive my car.

After finding a lot and charging up my cell phone, I locate my Cousin Shawn's number. He's the only person I'm comfortable enough to call although he's still pissed off at me for getting involved with Wes after he told me to leave his baller ass alone. After I scroll through the numbers stored in my phone I summons the number to Shawn's two-way that I haven't used since last year. As promised, he doesn't let me down. He tells me to meet him at his place not far from Lexington Market, and prepare to spend the night and come up with a plan on my behalf. In addition we have some family housecleaning to do anyway. Hopefully we can let bygones be bygones and clear the air. Perhaps we can kill two birds with one stone. I'll see.

When I pull up to Shawn's two-story row house I see him standing in the door. My nerves relax slightly and I'm thankful that I can depend on Shawn having my back once again. After I push anything exposed under my seats and secure my whooptie with a club, I walk up the three steps and greet Shawn. He still looks exactly the same, and we share an odd moment.

"It's about time you came to see your cousin, girl," he says with a grin, breaking the ice. "Did it take you getting sick again for you to stop by so I can remember what you look like?" He hugs me, releases me from our embrace, then holds the door open as I walk inside.

"I'm sorry for not listening, Shawn. I apologize for what went down last year."

"That's in the past. Live in the present and look forward to tomorrow, and the day after that and that and that—you get my point."

"Yes, I do. Are you standing on your tippy toes? You look a few centimeters taller, shrimp," I joke.

"Always the jokester," he laughs. "Girl, don't you start that short man stuff."

"I'm sorry. I just couldn't resist."

"Make yourself at home," he tells me.

"So, how's married life treating you these days?"

"It's fine. Great, in fact," he answers.

Just looking around in a short time my eyes observe fist holes in the wall and broken lamps that give me a clue that Shawn is lying his little ass off. He and Jackie's crib is beautifully decorated, and it's a shame that the leather couch has stab marks in it, obviously put there by large kitchen knives. Half of everything looks as if his wifey's temper has moved toward the over the top mark, including a door that must've been ripped off the hinges and is now resting against the wall. As I'm taking all of this in I hear Jackie calling out to him.

"Shawn, who came in here? I'm hungry. Bring me something to eat. You didn't finish cleaning the wheel chair. Get up here! God you're slow!"

"Umm, come say hi to Jackie. She's pregnant. I think she's going through hormonal changes," he says.

I reason otherwise and don't want to follow him to see Ms. Mixed Messages, but I do. I've always wondered who in the hell kept Shawn on a string the way she did. Now I'd finally have the chance to lay eyes on the woman who managed to fuck Shawn's cousin but still convince Shawn to take her back, and even follow through with marriage. After we walk up about eight steps I see who I assume to be Jackie laid up on the bed looking like a whale, she's so rotund.

"Jackie, this is my cousin—and—"

Jackie cuts him off. "Come over here and clean up this wheel chair so I can get around. You know I'm not supposed to be on my feet because of the blood clot. And I asked you to pick up a Triple Crown Publications book for me from Expressions. We live around the corner and your ass can't even do that either. If I have to be stuck in bed I may as well have something to keep me from wanting to get out of it."

I stand in the doorway and watch Shawn run over to Jackie's bedside. He grabs a rag and resumes cleaning a filthy wheelchair with a blue seat that slouches down in the middle. I swallow hard as I watch Jackie twist up her mouth like Shawn is moving too slowly.

"You don't do nothing," she insults. "Give me that rag—I'll do it myself, you idiot. This is why I can't stay off my feet."

"I'm doing it, baby," Shawn replies. "Let me finish please. Now go lay back down."

"You couldn't find your way out of a wet paper bag. I should've let Wes keep breaking me off. He won't want me now—I'm all fat and shit. It's just as easy to find a man with something as one without. That's what my grandmother used to say, and now I see the old bat was right. Did Jackie listen? Hell no. Now I'm knocked up again by another half-broke nigga that works at a gas station and hides sodas in the trunk of his car because he's too cheap to share anything with me. Hmmph. And the other one is taking me to child support court. Why do I do this to myself? Why, why, why?"

Jackie takes her big foot and pushes Shawn off the bed like he's the nasty wet rag headed for Monday's trash pickup. I'm embarrassed for him and begin to back away out of the door. When I do, I back into a small child about four years old. While Shawn is picking himself up from the floor I hear the child say, "Hi, what's your name?"

"Jalita," I answer.

"Come in my room. Will you play with me?"

She takes my hand and looks up into my eyes. I assume she's Jackie's daughter because she looks just like her in the face, but I have to admit she's as cute as a button. Although I'm winded I'm grateful to escape from Shawn and Jackie's drama. I hear them arguing as I turn the corner and enter the small girl's room.

"What's your name?" I say gently.

"Myra," she says with a wide smile.

"You're very pretty, Myra."

"Do you like my room?" she asks.

"Yes, it's beautiful," I tell her.

It is. The wall is painted two shades of pink, the darkest hue at the top. A light border accents the perimeter of the ceiling. Her white furniture looks delicate and feminine, and her personal computer sits on top of a kiddie desk in the corner. Apparently, Jackie and Shawn don't fight in Myra's space, which relieves me.

Myra scratches her nose and pats the bed. "Sit down."

"How old are you?" I ask after I sit down next to her.

"This many."

She holds up four fingers in my face then backs away from me. This kid has the feel of a little adult and it sort of freaks me out, but I remind myself that she is four years old as opposed to being a grown woman. She's one of those adults in a kid's body. I can tell that because I was one myself.

"Do you hear Mr. Shawn and Mommy arguing? They always do that. Mommy broke the mirror in the hall last week. It was right over there. Glass was all over the floor." She points around the corner then looks at me with her gorgeous large eyes.

I try to change to subject. "What's your favorite color?"

"Pink. Me love pink. I have pink slippers. Pink covers. Pink Spongehead Bob— "

While I'm listening to her, I hear Shawn holler. "OOOOw! Damnit Jackie!"

Instinctively, I run into Shawn and Jackie's bedroom. I get there in time to see Jackie scratch Shawn's face, and then bite him on the arm like his limb is a juicy chicken leg. I wince in pain for the brother as he snatches his arm back, shakes it, and rubs it vigorously.

"I'm trying to help you," he says. "Why are you so difficult? You left teeth marks in my arm. What's wrong with you? You've lost your mind!"

"Weren't you listening to me, you broke lazy ass? I should've stayed with your cousin, Wes. Get out of my room in *my* house!"

Jackie throws the phone across the room and it hits the big screen television, knocking out the screen. She continues screaming and cursing, although she's on bed rest and has a hard time moving because of her extreme weight gain.

Myra pulls on my shirttail, and puts her arm through the hole. She gives me a wide-eyed look. "Awww. Look what mommy did to the TV!"

"Don't do that. You might hurt yourself," I tell her. "Let's go downstairs."

I'm sad that Myra endures sights like these and has become used to being a third party to mommy demolishing what should be home sweet home. It's even worse when I hear Jackie call out to the little girl.

"Myra, spit on Shawn!"

To my surprise the little girl runs over to Shawn and spits on him like a pro. Her ability to turn nasty upon demand causes me to quickly scurry downstairs and sit on the couch.

"Now call him a stupid ass," she commands.

"Stupid ass!" Myra parrots.

Her tone mimicked her mother so much she could have been Jackie's evil twin. At that moment Myra appeared to be four going on about thirty.

The screaming continues and I hear a low rumble of Shawn weakly defending himself. "Jackie, how could you teach Myra to do something like that? What kind of mother are you? You're sick!"

After I process the scene, I close my eyes, exhale heavily, and then rest my head on the back of the couch. I'm suddenly feeling as though my problems are nothing in comparison to Shawn's. About ten minutes later the door opens. I raise my head and watch a man walk up three steps and move across the living room. His eyes are red and he's as skinny as a rail. In fact he looks as if I could wrap my pinky around his ankle.

"Hi miss lady," he says moving past me like he's familiar with the house.

"Hi," I say, with no clue of who he is.

He begins scanning the room, and I'm not sure what in the hell he's looking for so feverishly. I watch him pick up the VCR, toaster, and begin to take a large picture off the wall. I finally realized he's a crack head, his jittery presence indicates his desire to rob Shawn and Jackie blind.

Apparently Shawn hears him, and comes flying down the steps.

"Yo, B, put it down. Not this time you don't. I've had to put a padlock on my own refrigerator because of you. You're breaking my pocket. And would you stop picking the lock to get in? There's a reason you no longer have a key."

"I was just straightening up, Shawn. I wasn't taking nothing. You know me better than that. Now I steal? That's not right."

"Your sister broke up half of what we own," Shawn replies. "You're not going to steal the other half, so put my shit back under the Christmas tree, and the angel back on top of it. This has got to stop and it will right now. Someone told me they saw you getting high in a house down the street, and someone else in the neighborhood tried to sell me my own iron and hair clippers. Pretty soon I'll have nothing left. What's next, my car? And don't think I don't know what happened to Myra's missing piggy bank."

As the man pauses and places the wrapped goods down under the tree, Shawn snatches the angel and places it on top of the tree himself.

"I needed help. You don't do nothing, and you're not home half the time. I asked my brother to come over to help with Myra. I keep telling you I'm not supposed to be on my feet and you don't listen. Get off his back!" Jackie screams from upstairs. "He punched Myra in the stomach, Darrell," she lies. "Are you going to let him treat your niece like that? Do something to defend us."

While all of this is going on I see the man eying my purse. "Don't even think about it," I tell him. Although it's nearly empty I pick it up anyway and remove it from the coffee table. I clutch it tightly and hold it close to my body.

"I see Jackie bit you, and now this Darrell character is trying to wipe you out the old-fashioned way. Why don't you call the police Shawn?" I say. "I told you to leave her alone, but I guess we're even. I've got love for you but I'm trying to straighten out my ship and find my shade in this life. Thanks for everything. I'm rolling out. We'll talk at some point." I begin walking toward the door, feeling a burning sensation in my chest.

"Jalita don't leave," says Shawn. "You came here to rest. I've got your bed made up and everything."

I was about to answer when I hear Jackie bang on the wall four times. "Shawn, are you going to bring me something to eat or what?" she screams.

"Why, so you can lie to the police and tell them I put my hands on you?" he shouts back at her. "Ask your brother. He picked the lock to get in here, supposedly to help you. Or maybe he's down here robbing us blind. You're probably the one that drove him to crack in the first place!"

"You've got your hands more than full," I tell him, shaking my head sadly. "Damn, Shawn, your arm is bleeding. Take care of that and tend to your household. I told you girls born and bred in B-more City hold it down and that still hasn't changed."

74

He looks down and sees the blood dripping from his right arm.

"I called 911. I'm reporting you for punching my baby in the stomach. You're going to jail tonight," Jackie screams.

"Thanks for running my cousin off—now she's leaving. My own family can't even visit me, thanks to your Dr. Jekyll, Mr. Hyde ass," Shawn yells.

"You're the one with the record, you idiot. She probably ain't your cousin anyway. How long you been fucking her? I knew you were cheating on me. All black men cheat! I can't wait for *Diary of a Mad Black Woman* to come out at the movies because I'm going to watch it at least ten times. I am one mad black woman who could've written the script myself!"

I walk to my car, unlock my club and sigh as I plop in the driver's seat. I look toward Shawn and Jackie's place and watch Jackie's drug addicted brother flee the scene with an arm full of their possessions. I can still hear Jackie hollering and complaining so loud that her insults spill outdoors. Myra walks toward the storm glass window and waves at me with tears streaming down her face. A tear falls down my face too as I remember what it feels like to be in Myra's shoes. The only way I can cope is to pull off into the darkness and worry about where I will sleep afterward. Talking about a dysfunctional family, people don't know one quarter of my world. Everybody's got drama, down to the little kid who's just learning to talk good. While most people endure family squabbles, I endure wars that would make the strongest man fall to his knees and beg for just one person acting right in the name of getting along.

7

SHIT OUTTA LUCK

Wes

"Wes, it's Malik."

"Who is this?" I say like I don't recognize the familiar voice.

"You know, your brother," he says with frustration. "Look, I've been wondering how you've been getting along. Family sticks together; they don't separate under any circumstances."

"Malik, I don't have time for your bullshit. What do you *really* want?"

"You're always the skeptic, Wes. I got myself together, just like you said. I cut out my drinking and I'm clean now. Damn, is missing my twin such a crime? I don't want shit but your company. I fought with myself over whether I should pick up the phone or not, but I decided this is long overdue. I was going to see if you wanted to meet me for a little fun like we used to do."

I don't say anything right away because I'm still trying to figure out if Malik is bullshitting.

"I'm not going to beg you, but if you want to see some fat asses shake and do shit that can't be done in most clubs, come meet me in P.G. County where I am. Hopefully we can squash some things and keep it light," Malik says.

After riding around in downtown D.C. for a while, I still feel uptight and preoccupied from digging up emotions about so many downers in my life. The upside is the booming music coming through my speakers. I don't know why I'm rolling up to the address where my estranged brother is, but when I approach a banner that reads *Female Dancers,* it signals me that I suddenly find myself fiending for erotic pleasure and tension release.

Apparently Malik invited me to a garage strip club, which is a car garage by day and strip club at night. Maybe there will be no harm in it. I can pull a hat over my eyes, act like I'm a drug-dealing hustler that often frequents spots like this, and pretend I'm not Wes Montgomery, the baller with the long paper. Tonight I'll just be a neighborhood small-time shot caller who wants to watch booties shake. I'll stay for fifteen minutes or so to speak to my brother, then I'll be out and off to Florida to deal with Marquita's baby momma drama shit. When I get back in town I need to stop procrastinating and get a pole installed in my basement. That way these hos can come to me and dance 'til their knees give out, and I won't have to hit up hood spots like this to see some buck wild shit. When I approach and prepare to pay the outrageous fee for this type of operation, I see Malik.

"I got you. It's taken care of," he says.

I'm stunned that Malik looks fresh, clean and actually isn't trying to sponge off me.

"Thanks, man."

Although I'm still leery of Malik's invitation I follow my brother through the makeshift joint where the smell of car oil is heavy. A stripper quickly catches my eye. She must be able to smell money because I see her smiling from across the room like she's ready to go on the prowl.

Malik leans over and whispers, "Look at that right there. You getting play already, playboy. You the man!"

No sooner than I sat down in a folding chair, the same stripper walks over to me. "Don't say a word, just follow me," she says.

She's got a refreshing thickness I haven't experienced in a while—about a size 11/12, with double D titties and thick country girl legs. I feel my dick harden and I can't help but to be aroused by this chocolate sista with the layered blonde wet-n-wavy braids cascading down her back. I follow her to a corner of the garage.

"I know you can afford the VIP treatment so I won't ask."

I watch her wind her waist to a rap tune, wishing I could grip on her ass and lick those pretty, suckable breasts.

"You like what you see, don't you baby? If you do, tip me right."

She saunters over to me, puts her crotch up in my face and I find myself stuffing three hundred dollars in her silver and black

Andrea Blackstone

sequined G-string. Before I know it two other women appear from nowhere with my brother. He sits down next to me and they take turns giving us lap dances. By the time my penis hardens from feeling ass cheeks caress my crotch, the other stripper tugs at my pants, telling me that I should unbuckle my belt if I'm willing to throw some extra cash into the mix.

My brother must've forgotten that we're not in a high-class strip club where booties shake. He peels an extra five hundred dollar bills off a fat wad of cash that is in his pocket. After he slides the bills in her left hand, she tucks the money in her red platform boots, gets on her knees on top of dirty concrete, and gives me exactly what I like, just right.

"Take care of him, baby. You better do what you do to my twin as good as your girl gave it to me."

She looks up at me while licking, sucking, and caressing every inch of my manhood. It's times like these I'm glad I'm well endowed. I forget that I can smell oil and gas.

"Mmmm, baby. Don't stop. Don't stop," I say as the stripper sucks on my balls. I look at her two friends that begin to tongue each other. The real two-girl fantasy show begins when one stripper pumps a dildo in and out of the other's ass. When I hear a high-pitched sensual scream, I feel my body relax. At this point, the stripper going to work on me looks at me square in the eye.

"I'm about to cum!" I yell. When I say this she holds the base of my penis with one hand, positions herself under it, and opens her mouth as if she wants to begin swallowing every drop of my juices. Midway between busting a huge nut in between her plump lips, my cell rings. I look at the caller ID and know that Marquita is calling to deliver her final tongue lashing for me not showing up in Florida. I turn the power button off, and put my daughter on hold just a little while longer. Like I said, I'll be there, just after I spend some time with three freaks back in the cut of an industrial area, inside of a tin and brick building.

"I didn't tell any of you to stop," I complain. Then we all picked up where we left off since I'm the boss.

$

After relieving some pent up stress and frustration with my brother I get ready to leave.

"Malik, I know this was your way of reaching out to me. Thanks for taking the first step."

"You made me see some things, Wes. I guess this is my way of apologizing. You were right and just keeping it real with me. I should've invested my money because I knew my NFL career was going to come to an end. Shit, I had no credit and nothing to show for being the age I was. I take responsibility for myself now and have stopped being such a taker." Malik gives me dap. "Good looking out."

"Are you staying or leaving?" I ask.

"I'm going to watch them girls pop some coochie a while longer but you go on. A nigga's romantic life is on the rocks so I need to see all I can while I can. I haven't hit nothing in a while." He smiles. "I know you've got shit to take care of but I appreciate you coming out. Take care."

I'm speechless that my brother has extended the olive branch and admitted his shortcomings. I exit the garage feeling like I'm walking on cloud nine. When I get inside of the Hummer, I turn on my TV and my cell, ready to hit the road. As I'm checking my messages, I realize that I've forgotten to lock my doors. Just as I'm about to push the driver's side lock down with my elbow one of my back doors open and I feel a gun pressed into my temple. The passenger door opens and then slams.

"Drive, nigga, just drive!"

At this point I realize I'm being carjacked but comply with their orders by pressing the accelerator. Suddenly I'm wishing I'd taken the reverend's advice and gone straight to Florida.

"I'll do whatever you want. If you want the Hummer you can have it."

"I give the orders and I said drive. Follow directions!"

"Ok." I turn my head to try to get a glimpse of the armed man. He's wearing a black ski mask.

"Turn the fuck around and stop trying to look at my face!" he says full of hostility.

With his gun poked near my right kidney I begin to drive out of the parking lot. Before I know it we've reached Bladensburg, not far from New York Avenue in D.C. I hear him flip his cell phone open.

"Yo, C, I got me one. I'm on my way so get ready." Then he looks over at me. "If I even suspect you're trying some funny shit, you're dead before we get to where we're going. Got it?"

"Yeah, man," I feel the wheel becoming slippery from sweat, but I'm trying not to panic.

After a few more minutes we pull into an isolated, dimly lit area. I'm guessing it's in an industrial park but I'm not sure where I am from weaving through a maze the masked-man concocted. I'm sure it was to throw me off course. When I approach the building the man says, "Stop."

I smack on the brakes like an uncoordinated new driver that doesn't know how to gently ease down on the brake pedal. When I do at least eight masked men wearing all black appear and stand a few feet apart from one another. Half of them walk toward the Hummer.

"C, do you know who this is?" asks one of them after he gets a look at me.

The one they call C is cleaning his nails with a knife. After barely looking at me he says, "I don't know. Another nigga tryna carry it like he got shit going on I guess."

"This dude plays for the Blitzers. Oh shit! They'll be looking for him."

"Are you sure?" he asks. He looks at me, his eyebrows raised, forehead wrinkled, like he doesn't believe it.

"Yeah, I know what I'm talking about. His name is Wes Montgomery."

"Let's get him inside and figure out how we're going to make this work to our advantage then. What in the hell was he doing at a garage strip club?" He shoves the knife in his back pocket.

The three masked men pull me out of the driver's seat while the ringleader follows us. He holds the gun steady. They take turns shoving, pushing and kicking me, ordering me to walk faster into an opening. Once inside, the large door is padlocked shut. The cinderblock building is cold and dirty. I begin to fear for my life when one of them sticks the butt of the gun in my back.

"I can't stand you damn ballers, and I hate the Blitzers! You think your shit don't stink, don't you nigga?"

"No," I answer weakly.

I feel him search my pockets. He locates my wallet and rummages through it. He tosses some pieces of paper to the floor. He finds Dom Dom's school picture and stops.

"How *cute*," he says sarcastically. "Is this one of your illegitimate children?" All of them laugh.

I don't answer.

With attitude in his voice, he asks me again, "I said, is this one of your illegitimate children?"

"No."

"Liar," he replies. "If you want to see this kid again, do what we say." He hands my wallet to another masked man who starts rummaging through it.

"Well, well, Visa, American Express, MasterCard, and Discover. I hate rich people. I'll take these. Shit, I bet I can run ball better than your overpaid ass. You won't be needing these so I'll consider it my back pay. Thanks for putting me on your payroll, G." He pulls each card from my wallet, then sticks them in his pocket.

"Now what? I didn't mean for things to get this complicated."

"Let's get paid, that's what."

"How?"

"Extortion?"

"Yeah, extortion. I'm sure you heard of it."

"Are you crazy? We don't know nothing about no fucking extortion."

"Don't let me find out you don't have heart enough to be in this gang."

"I didn't say that. I'm just saying—that's all. I mean, the worst we done is car jack and contribute to PG. County's missing car list, send the cars to the chop shop, rape a few hos, and snatch a few purses."

"Then think. Shut up and think about how this should go."

"Let's text message someone our demands. Or better yet we can take a picture of him with the camera phone then have him call someone for help."

"Do you have rocks for brains? There's too much of a chance of that being traced. It's too risky. ISPs are traceable. Don't you know anything?"

"What's an ISP?"

"Never mind. Just don't do that, okay? The police can track down who sent it."

Another masked man says, "Take care of the H2, Wild Man. You're slipping." One of the masked men steps forward and I assume he's off to secure my vehicle and move it from plain view. When I hear the hum of the engine I guess he is driving it inside of the warehouse. My guess is correct. I hear a huge sliding gate open, then close. Afterward my Hummer is parked inside and the glare of the lights shine in my face, nearly blinding me.

"Little Murder, collect his ice," says another one.

A small-framed masked man snatches my Rolex, championship ring, and rips my diamond earring from my ear.

"Ouch!" I feel my earlobe partially tear and it begins to throb.

"Oh, so you're not so tough after all." They all laugh.

I see the first masked man bring some thick rope my way. He begins wrapping me up into a makeshift mummy. After about thirty minutes of having my possessions examined and stolen, someone sticks me in my right arm with a needle. In a panic I say, "What are you doing? What is that? Don't stick me, man. Don't!" I attempt to pull away from the masked man but I can only do so much since I'm bound.

"It ain't insulin, but I'm sure you already figured that out. Apparently, you're a fan of getting high. We found weed and X in your glove box. Now you can use grown folks shit. The high will help you mellow out and shut the fuck up! Welcome to the world of a junkie."

I shut my eyes, wondering what's in the needle and who may've been infected with what. It's the first time I've seriously thought about contracting AIDS despite constant reminders for me to take good care of my sexual health. When sedation causes me to end my protests I drift into a zone I don't want to be in. I suddenly realize that I was using my fame, the Hummer, my mansion, and all of my assets as a crutch to behave as though I was something that I'm not. Now that I realize that I'm not invincible, I hope I'm not shit outta luck.

8

FRESH MEAT

Malik

Keeping fit does have its benefits—you meet all kinds of people in a weight room, from lawyers and judges, to preachers and teachers. Although 98% of the brothers in the gyms in the Nation's Capital swing both ways, or either swing the *other* way they shouldn't be swinging, every now and then you meet one of the rare two percent who don't come on to you in the locker room. After weeding out the ones on the prowl you could find yourself holding a conversation with anyone from Benning Terrace to the White House. People in the hood don't understand that giving dap and dressing in hoodies and Timbs is all good, if you want to limit yourself in life and settle for Diamond's type of life. If you want to put yourself in a position to get out the hood you have to know how to relate to people other than the type you typically associate with. As a result of my understanding how to flip the game, my part-time hanging partner, Hakim, invited me over to Sunday dinner at his pops' place in Hillcrest Heights, which is about six miles from D.C. and one from Marlow Heights.

After a while, fast food and complimentary continental breakfasts from the Motel 6 doesn't cut it anymore. Kale, freshly baked rolls, roaster chicken, rib tips, and corn has been a long time coming for me and my suffering stomach, and finally we're getting something worth eating. When I come inside the house and greet Hakim he calls everyone into the dinning room.

"Come meet Malik, everyone. Remember the one I told you about that plays ball and is going to play in the European League?"

One by one, people begin to appear and offer smiles and handshakes.

"My sister will be down in a minute. She's always the last one to come sit at the table. You know women," he says.

We talk and shoot the breeze for a few minutes, and then a familiar face turns the corner. I try not to appear stunned.

"Oh, this is my sister Monica. Finally we can eat."

She and I pretend not to know each other. I'm amazed that I hit my best friend's sister while in Atlantic City. After I get over the shock, I try to pace myself and not gobble up everything like I've never seen food before in front of Monica, her father, Hakim, and his date. As her father tells me story after story about life back in the day, I eye Monica, who looks as if she doesn't give a shit I'm here, and isn't interested in trying to impress me. I watch her shove food into her mouth, never glancing at me or pausing to join the conversation that amounts to little more than polite bullshit.

"So where'd you attend college, Malik?" asks Hakim's father.

"HU. Only the best for the best. End of story."

"I'm a Morgan man myself," he replies. "I won't hold it against you. I'm sure you didn't know any better when you set foot on Howard's campus."

Hakim and his date laugh.

"And I won't hold the Morgan thing against you so long as you're not an Alpha. Being my brother is your last chance to redeem yourself. So what's the deal?"

"He's an Alpha," Hakim says. "You started it now. I think it's time for me to take my date into the other room and let you men duke it out over the dinner table. I'm out of my league since I pledged Me Phi Nothing."

"Being that I attended a white school in the Midwest I really don't have anything to add to this Historically Black College chat. Excuse me. Dinner was delicious, Mr. Jones," Belinda says, getting up from the table.

Mr. Jones replies, "Son, I don't know you. In fact, I just laid eyes on you. Just remember this: We all make mistakes and I give you credit for at least admitting two of yours. I'd love to stay and rip your theories to shreds but I've got a very important date. I may be old but I'm not dead. And for the record, my plumbing still works just fine." He picks up his plate, managing to flee the scene while getting the last word in.

Monica rolls her eyes at her father in disgust, when he leaves the room. I hear him rattling pots and pans in the kitchen, which prevent him from hearing what I say next.

"I can't insult a man who just fed me, but the next time I see you I'll be decked out in my Q dog and Howard gear, then we can pick up where we left off. Everyone knows the truth, and if they don't know they better ask somebody. "

When I finish I eye Monica dishing more food on her plate.

"Damn, shortie, how does anyone as little as you pack it in like that? I'm a football player and you eat more than me."

"Drop the act. You didn't do so badly yourself. Mind your own business and stay out of mine," she mumbles.

I feel my temper rising up and quietly reply, "What are you on your period or something? Why the extreme attitude change? You were pressed before."

"Look, when the clock strikes one minute past twelve tonight I'll officially be an twenty-eight year old, bitter, black female, in credit card and student loan debt with a ticking biological clock. Any more questions, Inspector Gadget? I got into an argument with my boss and I quit after telling him what a broke-down administrator he is. He didn't even care about parents banging on my classroom window cussing at me, or the last stunt a hoodlum pulled. I didn't even have a staff bathroom key, and there were bullet holes in my classroom window. That place was a dump."

"I'm sorry you're having a hard time right now but I told you when you dropped me off from Atlantic City that I could take care of you. There's no reason to put up a wall with me."

"Two degrees and one certificate, and all I get is the typical you have no experience but excellent credentials speech," she rambles. "I'm worn out and worn down. College is important but definitely overrated. People think your life will be perfect if you have a degree. Look at the people with records complaining they can't get jobs when they come out of prison. What about those of us who have never been to prison and still can't get our due? You have no idea what I've been through, and how humiliating it is to earn $10.00 an hour to substitute some off the hook teenagers in schools that no one wants to touch. And how can you take care of me? I paid the room tab, remember? I do what I've got to do."

"I know all about what happened to you and why you didn't finish law school. Hakim told me. At the time I told him to take sixty grand and help you out. I cared about you even before I knew who you were. As far as the rest, you'll find out what the full deal is with me if there's a need to go there," I say. "Do you have birthday plans?"

She wipes her mouth. "Would I be here if I did?"

"How about I take you out for your birthday? Maybe some fresh air will do you good, Monica. Maybe we can air out that negative attitude of yours."

"I can't so stop pushing the issue."

"Woman, what does it take to change that to a yes?"

"I don't have anything to wear. I can't afford to go shopping now, and I don't have any party clothes."

"Let's go to the mall and make arrangements for you to have a nice dress and heels to match. Girl, you got to live a little. You're not getting any younger. Pretty soon that biological clock won't work anymore, let alone stop ticking. Now if a man is trying to treat a woman like a lady the most logical path to follow would be to cooperate. Look on the bright side, I already hit it so you don't have to worry about me trying to get some while we go out on our little date."

"Shut up," Monica snaps. "Watch what you say. And for the record, I don't date, I *mingle.*"

"Let's just get out of here and pick something up for you, ok?"

"Whatever."

She's still got an attitude, but even so she follows me out the door to head for Pentagon City Mall. Even if this middle-class shortie doesn't have much, I have a feeling there's something she can offer that will turn out to be to my benefit until Wes's body is found and I can collect the insurance payout.

$

It's now 12:15 a.m. and we're celebrating Monica's birthday at one of the hot new clubs in the city. From the get go I show off for her, trying to impress her and prove that I still have my NFL props. After I park the truck I look at the sea of people standing in a long line, shivering and waiting to drop fifteen bucks and get inside of the club. I walk up to the doorman, whisper something to him, give dap and interlock Monica's fingers in mine. I love it when I hear, "Hey, why that nigga get to skip in line? Who the hell is he?" There's at least a hundred people trying to shield themselves from the blistery weather, and I walk past and don't even blink. I feel like I'm the man when I can pull rank this way.

Within a few moments I'm sitting on the barstool, slurping drinks, getting twisted like I always do. Monica's in between my legs dancing to *Lean Back* while I'm smoking an imported cigar, enjoying the sweetness of the flavor. Drinking has a loosening effect on her. She ended up telling me a guy she really wanted wasn't giving her relationship vibes, so it was time for her to find someone who was ready for one woman, all the way. I know before the night is out I'm going to hit it again and prepare her for Malik's *your my ho now* training camp. The first step was to explain that he was just using her and would never do more than tap that ass once a week. A man can get most any woman to do anything if they hit the right chord with the right pressure when she's emotional and feeling like she doesn't know which way is up. Since I know this to be true, I begin strumming those chords.

"Here, drink some more. Bottoms up, Monica." I hand her a glass of Grey Goose.

Already half bent, she smiles and asks, "What's in this one, Malik?"

"It's your birthday, just drink it, but slower than the last one, ok?"

Monica takes three long gulps and the drink vanishes. She hands me the glass, loosens her ponytail, swings her hair loose, then starts bumping up against my crotch like she's a world class stripper. She turns around toward me.

"The music, this club, the atmosphere, you—it's all just making me feel like a million dollars. It's something about the city that just turns me on."

Monica gives me the sultry look of a temptress, purses her lips, and then blows me a kiss while mimicking a Marilyn Monroe stance. When she turns around yet another time I rub on her ass. I begin to salivate over the round yellow booty that's close to Diamond's size and suddenly realize that I'm purely attracted to her. I smack her on the ass and say, "Dance for daddy!"

Monica turns up the boogie a notch and gives *Lean Back* a whole new meaning. She jumps in my lap and straddles me, and I notice she isn't wearing any panties. I feel myself harden as she leans backward, thrusting her hips against my middle while singing along with Fat Joe.

"I think I've had too much to drink," she says. "Oops. This is why I never drink in public. I have a low tolerance to alcohol and I know better than to have had so much to drink."

"It's ok by me. I didn't know you had all this freak up in you. I thought the first time was an accident and I wasn't sober enough to realize what I should've remembered that I enjoyed," I tell her. I feel her jerk upward then hop out of my lap. "What's up with you? I thought you were having a nice time."

"Oh, I am," she says.

I can sense her mood has changed. High blood alcohol content or not something put a damper on my show. A minute later a nigga steps to Monica, kisses her on the cheek, hugs her and starts feeling her all on the ass like he's laying claim on my date. He eyeballs me with a territorial attitude, and then turns back to Monica.

I tried to call you to take you out for your birthday but *you* didn't call me back. I had plans for you and had to break the reservations I made."

"I, uh—well. You did? I didn't know you called," she says.

She's standing in between us and I feel like reminding the nigga that I'm on a date, and I don't appreciate him trying to carry me like he doesn't see me sitting here.

As a new song begins, the volume and bass increases. Yelling over the music, he adds, "Apparently you may have checked your messages and just didn't want to call me back. I'll get at you later, Monica. I see you're a bit busy at the moment. Think about this shit— if you're not *too* busy having a nice time. Don't let me stop you from dancing. It looked like you were really into it. Peace, mami."

When the pretty boy nigga turns to walk away I tell Monica, "He don't know me. I got money to get out of jail!" I draw back my arm to hit him in the back of the head but instead my elbow knocks over my drink in the martini glass that's sitting on the bar.

The remaining contents of the drink splash on a man wearing a blue, silk shirt who looks ready to complain until he sees the size of me. When the glass rolls off the bar and shatters on the floor his date rolls her eyes and sucks her teeth but the man nudges her and she stops rather suddenly.

I'm angry that the pretty boy was so smooth yet still made his point loud and clear. Me, on the other hand, I've got an explosive temper that's about to blow in front of the whole damn club since the first few onlookers seem interested in what's happening in my world. I rear my arm back a second time and hold my fist about six inches from the man's head. Monica screams over the music.

"No, no! You don't want to do that." She tries to push me down back on the stool and rips one of the straps on her dress. Her size D titties are half hanging out but there's nothing she can do to cover herself much more. She holds the half torn dress up with one hand.

"Move," I say. "I'm gonna handle this shit! I don't play that. Like I said he don't know me. I will wax that ass like that cocky motherfucker stole something!"

The bartender runs toward the end of the bar where we are. "Malik, are you all right?

I nod my head. "I got this."

The bartender is half turned in my direction as he continues to pour drinks but I'm sure he doesn't summons security just yet because he knows me.

"Don't hit him, Malik. Leave it alone!" Monica screams.

People stop clicking their fingers and holding drinks to their mouths. I feel more pairs of eyes watching us as we argue.

"Why you trying to protect the nigga? You care about him more than me or something? Is that what you're trying to tell me, huh? What you trying to say, girl?"

By now I see that the pretty boy is half way across the room. As I start to go after him Monica attempts to push me backward as hard as she can to prevent me from following him. Her dress falls to her waist and she breaks one of her stiletto heels. She grabs the front of her dress and holds it up with her fist, and starts screaming at me.

"I'm fucking him, ok? He's the one I told you about earlier. That's the one that I get with when I want some."

When she shouts this information out in the open, the whole corner of the club begins to chatter and the music stops playing. The nigga that almost got clobbered for starting the static was spared since he disappears around the corner but apparently the scenario is still interesting to many who came out to have a good time.

"What ya'll looking at? Turn your asses around—this ain't no movie set! If you want something to watch, go to a fucking theater! Now turn the damn music back on and keep doing what you all were doing."

As they turn around and the music resumes, I remove my sleeveless black sweater and put it over top of Monica's head. I dodge pieces of glass, pick her up, and carry her to the coatroom. When we get away from the booming music and all those ears, I summons our coats and bundle Monica up. I pick her up again and kick the front door open. After we reach the chatter of people too cheap to pay to get into the club, I break the new rules down to her.

"I almost had to bust a nigga's ass over you in there, so from now on there will be no more going out with other people. You have a man now and that's me!"

"Don't I have something to say about this?"

"Let's talk about this shit when we get to the truck." When we reach the Escalade, I put Monica down on the pavement. "Get in."

After Monica gets in I pull into the back of the lot and turn the truck so the back window is facing the street. I look at Monica and decide I'll give her the silent treatment. Every time she looks over at me wondering when we'll talk about what happened in the club I change the radio station. She doesn't know it yet, but this is part of her training to become a committed woman who'll soon learn my rules. I can't believe she tried to play a brotha and use me as her back up plan. She needs to trust and believe that she'll never see that other nigga again. Let the games begin.

9

WHATEVER HE DID IS HIS FAULT

Wes

"Malik, it's Wes. A little situation came up after I left the club," I say as C firmly presses the cell phone to my ear.

"Who is this?" Malik asks like he doesn't recognize my voice.

"You know, your brother," I say with frustration. "Look, I need you to do something for me," I say calmly. "Can you do that, bro? I'm counting on you. This is serious. Please listen carefully to what I'm telling you I need done."

"Me do something for *you?*" he asks. "You must be on something, man. Remember putting me out of your house and leaving me hanging last Christmas when I went broke? I didn't have two pennies to rub together after I was injured and cut from the team. You have a lot of nerve even calling this number after you turned your back on me."

Little Murder appears in front of me and mouths the words, "You better not fuck up." Then he makes a motion across his neck with his fingers like he's slitting it.

I get the message, and start trying to talk to my brother again.

"Now, Malik, I know we've had some misunderstandings in the past but please, I need you to contact my new accountant and ask him to get all of the cash out of the safe. He'll know what you're talking about. All I can say is *please*, I'm begging you, contact my man and let him know my emergency message. Then tell him to—"

"You're just like one of them backstabbers you gotta watch for out here. I can't trust you and you can't trust me. Not even for a hot minute."

"I thought we straightened out some things out. What are you saying?"

"You have no idea what I've been through since the day you took the key to your house from me—the butts I've had to kiss, and the lies I've had to tell when you could've spared me from the humiliation. That hurt my heart, man. It was the lowest thing to do of all time lows. In my book, you're no longer my brother."

"I could talk about you screwing Tomi in my bed when I was on the road but I won't. We've both done hurtful things to each other. Like I said, I thought things were better between us."

"Had you given me help I never would have touched that crazy broad. She came on to me. I didn't come on to her. If you want someone to blame, blame her."

"I don't want to talk about that anyway. Look, I'm begging you. Find it in your heart to do me this favor. I was a jack-ass. What can I say? I'm sorry. I'll make it up to you later."

"I think whatever is going on wherever you are is your problem, not mine. As you suggested, I cleaned myself up, and that included weeding out judgmental motherfuckers like you. Don't call me no more! You'll be okay I'm sure. Call one of your NBA brothers, or one of the male groupies you throw tickets to, and drag around the country with you while you throw money away on people that are damn near strangers. If they got love for you they'll take care of it. Whatever you did is your fault and whatever I did is mine. I don't feel like arguing. Your gambling probably got out of hand or some shit. I don't know. Whatever is going on, I've got to go. I'm wasting my airtime minutes now. Peace, Wes. Good luck with whatever."

"Malik! Malik! Don't hang up. They'll kill me. I'm not playing," I scream, but he's gone. I can't figure out why my brother acted as if we just didn't party together and sort some issues out between us, but I know these criminals won't give a damn about that.

"What a shame," he says. "You hit your call list limit. Shame, shame, shame. It doesn't sound like you didn't treat your brother too well, because he doesn't give a shit about your ass. We can't get to phase two, which was telling your accountant where the drop off point was supposed to have been. If your brother cared about your ass, maybe, just maybe things could have turn out much better for you. Well—this is out of my hands now. You know that right?"

I watch him slide tight black gloves over both hands. I can't manage to form words to respond. One masked person swaggers into my space and I gulp hard. When the person stops about four feet in front of me, the mask is removed. I realize it's one of the strippers from the club. My lip nearly drops to the floor as I realize she tipped some criminals off and set me up. I look at her like a deer caught in headlights.

"Before we take the last stop on this trip we may as well explain how you ended up here."

In a mental fog, I begin turning my head all around frantically. My chest feels tight and it hurts to breathe. The woman's wearing a smirk on her face and for once in my life a woman's physical attributes don't stick in my mind. She sits down on a metal chair and lights one of my imported cigars.

"You've got good taste. An imported Cuban. This is some good shit, Wes." She exhales the smoke then twists out the amber flame on the cement floor. The stripper looks up and tells me, "I guess you met my crew. You think what I do at low class clubs like the one you hit up keeps me fed? If you haven't guessed, garage strip clubs don't pay top dollar. I've got to eat too so this right here is part two of my gig. If your dumb ass hasn't figured it out by now, your brother set you up, Wes. After we take you out we're going to get a cut of the insurance money he'll be due. That's right—he took out a policy on you. Now that you know the whole story, you know what that means, right?"

I shake my head no and swallow hard. She moves close to me, puts her hands on her knees and is about an inch and a half away from my face. She's so close I can feel the heat of her breathe on my clammy skin.

"No mask, so you die, baby. Your luck just ran out, so say adios to all that baller shit. Little Murder is gonna hook you up. And, for the record, that was heroin in the needle. Everyone will think you overdosed. It's been a pleasure doing business with you." She shakes her head. "All of this over a peek of a prostituting dancer's pussy. You did it to yourself, baby. Look at you still fantasizing over my tongue and hands sliding down your cock. What a damn

94

shame!" She stands upright, backs up, winks, and then switches away, delivering a diabolical laugh.

"Wait! Wait!" I call weakly. "You don't want to do this, sweetheart. Please don't. I'll give you anything—way more than whatever cut you were promised."

The stripper doesn't flinch, and I hear her laugh even harder. I sense her cold spirit and mercilessness.

"Thanks for offering but this right here is a done deal," she says.

When she stops next to one of the masked men, someone runs up behind me from the other direction. I feel a shot puncture my skull at the base of my neck. As I slump forward, the volume begins to fade but I make out someone talking.

"Shoot him again! Finish him off now and let's get it done!"

I feel another bullet penetrate my heart. As my blood flows across the concrete of the warehouse floor I mumble softly. "Dom Dom, daddy's sorry, my angel."

After those words fall from my lips and float into the universe I verbally pray that God will forgive me for cursing His name, and that my troubled soul will find its way to heaven. Gasping for air, I continue to pray silently.

Things just didn't turn out as I would have liked them to. I should've acknowledged you no matter what. Please forgive me of my sins. I've been a fool, Lord. Take care of my precious baby girl for me, and make her childhood much better than mine. Spare my soul, for I have sinned against my Father. I—I—I—repent. Malik, my own brother. My own—.

I take my last shallow breath. Blood streams from my mouth and creates a widening puddle. With those thoughts, my life on earth comes to a tragic end. All I can do is pray that God will accept my profession of faith and let me into the gates of Heaven.

10

BURNED OUT

Jalita

Unfortunately, I used my last sliver of Dove deodorant yesterday. My pits are humming like I'm Ms. Geraldine's relative all because I can't afford a razor with a decent blade, a fresh batch of deodorant, and shaving cream to help weed the forest growing under my arms. And if that's not bad enough, my period came on last night and I couldn't afford any Playtex tampons. So I did the next best thing. I went to a public restroom and dropped a roll of toilet paper in my purse so I could make a huge ball every hour and create a makeshift pad. After sliding into a sleeping bag in my car last night I feel as though I have no choice but to tuck away my pride, and take me and my cramps to the welfare office. I already scolded myself for backsliding, and vowed I'd try to behave myself, no matter what. I found out that I might be eligible for some type of assistance since I'm halfway ill, so I figure I have no choice but to find out what Uncle Sam may be willing to do for me.

I pass a security guard that's reading *USA Today*, and walk up to the desk.

"I need to speak with someone about some help."

"Do you have kids?" asks the receptionist.

"No I don't."

She looks at me over her glasses like she's inspecting me, as if I shouldn't be interested in getting a help me up if I don't have extra mouths to feed.

"Well, I don't know what can be done for you but sign in and have a seat. Someone will be out to see you shortly."

After I scribble my name I feel the wad of thin, cheap toilet tissue shift and I wonder if blood will begin dripping down my leg, or if my jeans will become stained and let everyone know that my period is on. Feeling bloated and achy, I sit down in an ugly, plastic orange chair and watch the hands on the clock. They barely move since I'm staring at them so much. Since at least seven people are ahead of me I tap my foot and try to keep myself calm as kids run around like they've lost their minds, rude women smack bubble gum like cows chewing cud, and chatter about hard times fill my uninterested ears. To dull my senses I pull a piece of paper from my pocket and search for a pencil in my purse.

I begin to write:

It's funny how life goes around in circles. My mother abandons me in a welfare office and all these years later I find myself in one again. I said I'd never return to the system. I said I'd become a fully sufficient, independent, woman. I said I'd work hard and finish college so I could turn my fate around. Almost a year later after revisiting what I said, my whole plan has fallen apart, along with my heart, soul, and mind. Is this my fault? Did lack of ambition cause me to close the case on my pride and convince myself to beg for food or shelter? I don't know. But what I do know is that I shouldn't be here. I hate the system and it hates me back. I worked three jobs to prove that, but it didn't pay off. The honesty, the reform of self, the attempt to earn my due from the labor of my own efforts was all for nothing. Where's the sunshine, the pay off, the encouragement to make money from my mind and not my ass? I don't see it. I feel like I'm going backwards. There's always an obstacle to get over in life—always a mountain to climb. There's always a tear to dry over a twist or turn you didn't see coming. At least for some of us, that is. I ache for peace, I ache for love, and I ache for prosperity. I ache for making it to the top of some mountain and out of the valley.

I hear someone call my name as my emotions begin to pour like a flood. Suddenly I feel the value of Brenda Brown writing her story and Seth making a living at putting together words. What I can't admit to others I managed to admit on paper. So long as no one sees it, I'm straight.

I follow a large pear shaped woman with a run in her sheer black stockings down a hallway. As her heels make a clicking noise and her legs, which are rubbing together, make a swooshing noise with each step, my courage to tell my business waivers. When we turn into a small office I watch her sit down in a wooden chair that could use a good refinishing.

"So what can I do for you?" she asks after I take my seat.

"I need to find out if I'm eligible for benefits."

"And what kind would that be?"

"Anything. I don't know much about this sort of thing and this is your territory."

"Well, why do you think you should receive assistance?"

"Because I can't work and I'm ill. In fact I just had a nervous breakdown," I admit.

"Having a nervous breakdown doesn't make you eligible for anything," she says with an attitude.

Remnants of the old me rise up, but stop at my lips. I decide to keep pulling teeth with her as opposed to sucking my teeth and explaining what her proper attitude should be as a servant of the public. I refocus on the reason I came there.

"Look," I tell her. "I must not be asking the right questions. I don't want to take up much of your time, so maybe this would work best if you ask me the questions." I sit back and wait for her to start asking, and try hard not to stare at the mustache growing on her top lip.

"Do you receive disability benefits or SSI?" she asks.

"No, I don't."

"Well you have to apply for it. If you're deemed disabled and unable to work by law you may be eligible for a monthly check. After that, you can come back and apply for medial benefits and food assistance."

"How do I do that?"

"Apply for it."

"Where do I do that?"

"Go to the Social Security Administration. You can get the paperwork from any branch."

"What about emergency food or shelter? I understand about protocol and everything but I'm in an emergency situation that can't wait to be addressed," I explain.

"Did you fill out an application?"

"What application would that be?"

With an attitude, the worker says, "There are procedures we have to follow. Fill this out and come back. Call this number and it will explain what you need to return with. Until I can verify some information, there's nothing I can do for you." She hands me several papers and I can tell she's ready for me to leave her office. I notice she keeps eying her Styrofoam Cup of Noodles container like it's lunchtime.

I feel my emotions heat up. "Why can't you just tell me what I need?"

She blows her nose on a wrinkled Kleenex. "I gave you the number," she says. "There's a pay phone around the hall if you'd like to use it."

I sigh as she lays her balled up snot rag on her desk. "Do you have any other suggestions, in the meantime?

"Call homeless services. That's an option. That's what everyone else does," she says coldly.

"I did that already!" I snap.

"Then no, I don't. Go see what can be done on that end or make it the best way you can."

"So that's it?"

"I don't know what you expect me to tell you. You don't have children. You don't have a disability by law. And you don't have your paperwork completed."

"And if I were you I'd wax that mustache before someone mistakes you for a dude with after shadow," I mumble.

"Did you have something you'd like to say to me?" she asks. I hear her grabbing her Cup of Noodles and preparing to add water into it.

"I think I already said it. Thanks for nothing." I gather the small pile of papers and leave the office. As I walk past the security guard I feel tears building up in my eyes, and the room becomes blurry and out of focus. I know I need a plan but I'm not sure what to do. All I do know is that I'm jittery, nervous, and officially burned out. All I can say is life is a bitch, and then you die. Maybe I would've gotten more empathy and speedier service if I were an immigrant or toting a screaming, snotty nose rugrat on my hip. Since neither is the case I got tossed out on my ear like a redheaded stepchild.

11

TWO THOUSAND KISSES DEEP

Malik

The day after Christmas the sun shines through thin lace curtains and awakens me in the Jones' household. While I stare at the beams that run parallel across the vaulted white ceiling, I think about how Monica thought she was regulating me, but how I could flip the script and regulate her without her realizing what hit her. After the episode that unfolded at the club, Monica caught an attitude and went to her room without giving a nigga a thank-you, nigga I had a nice time, an apology for putting me out there— nothing. Determined to get in the last word I sat up with Hakim and talked about how I almost had to clock the yellow nigga and set the record straight. After that he told me to stay put for the night, blew up a large blue air mattress in the living room, and threw me a pile of blankets to cover myself with. Hakim not pushing me out of the door works perfectly because it gives me access to his crazy-ass sister.

After I walk upstairs to the bathroom and pee out my last evidence of liquor from the club, I go to the end of the hall where Monica's room is. I knock on the door three times. I'm about to knock a forth time when she comes to the door and sticks her head through the crack. She's halfway squinting at me like she can't quite make out who I am.

"What is it? What do you want?"

"What happened to good morning? Shortie, you've got an attitude problem up in your camp."

"I have an attitude with anyone who almost knocks out a friend of mine and embarrasses me in the process."

"Well the last thing I heard was that he was just a fuck to relieve stress, so you said. What, now you're catching feelings for him? Get your story straight and make up your mind about it."

"What I told you was true, but no one said you had to go off like that."

"And no one said you had to forget to mention you were fucking someone until after all that went down."

"That was none of your business."

"*You* are my business."

"I'm not trying to argue with you. I don't even know what you're still doing here."

"Hakim invited me to stay."

"Good ol' Hakim. Leave it to him." She rolls her eyes.

"There you go again. Why do you act like that?"

"Act like what? I told you. Now get out of my face unless you've got something different to say."

"I want to take you somewhere so get dressed."

"Who do you think you are ordering me around? Even if you asked me I—"

"Will you please ride with me?"

"Take Hakim with you. You're his guest, not mine."

Monica won't admit it but I feel the sexual tension between us. I grin at her. "I asked you, not him."

"Will you promise to leave me alone if I go?" she asks.

I can tell she's getting turned on but is trying her best to cover up her annoyance by acting cold.

"Shortie, I ain't sweating you. Whatever is whatever. I'm not even slightly jealous of that freak in the club. I've got plenty of options on lockdown. All I asked you to do was ride with me."

"Fine. I was just going to sleep anyway. But have me back before dark. I have plans."

"With who? That gay looking nigga whose ass I almost waxed?"

"He's definitely *not* gay, and that's none of your business. I thought you said you weren't jealous."

"Look, get dressed, make your call to your man, and let's roll."

Monica's eyes opened wide. " Damnit—I don't have a man! I told you that!"

"Whatever you say. Just be ready in twenty minutes."

Monica doesn't answer me, but she ducks her head back inside and shuts the door. Since she admitted she didn't officially have a man I know I'm about to lay it on thick as chunky peanut butter.

$

As I turn the corner of the street to my development in Virginia, I feel relieved. The whole thirty minutes Monica keeps her jaws locked tight like an obedient pet. Normally I can't stand a woman's running mouth, but it is nice to have some degree of conversation. All she did was alternate between shutting her eyes taking a nap, and blabbing on her cell phone to one of her female friends. What does she think I am—her chauffeur? I don't think so. She should at least make an effort to act like she knows I'm somebody worthy of impressing not stressing.

When I turn the corner I nudge her. "Would you mind paying me some attention and giving that damn cell phone battery a chance to rest?"

She rolls her eyes at me. "I'll call you back," she says. "No, that was nobody. I'll tell you about it later. Ok. Bye girl." Then she turns to me. "That was so rude. You were listening to the radio anyway. What was the harm in me talking to my friend?"

"I'm not trying to argue with you. I didn't bring you out here for that."

When we pull up to the guardhouse the guard tells me, "Have a safe New Year, Mr. Harrison."

"You too, dawg," I say.

The arm of the gate lifts upward and I drive through the entrance. Monica looks confused and it feels lovely to have made her start guessing about why I'm getting these props. She suddenly becomes attentive as I drive slowly down the street, make a left, and stop in front of my house.

"Where are we and why did we stop?" she asks.

"This is what I wanted to show you. This is what's bothering me," I tell her in a frustrated voice.

"And what is this?" she asks, putting her cell phone inside of her purse.

"My home—the one that I can't live in. My home that I'm paying a maid to clean, but I'm sleeping in a sixty thousand dollar truck. My home that has an indoor pool, a game room, six bedrooms and every piece of furniture within it that I paid cash for."

"Slow down. What are you talking about?"

"Monica, when I was playing ball it was long enough for me to get all this. Then I met *her.*"

"Who are you talking about?"

"The bitch. My baby's greedy momma."

"Is that any way to talk about your baby's mother?"

"She had the smarts and I had the contacts. She was one of the top computer science people in the area. I had the money and so we started a business. I moved her in. The first time she got pregnant she lost the baby. She got pregnant again. We had what I thought was my son. Come to find out she was cheating on me with one of the other players. We all used to bowl together and she was always up in one of their faces flirting. I should have known her groupie ass was no good before I got with her. Now she's got me paying for some kid that probably ain't even mine. Not only that, but my assets are frozen and it's a big mess. I paid a law firm $60,000 to straighten things out, but they aren't working on things right. I get an allowance every week so I can live. It's not right. I hate that bitch! I want to kill her!" I begin to open the door of the truck.

"Get back in here, Malik! You're not going anywhere."

"Monica, do you see the maid upstairs looking at us? I'm paying her check—it's coming out of *my* pocket yet I spend all my money living in hotels. I can't believe I let her do this to me. I've been in every hotel around the beltway to try to keep peace in my own house. Some days I sleep in my truck. I'm tired of living like this!"

"Why can't you go in if it's your house?"

"The judge ruled that she gets to live in it until she gets a place. I left after we had a fight. She threw my ring out of the window and I started to whip her ass—I'm not going to lie about it. When the police got here they didn't take me in because of my title and everything. I just left though. After that she threatened to make trouble and by law she could because she'd been living with me for so long, with my so-called son. I'm doing the DNA thing now. I don't know what the truth is anymore."

"It's not the end of the world. Get yourself together, Malik. Start a new life. Even if you don't get all of your money and material things back you can get more. You're intelligent so don't let this stand in the way of moving forward. You're bigger than that," Monica says sympathetically.

Tears begin to drip slowly down my face and onto the steering wheel. "My mother turned me out on the streets when I was young, all because I didn't agree with her having men run in and out of our apartment when my dad left. The drugs and the drinking got out of hand. The next thing I knew I was being taken in by my aunt. I don't want to get into all of that, but let's just say my family ain't shit, starting with that woman. The last time I saw her I didn't call her mother to her face because I don't remember her that way. I haven't seen Vikki in years. She's selfish and I hate her, too!"

"Don't say that. Hate is a very strong word, and she did birth you. That counts for something—actually a lot."

"That's all she did for me."

"Malik, you can get even by becoming successful again. Have you thought of that? Being stuck in bitterness won't get you very far. You've got to shake this off and let it roll off your back— completely and wholeheartedly, not just part of the way."

"Actually, I have. I was thinking about going back to sports for a few years. I want to get back in, make some money, and then get off the field."

"So do that then. Make it happen! Don't let bitterness destroy all the good. Life goes on no matter the hand you're dealt. We all could manage to generate a list of what wasn't fair at some point. I'm no different than you. I need to let some past hurts go myself and get my shit back in order. Working things out and getting them straight can be exciting some times. I mean, as far as the challenge of working hard and making yourself blow up. Then you can say *kiss my ass* to everyone that hated. Any questions?"

"Damn you're smart when you're not drunk or got niggas starting fights over your ass. Will you help me train, Monica?"

She laughs. "I don't know anything about that whole deal of athletes getting in shape. I just gave you a little pep talk, that's all. I need to take my own advice before I do anything else."

"I'll teach you what you need to know. You'll catch on to the program."

"Ok. I'll do it if that's what it takes to help you move forward."

"Now one more thing—will you be my girl? You're going through shit and so am I. We can be a team and be there for each other. Whatever I make in this game I'll share. When I get my money back I'll keep looking out for you no matter what happens between us. All I'm asking you to do is stand by my side through this so I can get back to the show. I'm getting older and this may be my last chance to play football. Please say yes. I need your help and a commitment." I lean over and kiss her lips.

I know Monica's walls came tumbling down when I hear her say, "We can try to date a while and see what happens, Malik."

"Well, do you want to fuck a whole bunch of niggas or something?"

"No, that's not it," she says hesitantly.

"Then I think you need to think about this from my point of view. I can't get ready to put you on and have you on my team if you're fucking a whole bunch of niggas. I just told you I've already been through that," I say, looking in the direction of my house. "I need assurance that we're on the same page, Monica."

"It's been a while since I've been in a real relationship, and I don't trust easily. I'm telling you right now that I don't have good luck with men. This has nothing to do with wanting to have sex all over the place. I don't roll like that."

"Look, I'll take good care of you, I promise," I tell her. "Whatever you need, I can get it. I told Hakim to take sixty grand from the last check I had before my stuff was frozen, and pay some of your bills down because he told me some things about what's happened to you. I don't know why he never did it, but it just shows that I cared about you before we even met. I can get mostly any woman I want, and I know you can get mostly any man you want, but we need to commit to each other. That player shit is out, and if you really don't roll like that, you know what should come next."

"Okay already. I'll be yours exclusively, but don't make me regret doing this so fast."

"The only thing you'll regret is not having met me sooner. I used to ask Hakim if I could meet you when I came by, but he always said he didn't know if you were home. Your car was always in the driveway though."

"Well, that's over now. Let's go. We shouldn't be sitting here having this type of conversation. This is not the place for that. I think the maid is calling the police or something. I see her holding a cordless phone and staring in our direction."

"I wouldn't be surprised if she is. Me and my new girl have some celebrating to do. Bye, bitch," I mouth, driving past my house. I throw on the brakes and begin to back up.

"What are you doing?" Monica asks.

"I forgot something."

"What's that?"

I push the button to lower the window. "You'll be off payroll soon," I yell. "And tell that other bitch her free ride is coming to an end, too!" After I raise the window I pull off.

Monica strokes my neck softly. "Everything will work out. You'll see. Maybe I can talk to my dad and see if you can stay with us while you train. But the first thing you've got to do is leave your ex on this street. We just talked about moving on. I can't help you if you refuse to meet me halfway."

"You're right. I guess the talk hasn't completely sunk in yet."

"Well you don't have a whole lifetime to do it. I advise you to get started." I stop the truck again. "Now what this time?" she asks.

"Kiss me. Maybe that will remind me to get with the new program."

Monica and I share a long, passionate French kiss that's so sensual that I feel something I've only felt one time before, and that was with my very first sweetheart, the girl I fell in love with. When our licks and tongue swirling stops I say, "Let's bring in the New Year with me giving you something I think you'll enjoy. That will officially mark both of us moving forward."

She wipes her mouth, sucks one of her fingers seductively, and lifts her dress to the edge of her thigh. After that I begin to visualize Monica naked.

"Damn. I've got me a lady in the street and a freak behind closed doors. That's enough to make any nigga make that paper and get back on the map!"

As Monica giggles I pull off for the last time. I think I need to cry and act hurt and bruised more often. Apparently it's earned me enough sympathy to buy myself some time while I'm using this whole situation to my advantage. Either way, I ain't working because I'm allergic to pushing a broom, reading through a stack of papers behind a desk, or doing whatever at a regular nine to five with a boss telling me how to do shit. Even ex-ballers have privileges, and people should still be kissing my ass like it's golden. I'll start by breaking in her whole damn family, and even have the nerve to screw her under everyone's nose.

My first move is to give her two thousand kisses deep, and put it on her something terrible so leaving my ass won't be an option. The next stop is somebody's bed and I don't care who it belongs to. I may be preoccupied over my baby's momma but I'll clear my mind enough to hit my new girl's ass properly, because if I don't say so myself, I'm the boss. I'm sure Wes has realized by now that I can be one ruthless, deranged motherfucker.

12

THE DISAPPEARING ACT

Wes

The Blitzers are on a winning streak. In our top sport story today, one of their star players, Wes Montgomery, may be missing. In a statement issued by his publicist, Patty Bingham, she said: "We are making every effort to uncover the details behind Mr. Montgomery's disappearance. I cannot comment any further at this time."

Police have begun a search for the point guard who didn't show up for Monday's game against the team's biggest rival, and hasn't been seen for days. His coach alerted the authorities after he missed several practices and tonight's game. Coach Anderson said that Wes is normally a punctual, responsible player and this is the first time he's ever been missing or unable to be reached. Teammates are also concerned about their fellow team member.

Newcomer, Gerard Stanton said, "We hope Wes is all right wherever he is. We love him like a brother and look forward to his safe return."

Montgomery's black Hummer, license plate, Bgblr#1, Maryland tags, was last spotted near Bladensburg Road and has not been seen since. If you have any information about the whereabouts of Mr. Montgomery, please contact The District of Columbia Police Department by calling the crime solvers Tip Line at 1-800-673-2777.

13

CAUGHT IN THE MIDDLE OF BAD AND WORSE

Jalita

Last night it was forty-seven degrees, and tonight the weather is calling for fog and rain. It's getting harder to keep shivering my ass off and sleep in my car. I'd better find someplace quick if I expect my physical health to hold up better than my dwindling mental health. My throat's getting sore from a pending cold, and I'm almost out of gas from cutting the engine on and turning it off every half hour. I can't cook a decent meal or keep my personals clean and in order. Something's got to give, and as much as I hate to follow up on the Uncle Sam tip, I'll make a second effort to stick out my hand.

After I dial the number Ms. Mustache gave me, I hear, "Hello, this is the department of social services for Prince George's County, MD. Our hours of operation are 8:00 a.m. to 5:00 p.m., Monday through Friday. If you're calling about your temporary cash assistance time limit, please press zero now. If you're calling for information about child related services, please press one now. If you're calling about eligibility requirements for food stamps or medical assistance, please press two now. To find the nearest office in your location, please press three now."

I press three. I'm fuming mad because Ms. Mustache intentionally gave me P.G. County's number as opposed to Baltimore's. I continue to listen because calling information from this phone is out, plus the rules from one county to the next aren't drastically different.

The recording continues to play. "If you need information about homeless services or emergency assistance, please press four now. Our regular business hours are 8:30 a.m. to 5:00 p.m. You can come in, mail in, drop off, fax, or have someone drop off your application for you. If an interview is not possible on the day that you apply an interview appointment will be scheduled for you. All food stamp applications will be screened for expedited services. Bring copies of a birth certificate and social security card for each household member. You will also need to bring verification of income for the past 30 days, a copy of your vehicle registration, and verification of rent or mortgage."

The man's recorded voice doesn't spit information fast enough and my prepaid cell phone cuts him off in mid sentence. I consider it a sign that I should leave government begging alone. There's no way I can produce all of this documentation on the fly, plus I don't even have a current fixed address. If I'm up shit's creek without a paddle, how in the hell can they expedite anything? This is all Ms. Geraldine's fault and maybe she should help me find a solution. If she doesn't, maybe I'll take her downtown after all. If I have to go to hell and back because of her shady dealings, she may as well come with me. Put away your black-eyed peas and fatback, Ms. Geraldine. You're about to have a lost visitor to accommodate on New Year's Eve.

$

Since Ms. Geraldine is nowhere in sight, I walk up the steps and knock on her tenant's door. I don't know why I'm standing in front of my old apartment, but I am. What am I lying to myself for? I don't feel like I can go back to Shawn's looney world, and I'm getting no where with Uncle Sam's emergency services. There are too many crazy asses out for me to sleep in the car tonight, and my stomach is growling like nobody's business. Maybe the man who took my spot will feel sorry for my ass and agree to move out or deliver me from this fiasco. If the government can seize homes, cars, and miscellaneous goodies from criminals, I see no reason why I can't seize my spot. It's mine. I paid for it and I want it back. Fair enough in my book.

"You're back," the man says when he opens the door. He's in the middle of eating a donut and my eyes follow it up to his mouth because I'm so hungry. As he chews and swallows the last bite I long to brush the powder from around his mouth and eat it. I'm that famished.

I snap out of my episode of daydreaming. "Yes, I'm back."

"Let me guess. You got the royal run around," he grins.

"Maybe, but don't gloat. I'm sorry to disturb you, but I just didn't know where I could—"

"It's all good. Come in." He wipes the powder from around his mouth then brushes his palms clean. He turns around and tells me, "The offer still stands. You can crash here tonight. I'm not trying to be your daddy or anything but I just want to remind you that someone who just got out of the hospital shouldn't be roaming around the city in the cold."

"Don't I know it," I say, shaking my head. "But I can't do that. I can't afford to pay you, and I can't infringe on your privacy either. I paid Ms. Geraldine to be here, and I was hoping that I could find her and work something out because this isn't fair to me. If she has to give up her own unit to accommodate me, I think she should. I can't keep floating around like a vagabond, living out of my car like this."

"I agree with you 100%, but I did offer to help you out. Look, I have sisters and I would want someone to look out for them if I wasn't around." He sits down on the couch and I sit in a black pleather chair across from him. I notice all the shades are drawn.

"That's nice of you, but no. This is her problem, not yours."

"Ok, be stubborn all you want to. Have it your way, but you're not going to get anywhere by chasing around a crooked landlord. I think she went away for the weekend—at least I saw some old geezer pick her up and she was carrying her suitcase to his stinkin' Lincoln. Look, the very least I can do is feed you."

"I don't need your charity!" I snap in embarrassment.

"I didn't say you did. I don't even know your name and I'm still trying to help you, shortie. I'm on your side so remember that."

"Sorry. By the way, I'm Jalita. And you are?"

"The name is Clyde. Look, Jalita, I haven't had lunch yet either. How about you run to the store and get us something.

When you get back we can work on your situation." Clyde hands me a one-hundred dollar bill. I look at it. "Keep the change," he adds. "All I want is anything that doesn't require cooking and a bottle of Coca-Cola."

Without saying a word I take the money, admitting in my silence that hunger has set in. I walk out of the door. I don't know Clyde, but if he's willing to feed me maybe I better drop my tough girl act long enough to get fed.

$

My mouth is watering and I don't know what's holding up the line at the grocery store. I crane my neck and see a cashier that looks to be about twenty-five, with her hair brushed back into a broken off ponytail. Her edges look overeaten by a super perm, and her skin is full of dark splotches. She realizes the magnetic strip of someone's food card is screwed up and whips her head toward the right side of the store. "I've got a welfare food card on isle number three and it doesn't work. Manager to number three!" she screams into the microphone.

I feel sorry for the woman on welfare who must've filled out her whole life's story on a couple of forms, and is now being humiliated in front of an entire store of customers. No one appreciates having their business out in the street, and to some people, telling everyone you receive welfare benefits are fighting words. After her slow supervisor keys in the information the way she could've in the first place, the woman snatches her receipt, rolls her eyes, and grabs her bags. As she walks past the eyeballs that were burning holes in her back I decide that I was fortunate to have been rejected for help from Uncle Sam. Like it or not I'll keep Clyde's change and listen to any suggestions he makes when I return with his hoagie, cheese doodles, and Coca Cola. I know it sounds greedy, but I'd rather take a handout from someone like Clyde than Uncle Sam.

$

After Clyde and I finish lunch my mood is much lighter, and I'm not in a royal rush to leave my old spot.

"Excuse me a minute, that's the door," says Clyde. He gets up and I hear him ask, "Yo, what's cracking?"

"Not a thing worth talking about," replies the voice at the door. "Just getting ready for tonight." Both men walk toward the living room area. The newest face points to me. "Who's that?"

"Didn't your momma ever tell you it's rude to point?" scolds Clyde. "Ask her who she is—she has a mouth. And don't hit on her either, trying to be no playa playa."

"You always gotta be smart, man. What's your name?" he asks.

"First of all, who the hell are you?"

"Damn, girl. You don't have to be so cold. I'm Reggie."

"The name's Jalita. Next time don't point. Just like your man said, it's rude."

"Excuse me for that. Nice to meet you, Jalita. So, are you a new girl?"

"Excuse me? What in the hell is that supposed to mean?" I snap. I sit up straight and feel my heartbeat quicken. My relaxed vibe turns toward another direction.

"A new girl," he repeats. "You know. One of Clyde's girls."

"She's not here for that," Clyde answers.

"Well she should be. For all intents and purposes, she'd be good. No—great." He looks my way again.

Clyde clears his throat, gaps his legs apart, strokes his goatee and says, "I see what you're saying. You do have a good eye; I have to give you that. Now I have an idea that can kill two birds with one stone."

"Why are you looking at me like that?" I ask.

"Just get up and turn around for me, shortie." I do. "Yeah—yeah. This can definitely work," he says, nodding his long head up and down.

"What?" I ask.

"You need money, right?"

"You know I do, Clyde."

"Well, I can use you for what I do."

"Use me how? Tell me that. I'm not into illegal dealings so don't even think about it."

"Nothing illegal is to it. I'm a manager."

"Get right down to it. A manager of what?" I snap again, eying the knock off purses, shoulder bags, hats, throw back jerseys and designer jeans.

"Upscale strippers, escorts, topless maids, and nowadays video girls," he answers. "Sex sells and I do it all. I'm starting to branch out because there's no shame to my game, and if there's an opportunity looking you in the face, a smart man like me takes it. I just got here from Atlanta and this place is where I work out of, make connects, and set up appointments and things of that nature. Now you know, baby girl."

"Oh hell no!" I say indignantly. "Now wait a minute, I don't get down like that and you forgot to mention your little knock off stash here."

"Hold on now, shortie. I'm not a bad guy, and I'm not forcing anything on you. I'm just letting you know this can be mutually beneficial. I like money and you need money. You got a pretty face, a fat tail, and a nice pair of knockers that can bring in some nice cash. Sounds like a formula for a win-win situation to me. As far as the knock offs, my man here gets the things from New York to hit the local flea markets on weekends. Don't act like you've never bought or listened to a counterfeit CD, or watched a bootleg movie. I let the young boys sell it; let them take the chance now that the feds are clamping down. My main hustle is big things."

Before I know it I say, "Keep talking then. I'm listening."

"I always start my girls off with a test assignment. If you handle this one all right then I have an audition for a video shoot coming up just after the New Year. I'm pretty sure this rap artist would like you, and I kinda sorta have the final say so in the casting department. Consider yourself lucky because most of my new girls get sent on that topless maid shit and have to let their titties hang out while they push a vacuum and wipe down counters, or either do those web cam gigs and have pictures of their body parts pasted on the web. They'd be mad if they knew you didn't have to go there," he explains. "Let me see you move," he tells me.

I place my hands on my hips. "Move for what?"

"Look, now is not the time to be shy. This is your audition. I'm the man but you have to follow what I'm asking if you want me to give you the hook up. Let me put some music on to help you along." He puts on Ciara's *One Two Step* and says, "Move it and let your blouse hang over your shoulder just a little bit."

I move my shirt to the side, close my eyes, and move my hips.

"There you go. But give me some more like you're really feeling it. I know you've been clubbing before. Get into it, baby girl—work it like it means something to you."

After I consider the stack of bills I can't pay, having nowhere to go, and the food stamp incident, I drift back to the old Jalita again. Before I know it I'm doing my famous booty shake, snapping my fingers, and mouthing the words to the song with a seductive look on my face.

When I stop, Reggie says, "Damn that was good!"

I look at his crotch and notice the bulge in his pants.

He looks at Clyde and says, "Now she's a definite money maker. You need to use your connections to the modeling industry, send her to South Beach in Miami, get her a test shoot with a photographer and take things from there. Fuck the local shit—this girl is print, video, movie, and TV material."

"I know, B. She's too short for runway, but she damn sure can fit in somewhere else. One thing at a time though. Before you got this chick staying up on the beach at Ocean Avenue, I've got to find out if she's one of those types who's gonna be a drama queen on a set and mess me up with my peoples."

"All I know is that you need to jump on this opportunity, and I need to ask her a question before I explode." He walks over to me and says, "Hey sweetheart, do you have a man?"

"I sure do," I lie. "Where there's smoke there's fire, right?" I decide the next bum that asks me that is going to get told off, but I know I can't unleash my classic feisty style if I'm talking about making money with his boy.

"Forget him," says Clyde. "Do this gig I have tonight and I'll get you on the video set. Do it and you'll be getting paid before you know it."

"Well what is it that I have to do?"

"Are you doing it or not," he asks. "If you are I've got to make a call right about now. Then we have to get something hot for you to wear, and let you get cleaned up."

I know I shouldn't agree to something when I'm not sure what it is but I nod yes. Clyde smiles, dials a number on his cell phone, and before I know it he's telling someone, "She has that *look* like one of those Ethnicity Models in Miami. I'm telling you, she's straight, even without makeup. Yes, she's young. In fact she just turned eighteen and is fresh on the market. Right, ok, she'll be there. You won't be disappointed." He closes the cell phone. "I got a call for a girl earlier. All I need you to do is just show the gentleman a good time and satisfy him. Make him happy—it's easy money. All he wants to do is go to a New Year's party with a date."

"I don't know. Maybe that's not a good idea."

"If you don't want the gig I can get someone else. It doesn't matter; just let me know. If I give your assignment away that's it though. There's no turning back."

"I'll take it but I was eighteen two years ago."

"What's he going to do? Ask you for ID? You ain't far from it so you can pull it off." He looks me over, and suddenly he's all business. "Now here are the rules for my clients: No photography or video. He's not to take pictures of you in any form. No touching, no verbal abuse, discussion of money, and he's to stay fully dressed at all times. Lastly, make up some sort of sexy name for yourself. Men that contact me love that corny shit. If you have any problems, call. I'll be around to take your call on the first ring if anything jumps off. Do you have a cell phone?"

"A prepaid one but all my minutes are out right now."

"Here, use this one. It's fully charged. My number is already stored in it. Just find the phone book feature and you'll see it." He passes me the phone. "I know I just told you all of these rules but don't think that doesn't mean you shouldn't stroke his ego. Make him feel good. Smile a lot, be friendly, act like you're having a good time, and flirt. Do you think you can do that? This is a new client and I hear the dude is loaded."

"Yeah," I tell him. Obviously he doesn't know whom he's dealing with. "I can do that better than you could ever imagine," I add.

He smiles. "I'll drop you off around the corner and his limo will pick you up. I keep my business and where I lay my head private, even at my part time crib. You straight as far as the instructions?"

"Yeah, I'm straight."

"Ok, then. My topless maids get $90 an hour so that should tell you I'm gonna look out for you. When you come back you'll get your $1,000 cash. And don't worry you'll get your money. Let's go. I have a boy who will open his boutique up if I can catch him before he rolls out." He heads for the door then stops. "You don't feel sick or nothing do you? I forgot all about that hospital stay."

"I'm ok. It wasn't anything like you may think," I explain.

His friend asks, "You still rolling with us to The Big Apple, right?"

"Yeah, man. Money first, hos second. You know the order. We got time and you know I'm in there. I'll be back with a quickness."

After Clyde closes the door behind him I realize that I just signed up to take a stranger on his word that this assignment will be kosher, and I'm assuming I'll get my cut in the first place. Either way, Jalita is stuck between bad and worse so she'll just have to take the chance that this whole scenario will turn out to be harmless. Spreading my legs eagle is off limits and that makes all the difference in the world. I don't know how those strippers and the rest get down in the ATL but my legs are staying closed, even if the price is right. At the very least I will get another meal out of the trip to flirt with some old dried up prune.

14

FANTASY FOREPLAY

Malik

"Malik, where have you been?" Monica asks.

"Out," I tell her after returning to the cheap hotel room that fits my budget.

"*Out?* That's all I get for a reply is *out?* I know that much. You said you'd be right back and you've been gone for the last three hours. What, you don't know how to tell time?" she says sarcastically. "If you were going to be gone that long I could've come with you, instead of sitting in this room with the tile falling off the walls and mold in the bathroom."

I ignore Monica's bitching and set an assortment of bags in the corner, and one on the small circular table. I ran around D.C. in search of a necklace, a banging love making CD, some Victoria's Secret lingerie and shower wash, some massage oil, honey, shampoo and conditioner, a picnic basket, Gatorade, strawberries, cantaloupe, a bottle of chilled wine, and three orders of Chinese food that is bound to taste like something worth eating.

"I need to take a shower, Monica," I say without further explanation of my whereabouts. I grab the body wash out of one of the bags and then strip, letting my clothes fall to the floor. Then I walk to the bathroom and turn on the shower. "Come in here, Monica," I call out.

"Why, you're in the shower. I'm watching something on TV— hopefully it'll stay on long enough for me to finish."

"I asked you to come here. Stop being difficult. What's more important, me or some pre-recorded TV show?"

"What? I didn't hear you," she yells, her eyes glued to some corny sitcom.

"I said come here," I shout over the running water. In a few seconds Monica appears. "Could you put some soap on my back?"

Without saying a word Monica takes the white washcloth and begins to rub my back in small, soapy circular motions.

"Lower."

"How's that?"

"Lower," I say again. I want Monica to notice my ten-inch penis that's sticking straight out. When she does I know that her indifference won't last. I turn around and face her. "Could you put some soap on my chest?"

She lathers my chest without so much as a glance down below. "How's that," she asks.

"Higher, you missed my nipples."

"They could only be but so dirty. You're a man. Am I finished yet? I was trying to watch TV, Malik. The show was almost over. You might make me miss the end," she complains.

"Not until you get in. After that you can finish watching TV. Now take your clothes off and shower with me."

When she steps into the shower in front of me I grab the soap and another washcloth, I begin using Victoria's Secret Body wash to cleanse her soft-looking skin. When my dick grazes her Monica's voice softens and she forgets about that TV program.

"That smells good," she says. "What is it? It can't be the motel soap smelling like that."

"Don't worry about that. Do you like how this feels?"

"Mmm-hmm," she moans.

I continue caressing her body. "I want to love you, Monica, and I want to make love to you. I want to be your best friend and confidant. I'm going to spoil you and give you every advantage you deserve in life. I'm going to make up for any and all bad times you've experienced. Tonight is my first night to prove my intentions. Some time alone is what we really needed."

She turns around and we begin tongue kissing. The water wets her dark hair and it falls down her back in very large waves that are nearly straight. I imagine her standing under a waterfall with skin bronzed from a warm summer's sun. I grab her around the small of her back and begin sucking her nipples with the gentle motion of an erotic lover. She begins moaning by the third suck.

"Mmm."

I step closer, grab her tighter, and let my hard dick press against her belly button. Steam begins to form on the mirrors and it feels as if we're enclosed in a sauna. I take my left hand and play with her clit. "Tell me if you still want to watch TV, baby."

"I—uh. Mmm."

"What, cat got your tongue, baby? I can't understand that shit you're mumbling."

"No. You know, you—you know what you're doing to me. It's hard to talk right now. Mmm. Mmmm. Mmmhmm," she moans softly.

I begin rubbing my dick across the lips of her pussy. Monica sounds as if she can barely breathe. I watch the color in her face deepen and she now looks as if the sun has indeed kissed her light skin and warmed her hue to a much richer yellow.

"Fuck me!" she blurts out. "I need you to fuck me, Malik. Do it right now! Fuck me. I want you. Come on. Do it!"

As I listen to her breathe heavily, I tell her, "Nope."

She pants and whines, "Please, fuck me. What do you want me to do, beg? I want you." She grabs me around the neck and presses her breasts against me like she's losing control of herself. I laugh at my ability to guard my urges while Monica is panting like a dog in heat.

"Why are you teasing me? Why are you doing this to me?"

"Because you're not ready for that yet." I bend down and turn off the water. I step out of the shower, grab a towel, and look into the mirror as I dry myself off.

"What about me?" she asks. She smoothes back her hair and squeezes the water from it.

As droplets fall from the ends I reply, "What about you?"

"Are you going to leave me like this?" she snaps.

"No." I throw her a towel. When she catches it, I add, "Now dry off. Of course I can't leave you wet. I can't have you getting sick, and I can't afford to catch a cold from you either."

Monica's sultry appeal disintegrates and is replaced with anger and frustration. She steps out of the shower with heavy steps, like she won't have much to say to me for quite a while. I walk into the room and sit on the bed. She crosses her arms, letting her hair drip onto her shoulders.

"You better get another towel for your hair before you get everything wet."

She starts slamming things around and returns with a towel tightly wrapped around her head, looking like an Indian swami.

"Lose your attitude. There's no need for all of that, Monica."

"I have every right to have one. You know what you did to me and that was cold."

"No, it's what I *didn't* do that you've got a problem with."

"Ok, fine. You get the point. Same difference," she tells me. Monica grabs a bag of corn chips, sticks her hand deep into the bad and begins eating them, crunching loudly like her emotions are driving her to take out her hostility on the Fritos.

"Put the bag down and close your eyes," I say softly.

"What? I'm hungry, and you're not trying to give me any attention or feed me a meal. Why should I?" she says as she continues to munch on the snack.

I put some base in my voice. "Put down the bag and close your eyes you stubborn woman. Maybe if you do your luck will change." She does.

When Monica complies I lift her up, place her on the middle of the bed, and unwrap her towel. I begin to lotion her feet, remembering to let the liquid flow between her toes. Then I work my way up to her graceful long neck and delicate shoulders. Next I begin to softly kiss her on her hips and thighs. After I stop my hands continue to massage in the lotion. A sense of calmness falls upon her. "Turn over."

When she does I pour massage oil down the crack of her ass, periodically grabbing handfuls of her flesh and squeezing her full cheeks. Monica begins to squirm and I can tell that I am arousing her with my touch. She attempts to turn over and look at me. "I didn't say you could open your eyes. Turn back around and relax."

Monica closes her eyes again and resumes moaning.

"Since it appears that you want to moan, big daddy will give you something to moan about, girl."

I part her legs and begin to lick her softly with my tongue. When she's wet and slippery I lean over top of her and whisper in her ear. "You're about to have the best sex you've ever had in your entire life. Did you think I brought you here for nothing? To think you were upset because you thought I wasn't capable of using a cheap hotel room on New Year's Eve properly. I tell you what—I'll let this one slide but the next time it happens I'll have to spank you until your butt stings. Now you can turn around." When she does I say, "Look at me in my eyes." She does and I obviously have her full attention.

When I realize I've emotionally connected with her, I say, "Already, I feel as though life without you would be like taking away sunshine. You make me smile. You make me happy. Now I want to make you feel just a little of the way I feel inside. I need to wake up in your arms every day. Every day I can give you orgasm after orgasm if that's what you need. Thank you for what you told me the other day. I feel like a new man. I got you something." I reach down and grab a fourteen carat gold necklace with a heart dangling from it. "Here, I want you to wear something and never take it off unless you have to." I place the jewelry on Monica's neck.

When a shady brother whipped the necklace out of the inside of his jacket pocket and dangled it front of me, I just knew I had to have it to top off my evening with Monica. I was fortunate enough to talk him down to twenty dollars for it when I was in a parking lot at a shopping center in the hood in Forestville. His loss, my gain. That's life.

When I fasten it on Monica's neck she says, "I can't believe you did this for me, Malik. That was so thoughtful. I love, it. It's beautiful."

"It's nothing," I say. "I wish I could do more, but then again I can." Slowly I slide down her body and kiss her flat stomach. I reach over to the portable CD player and press play. Mario's *Baby Let Me Love You* begins and I reach into my bag for the small bottle of honey. When I squeeze out the first swirl onto Monica's belly button she flinches at its coolness. As I begin to lick it off her soft moans resume. Next, I drip honey onto each nipple and suck it off gently.

"I've never had anyone do this before," she sighs. "Oh, Malik. Damn! This feels wonderful."

I know it does because every woman I do this to reacts the same way.

"Shhh. Relax and enjoy this. Let me do all the talking, and redefine foreplay in your book. Pretend this is your fantasy and I'm here to fulfill it for you."

Next, I pick up a strawberry, place into my mouth, bite it, and then move toward her lips. I use my tongue to push the strawberry into Monica's mouth. "Eat it," I say. While she does I pick up a piece of cantaloupe and carefully stuff it into her pussy.

She swallows the strawberry, and raises her head. "What are you doing?"

"Eating dessert," I answer. "Where's my manners? Want some, baby?" Then I use my mouth to gently lick on the piece of cantaloupe and pull it out of her pussy. "Here. See how good you taste and find out why I don't mind taking control. You taste so sweet, Monica."

After she chews it, I stick my finger into her mouth. She begins to suck it. "Pretend it's my dick," I tell her. "Suck it like you'd suck me, because this is the last one you're going to have." She sucks harder and I feel my erection grow as I imagine how good it will feel to have her luscious lips wrapped around me.

She moves her mouth away from my finger. "I'm ready, Malik," she whispers.

I smile. "Not yet. Slow down." I take her right hand and pull her to her feet. After she stands I get up too. We begin to slow dance. For the first time I realize how well Monica fits into the middle of my chest. I hold her tightly while touching the small of her back, then her ass. We begin to kiss again, first flicking our tongues, and then taking turns sucking on them. I move my mouth away. "You know I care about you, right?"

"I think so, Malik," she answers timidly.

"You'll see. One day you're going to be my wife. We're going to have everything. Make babies. Have a nice home and money in the bank. You'll see, Monica. The world is ours and that's that.

You don't have to worry about anything, and you can tell me anything. If there's no place or no one to turn to, turn to me. I am here for you, girl. It's just us from now until a very long time. There was a time when I was out there but it's not like that now. I have my mind made up—I'm already sprung and I care about you. I'm going to teach you to follow your heart and let some of those walls of yours down." I gently push her away, take her hand, and lead her back to the bed. "Lay back," I say softly. She does. I roll down a condom on my dick.

I stand over her and look her right in the eye. "I don't want you to have me until you're ready to make love to me. I didn't say fuck me, I said *make love to me*. Before it was a lust thing but this time around I need to know something. Do you love me, Monica? Tell me the truth."

"I think so but I can't tell yet," she answers. "We have to grow a whole lot before I can determine that."

"If you love me, if you think you love me, tell me I'm not a rebound. Tell me you'll never fuck no other nigga but me, and tonight is something you'll never forget."

"I promise. It's just us. I won't do you wrong, Malik. You don't have to worry about that."

"Then you do love me. It doesn't always take years to fall in love with someone. That's bullshit. Love is action, doing—a feeling like what we've got. You're starting to love me. I can tell. This is good." I twist her long dark nipples with my hand and continue, "This will only get better and better on all levels. Now that you've proven you are my baby, the rest is up to you. Now what do you want?"

"I'm now in a monogamous relationship, so I want my black dick—that's what I want, right here, right now. Not tomorrow, not next week, but now! Stop teasing me and give me every inch. I'm ready for you and you know it. Keep touching me, baby. Don't let this good feeling stop. It's been so long since my body's felt this good."

"Then that's what I'll do. Daddy's dick is ready for you too. Come home to me, Monica. You and I have some unfinished business that we started in Atlantic City. This is like a dream come true, to be behind a locked door with you when I'm completely sober." I push my erect ten-inch dick inside of her, and Monica begins to gush instantly. Our words are few but our noises of lovemaking resound throughout the room.

We bring in the New Year the best way any one can bring it in—fucking, making love, and screwing in every position I feel like contorting Monica in, pushing her imagination to the limit. Gatorade will replenish us when we're finished because it's going to be a long night. Little does she know I plan to put it on her and talk shit the whole night, because a pussy whipped woman will stand by her man, even if he turns out to be trifling. And I know how to work what I've got that well. Every woman has a fantasy and it's a smart man's job to find out what it is, or at least impress her by attempting to guess what it could be. I'll top off my performance with a picnic dinner on a blanket spread out on the floor. Although it may seem like a complete waste of time to brothers who are accustomed to booty calls, real players take it slow and know that things like this are worth their weight in gold because it helps a man get into a woman's head. I'll lead Monica into believing I'm sensitive and into that talk after sex, that bonding, and cuddling shit. I've got plans and more tricks than I can count up my sleeve including lying to her that I wrote two poems about the first day I saw her. I actually recopied them in my own writing from a few ethnic card lines in Safeway a while back and keep them on hand for occasional use. Now that I've laid the groundwork, it's on like a pot of neck bones. By now it doesn't even matter that I couldn't take Monica to the Ritz Carlton, Marriott, or Hilton. Her feeling sorry for me and my broke pockets fits into my master plan.

15

IT HIT ME FROM BEHIND

Jalita

A clean white limo quietly pulls up to the side of the curb, and I know I look the part of a woman who should be paid just to be seen with a man. I'm standing on the sidewalk decked out in a dark brown faux fur, three-inch heels, and an authentic, long, strapless Vera Wang gown. My lips are coated with just the right amount of lip-gloss, making them look sexy, tempting, and delicious. When the driver gets out to open the door my mind flashes back to the Tomi limo fiasco, but I shake it off and smile as I step into the back of the limo.

As soon as I peek inside I hear, "Am I in Heaven? You are absolutely beautiful. You must be my date."

"Thank you but you're still on Earth, indeed," I say shyly. "Yes, I am your date. Are you going to leave me standing out here on this curb, or are you going to take me along with you?"

"Oh, I see you're witty. Please step in." After I get in he pats the spot next to him. "Move closer. You're so far away from me. I don't like to talk too loudly."

My heart pounds as I slowly slide across the leather seat and invade his personal space. He's a dark-skinned black man, nearly fifty years old, with the beginning stages of salt and pepper gray hair cropping up sporadically around his temples. He looks to be in good shape and likely uses a personal trainer to keep him looking fit, trim, and tuned up.

"It's a pleasure to meet you. I'm Ginger," I say, offering him a handshake. Instead of shaking it he kisses it and releases my hand.

If I didn't know better I would call him an older version of Wes, but I won't.

"I'm Kyle. Let me tell you a little about myself. I'm a very prominent businessman, the CEO of a well-known company with offices in D.C., New York, and Tokyo. I just relocated from Tokyo a few months ago. You may wonder why a man like me is using a service like this. Well, I'm paying to keep my name clean and my business out of the street. Whatever I want I pay for it, and when I pay for it I expect the best. Although I have money, I spend it wisely."

"Yes, sir," I nod. "Just to let you know, I'm worth every penny and then some. In fact, you're getting quite a bargain, but then again I am lucky to be in the presence of a well-established man like yourself. I'm sure you will tell me all about what you do this evening," I reply. Apparently he's an ego head like Wes, but I know exactly how to deal with him for the next few hours. After that I never have to lay eyes on his arrogant ass again. Charm and flattery goes far with these types, but I get tired of ego rubbing and eyelash batting after a while.

"You seem rather intelligent but I just want to remind you not to split any verbs or butcher the King's English. Act like you've known me for a long time because I anticipate running into some of my colleagues and clients. Stay by my side at all times. I'm paying you to be with me, not wander. Whatever I do, follow my lead. I do the drinking, you do the watching. Do nothing of the sort to embarrass me. Follow those directions and we'll get along just fine. Have I made myself crystal clear?"

Although I'd already like to smack his pompous ass into a tailspin I don't. Instead I nod. "I fully understand your position, sir."

"Good. The affair we'll be attending is very nice. I go every year. Call me Kyle, my dear. There's no need to be so formal with me."

"Yes, Kyle." I flutter my eyelashes and smile.

For an entire forty-five minutes he bragged about himself. He made it clear that he's a member of D.C.'s in-crowd. All that did was prove that he's probably having a mid-life crisis and wants to be seen with a young dime piece. When the limo pulls up at a hotel in a location I don't recognize, I'm more than ready to get out and enter the hotel lobby. Music flows into my ears and instantly puts a sweet spell on me. Tall ice sculptures are everywhere, and as I wonder why they haven't melted, I'm so impressed by the time and skill it took someone to carve out the various shapes and figures. My eyes drift toward all of the beautiful decorations that set the mood for good times in an elegant setting. People dressed in formal attire, donned in tuxedos and formals dresses laugh and talk while holding drinks. I've never seen anything like it, even on Wes's arm. The event is truly captivating, and I think that maybe listening to Kyle brag on himself for a few hours won't kill me after all.

After we ride the escalator, push our way through the thick crowd, and find seating in a sophisticated ballroom with low lighting, we eat as Kyle converses with a few clients. He does a little ego massaging of his own, conveniently reminding each of them of their remarkable achievements. I am so nervous I watch which fork and spoon Kyle uses and when, so I won't give away the fact that I've never kept up with formal dining etiquette. The only thing I know I should do is place my gold cloth napkin in my lap and avoid belching, slurping liquids, or eating like a wild animal that's just been released from a cage. Kyle must detect my nervousness because he points to a freshly poured glass of water and whispers in my ear that I should take a sip and wet my throat.

After an hour or so, I hook my arm in Kyle's and we circulate around the room so that he can make his socializing rounds. In fact, I get the feeling he is "showing me off," and flaunting me like the young arm piece that I am. Before long I notice people whispering and looking at me coldly as if I've done something deplorable above and beyond being seen with a pompous older man. I'm not sure if they are staring because they sense that he drank like a fish, or because I'm making such a wonderful impression since I'm so easy on the eyes. When I mention it to Kyle he feeds me some information that I'm not at all happy about.

"I'll be up front with you. I'm married and I'm not planning on leaving my lovely wife, even though she won't have sex with me. We have a good life together, except for a few minor things.

Ignore my wife's friends because what they think doesn't count for much."

I'm livid that he failed to mention all of this shit before I stepped my ass into the limo. But he didn't, so I'm stuck making my buck to fulfill my agenda. The meds for my nerves must've had a real effect on me because my tongue stays still. My ability to quickly conjure up an episode of revenge kicks in, but I push it back down into the pit of my smart-ass memory bank where I store appropriate one-liners to fit any occasion. Instead of cussing Kyle out I look at a huge ice sculpture and listen to the relaxing piano tune that's being played by a very talented musician. What else can I do without causing a scene and going back to sleeping in my car broke?

$

Kyle insists that he venture to his room to freshen up, so we do. I can hear the water running in the bathroom as he washes his face. "Ginger, can you hear me?" he calls out.

"Yes, Kyle. I can." I notice I feel lightheaded but I'm not sure why.

"Good. I brought you up here because I want to tell you something. Let's just say I'm trying to pick up the pieces of being married without the kind of sex that can make me abandon my viagra. I'm tired of all the money and time spent in sex therapy so it's time to try another approach." I hear him turn off the water.

When he walks out of the bathroom and stops in front on me, I tell him, "I'm sorry about all of that but that's not in the job description. Are you ready to go back downstairs to the party?"

"No, I'm not ready to go downstairs, and it's not your place to rush me. I like you and I don't want things to end here. What will it take? What is it that you want? Sex is certainly in *my* job description, even if I have to pay you for that, too."

"With all due respect, Kyle, I wouldn't like any of those things from you and I don't think your wife would approve of you offering them to me."

He laughs, unties his tie and begins dialing on a room phone. "Yes, darling, I miss you, too. Are you having a nice time in New York? Wonderful. I'd like you to say hello to someone. Come say hello, Ginger. It's all right—speak to her." He hands me the phone.

I think of the fact that I'm probably wrecking my cut and take the phone. I figure the woman can't see who's on the other end so I'll play his little game.

"I know where this is leading," said a calm voice on the other end. "I don't care if you sleep with my husband. I'm not interested in him that way, so go on and have your little affair. Now put him back on the phone. Maybe we'll meet at some point. Happy New Year!"

In shock I hand the ivory colored room phone back to Kyle.

"Doesn't she sound sexy?" he asks. "She looks as good as she sounds, Renee. So, is your girlfriend there? Oh, she is? Let me talk to her—I want to ask her what color her panties are. Oh, thongs, huh? Yes, I know. Don't you just love Renee's body? You're doing what to my wife? Mmmm, that sounds delicious. Well you girls have fun. I'll join you in the morning. I'm looking forward to visiting. Have fun but don't stay up too late. Goodbye." Kyle turns to me. "Now do you believe me? I told you it's ok. I have a wonderful wife who doesn't mind me meeting my needs elsewhere as long as she's taken care of too. In fact, I've been in search of someone like you. My wife and I are willing to share our new home with the right young lady. We would give you a free room in our beautiful home, and even pay generously for you, let's say—spicing up our love life. You would have your own private bathroom, and of course a large second master bedroom. We have an enclosed back yard that has a grilling area and hot tub. The house has every amenity you might need or desire. There is a small catch though. We spent ten years in Tokyo and we grew to adore our housekeeper. We are looking to form another relationship with the right woman."

I gulp, remember my days of getting beat down for messing with other people's property, and say, "I think you've misunderstood our meeting tonight. I hate to get in your business but that's not my cup of tea, so I don't prefer to continue this conversation with a *married* man."

Andrea Blackstone

Kyle takes his wallet out of his pocket and pulls apart a stack of hundreds, forming a fan with them. After charming me with it he pushes the stack back together and stuffs it in his wallet. Then he looks at me. "No, I haven't misunderstood anything," he says firmly. "I've been watching you—you are obviously young, educated, easy-going, loyal, and a good conversationalist. Most of all you're naturally sensual, and I believe you're someone who could turn my wife on enough to have sex with me. All you'd have to do is watch us become exhibitionists in front of you in the bedroom and out. My wife and I don't always wear clothes inside of our home. We expect that you would respect our choice although you are not required to do the same. If you choose to wear clothes sexy lingerie and heels would be appropriate. Your responsibilities would be to keep your living space clean, help out with chores, and cook. My wife and I are sexually open. She has her girlfriends and I have mine. We're both swingers. Although we would respect your privacy, we hope you are open-minded as well. I'm serious about this offer and would be happy to schedule a time that my wife can meet you. Since we do have a child I'll need your real name for my own personal comfort and the safety of my family. Let's start off the New Year right with our first episode of foreplay. I want to suck your toes. I know you have beautiful feet; I can just tell. Let me see them, Ginger. What color did you paint them? Don't make me beg. Give me your young, supple feet so I can suck your sexy toes."

When I notice that he's staring at my shoes, I put up my hand. "Stop right there. I'm not agreeing to any of this. Excuse me, but I need to use the restroom." When I drop my arm, get up and make it into the restroom, I lock the door and call Clyde to inform him that this psycho is in need of head medication more than I am. The only problem is that each time I scroll through the stored number section and push send I'm connected to his voice mail. After the sixth attempt I know that I can't stall much longer.

"Is everything all right? You wouldn't happen to be on the phone would you?"

I cuss softly to myself. "No, everything is fine. I'm just using the restroom."

I flush the empty toilet and then turn on the faucet as if I'm washing my hands. When I unlock the door I am startled when Kyle grabs my wrist. I get that dizzy feeling again and my equilibrium is definitely off kilter.

"If you had to use the bathroom, you should've pissed on me, Ginger." I gulp hard when I realize Kyle is some kind of aggressive sexual deviant. Then he continues, "I don't think you understand what's going on here. I get what I want and I suggest you comply with my wishes. Don't lie to me. I know what you were in there doing. If it's one thing I can't stand it's a lying little bitch who plays hard to get!"

"Stop! Let me go," I yell, my words half slurred.

Before I know it Kyle wrestles with me and manages to tear my dress and expose my black stockings. I break free and he chases me around the room. The thing is I can't run very fast and begin to stumble, but I'm still not sure why I'm so woozy. When he catches me again he throws me against the wall and pins me.

"You know you want it, you little slut. Tell the truth! You want to come home with me and sit on my face every day, don't you?"

I smell the liquor on his breath and grimace at the pungent odor. He's more inebriated than I thought and his slurred words are evidence of that.

I'm surprised by his strength. I jerk in all directions but I can't shake myself loose. Although my mind is telling me to resist him, I can't figure out why my body isn't responding to push Kyle away.

He covers my mouth with one hand. "You want me to tear your little asshole to shreds while I fuck you—you want me to look at my wedding picture while I'm doing it, right? You want to fulfill my fantasies and rub my wife's nose in it, don't you? Where would you like it—on the floor, the table, the counter top? Let me put you on my slut list, Ginger!"

"I can't think," I mumble. "I don't know why I can't say things right." I look into his eyes deeply and intently, searching for clarity as my confusion grabs me in a cloud of haze.

Kyle ignores my garble. "I see the Super K ecstasy has started to kick in. That was ketamine you were sipping at dinner, not water. Funny how it's clear just like water, huh, Ginger? Even if you could still let out a scream or two, no one is up here anyway.

Andrea Blackstone

They're all downstairs at the party." He roughly thrusts his fingers into my vagina, and I feel my stomach turn. "I asked for your panties and you wouldn't give them to me," he rasps in my ear. "So now I think you're ready for this and I expect you to get used to it. You're a bad little girl, Ginger, so I'm punishing you." Kyle straddles me, unbuttons his tuxedo and before I know it he's deep inside of me.

I cry the whole time, tears streaming down my face although my senses are dulled. I feel helpless because I can't form the words to tell him to stop having sex with me. Before I know it I drift off to sleep and none of this matters. My body shuts down against my will, and Kyle lies next to me enjoying the fact that he gave me a date rape drug and took what he wanted instead of letting sleeping dogs lie.

When he gets up he says, "Go clean yourself up and get yourself together. I'll stand by the door while you do it. I begin to shake as I feel the humiliation of being raped. I'm overcome with weakness and don't feel up to fighting him to get out of the door. Instead my crying spell turns into a panic attack and I begin shaking. I want to run, but instead of running I can't move. Kyle ran better game than me and I'm in shock about everything that just spiraled out of control. Despite my desire to decipher what in the hell just happened to me, I begin to feel sleepy. My eyes slowly shut, whether I like it or not.

16

POCKET CHANGE

Malik

It's been one month since Monica and I have been kicking it, and it amazes me how many women are capable of setting their standards so low, tolerating the most ridiculous lies ever told. No matter how you treat them they don't seem to realize that they were the plan B, and that there's always a plan C. When a better offer comes along, the crisis is over, or the purpose has been served, men with an agenda don't give a damn about who was there when. But these women just keep on giving, investing emotional energy and time in a lose-lose relationship. Maybe it's hard for them to admit to themselves, even when they see it coming. I don't know.

If women would learn these four facts about men they might not find themselves being taken for a ride all the time: 1.) You can't change a man, even if it seems like we need fixing. In fact, we despise the thought of someone trying to set us straight and make us over their way. If we're a mess when a woman meets us why expect us to fly straight? 2.) If we give private information freely or quickly, it's probably a set up to gain sympathy and make ourselves look good. 3.) If we want something bad enough we're willing to go the distance to get the job done. We don't need to be reminded or assisted to be considerate or get on the ball. That's all a choice. 4.) The truth falls apart when lies hold it together. One lie leads to the next lie and the chain of little lies string together to form one monumental lie. A woman may never know the truth, and the art of lying is designed that way. The thing is a woman will keep asking us about a lie as if we'll ever own up to the truth. What sense does that make? Women—you've got to love them and their naïve innocence.

Wrap all of these points up into one and what I've got is the makings of free labor, unwavering support, and maybe even some pocket change from Monica, who has just begun collecting unemployment after quitting her long-term substitute teaching gig. Apparently the last straw for her was some kid putting a tack on her chair, Monica sitting on it, and then falling out with the principle because he didn't do shit to discipline the kid. Monica gathered her belongings and never went back, but I'm not mad because I can see that taking her for a ride will be an easy thing. My goal is to work the fool out of Monica—for free. Former honor student, good head on her shoulders, responsible—just the kind of ho I can exploit from brain to ass, and now her schedule is completely open.

I already showed her how to do my bio. She updated my numbers and stats, and typed a personal introductory letter to accompany each one. I got a hold of a fresh list of teams and we addressed a letter to various coaches in the NFL. One night we sat down with a pile of bios that Monica printed out in color, a stack of business envelopes, and a book of stamps. When we were done she even drove to the post office to drop them off for me while I slept before going to the gym for my evening work out. Then when she hit the door she peeled off her coat, washed her hands, and prepared my baked chicken breast, cooked me brown rice, and boiled fresh broccoli. When she finished cooking she cleaned up the kitchen while I watched television and prepared to train at the gym the next morning.

Couldn't she see the pattern? Even a blind man could, so you would think. If anyone should've been resting it should've been her because she knew she'd be the one driving me to the gym. Even so she allowed me to fuck her brains out and drain the last drop of energy she had from her body. I know she can't cheat on me because she never has the time or energy to break away from her duties of making love to me three times a day and running my daily schedule.

Her training is coming along as well as mine. Today I'll prove my theory even further, by testing Monica's ability to say no. The thing is, I don't expect her to say no, and to keep it that way I'll train her to keep her standards low—much better than I did with Diamond.

$

"Hey baby, what's up?"

"I just got back from shopping and putting the groceries away, Malik. What's that in those bags?"

"Vitamins, protein, and supplements. I need these along with my training to keep me strong as a horse."

"Where'd you get that stuff? You didn't have money this morning when you left."

"I met this white guy at GNC. I just went in there to buy some glucosomine, but we got to talking and we hit it off. Before I turned to leave he said I could pay him later. It was a blessing. I needed so many things."

"That's at least four hundred dollars worth of goods, Malik. You shouldn't borrow from people or ask them to do favors if you don't know how and when you can pay them back. I told you that before," she scolds.

"I know, but we started talking and he's cool. You'll meet him. Do you want anything for yourself, baby?"

"No way, Malik. That's not my style. If I don't have money for something I just can't get it. I don't like it when you do this. It makes me nervous. It's just a very bad habit you have."

"Don't worry about it. It's just perks, baby. I have to get ready for the show. Let me check my messages."

After I dial into my cell phone voicemail from the landline phone, I hear my son screaming in the background in between his mother yelling, "Come see your son! If you don't fucking come see your son, Malik, you'll be sorry. You'll never get in your house again or see your money. I'll see to that. Get your black ass over to this house tonight, motherfucker! Where are you? I don't even know where you live, or have a real phone number for you. Put that down, little Malik. Get over here before I warm up your butt. What was I saying? Oh yeah. What if I need to get in touch with you in the middle of the night, Malik? What am I supposed to do? Call me back as soon as you get this message. I'll see to it that you pay some attention to your son!"

I calmly motion Monica to come over to the phone. "Listen to this message." I hit replay on the message and hand the phone to Monica who carefully presses it to her ear like she's afraid. After she listens she makes a sour-looking face. "That's your child's mother?"

"Yeah, I told you she was off. Every now and then I slip up. I didn't want to tell you but she showed up at Bally's in P.G. Plaza when I was there earlier and brought the baby down but they wouldn't let her past the counter. She told someone that I was supposed to meet her to pick up my son so I could baby sit him. I better tell you her name. If you ever run into this girl named Sandra Greene, do yourself a favor and stay away from her."

"Damn, she *is* nuts. Why don't you let your lawyer know what's going on with her?"

While the ball is in my court, as far as appearing to be the victim, I reach into my old red and blue NFL bag that was issued years and years ago, and pull out a group of papers. I push them into Monica's hands. "I've got bigger problems. I got this credit report today. All of this mess is from women—jewelry, trucks, gifts— all sorts of shit. Seven pages worth. And now the dealership is calling me about the truck payments. What should I do?"

As Monica looks over each page I follow her eyes. Her expression is intense and serious. After she reads a while she answers, "You don't own the truck? I thought you did. You seemed like you did. In fact you drive it around like it's paid for." Monica looks at me and folds up the papers.

"I lease it," I answer as she hands the papers back to me. "That way I can change to a new vehicle every year. A lot of athletes do that."

Monica shakes her head disapprovingly. "Then send the truck back to the dealership," she says. "You have to try to make arrangements with them if you can't make the payments right now. Do it before it becomes a collection issue and then you'll have that on your credit, too. Leasing is a rip-off anyway. Just call the dealership and tell the truth. Maybe you should consider declaring bankruptcy because you'd spend I don't know how much paying off these debts. And if you don't have full access to your money it makes no sense putting undue pressure on yourself by trying to live a life you can't afford to lead. I had to do it—it's not fun but it's not the end of the world either. You need to get all of these things in order, Malik. I'm surprised your business manager didn't help you with these things. Didn't you hire one when you were playing ball? What was he or *she* being paid to do?"

"I've had several," I answer vaguely. "But I don't want to get into that right now. I don't want to talk about it."

Monica sighs. "Whatever. We better go prepare to return the truck before we call the dealership."

"Yeah, I've got to vacuum the truck out, call a tow truck, gather all my keys, and clean out the inside. This shit is ridiculous. I'm losing everything."

Monica gives me a look. "How do you know so much about this procedure if this is your first time trying to do this?"

I'm quiet because she's picked up on something she wasn't supposed to. This isn't my first time. I have to talk myself into feeling that SUVs suck up too much gas, and now I can stay out of her change bag in the closet when my allowance to live runs slim to none. If she hadn't managed to save so many dimes, quarters, and nickels, many days we wouldn't be able to buy groceries, rent Blockbuster movies, and do whatever needs to be done, here and there. It must be holding at least eight hundred dollars worth of coins.

After we talk, I go upstairs and fill my hands with change so I can go to the gas station to vacuum out the truck. Monica follows me and sits on the bed. After I drop at least fifteen quarters in my pocket I walk over to Monica. "Baby, I'm not trying to overwhelm you, but I've got another problem on my hands."

"What is it, Malik? What's wrong?"

"I'm short. How am I going to get to Minnesota to my team workout?"

Monica rubs her temples. "You called all the people that owe you money?"

"Yeah. I can't get anyone right now. The bitch would love this. You know I found out teams had been calling me and she wasn't giving me the messages. I'm trying to get back to the show without her help just to prove a point. She thinks I'll fall without her."

"What about your frat? I told you, if you're a Q and a Mason your brothers should step up to the plate and support you. That's what those organizations are for, not just socializing."

"I got a little but not enough," I say.

Monica balances her chin in her right hand. "Well, what about your Mason brothers?" she asks again.

"One came through but not for much. Shit. Uhh, baby. I have an idea. Can you ask some of your friends?"

Monica suddenly perks up. "You don't even like them, and don't even want them to call me. I can't ask for you. I don't borrow money from my friends, not even for myself. As many friends as you have, and as well connected as you're supposed to be, it would seem you could turn up more than you have."

"Well I can't. I tried. People turned on me when my money was frozen and I quit playing ball. I told you how my brother acted and he wasn't the only one. That's why I cut most of them niggas off."

Monica sighs. "We don't have time to debate this. You're my man, it's my place to help you, and you've come too far to have to quit. I'll just pawn my stuff, I guess."

"No, Monica. I can't let you do that."

"Malik, it's just material things. All I ask is that you get it out as soon as you can. I let you hold my cell phone and you ran it up. You promised you would pay it and I had to cut it off, but you got one cut on by getting someone else to get one in their name for you. I'm not trying to nag you but you also said you'd put money in my bank account after you told me to write those checks. The bank wrote me a letter and my account is in the negative, Malik. I'm going to have to close that too *and* pay them back. Things are getting out of hand very fast. I'm trying to support you because too many women want to enjoy what a man already has, and won't even look at an up and coming brotha. I'm trying to do right by you because you say you want to do right by us," Monica explains.

I give her my famous smile and say, "I will. I promise, baby. You're the best. I know I said I'd take care of those things and I will. Think of what we stand to gain. We're almost there. You

140

know I want to marry you, and I'm going to give you the life you deserve. You're a good woman, baby, and I won't forget all of this. Why do you think I tell everyone we're already married? I can't imagine life without you. I told you I want a future with you. I'm going back to ball for us, not just myself. This is a quick way for me to make good money and put some away to invest."

Monica doesn't answer. She sighs, and then scans the room for valuables. She unhooks her computer scanner, unplugs her Sony sound system, unplugs a medium-sized color television, and then walks to her bureau and takes out two gold rings.

"These are my sister's wedding rings and I'm holding them for her children to have when they get older since she got divorced," she says. "I can't replace these, Malik. My stereo was the first thing I bought when I started working, so that has special meaning to me too. Now, Malik, you know my situation and why I'm doing this. I don't have much to share, and I don't have anyone that I can go to that can do me favors like you do. Don't play around. I want you to know that I'm trusting what you've told me, and I'm putting myself out on a limb for you."

When I look at her face I notice the bags under her eyes, and I can tell I'm already wearing her down this early on in our relationship. "I'll get it out, baby. I told you that," I tell her.

Monica dashes to the car with an armful of goods so no one will see her toting anything of value to the car. Although she thought she was doing this on the down low, her family members frowned as they watched her carry her things to the car. I know she doesn't want to have to explain what she's doing but they'll figure it out provided that they know about my ticket dilemma. I have no shame, and stroll along carrying the lightest pieces, forcing her to struggle with the heaviest ones. I figure if women want equal treatment then they should have it. Let them do what men do and not pick and choose what's appropriate when it's convenient.

"Let's take your car," I say although my truck is nearly spotless. "You know we have to take mine to get it cleaned when we get back. There's no since in dirtying it up any more." I figure her car is best suited for seat rips, tears, or whatever could go wrong when the heavy equipment is placed in the car on our way to the pawnshop. I take her keys and unlock the back door on the

141

passenger side. After we load up the car we both get in and head downtown in search of a pawnshop that is willing to accept Monica's cheap-ass shit.

$

"What can we get for all of this?" I ask the pawnshop owner. He's a middle-aged white man dressed in Levi's and a plain, purple generic t-shirt. His beard is thick and brownish blonde. Overall, he has that bland, mid-western white man look.

After he inspects everything we bring in, he says, "Two hundred dollars is about what I can do."

Monica's eyes widen. "Two hundred dollars! The rings are worth three grand alone. What a rip off! You know good and well everything is worth more than that. Come on, man, this is some shit you're trying to pull on us." She walks away from the counter in disgust, and stands by the door like she wants to push it open and leave.

I lean over the counter, smile, and put on my charm. "Look, man, I'm a football player. I'm trying to go do a little something for the Vikings while I can. You know how it is—one shot may never come again. Can you do anything better than that for me? Under the circumstances I mean."

The man beams and suddenly comes to life. "The Vikings? That's my favorite team! I'll see what we can work out. How much do you need, man?"

"Four hundred."

He strokes his beard and thinks for a moment. "Give me the gold necklace the girl is wearing and I can make that happen. Hey, I'm a nice guy."

Monica hears what he says and walks back toward me. I can't help but notice that her face is filled with disappointment. She caresses the heart with her fingers, and then drops her hand from her neck. "But Malik, this was the first piece of jewelry you gave me with the heart and everything. I can't give this up. It's the only sentimental thing I have from you and it means so much to me. This man is trying to snow us. Let's try somewhere else."

I touch both of her shoulders and turn to face her. "I'll get it out in time. Don't worry about it. Besides, I'll be giving you real jewelry after a while. Give it to the man so we can go buy my plane ticket and take care of the rest of our errands. The longer we wait, the more the ticket fare will go up. Now come on, Monica. Look at the big picture and stop sweating the small stuff in this situation."

Without saying another word she turns around so I can unhook the necklace. I take it off and drop it into his pale palms. Then I say, "That ring you have in the pile is my championship ring from college. Do you have to take it? Come on—help a brother out. Maybe I can get you a few autographs when I'm up there or something. Who's your favorite player?"

"Randy Moss."

"I'll see what I can do." I smile and look him in the eye.

"Here, I don't really need this," he says. "Go ahead and keep it."

I take the ring, put it back on my finger, and then ball up my fist and knock knuckles with him. When he bumps knuckles with me I feel fortunate that my shit is safe so it doesn't matter if I don't get the things out of pawn. Plus, the ticket will be in brain's name, not mine.

Monica looks despondent, like she has mixed feelings about filling out the paperwork and registering her things. I put in one thing, got it back, and she was dumb enough to clear out half of her room. As I shoot the shit with the pawnshop owner, I'm thinking that all I know is that I have the money from his cash register drawer, and I'll be getting on that plane, thanks to Monica. When I get back from Minnesota I can take over her car. Thank God this bitch is getting trained and it's spreading like wildfire throughout the household, beyond her bedroom doors. Her father charged luggage and vitamins, as cheap as he is. Her sister bought me new tennis shoes, and she lives way in Baltimore. Her mom has even kicked in a few dollars to take care of my miscellaneous necessities. Hell, the whole family is taking care of me and I'm enjoying every minute of it.

17

THREE FEET DEEP AND SINKING

Jalita

I awaken tangled in soft white sheets and a velvet maroon blanket, with Kyle passed out on the top of the hotel bedspread next to me. When I realize what went on during the previous night I grab the covers, and pull them around me, hiding my body parts from daylight. When I sit up I can feel Kyle's semen dripping down my thighs. I reach for the telephone. My eyelids grow heavy again but I still begin dialing.

"I'm not asleep," Kyle says groggily. "Ginger, put down the fucking phone! I know what you're thinking of and you shouldn't even think about it. What will you tell security? What will you tell police? That you were a paid escort who told me no and I took advantage of you? I know you're smarter than that. Think about it. They'll take one look at you, find out who I am, and dismiss you for a cheap black whore who decided to cry rape on an older, established man in a hotel room after she got laid for a few bucks. I'm connected, *Ginger*. From judges to lawyers and policeman, I have friends in high places that will look out for me. I think you'd like to reconsider. You don't make the wisest decisions, do you? You couldn't keep your panties up until the trial date. You're the one that was involved with that athlete last year. I remember your face. I say you needed this. Some women enjoy being taken by force, and from the way your pussy felt you're one of them. In your book, no means yes and yes means no, doesn't it, Ginger?"

I look at Kyle and his eyes are still closed. I'm so livid I want to reach over and kill him with my bare hands.

He eventually rolls over on the bed closer to me and caresses my face. "Get cleaned up, and leave your clothes with me. I'll have something else for you to put on when you come out. And as far as our little arrangement, the conversation isn't over."

I stumble into the bathroom, crying. Everything is beginning to look distorted all over again. As I shut the door I'm thinking of how cheap and dirty I feel. Not only did I humiliate myself once again, but this time I got date raped in the process. Lucky me. I scrub my skin, trying to eliminate the dirty feeling, but I can't rid myself of it. As I scrub and scrub my skin into a tender state I think that this is my tumultuous start of 2005. I don't know how I'm going to do it just yet but I will get my revenge on this Kyle person who stuck his raw dick up in me by force and trickery. I may be depressed but I'm not dead. I hope he enjoyed his date rape moment, because I'm going to see to it that he pays the piper after this damn Ecstasy gets out of my system. Come to think of it, revenge is still my specialty.

$

"Walk to Clyde's and give me a call by eight o'clock tonight," Kyle says sternly.

The limo halts and I awaken to those specific instructions. I look around to get my bearings and notice that Kyle and I are sitting on a side street not far from where he initially picked me up. Kyle moves close to my ear and says, "I'm late going to see my wife. Call me later or else. I put my number in your purse—use it." When he leans back into a seated position I squint and look at his face trying to recall everything that transpired at the party and in the hotel room.

I hold my head with one hand and step out of the limo. I don't know how I do it, but I manage to put mind over matter and ignore my throbbing head enough to make it to the front of Ms. Geraldine's building. I rub my eyes, rest on the side of the concrete wall a few minutes, and then slowly walk toward my old apartment. Just as I get ready to ball my fist to knock on the door someone says, "Are you looking for that dude that was in there the other night?"

"Yeah, I am," I answer in a raspy voice.

The woman, wearing a multi-colored head tie and old scuffs with exposed yellow foam, has a cigarette hanging out of the side of her mouth that looks as if it will drop from her lips. She takes a drag from it, removes it from her mouth. "I went to ask him for a light this morning. He's gone, baby girl. The old man across the hall said everything is cleared out. Ain't nobody in there that I know of."

I shake my head in disbelief and knock anyway. When I look around for the woman to question her, I see her door slam and decide not to follow anyone else into their apartment. After hearing this bomb drop I walk down the steps and head for my car. When I reach it I find an envelope on my windshield.

I open it and it reads: *You'll never get a job in this town, this entire state, or any neighboring one. You'll never have PEACE if you make trouble. I'll tell your little friend from the building goodbye, and pay you a bonus, on his behalf. This is your last warning, Ginger. Call me at eight o'clock tonight and don't keep me waiting. Ciao.*

Just as my lip drops in astonishment and I realize that Kyle's psycho ass has set me up, I see a tow truck driver walk toward my car and begin hooking it up to some chains. I cram the note in my purse. "Wait, what are you doing?" At first he ignores me and doesn't respond. I run up to him. "This is my car. What the hell are you doing?"

"I've got a work order to have this vehicle towed," he finally says.

"For what reason?"

"There's no resident sticker, and you're also blocking private property."

"But I live here. I mean, I did live here. This must be a mistake," I ramble. "These other cars have been here just as long as mine. Why am I being singled out? Who sent you to do this?"

"I'm just doing my job. Excuse me, ma'am." He hops into the truck and pulls off before I can ask him where he's taking it.

Frenzied, I reach into my purse and search for the cell phone that Clyde let me use, and then find a phone book I started but never completed. When I find these things I sigh with relief because there's still some charge left on my cell. I dial Shawn's number. It rings and when it stops because someone is on the other end I breathe a sigh of relief again. I'm thankful for this small break through as fucked up as it is to be standing on the street trying to paste details of what a wacko did to you, and having no transportation to drive anywhere, on New Year's Day.

"I don't who know this is but whoever it is Shawn can't talk on the phone," says the voice on the other end. "But if you're willing to keep him from running the street, come over to help me take care of Myra, and wait on me while I'm laid up with this damn blood clot, then come on. If you know where we live show up ready to contribute or don't call back. Shawn is with his family and you should be with yours." The line goes dead and I wish I could've cussed Jackie out, but she hung up before I could manage.

I shake my head in denial of what has occurred so far, and find the last number I had for Seth. When I dial the number I hear, "Hello, you have reached the mobile number for Seth Culligan. Today is January 1ˢᵗ and I'd like to wish everyone a happy New Year. I will be unavailable until January third but you may email me at seth@mariposapress.com, in the interim. Thank you and have a safe holiday."

Tears begin to form when I hear my crush's voice—the one that I evicted from my life to spare him from drama-filled reports such as the one I'm living. I don't leave a message, I just hang up.

Just as I'm beginning to panic over having two dollars to my name, trying to figure out how I can make my way to an ATM to drain the last few bucks out of my account, the cell phone rings. I wipe my nose on my shaking arm. "Hello."

"I imagine you're good and frustrated by now, Ginger. I have your car. If you'd like to come pick it up I'd advise you to cross the street and request for the driver to bring you and your little car to my home so that we can have our talk early."

Before I can respond the line goes dead. I look across the street and see the tow truck driver looking at me as if he would like me to make up my mind in a hurry.

I cross the street and walk up to the window. Before I can open my mouth to speak the tow truck driver looks in the opposite direction from me. "Yo, sis. Don't look in my direction. I have to say this fast because someone might be watching. I don't know how you got mixed up with old boy but he's a very dangerous man. You didn't hear it from me though—don't be stupid. I'm not supposed to talk to you and that's all I can say. You want to go see Kyle, right?" he says like he's throwing a huge hint for me to comply, as opposed to calling the police or digging deeper into this matter while stranded alone with no idea where Kyle is or if he's spying on me.

"Yes, I do."

After I hop into the passenger's side he turns his head straight toward the street and takes the emergency brake off. When we pull off I scan my purse for one of my antidepressants to keep me calmer and desensitize me from the newest drama. Meanwhile, I close my eyes and ride, wondering what I'm going to do when I face the psychopath businessman who put an unwanted twist in my already crazy life.

18

SEX, LIES, AND FOOTBALL

Malik

"You better be in for the night. You weren't out with your man were you?"

"So how's it going in Minnesota, Malik? You know you're the only man I've got," she answers, thinking I'm teasing her, but I'm not.

"Baby, they're not treating us right down here. That's why I wanted to call you."

"But you've called me every night since you've been gone. Are you afraid I'm out in the streets or something? If that's what you think I don't have time, energy, or money for that. All I'm thinking about is you, and hoping we can make this thing work."

"I know but the other times it was because my dick was hard and I wanted to hear your voice. This time it's because of the way the guys and I are being treated. I know my woman is home where she belongs."

"What do you mean they're not treating you right?" she asks, just like I knew she would.

"The conditions are terrible. I can't eat this food—it's so nasty. It's cold. The heat isn't even all that good. We're staying in these dorms at this university and we're practically stacked on top of each other. I want you to fire my agent. I'm not going to put up with this. I called him and he's done nothing about anything."

"What? You're lucky he's working with you. That guy is legit and he's good. He did what he said he'd do. You're a retired player. You were lucky to get an invite for a workout and the opportunity to play a little ball for the feeder team. Don't make any rash judgments, Malik. This is a business, not a game."

"Stop your preaching. I don't want him anymore. I've already made up my mind that I'm going to fire his ass. I want you to type up a letter to NFL Player's Association releasing him from our agreement. You have his address and you know how to word it. You're good at that kind of thing. We'll mail it off when I get back."

"But he's the one that got you the workout and the spot for the combines. Do you really have to fire him so close to gearing up for mini camp as a free agent? I think he's doing a good job. You're making progress with him on your side."

"Look, I know what I'm doing. I've been in the NFL before, remember?"

"If you say so, but I think you're making a huge mistake. What's all that noise? It sounds like someone is having a party over there."

"Oh. That's the guys. They let some hos in here. We haven't been here a week, and already they have women running through the halls and acting crazy. I've got you at home. I don't need to cheat. One came at me and I told her 'no thanks, my girl looks just like you.' I tell these guys they shouldn't be fooling around on their wives and girlfriends. And letting those white girls in the room is trouble. They must've forgotten where we are."

"Well you just keep your nose clean. That's all that's important to me. What they do is their business if it doesn't involve Malik Montgomery."

"Hold on, baby. Will you keep it down? I'm on the phone. Shit! Sorry, I'm back."

"Did you send your payment in to the dealership? You know that you still have to pay on the truck even though you returned it."

"I took care of that from here."

"Okay—that's good."

"Oh yeah, I'm coming home early."

"Why is that?"

"I got my spot. They said I can come back to Maryland. All I've got to do is show up for mini camp in the summer."

"You're going to be on the team?"

"Yeah, baby. All I've got to do is stay in shape. I'm ready."

"You did it!" Monica exclaims.

"No, *we* did it," I corrected her. "I'm flying back home in two days."

"I can't wait to see you. I'm so happy!"

"Me too." I let her get all happy for a minute. "Hey, Monica."

"What?"

"I need you to do something for me."

"What is it?"

"Wire me some money."

"Money for what?"

"I need spending money, and I have to buy something decent to eat."

"But you just said you're almost ready to come home. Can't you take it just a few more days?"

"I can but it could set me back if I don't keep eating right. I've eaten so much pizza and junk food that I feel sick. You know I can't afford to get sick at a time like this."

"Well how much do you need?"

"Three hundred."

"What! Why so much?"

"I have to have money for a cab from the university to the airport, buy some Vikings gear to give to your family, and do a few other things like pay someone I borrowed money from down here to get the things in the pawn shop out. You're always telling me to be responsible and I'm trying to listen to you. I wired the guy his money and as soon as I get back we can pick up your things."

"Malik, I'm not made of money. I keep telling you this. It's good that you sent him the money, but why would you borrow it and generate another debt with someone else?"

"I'll pay you back. You know I'm good for it. All I need to do is get straight on this end."

"I'll wire you one hundred dollars. That's all you're getting. Once I send you that I don't have much left over for myself. You'll have to work the rest out on your own, and start asking these Negroes you lent money to pay you back. The only letter I should be typing up is a stack of I-O-U's. When you see these people out in public like you do when I'm with you I think you should start stepping to them."

"I keep telling you you'll be taken care of. If we can just make it until the season starts we'll be living large. Come on, baby, this is for us. Remember our deal."

"Give me the information I need because I've never wired anyone money before. I'm still going to type up those papers for you to keep on hand because this doesn't make any sense."

"Okay. And as for the wiring part, it's easy. Just find a Western Union. Safeway has one. You can go there since its close. Thanks, momma. I love you."

"Yeah—whatever, Malik," Monica says.

That's what I say, too—whatever. What's wrong with those coaches on the team? Don't they see I still got the juice? I'll keep rolling like I made progress with going back to the game and keep buying some time while I'm waiting on the results of my master scam to jump off. I ain't telling that bitch shit about me getting sent home.

$

When Monica and her father pick me up at Ronald Reagan National Airport, I can't wait to wrap my arms around every inch of her. I truly missed her, and when I see her sporting that mini skirt with her hair pulled up in an upsweep hairdo, it makes me want to throw her down and screw her right there in the middle of the terminal. After I brag about how well I did in Minnesota and give my full report about my prospective contract, my mind drifts back to licking, sucking, and fucking Monica. Although I cheated on her in Minnesota she doesn't know any different. Who in the hell expects a man with a "contract" to be faithful and not slip up, ever? Pussy I don't have to work to get is also a part of the perks of being an ex baller, and I ain't turning down shit 'cause this is one nigga that ain't gay or bisexual.

"Quiet, Malik. They'll hear us," Monica hushes me. "You're not even supposed to be in my room."

"So, I don't care. They know you're getting dick. Your man's been out of town, and now he's got to lay the pipe. This is what you get for wearing that sexy mini skirt for big daddy." I part Monica's legs and begin to lick her clit. I look up at her and watch her bottom lip drop and feel her caress my smooth baldhead. I know she's holding in her screams because her room is over the kitchen and someone's decided to make something to eat. The thrill excites me and I lick her harder and faster.

"Stop," she whispers. "What do you want me to do, get caught screaming?"

When I hear this I lick her even more. I feel cum gush into my mouth. I rub my face in between her legs until my whole face shines with her juices. I come up for air and say, "I went to Minnesota with frozen assets and came back a nigga with a two million dollar contract. So technically, I've got a two million dollar dick. Them niggas in your family ain't gonna cock block at a time like this. In fact they'll be kissing my ass and hinting at you to give me some whenever I want it. Even your daddy, I'm sure. He smells money like the rest of them. Did you see how he was smiling and calling me son all the way back from the airport? He's no dummy."

"Malik! I can't believe you said that!"

"You know it's the truth." I resume licking, and feel her wetness. I harden after she grabs the side of the mattress with her left hand and has her second orgasm. After she exhales and sits up, I push her back down on the bed and stick my dick inside of her.

"What are you doing?" she asks, trying to sit up again. "Do you have a condom? Where's your protection?"

"I know where I've been. I've done this with two women in my life, that's it. You told me about your history. We love each other and we should act like it. I want to feel you, Monica. Condoms fuck with my hard-on too much."

"I don't think this is a good idea, Malik. I could get pregnant. We can't afford a baby right now, and we're not married yet. This just doesn't make sense to me to take a chance."

"If you get pregnant, it's God's will. I'll have money soon enough for a baby."

"I don't want to have sex without protection. I'm on the pill, but I'm just not comfortable with this."

I lose my patience with Monica. "Look, I'm going to tell you straight up. If you don't do this I'll find someone who will. And I expect you to eat *my* cum tonight if you love me, Monica. You said you want to get married. So since this is the last dick you'll have, you have to get more adventurous and trust me. Shut up and fuck, you freak! I know what you need—what you need is this big black dick up in you." I see small tears form in her eyes. She turns her head and I push my dick inside of her. "I love you, Monica. Everything is going to be all right. Now stop crying and call my name."

Before I know it I'm thrusting my dick inside of her, watching her breasts bounce up and down. I fuck her so good she can't think straight, I can tell by the way she moves her head from side to side. What I say goes, and what I say is love can enslave a woman, keeping her tied up in bondage on so many levels. Monica will learn the hard way that I'm Master Malik.

$

I sit up in bed in the dark and poke Monica in the side. "Monica, wake up. Get up, girl. I need you."

She jumps up startled. "What's wrong? What's going on? Why are you in bed with me? You're supposed to be in the living room on the air bed."

I can see the silhouette of her head moving around in all directions. "Fuck the airbed! I'm sleeping with you every night from now on until I leave. I want a sandwich, little momma. Whatever kind your father was making in the kitchen earlier is fine, but no mustard. I want mayo. Don't forget to cut it in half and bring me something to drink to wash it down."

"A *sandwich*? Malik, are you for real? It's three o'clock in the morning! Can't you wait or get it yourself? You know where the kitchen is, and you know I don't eat in my room. Crumbs will be everywhere."

"Man, I should've known you didn't have what it takes to get me where I need to be. If I had my money I—"

Monica cuts me off. "You fucked my brains out, and then you had me rubbing your ear for the last hour because you say it puts you to sleep. I'm exhausted and I need to get some sleep. My life should not revolve around you, contrary to how it seems."

I look at her like she's the one that's crazy. "You're making my blood pressure go up. I'm supposed to be stress free while I'm training. I'm going to be the one making all the money for us, not you. Do you realize the pressure I'm under? You're not doing any more than any of my other women did when I was training. If you don't want to do what it takes to get me to the show I know plenty of hos and bitches who won't mind doing it for me. If I want my asshole licked, you should bend me over and lick it for me—and that's the truth."

"Oh, so it's like that now? If I'm not mistaken slaves were freed long ago," she says, her voice dripping with disdain.

"Yeah, it's like that. Did I stutter, Monica? You don't understand your role or something? You said you'd help me train. I had no idea you were so fucking lazy. This isn't a joke."

She begins cussing as she rolls out of bed. Then she puts on her robe, goes into the kitchen, makes me a sandwich, and brings it to me on a tray. As I'm eating it she sits on side of the bed yawning.

"Are you hungry?" I ask between bites.

"No, not really," Monica answers.

I've noticed that too many niggas of all races are trying to holler at my girl since she put on a few pounds in the right places. I'll keep her self-esteem low and see to it that she doesn't go anywhere, because I'm not up for training a new bitch so soon. It takes way too much work and energy—knocking Monica down a few pegs is much easier. Here comes a little preventative maintenance on her ego just in case she's trying to gear up to drop me while I need her help most.

"That's good because you need to cut back on your meals. You shouldn't be putting a damn thing in your mouth past seven. Your friends won't tell you, but you're getting fat. You're not flexible like you used to be. I can't hold your legs up when we fuck. The pussy isn't as good as it use to be—my baby is heavy. When I first met

155

you, you looked good. You've gained weight and you're on the verge of shopping in the big girl's section. Maybe you're not active enough now that you're not working."

"I'm not fat, and I'm in shape. I work out with you, *and* I wait on you, remember? My job is hauling the groceries in all by myself after I do all the food shopping. I'm using my unemployment money to pay for the chicken breasts, sandwich meat, snacks, and all of the other things you say you need to train. All you manage to do is insult me and point out what you perceive to be fault after fault. I've got curves and hips now but that's what black men like. I'm not slim anymore but I'm definitely healthier and proportional. A scout for a *Jet* photographer gave me his card and asked me to get in touch with him the other day. If I wasn't spending all my money trying to help you maybe I could shop, *period.*"

"Say what you want to, but you're fat. You think you look good, but when you go out of here sometimes I just laugh at you. You wouldn't make it past a test shoot for *Jet.* Do you know how many girls want to get into that magazine and be the beauty of the week? You'd never make it, so I hope you don't waste your time thinking you're something that you're not." After I finish eating I hand her the tray then wipe my mouth on a white paper napkin.

She snatches the tray from me. "I don't see you complaining when you're sucking on my titties, feeling on my legs, or ramming your dick up in this." Monica storms out of the room with the tray. When she returns she gets dressed in a tight outfit and grabs her purse.

"Where do you think you're going?"

"Out for some air. I'm fat, remember?"

"You're not going anywhere."

"Oh yes I am. My father's downstairs and my mother's up the road in her house. You can't tell me what to do. Who do you think you are, Malik?"

"Get your ass in this bed, go to sleep, and shut your damn mouth, big girl!"

"Nigga, you can't make me do any of the above. In fact, you've been an asshole ever since you got your little contract and shit. I've got something to tell you about the way you've been acting since you stepped off the plane."

"Talk, bitch! I'm not stopping you."

"How can you treat me this way after I was just trying to be supportive? I'm just an ordinary girl and this whole life is not my style. I don't know how I got mixed up in this mess or with you. You said you wanted to make me happy when we met but now I'm confused about our future and I have damn good reason to be. You act like you don't give a shit about me now. You cuss at me, insult me, lie, and I am sick and tired of it, Malik. These days you think tearing me down makes you more important than me. Like I said, I need some air. This is all too much. I thought this would be a good night for us and here we are fighting like cats and dogs. Something is wrong with all of this."

Before I know it I knock her down on the bed and pin her down. I grab her neck tightly with both hands and stare into her light brown eyes.

Her eyes begin to water. "I can't breathe. Get up, Malik. I can't breathe. Please."

"I'm not to be played with," I tell her. I'm silent for a few seconds then I continue, "Some nigga called you tonight. I know you paged him, and that you've been talking to niggas the whole time I was gone. Your pussy felt funny, and you shaved those hairy legs I like too. I'm going to tell you again. I'm not to be played with, you freak. I threw away my book of numbers with the finest collection of hos for you. Don't you back talk me! I just got home and you're starting to act up already. You know I love you and everything you said is a damn lie. And when I move to Minnesota you're coming with me and getting from up under your family. We'll get my frat and a moving truck, open this bedroom window and throw everything you own out of this bitch. Then I'll teach you what it means to be a real woman who can stand on her own two feet. Now stop all this shit and act right." When she begins to turn red I abruptly take my hands from her neck and let her up.

That was the first time I put my hands on Monica but her ass deserved it. A man has to set the tone for respect by any means necessary and I did just that. Right or wrong the bitch took off her clothes, got back in bed, and wasn't talking about driving anywhere

Andrea Blackstone

anymore. The rest of the night it was quiet and I felt good knowing that I was running shit in another man's house. Malik Harrison rules the roost because everyone thinks he's about to lay a golden egg in the NFL. Whether I do or don't is another question.

19

KINKY LIVING

Jalita

Just when you think you've seen it all something new unfolds before your eyes. Although I can think of at least four thousand places I'd rather be other than standing in the doorway of Kyle's study near Rock Creek Park in D.C., that's where I am. He's wearing a silk paisley robe, and his glasses are hanging off his nose. A glass of what I guess is cognac is halfway full, and I can see ice swimming around in it, slightly diluting the normally rich brown color.

"I've got to go. We'll continue this conversation later," he says. After that he hits a button on the speakerphone, takes a cigar out of a box, and lights it up. I watch a thin, steady stream of white ascend into the air, and the entire room begins to smell like cigar smoke. After taking a few puffs on it he says, "How nice it is of you to join me. You don't mind if I smoke do you? Sit down, Ginger. Are you looking for these?" Kyle dangles my car keys in the air then puts them inside of his top desk drawer.

"Give me my car keys," I blurt out angrily. "They don't belong to you. Take your dirty paws off of them."

"You know what you must do to get them back. Have you made up your mind yet? The clock is ticking."

I sit down in a gray wing back chair seated in the corner by mahogany colored lawyer's bookshelves.

Kyle sets his smelly cigar down in an ashtray and calls out to someone. "Raul, shut the door. Raul," he calls. The tall, young, lanky Hispanic man that led me into Kyle's home appears and shuts the door to his study. Once the door is closed, Kyle continues.

"Some things are better left unsaid while others have to be spelled out in black and white. You're young so I'm going to give you the benefit of the doubt and take the time to spell out a few things. I can make people disappear, Ginger, and I don't mean because I'm a magician. Don't go to the police, running your mouth about the little disagreement we had in the hotel room. If you do you wouldn't be making a wise decision. You're here because I want to make you an offer, and I'm not usually a man of compromise. If I were you I'd consider myself fortunate." He twists the cigar in the tray and the smell of it stops.

While he takes a long sip of his drink, I respond, "I don't want to talk to you about any offers. There are no deals to be made. I'm not interested. You're a crazy man. How dare you have my car towed here and use scare tactics to make me talk to you. I'll get someone to kick your ass and take care of you!"

Kyle puts his drink down and grins. "Now, Ginger, I see you've got a little too much spunk. By doing that you would only get yourself into deeper shit—three strikes and you're out."

"How can I be out when I haven't even been up to bat yet?" I snap.

"Clever. You're a clever one, but not more clever than I am."

"Why are you doing this to me? I don't even really know you."

"Because I can," he said smugly. "I see something I want. Besides, you had no business out with a man like me. I won't allow you to destroy my reputation over this, so we must resolve this between ourselves. I can't take a chance on any other way because like you said I don't know you. I have no idea what you might think you're capable of, or if you would attempt to take on a losing battle."

"You raped me. There's no mistake about that, Kyle. Let's not forget what really happened."

"Don't you ever use the word rape and associate it with me again!" he growls. "You're not listening, are you? If you go to the police the evidence they gather won't be accurate. Too much time has passed. If you go to the hospital the clothes you were wearing that night can't be taken to a laboratory because I destroyed them while you were sleeping off the ketamine. Why do you think I had you leave them with me, and conveniently had another outfit for you to wear? You have no bruises or lacerations. Even if you did scratch me just a little bit I had you shower for a reason. So be my guest and agree to a blood sample, clipping your hair and everything needed for a rape kit but your chance of prosecution is shot. Even if this alleged event makes it beyond where it should I told you I have friends in high places. Look at my wall, Ginger. It's full of politicians, judges, lawyers, CEOs, and other important people. Do you really think anyone would believe a half-homeless, tawdry little whore who had a nervous breakdown? Your hospital bills are starting to stack up, aren't they? How will you pay them at a time like this?" he snaps.

"I knew you were low but not this low. How did you know that about me?"

"Ginger, Ginger, Ginger. At the snap of a finger I can know most anything."

"What do you want from me?" I ask, scanning the photos on the wall.

"I want your allegiance, that's what. I told you last night what I was looking for, and I wasn't saying it to waste my words. What I want, I get. Now, let's move on with this conversation." Kyle's demeanor changes and he leans forward in a threatening manner. "I'm not what or who you think I am. At any point in time I can make this matter a whole lot more complicated."

"You're threatening me?"

"No, I'm warning you, if you want to call it that."

"In light of what you've done this is just plain crazy. Who are you to blackmail me?"

"It's plain and simple. Do what I say or face prostitution charges. I can frame you for more to go along with it. I don't think that would be good considering your character is already in question in light of the trial you're wrapped up in, Ms. Jalita Harrison. What I want to know is—are you a fan of incest? What's it like screwing your own flesh and blood? Did Wes fuck you better than I did when he thought he was getting some groupie pussy?"

My heart begins to pound and my throat feels as though it's dried shut. Eventually, I manage to squeeze out some words. "This is too much for me to take."

"I thought you'd be a little overwhelmed. Go ahead and be shocked if you need to be. Do a personal favor for me and I'll do one for you."

"What do you want?"

"What I want is a tender, young, piece of ass to inspire my wife to spice up our sexual love life. Her girlfriend is ruining our marriage, and the hell if she will stand in the way of me staying married to my wife. I have my reasons, which are not worth mentioning, why that's so important to me."

"What are you talking about?"

Just then a tall, slender black woman with legs for days and a high waist walks into the room completely nude. The only thing she's wearing is a straight face and a tattoo of a rose on her hip.

"This is the young lady I was telling you about," Kyle says. She looks at her husband, then at me. She stares at me while undressing her husband. "Do you like what you see, Renee?" he asks.

His wife doesn't say a word but begins licking her lips and stroking her vagina. Kyle watches his wife heat up with desire while staring me down seductively, and begins caressing his bone hard erection. Surprisingly, "frigid" Renee braces herself on Kyle's shoulders, gaps her legs open and slides down on his dick. "I want to have sex with you now," she whines with desire. The couple begins having sex in front of me like I'm a voyeur. I gulp and feel my face grow hot as Arizona sunshine.

Kyle leans back in his oversized black leather office chair and rests his head back. "Ohh, baby. Ohh, baby," he moans. "You haven't fucked me in three years. I knew you still wanted me. Mmmm. This feels wonderful. Oh baby. Oh baby. Yes." Renee quickens her pace, moving her hips up and down on Kyle. I watch cum drip down her slender thighs as she looks at me with lust in her eyes.

What I hear next is just plain crazy. "You are not worthy to moan. Stop it! This pleasure is for me. Submit and remember your proper place," Renee says, abruptly hopping up off of Kyle's dick. "Look how you make me chastise you instead of enjoying your much-deserved reward."

"I'm sorry, Mistress. I'm not worthy. You're right."

Renee looks at me and smiles like she's flirting with me nonverbally. Then she turns back around, drops to her knees, and sucks on her husband's penis. "Put me on speaker phone," she demands between slurps.

Obediently Kyle dials a number. Renee gets up and lies backward on top of his executive desk and begins stroking her clit. A female voice answers on the other end. "It's over," Renee says harshly. "You've been replaced. Stop the noise—you knew I was married and that anything could happen. Get over it, you nasty little slave. Don't you dare cry! Listen to your Mistress! Don't call me again!" After she presses the speakerphone button and ends the call, she continues pleasuring herself as her husband sucks on her nipples. "Oh my! Oh my! Fuck!" she screams.

"You like daddy's present, don't you?" Kyle says as Renee sticks two fingers into her vagina. She begins masturbating so wildly she knocks Kyle's nameplate off the desk. "Can you imagine her sucking on your nipples and you nibbling on her clit?" he continues.

"Yes!" she screams in a heated frenzy.

"Look at her again," Kyle suggests.

When she does, she gets up, bends over, gripping onto her husband's mahogany desk. Kyle stands and rams his penis into Renee, pounding her steadily from behind.

"I want her. I want her. Honey, I want that sexy bitch!" she screams.

"Daddy knows you do, Mistress. I did this for you. She's going to be ours. The three of us are going to have lots of fun together," Kyle says, grinning at me.

Renee screams out an orgasmic noise. After her hips stop grinding on her husband's dick, she breathes heavily, opens up his desk drawer, and takes out a stack of cash. The tall woman with sweat still glistening on her body walks toward me, and waves the smell of fresh money under my nose back and forth like she's charming me—the same way Kyle did the night he raped me. The stack of cash is so large I can't help but follow the dead presidents with my eyes as she taunts me.

"I'd like to pay you for your services and discuss something with you in the other room. It was *very, very* nice meeting you, and it's time to thank you for making me nice and wet."

When she shuts the door I scan my purse yet another time for one of my antidepressants. Since I can't find one I close my eyes and scan my mind for any indication that this bizarre domme and submissive couple shit is all a terrible nightmare—but it's not. It's real as real can be, and on top of that Kyle just upped the ante by blackmailing me. I need all of this new drama like a fucking hole in the head.

20

KEEPING UP APPEARANCES

Malik

Too many women like bad boys. They say they want a man with all of these wonderful qualities but when it comes down to it they like keeping company with knuckleheads like me. In fact, it takes an act of God to make some bitches see the light and accept what is. If a man can get away with X,Y,or Z then he will. What incentive is there to act right if you don't have to? So in my mind no is not an option. I say what I want when I want to say it, and do what I want and lie to cover my tracks later. It's that simple. Get what you want or need and then roll out.

And lately I've been rolling out all right. Since I lost my truck I've been driving Monica's car any and everywhere under the guise that I have to do business to prepare for ball. A few times I've peeped her pops touching the hood to see if it's warm, and even having the nerve to check the mileage after I park the car in the driveway. So what if he has Monica on his insurance, the mileage I rack up comes with the territory of taking care of me. Most days Monica is trained to sit her ass home or catch a ride to the store when I'm out and about. Today is a rare day that I'm waiting on her to come in.

As soon as she did hit the door she started running off at the mouth. "Malik, I just came back from the pawn shop."

"And, what about it?"

"You told me you straightened things out—that you were getting my things out of pawn immediately after you returned from Minnesota. The pawn shop owner said he never talked to you. In fact, I just found out that my gold jewelry was melted down to

Andrea Blackstone

make new pieces for sale, and the rest is going to be used for scraps. Not to mention that all my other shit has been sold. Now I have no stereo, no scanner, no TV, and whatever else I was dumb enough to throw into the pot because your ass couldn't act like a responsible, appreciative adult. I told you that some of those items were irreplaceable and those that aren't I can't afford to replace. You're a habitual liar! You never do what you say."

"First of all, I talked to the man and he said he was holding it for me. It's not my fault if he didn't do what he said he would to help a brother out. Second of all, if you had some sense, logic would tell you that all of you cheap shit is about to replaced with real ice and much better electronics and gadgets. You're always reminding a nigga what you've done and I don't appreciate you throwing it up in my face. I don't need that. How am I supposed to concentrate with you bitching and complaining like this every time I turn around?"

"Throwing it up in your face? Bitching and complaining—are you for real? You put your hands on me the other day and now me speaking up about what's mine is throwing something up in your face?"

"Girl, I was just kidding with you. If I wanted to hurt you don't you think I could've? I was play fighting. I thought you knew the difference."

"Then you called me fat and insulted me. Is that my imagination, too? You're always talking down to me."

"Girl, I only date the finest. That's what I'm known for. You need to stop putting your feelings into every little thing. Now give me the keys so I can run some errands, boo."

Although Monica is pissed, she drops her car keys in my hand like they belong to me. Fellas, this is how it should be done and this is how I do what I do. But just in case she gets any ideas about cutting me off from the car, I'll make an extra set of keys while I'm out.

Just before dusk I roll up in the driveway at Monica's dad's crib with Luda's Song, *Get Back* blasting like I don't need my ear drums for the rest of my life. Since I have some of the windows in the car rolled down, the brisk air hits my skin but I don't feel the chill of it because I'm so hyped about what transpired not even thirty minutes before. When Monica opens the front door I sing Luda's lyrics, do my Q-dog steps complete with hand action, and a frat call bark.

"Malik, why are you dirty?" Monica asks. "You look terrible. What have you been doing, rolling around in mud or something? Why are you making all of that noise? What are you trying to do, disturb the whole household?"

"Baby, I got me one! I'm happy, that's all," I tell her as I grin from ear to ear and resume dancing around the foyer with my baseball cap sitting on my head sideways and one pants leg pushed up.

"Got me one what?" she asks, looking me up and down.

I stop dancing. "I caught me a nigga that owes me a big stack of cheese! I didn't want to tell you, but sometimes I take those papers you made for niggas that owe me, put them in my book bag and then go out and park near my house waiting to run into somebody. Today I caught one that's been ducking me. Look outside."

Monica walks to the front door, opens it wide, and then turns to me. "What's in all of those boxes coming out of the car windows and trunk? What did you do?" She crosses her arms and gives me a scolding look like she's my mother.

Half laughing, I close the door. "Seven thousand dollars worth of whatever I could grab from Best Buy. Go get your father and brother. I've got to tell them what happened." After pacing up and down the hallway a few times I call out, "Hey Dad, Hakim, come here. I got something to show ya'll. You're not going to believe this!"

I walk into the kitchen, grab a carton of orange juice, tilt my head back, and begin to drink it. When I come up for air, Monica's father appears from his room. "Hey, Dad, your son saw this nigga that's a doctor at the gas station near my house, right."

"Yeah," he says, looking me up and down the same way Monica did.

"When he saw me I walked over to him and asked him about money he owes me. He told me he wasn't paying me back for shit, then he swung on me like he wanted to get something started. He ran over to a field across the street and I followed him. I hit him

167

back and we started getting down. I grabbed whatever I could in the field and started whipping his ass with it in between using my hands. A crowd gathered around and the next thing I know after I put these big old guns on him his wife was screaming, 'please don't kill him! Stop beating my husband! Get up off him. Get up!'"

I laugh so hard I can barely squeeze out the next row of words. After I catch my breath I continue in a high-pitched voice mimicking a female, "We've got credits cards." I lower my voice to its normal pitch and add, "I said, did you say *credit cards?* That nigga's fake Jheri curl was all over his head, and his white lab coat was covered in dirt and debris. I pulled him by the stethoscope over to his car and took his wife's pocket book for collateral. They followed me all the way to the store. I went, and the manager saw me and asked if he could help. I turned my hat backwards, had his woman's pocketbook on my arm and explained what was going on. After they didn't dispute what I was saying he personally helped me pick out as much merchandise as their credit limit could hold. The nigga owes me three thousand more but it's a start. They left embarrassed and looking like they both wanted to cry."

"Is that right?" Monica's father remarks.

"Yeah, Dad. And little momma, I got you some things. I'll put everything together for you—it's yours. You've got a plasma flat screen television, a state of the art stereo system, and few other things. I was trying to get through on the line and ask you what kind of computer you wanted but I couldn't. I had to take care of my girl."

Monica looks at me half disgusted. "I'm going upstairs, Malik, I don't know what to say about you," she tells me.

I wave Monica off like her words mean nothing. I put the carton back in the fridge. Hakim comes flying down the stairs like a bat, all in one swoop. I grab his shoulder, grin, and laugh while repeating my account of events to him. We walk to the car to take the boxes out and carry everything in the house. After everything is assembled, I rearrange the room and test out each piece of equipment to make sure it's working properly.

After I've checked everything I walk over to Monica and embrace her. "I won't let go of these feelings I have for you. I appreciate everything you do for me, little momma. I'm sorry about earlier. There's just a lot going on while I'm trying to get where I need to be. You know I love you, baby."

When I release her from my grip and look into her eyes I notice that they're full of tears—partly from what I assume is hurt and the other half from humiliation. I know her self-esteem is almost shot to hell, and she doesn't know whether she should thank me and act like a happy camper or curse me out like a sailor. Instead, silence overcomes her until I say, "Oh, I got you a little something else." I hand her a cheap, stuffed duck. I grabbed it off the shelf when I stopped in CVS to give this chick I pumped a while back some free loot. Since she gave me such good head and I may be needing it again, I let her have a new telephone and answering machine. After all, I need to be sure she has something to call me on and that I have a way to leave her horny ass a message.

"Malik, this was thoughtful," Monica says. "I like this the best because you gave it to me from the heart. He's cute." She puts the duck on her dresser as if it's something to be proud of, worthy of putting on showcase. I'm stunned that a seven dollar stuffed animal could move her to open her mouth. She's one crazy bitch but I'm not stressed about the fact that she never makes good sense to me.

"I'm glad you like it. Look—I'm taking you out. We're going to eat at the ESPN Zone and then we're riding up to Winchester to see my cousin. Get dressed."

"That sounds good, Malik. It won't take me long to get ready."

As I watch Monica move about the room preparing to leave, I figure replacing some of her things will keep her quiet and happy for a while. It also gives me an opportunity to remind her that I've done something for her, as well. Of course I'll forget that I owed it to her—that's irrelevant. She better be happy that I'm letting her use shit that really belongs to me. If the truth be told, all of what I just brought to the table is nothing more than a temporary loan, minus the funny looking duck that I stole from CVS and shoved in my pocket, *from the heart.*

21

WHEN IT RAINS, IT POURS

Jalita

The more this kinky living tale Kyle and his wife own unfolds, the more I feel the need to just ask these folk not to tell me any more shit about a sexual revolution that I had no idea existed on this planet. Even though Renee has made it clear that she's one half of a prominent Washington couple—bragging on who she rubs elbows with, how many countries she vacations in, how much fun she has driving her Porsche, and how her husband spoils her with expensive diamonds and pearls, I'm still not remotely interested in her take on the one-sided view of the down-low saga.

Despite the fact that she reveals to me that she and Kyle belong to some exclusive members only swinging club where the two of them can discreetly get buck wild, the bottom line is that her life as a trophy wife who doesn't work, sounds boring as hell. If her husband didn't have my car keys locked inside of his desk I'd gladly get up out of their crib with no regrets, but since he does I feel my options are limited.

After a ten-minute crash course on their *lifestyle choice*, Renee feels the need to vent about why she signed up for couple swapping, orgy fests, and being watched while screwing. As I sit in the presence of a completely nude woman I tell myself, what the hell, she doesn't have nothing I don't, so let me patronize the flake and find a way to break out. Especially since I'm waiting for her to reward me for inspiring the freak in her, as promised.

"Five years ago my husband left at five-thirty in the morning, supposedly to go to work. As any wife would do, I sent him out of the house with his lunch and a kiss on the cheek. Later that Friday,

I called his extension and heard a message he'd recorded, telling his clients and co-workers that he would be out of the office that day in honor of the holiday, and that he'd return on Monday, the eighteen of January. I was livid! I had my suspicions, but that was the first time I realized things had come to this. I did everything from overeat until my stomach ached, to calling my girlfriends ranting about what kind of fool he was taking me for. Somewhere along the way during my fit of anger I logged onto the net. He didn't know I had access to his email but I did. I saw strings of emails from women flirting inappropriately, so I decided to have affair and retaliate. What I didn't know was that wanting to find a discreet way to meet men would lead me to an alternative lifestyle. I came across an ad where four couples were getting ready for a very hot swingers party. All the women were described as bisexual, and all the men were straight. The poster desired one more couple to complete the adult fun. Without Kyle's knowledge I sent our pictures and made arrangements for us to try it. I told Kyle we were invited to a card party, and he had no idea what I was up to since I never said a word about my email discovery. The evening started with Strip Trivia in which we all took turns asking each other questions. When someone answered incorrectly, he or she had to remove an article of clothing. Before long we were all naked, aroused, and ready to do more than play cards." Renee grabs a few pieces of wrapped starlight mints from a dish and hands me one. I don't bother to thank her because I don't want to interrupt her confession. We both unwrap the candy and pop the pieces in our mouths.

Renee continues, "The meeting turned out better than expected. At the end of the night one of the black couples pulled me aside and gave me a website address that provided information on a club they were thinking of joining. It was for a local club where elite blacks get freaky at undisclosed locations several times a month. After we passed a rigorous interview process we explored this lifestyle and it became a mutual addiction. Our marriage improved and Kyle got as deep into it as I was. He started coming home on time every night because his reward, of sorts, was to attend one of the themed couple events twice a month. I figured if he was going to cheat then I should see who he screws in a controlled environment—that way it would be something I was aware of. Likewise, he occasionally had the pleasure of coming home to me getting licked and sucked by another woman, or vice versa. Today I can get that man to do whatever I wish without blinking twice because I'm smart enough to know the power of sex. It's a great set up, Ginger—a very nice position to be in. This is all so habit forming and sexually empowering for me because now I'm in control. The tides turned when I met a single woman who hit it off with me at one of the swinging events. My husband became jealous when he discovered she was into Mistress worship, and that we were getting close in a way that he wasn't involved. I told him his Mistress would stop seeing this slave, give up the domme part of the lifestyle, and go back to *only* swinging with him if he found a replacement or some new young lady to spice up our love life— because without some juice in this whole game, I'm not the least bit interested in him, really. He's just a security blanket and front of sorts. Behind closed doors, your duties would be quite simple— walk around in heels and sexy clothing, watch us having sex, and let us watch you. But, the pay will be much higher if you let me get my thrills off with you. I'll never let him touch you unless it's discussed because you would primarily be for my ultimate pleasure. I bet I could melt your heart if you allowed me to. You could grow to enjoy all of this too, and when the time is right you can experience the club scene as our guest. Once you experience what I can give you, you'll never completely be able to go without having dick *and* pussy."

I swallow the rest of my candy whole and nearly choke.

"Straight women are a challenge, and I love a good chase if I think it's worth my time. The money I offered you can be yours, plus you'd get paid a regular salary. All you have to do is let me know you want me, and that you want this." Renee looks at me lustfully, begins to move closer, and rubs her head on my arms and in between my breasts. She caresses my neck and runs her fingers across my lips like she wants to taste them. Without hesitating I push her away and smack the shit out of her like she stole something. I hit her so hard the candy flies from her mouth. After I do it I realize I should've smacked her after she dropped the bills in my hand, but she hadn't done it yet, and I'm sure that was intentional.

"How dare you!" she screams, holding the side of her face. "I'm Mistress of this house."

I lose my temper and scream back, "Maybe you buy into this fantasy bullshit but you're no Mistress of mine. I live in the real world. Just for the record, I won't be swinging with your hot and horny ass. As far as I'm concerned pussy is as much trouble as dick, and quite frankly I'm not interested in experimenting with either of you. Keep your hands to yourself, you crazy twit! I'm not down with all of this mess. You've got the wrong one and that's for damn sure! I can't believe you went through all of this to keep that cocksucker of yours around. If I were you I'd be pushing the other way and leaving him on the curb for trash pickup!"

"Raul, Kyle!" she hollers. When they come running she continues, "I want this little bitch out! Get her disrespectful ass out of here!"

"I would gladly leave, but your nutcase husband had my car towed here and won't return my keys. I don't know who's crazier—you or him."

"That's not my problem, I just want you out or I'll call the police."

"Don't worry or be upset, dear. It was all a misunderstanding. I'm sure she'll be coming back," Kyle apologizes.

"I'm not coming back here to be with you sick freaks," I yell, forgetting all about the money. "I had no idea black people were into any shit like this!"

As I scurry out of this house I have no idea how I'll make it across town, or even where I'll go. All I know is that I refuse to be anyone's sexual slave. I can't keep up with this twisted logic of spicing up one's love life or retaliating by having a *who can get freakier* contest. Now that a new year has come, why won't drama just leave me alone and go pick on someone else?

$

I pull a cheap black skull cap down over my ears, cram my cold hands into my pocket, and walk at least six city blocks until I find a bench to stop and rest my tired feet. When I do I rub my hands together for warmth I find myself wishing that I had gloves to keep my fingers from feeling like icicles.

"Shit," I mumble. "As much as I hate to admit it, maybe a shelter is my only option. Stay calm, Jalita. Don't panic. You've been through worse." As I continue to rub my hands I start rocking back and forth, rubbing on my coat sleeves trying to take my mind off of the bitter cold.

Out of the blue I hear someone say, "I know someone who can take you in. She'll get you fed, and help you out. She's a good-hearted woman, sis. Ask around once you get to Georgia and Military Road. I spent some time there myself. Good luck to you." Then the man with a matted beard, tattered overcoat, and shopping cart full of belongings continues pushing his unmentionables up a steep hill on Connecticut Avenue.

I know he's the one who said it, and I wonder how he ended up in his position. But it isn't my right to ask or pry, so I just stare until my neck no longer appreciates being turned almost completely around over my shoulder. Now the last time I took the advice of someone based on a referral I ran into Kyle. Even though I shouldn't believe in what the man is saying I haven't learned my lesson, and I take all the details in. When I arrive at the doorstep of where I was told I could find this mystery woman, I knock, and moments later hear three deadbolts being unlatched. As I wait I notice timetables and poorly drawn pictures in crayon lining the front siding of the house. The weather beaten oak door opens and a child carrying a baby appears. One half of the girl's head is uncombed—lint is sticking out like it hasn't been combed for several days. The other half has synthetic hair extensions hanging from it. The girl looks like a Martian, big eyed, with a droopy bottom lip, that looks heavy and hard to keep pulled up and pressed against her top one.

"Is the lady of the house here?" I ask.

The baby whines. "She, uhh. She—I'on know," she stutters. "Hold on." When she swings her head around, I end up staring at the wax build up in her ear, and nearly vomit when the baby begins digging in its nose. She balances the baby on her tiny hips and yells, "Grandma, some girl at the door. Are you home?"

174

"Who's down there?" a woman screams.

In a fluster she huffs and puffs. "I don't know who it be? She didn't tells me nuffin' else."

The woman appears, mumbling under her breath at who I assume is her granddaughter. She shakes her finger at her. "What did I tell you about answering the door when you don't know who it is? If I didn't want to be at home it would be too late now, child. And where do you get this who it be, mess? You know better than to talk like that."

"Dang, Grandma, you be trippin' sometimes," she snaps as the baby drools on her arm and grabs a small fistful of her extensions. "Ow. Get off my head, Nunu."

While the girl pries the baby's hand from around her braided hair her grandmother remarks, "I won't have any dumb children in my house. Go find an English book and put your nose in it if you want those braids finished. I mean it."

The girl huffs and puffs again. She rolls her eyes. "But Mishi is coming back to finish my hair in a few minutes. Grandma, you said she could. Now you gonna act like you didn't tell me that."

"Girl, I'm not playing with you. I told you about your fresh mouth, and since you can't respect your grandmother I'm not paying for her to finish your little nappy head—you'll have to work it off now."

"But Grandma, you bugging!" the girl complains.

"Who's the child and who's the adult here? Unless you want to go out and get a job, and pay for your living expenses on your own, I said not until you do your homework. On your way, pour the baby a bottle and give it to him when you get upstairs. Give my legs a break for once. And if you stomp up those steps I'm going to come up there and smack you upside your head real good." After her granddaughter and the little baby fade into the background she looks down at me. "Yes, may I help you?"

"I'm looking for the owner of this house."

She looks at me for a moment, takes a sip of the forty-ounce beer in her hand, and then leans against the door. "What do you want with the owner?" she snaps.

In my opinion the woman is too young to be a grandmother. I'm shocked that she's not old and withered, or the slightest bit aged. She's wearing a dark flip wig, has blue painted nails that are curved over, a face full of make-up, tight jeans, a hot pink sweater, and several shiny gold ropes of various sizes hanging around her neck. The most prominent feature is her right earlobe because it's split and appears to be three times larger than the other one.

I put on my saddest, most miserable face. "I know you don't know me, and I know I'm just some stranger showing up at your door, but I desperately need to rent a bed from you. I was told you do that sort of thing, and I would be ever so grateful if you could help me out, if even for a night."

She puts her right hand on her hip, leans forward and says, "There's no use in my answering your question until I find out one thing." I smell beer on her breath and wish I could tell her to go gargle or invest in a more expensive brew, but I don't. "What's that?" I ask.

"Do you have a job?"

I feel the lump in my throat enlarge but I don't panic. I remain calm and lie. "Yes, ma'am. I start it tomorrow, as a matter of fact. I was off for a while because of the holiday."

"Whereabouts do you work?"

"I temp at a day labor place."

She continues to interrogate, looking me straight in the eye. "Do you work days or nights?"

"Days, mostly days," I lie. She belches in my face without bothering to excuse herself. I pretend like I didn't hear or smell the cloud of hop funk.

"All right," she says. "You'll have to pay by the week. I don't want no trouble. This is how it works—I'll rent a bed to you, and pair you up with someone who works nights. The cost is half that of room board so you sleep in the bed when they leave and vice versa. You'll have no cooking or bathing privileges, but there's a bathroom everyone shares down the hall. As I said it's a half bath so there's no shower or tub in it. Be considerate and tidy up behind yourself before you leave it because I'm no maid and you're not paying for maid service. In the afternoons and evenings you could very well come in and see me preparing home cooked dinners. Most of my customers are bachelors who don't cook. I move the furniture out of the living room into the kitchen and turn the place into a little restaurant at night. That's my side gig. Now if you're still interested, I might have a bed on a trial basis. It's up to you."

"I'll take it. May I come in—it's cold out here."

"Now wait a minute. Not so fast. How about my sixty dollars? I'll need some sort of up front deposit first." She tilts her head back and swallows the remaining drops of beer. Then she crushes the can.

"I can have it tomorrow because I get paid at work in the evening," I say, lying again.

"Young lady, how in the hell are you going to show up on my step with no money? You've got a Prada purse swinging on your arm and no money in it? What the fuck is this shit?"

"It's not what you think, really. It would take me too long to explain but I'm not trying to run game. I assure you of that."

"You've got until six o'clock to come up with the deposit. Don't make no fool of me. Since you don't have no deposit you can help me clean and serve meals tonight."

"Thank you so much. You won't regret this."

"I hope not. I'm not a fan of noise so don't make any. The grandchildren already work my nerves, as you can see."

"I won't."

"Take your coat off, wash your hands, and come to the kitchen so we can get started. I've already starting peeling the potatoes for the potato salad but I hope you catch on fast because I don't have time to spoon feed a slow learner. You can call me Miss Dee because that's what all the neighborhood folk call me. I don't care to know your name until you bring me that money, so when you put your money where your mouth is you can tell me." She throws the bent up can in the trash and it makes a clanking noise.

After about an hour and a half I had set up four card tables, and put the plastic knives, spoons, and forks on the table, when Ms. Dee's "customers" began to trickle in. Before long they were talking loudly, gambling, drinking, smoking, and of course eating. The little baby was running around with a load in its pants and a paper-thin white t-shirt on. He kept grabbing onto my leg, opening his arms begging for me to pick him up and give him some motherly affection. If I were his momma, aunt, grandma, or any adult that should give a damn I'd clean the dried up snot under his nose instead. After noticing that most of the dudes had holsters under their coats or stuck down in the front of the pants, and hearing a bunch of ringing phones and pagers accompanied by coded language, I figured out that many of the so-called bachelors are neighborhood drug dealers and pimps. I guessed that they must alternate between a home cooked meal, chicken wings, or lousy fried rice prepared by Chinese folk at the corner carry out joint. This area of D.C. is known for drugs, prostitution, muggings, and is a run down hellhole that the mayor is trying to revitalize. As long as they don't bother me, I won't bother them. If the door I'm sleeping behind has a lock on it, I'm straight.

If there was a contest for the world's worst rest, I'd be in the running—at least win as the runner-up. Without looking in a mirror I know that I have puffy eyes with the bags under them to prove it. I stretch and yawn. My back is killing me from the springs in the cot poking in me throughout the entire night. Yes, I spent the night tossing and turning on a metal cot, not a bed as assumed. Doors were slamming and bedsprings were creaking up until the wee hours of the morning. As soon as I tuned that out and fell asleep I was awakened by some bozo repetitively blowing a horn, then the driver yelling that he would leave if the person didn't hurry up and get their ass outside. After that unfolded, a domestic argument ensued very close by, as in next door. The police rolled up in the camp with sirens blasting and no consideration for anyone else in the neighborhood that may not want to hear about someone else's problems. The landlord's little angel of a grandson kept screaming and crying, and I could hear her yelling at him through the floor. Loud cartoons were the only compromise, but when he was finally quiet it was time for me to pee and get lost for the day. When I tried to get into the shared bathroom of course I could smell someone taking a shit through the door and there was no hope of me letting out some water, rinsing my mouth out, or making a washcloth out of toilet paper. As nasty as it is to sleep in my clothes, I had to go there. I had at least wanted to clean up by using a little hand soap and hitting all the vital areas. I have no way of brushing my teeth, and despite all of the cooking that went on I was never offered a crumb. Before I shut the front door this morning it was strongly *suggested* that I surrender my authentic Prada purse as a second half of my deposit. When I was gold digging last year that was one of few things I held onto. At this rate, before long I'll be stripped of my damn drawers! It didn't seem to matter that I worked the deposit off by any reasonable person's standards. Those Negroes didn't get up out of her makeshift restaurant until about four a.m., and guess who kept serving them and waiting on their asses? Me. The so-called cook spent most of her time flirting with her customers, who did everything but feel her up and take her pussy for a test drive. They did take turns taking other ones for road trips, talking about they were in need of "massages" for back pain. Yeah, right. I don't know which door it was coming from but I could hear someone complaining about not wanting to pay for dry pussy and the *landlord* had to go straighten out the matter by sending a young girl in the room after she made a telephone call. When she happily returned with a wad of cash, that was when I discovered she was also in the business of selling pum pum alongside of her crusty meals.

And as for locking the door to assure that I wouldn't be fondled or harassed—no deal. The room I slept in was divided from the hallway by a homemade navy blue curtain that was held up by two nails; one on the left side and the other on the right. Despite all of these *challenges* and compromised motivation, I roll out of bed and take my growling stomach out to look for J-O-B because my time is up on the cot. When a rough thug type with a cigarette stuck behind his ear pushes the curtain back and steps into the small space, I realize that moving fast had never been so important to me. He looks like he's just been released from a correctional facility, and I don't mean for having a history of throwing oranges at fake traffic cops. I can bitch to myself much, much later, after I got the hell out of dodge. Although my eyes still haven't adjusted to daylight, he doesn't have to wait for me to move my ass because I take the hint without him saying one damn word. But before I jet, the old Jalita can't help but leave Ms. Dee a lovely parting gift for her hospitality. Since I couldn't use the bathroom when my bowels wanted me to, I shit in a bag, tightly roll down the top of it, and leave the present at Ms. Dee's door with an anonymous note thanking her for everything. After all, it's the least I can do. She should rename her spot *The Best Little Whorehouse in Washington, D.C.* Yeah that would work for sure.

22

TOXIC LIVING

Malik

When I sit my ass down in the driver's seat, turn the key and watch the gas needle barely move off E, I complain. "Monica, what did I tell you about using the car and not filling it back up? Why do you do this every time?"

"It's my car, and if I didn't feel like stopping at the gas station on the way back home, that's my right don't you think? These four wheels don't belong to you, they belong to me."

"There you go again throwing shit up in my face. Who has time to stop and get gas if there's an emergency? I'm telling you this for your own safety. It's not for me, it's for you," I say, trying to make my lie sound completely logical.

"Why don't you shut up and get off my back! You said you were taking me out to dinner and already you're complaining. We can't ever have a nice evening. We haven't even backed out of the driveway yet. You're the one that loves to argue, Malik. You bitch more than a female."

I back up out of the driveway, look over my shoulder and reply, "And you are the bitch!"

"If that's so true why is it that I don't have this problem with anyone else—only you?"

"Shut the fuck up and suck my dick!"

"Have you forgotten you're driving *my* car? You have no respect for me. I don't appreciate the way you talk to me, Malik. I don't like it—you're so rude."

"The reason why you aren't driving is because you can't drive. The truth is the truth." I laugh. "Who taught you to drive anyway? Whoever did it should have *their* license taken away."

"You don't say that when I'm hauling you around everywhere. Since you've been sticking your foot in it you don't seem to realize how much extra mileage and wear and tear I have on my car thanks to you. It's not running very well, and now it needs a whole lot of work that I can't afford right now. I said you could use the car, not take it over. Give a Negro an inch and they take a mile!"

"This old piece of junk? Please. This car was already raggedy when you met me."

"You need to get your own vehicle, Malik. I've never been with a man without his own car. That's just a basic necessity," she says.

"I'm trying to do something nice for you and take your ass out to eat, and here you go bragging about your other man having a car. I can get my own. Shit, I can get whatever I want!"

"Do it, then. And stop that *your man* shit. If I had a real man I'd be riding in his car. He sure as hell wouldn't be riding in mine all of the time," she tells me, rolling her eyes.

"I will get another vehicle. The bitches will be on me then, too, so don't say shit when you see it."

"Well that would be a hell of an idea before you do any more damage. I keep telling you anything I share is all I've got. I can't run out and just get more, Malik. I don't have it like that. Among other things, I check the mileage on the car. You're supposed to be taking care of business and I don't think business requires you to travel three hundred miles in one day. If some airhead is dumb enough to chase a nigga with frozen assets and a host of other personal problems, she can have you. In fact, she'd be doing my ass a favor by feeding, clothing, and sheltering you."

"I don't need you to cosign it. Just close your mouth until we get to the restaurant. In the meantime there's nothing stopping you from buying a bike if you want to get out when I'm gone."

"Negro, did you just say what I thought you said? You must've really lost your last marble!"

I can feel Monica staring at me and it makes me uncomfortable. "You're making my blood pressure go up, Monica. I told you I have to be stress free while I'm training. Damn you're a crazy bitch! If you want to break up I can make that happen. I'm still one of the most eligible bachelors in the Metropolitan area, whether you think so or not. I've got the finest hos still chasing big sexy!"

In anger I run through pot holes on purpose, drive too close on people's bumpers, and nearly clip asses that cross the street much too carelessly. As I try to calm my nerves I'm thinking that Monica is bucking my authority, and isn't following her relationship training program as easy as the others usually do. Shit, I need to get back to the old me and stick to the three D's: dick 'em, demean 'em, and dismiss 'em. Although Monica is taking care of business and pushing me to get shit done that I wasn't on top of, if she doesn't watch it she'll be working on the third "d" faster than intended because a fine bitch in this area is a dime a dozen.

When we arrive at the ESPN Zone in downtown D.C., I pull my hat down over my eyes, stroll over to the hostess, and tell her that my *wife* and I would like to be seated. As usual, it doesn't take a whole minute before Monica and I are trailing behind her to one of the best tables in the house, all because she assumes I'm a Redskins player. She's more than happy to seat us ahead of the others who are holding those large square gadgets that light up to a bright red color when it's time to be seated.

After we sit down by a scenic window I motion to the waitress with my finger. "Hey, baby—come here a minute."

She comes over, stands off to the side of me, and then leans over so that I can see her cleavage. While she's shamelessly grinning at me in a flirtatious way I notice that her eyebrows have been completely plucked off. While I speak to her I can see Monica getting angry as a bulldog, but I ignore her mounting temper tantrum. If she's going to be around when I hit the field for the NFL again she better get used to the shit. This—and worse.

"Bring a glass of hot water back to the table," I tell her.

"Sure thing."

"I appreciate that kindly, dear."

When she returns with the hot water I drop my silverware into it. "Here, Monica—put yours in there."

"Don't you think that's a little extreme?" she asks. The silverware has been washed."

"This is what I do when I eat out, and since you know every damn thing I know some people that carry their own plates to restaurants." Monica drops her silverware in the glass and we proceed to scan the menu for something scrumptious and eye-catching.

When the waitress walks by again, I call her over. "Baby, I hate to bother you again, but could you come here?" I move my arm so that she can see the Rolex I collected from the vault when I snuck into my house a few days ago. "Could we have some extra napkins to dry off our silverware?"

In a perky voice, she replies, "Sure— that's not a problem."

"I know you enjoy flirting with the waitress and everything but I think that's enough," Monica says. "You never talk to me nice like that. Keep running her back and forth and she'll tell the cook to poison our food or do something to it. You better stop it, Malik."

"Girl, shut up," I snap. And I told *you* about facing other niggas when you sit down at places. My ex used to do that, and I told you I'm not putting up with it anymore. You hos just want to flirt all the time, at every opportunity. Now let's switch seats so you can put your back to those men at that table over there."

Monica slides out of the booth and we change seats. She rolls her eyes while we switch spots. Nevertheless, she gets her ass up and trades with me.

Within ten minutes our food is delivered to the table by a black female server. She's smiling just as much as the white girl and I smile back. When I see my entrée I say, "Baby, could you come here a minute?"

"Yes sir."

"My steak looks a little burned around the edges. Do you see that right there?"

"That's just the way it looks when it's charbroiled, sir."

"Baby, do me a favor and call your manager over for me."

She leans in closer and tries to shove her number to me without Monica noticing. "Can I get your autograph first?" she asks.

I grab the piece of paper she hands me and scribble something illegible.

"I can't believe I met one of the Redskins," she gushes. "My family is all fans. Wait until I get home and tell them who I met."

When Monica slams her fork down on her plate the girl tells me, "Oh, I almost forgot. I'll send the manger right over."

As soon as she walks away, Monica comments, "That bitch needs to wipe off that grin—she ain't slick. I saw her pass her number to you, Malik. You're not even back on a team yet and these gold digging groupie hos are at it already. Why don't you tell *them* about your baby's momma and the fact that you're not even a Redskin? In fact, you may or may not make it to the Vikings based on your performance in mini-camp. I'm sick of this shit already!"

"Girl, shut up! I'm doing this for us. Don't test me. I don't want that ho's number. I told you I threw out all my numbers of the finest when I met you."

"Well you sure didn't let go of your freak picture book with all of the women posing in it. When will you let go of that and the porn tapes, Malik?"

"I'm a dedicated man but a nigga can look if he wants to," I lie.

"If you're so dedicated where in the hell did her number go?"

"I pushed her hand back and gave it to her."

"I bet you did. Uh huh, sure," she says sarcastically.

While Monica and I are engaged in one of our typical long-winded arguments, a white man about forty years old with a slightly protruding belly walks over to the table. He looks at me with a warm smile and says, "How are you tonight, sir?"

"I could be better but I won't complain."

"What can I do for you this evening?" he asks.

"Oh nothing, don't worry about it."

"Please tell me if something isn't to your satisfaction, sir," he says, looking concerned.

"Well, it's no big deal. It's just the steak is so dry I can't eat it. My wife told me that I should say something about it being dry and tough but I tried to explain that it really wasn't necessary." Monica gives me an evil look and I hold my breath that she doesn't blow my cover just to fuck up my little scam.

"Well she's right," he says. "If something is wrong I'll be happy to take it off your check and cook you another one. How about some free gift certificates?"

"That's mighty nice of you. I really appreciate that but I didn't want to cause any trouble here."

"It's not a problem. I'll tell the waitress to calculate another tab. No, as a matter of fact, don't worry about any of the tab. Your meals tonight will be on the house. Before you leave I'll send those gift certificates to your table." He starts to leave and then turns back around. "What would your wife like for dessert? I'd like to give her something to take home."

I laugh. "Nothing for her, thank you. She's on a diet. But thanks for all of your hospitality. I really appreciate it." I reach out to shake the man's hand. He gives me a quick shake and then fades into the background of servers, waiters, waitresses, and the chatter of restaurant patrons.

When he walks away I shake my head and smirk. I was just given VIP treatment because his dumb ass thinks all black people look alike, and because he heard through the grapevine that one of the Skins was in the house. With no money in my pocket it's a good thing my plan worked like a charm. I don't know what Monica has in her purse but I'm completely cleaned out. Contrary to what many white people think about us being the worst tippers and the most demanding of A plus service, when I have it in my pocket I get attention by leaving a thirty buck tip and more—that is if I feel like showing off that I'm not some cheap ass baller who they shouldn't have waited on. It's nice to have a white person wait on a black person, from time to time. I feel that sort of bonus is justified for the way they're making the playing field uneven.

But these days I can't front because my pocket is hurting. The bitch that waited on me will get no tip since she slipped me her number. I'll slip something in her later and I don't mean some bill in her hands—especially since she was disrespecting my girl and trying to kiss my black ass because she thought I *could* give her more than the standard 20%. In case she didn't know, I'm an equal opportunity asshole who has no problems sticking my dick in her mouth as fast as any white girl's. As for Monica, she better not say shit to me about the diet I just put her on either. There's nothing wrong with her being a little on the thick side in the right places these days, but I can't have her getting full of herself, thinking she has it going on.

$

Monica and I swing near South Capitol Street and pick up my cousin and her husband who live out of town and are visiting some other relatives. During the ride to Winchester, my cousin's husband is leaning forward, looking in the rearview mirror and picking the in-grown hair out of his beard with Monica's tweezers. I could tell she wanted to tell him off for having the audacity to pick up her tweezers in the first place, let alone throw the tiny hairs around the car, but she doesn't say a word. Instead, she folds her arms and sulks like a good submissive woman would. Maybe her training is coming along better than I thought.

By the time we get to the gas pump I'm thinking she should have given him a tongue lashing. Both he and my cousin had the nerve to pretend they had no money. What did they think they were going to do—ride for free? That's my job and no one else's. After about fifteen minutes of sitting and denying he had any cash, he produced a twenty and we were on our way to our final destination.

We pull up to my cousin's old, all brick, semi-detached house and we all get out of the car. Although I haven't visited him for quite some time I notice that he still has his powder blue Jag sitting out front despite it needing a transmission and being inoperable. Let my cousin tell it though and he's got it going on. In fact, he's always been jealous of Wes and me. Wes because of his NBA fame, and me because I did a little something in the NFL. He could never get over the fact that we had a few big boy toys and shit. I guarantee he'll be out to try to show me up as soon as we set foot in the door. That's a ritual that I'm sure will never change.

"Man, next time ya'll need to call and say you've left because I had one of my guns cocked. You know I don't play," Calvin says, trying to sound tough.

"Boy, get out of the way," I tell him. We all walk inside, and he gets started right away trying to show out.

"Malik, you know I was promoted to manager at Jiffy Lube. I wouldn't be here if I didn't have the day off. They let me do what I want."

No one comments. I know that Calvin was most likely fired again, and that one of his baby's momma's is paying the rent and keeping him and his kids fed.

"What ya'll want to eat?" he asks.

Everyone shrugs and plops down onto the couch. Monica sits in a chair off to the side. I can tell she doesn't like Calvin one bit but I don't care.

Calvin picks up the phone. "Yeah, it's me. When you get off buy some food. Think of something to feed my family, aiight? Yeah, and hurry up. These kids are hungry too. You need to get your fat ass down here anyway because I'm tired of watching them." When he hangs up he smiles and tells us, "I told Tina to stop at the store and get something so she can cook. She got ya'll as soon as she gets off at Sheetz."

I really don't have much to say. I know that most of the performance will be for my benefit because Calvin is trying to prove to me he's the man and is in my baller league. The only thing about that is he'll never be in my league or have it going on like me. He dropped out of high school and occasionally deals cheap crack on the side, so he's small time as hell. Making babies is his main gig. The sad thing is, he doesn't have a clue about the fact that he ain't fooling nobody. He stands in the middle of the floor and continues bragging about himself. "Yeah, so, let me turn on the big screen in case ya'll want to see something." He picks up the remote. "This thing cost me a couple grand. I just got it. It's state of the art. Yeah, and if you know anybody that can use these couches and shit, let me know. I've got some new furniture on the way. Hell, I don't need the money, I'll give them away."

I shake my head and chuckle. I can see right now I'm going to have to break him down a notch, so I do. "Boy, you ain't getting rid of shit. We all know you got the furniture, TV, and everything else in the room from Rent-A-Center."

Everyone laughs except Monica. Just as he prepares for a comeback his daughter Imanni taps him on the leg. "Daddy, where's my kazoo? I want to play my kazoo. Can I have it?"

Calvin tries to look at her like she's bothering him, but I know he's glad she saved him from looking stupid after being busted out. "I broke that damn thing because it makes too much noise. I don't know why your grandmother would buy you some annoying shit like that." Calvin sinks down into the couch next to us. He gaps his legs open and sticks one of his hands down pants. When his little daughter begins to rub her eyes and whimper he tells her, "I don't want to hear it. Don't you dare start, Imanni. Do you want to go to bed until your mother gets home?" She shakes her head. "Then you better act like you have some sense. Sit your ass down and be quiet like your brother. He's a baby and he ain't carrying on like you."

The toddler looks around with his big eyes like he's scared to cry, but I can tell he knows he's being talked about. "And if you start showing off you know what you get, boy."

I look at the child and he's already sporting a fake little diamond in his left ear. "Man, why are you so hard on those kids? How do you get them to stay so quiet like that?"

"You got to train them early," he brags. "I'm not going to tell how I do it. Little man ain't no pussy though. I'm raising me a little pimp right here. I already taught him not to cry and he's just nine months old." Calvin laughs, takes his hand out of his pants and smacks both of them together in the air like he just heard the funniest joke. That's hard-core even by my standards but I can't judge the way the man raises his children because I don't even bother to visit my own.

About a half an hour later, after Calvin has made a small pyramid out of the beer cans he's polished off, the front door opens. Uncle Pete steps in with his famous brown-papered bottle and a pack of cigarettes. He always carries a taste everywhere he goes just in case no one else bothered to pick up a case of beer. A nip is his minimum requirement to stick around for more than ten minutes. He speaks to everyone and then walks into the living room singing the lyrics of some Smokey Robinson tune off key— he's obviously half loaded, and he hasn't even opened whatever is in the bag. With the drinking problem I used to have, I should know.

Monica stands up and walks over toward me. When she does Uncle Pete stops singing, clicking his fingers, and moving his hips. "Damn! She's phat as shit! Hey, baby. How you doing? You like old men?"

Monica ignores his comment and sits on my lap like she's scared of my family. Being sheltered in the suburbs hasn't taught her much about the streets and what's out here. Since she's been with me I've given her ass a crash course.

"Uncle Pete, this is *my* girl," I say, checking him.

"Oh, I'm sorry, dawg. Uncle Pete didn't know." He shifts the liquor bottle to the other hand and continues, "Pardon me, Miss Pretty. You got any older sisters?" When Monica doesn't answer Uncle Pete won't drop the issue. He looks from Monica to me. "Boy you keep an attractive woman on your arm. You get that from me. When I met Lou she looked just like her."

I keep quiet too because that's a damn lie. Somehow Uncle Pete thinks we want to see more of his a capella show. He starts clicking his fingers again, and does a lousy job of simulating some steps that the old school groups used to do on stage. It isn't until he does a drunken spin and damn near falls down, that my cousin Maria comments. "This isn't senior citizen Soul Train. Will you sit down? I can't see TV. You're not made of glass Uncle Pete. Stop showing off because Malik has company."

Ten minutes later, Calvin's baby's mother comes in carrying a grocery bag. She's no less than three hundred pounds, and still wearing her uniform from Sheetz. The funny thing is she used to be as fine as Monica, but since she started fucking around with Calvin, birthing his babies, and cooking for his lazy ass, she blew up like a helium balloon. Imanni runs to her and hugs her on the legs. "Momma, you're home."

None of the adults speak or acknowledge her—except Calvin. "What took you so damn long? We're around here with our stomach's growling. Would you stop taking your time and get in the kitchen and fix us something?"

She walks past us and doesn't say a word. I smile, thinking that Calvin's got her trained the way I plan on training my girl. These dumb bitches with college degrees—there's another prime example. I don't give a shit though because my stomach really *is* growling and I hope she can still cook like she used to. By the looks of her size, she still can.

$

A few hours later Monica and I have concluded that my cousin's baby's momma, their kids, and the two of us are the only ones that haven't been up and down the steps of the basement or even invited to move in that direction. Uncle Pete's bottle is one third away from being empty when he makes his seventh trip downstairs. Every time someone walks up out of the basement, someone else walks down the steps. Monica pretends like she's not watching, but I can see her looking from the corner of her eye. She stays silent when it becomes apparent what they were doing.

Finally, Calvin puts the proof in the pudding. "That stuff was weak. I want a refund, an exchange or something. That's a damn shame. I'm gonna see if I can get us something. Let me get in touch with my connect." He puts his hands down his pants and grabs his cell phone to make a call. By this time Monica and I can smell the aroma of weed traveling up the basement steps.

"Malik, could I speak to you outside for a minute," Monica says suddenly. I get up and follow her, which is an extreme rarity. After I close the front door she starts in on me. "How could you bring us over here knowing these people are winos, potheads, and God knows what else? I saw a policeman pass by when we came here, so they do patrol the area. If he smelled that shit and decided to investigate, we could go to jail and we weren't even messing with that stuff they've got down there. I can't believe you're foolish enough to jeopardize everything we've worked hard for over your idiot cousins and family. What's wrong with you?"

"This is my family, Monica. I can't tell grown people what to do. And I'm the one who's worked to get my ass in shape and train, not you."

"Well I'm not going to stand out here and debate all of that. What I want to tell you right here, right now is that your cousin and her husband are not putting one damn foot up in my so-called raggedy car. I suggest you inform them that they may have to hoof or thumb it back to D.C. I refuse to push my luck by letting them ride back with us. This visit has been enough to last me all year. If this is how your family acts why do you even visit?"

Andrea Blackstone

"Oh so now you've got the perfect family? Your peoples are crazy. They all need Prozac."

"You can say what you want but you're living with us and we're the ones giving you support. Your people have done nothing for you except put your goal in jeopardy. They didn't even want to contribute to gas after we rode all the way to D.C. to pick their asses up, so you need to watch the comments about my family. Yours is definitely nothing to shout about—at least the ones I've met so far. And why is it that you never go see your brother Wes, yet he's supposed to be big in the NBA? Something ain't right about that either."

"Bitch, don't you bring Wes into this!"

"I don't know why you're so touchy about that, but as I said you just better go in there and tell them they need to pay a cab or hitchhike back to D.C. and I mean it!" Monica crosses her arms and looks at me. I've rarely seen her stand up for her convictions this way and I know I can't back her down on this one. I'll never admit it but her ass is right.

After we walk back into the house I say, "Ya'll can't ride back to D.C. in my girl's car smelling like weed. I can't let you do that."

Maria, who is still half high, stumbles over to Monica and lets her hand drop on Monica's shoulders. "Hey, Malik's pretty girlfriend. I'm sooooory! I apologize." Then she laughs.

Monica's facial expression doesn't change. In fact she acts as though she doesn't even hear her.

Calvin's daughter Imanni says, "Daddy, I smell smoke."

Calvin hops up. "I'll be damned! That is smoke!"

Monica and I look toward the basement and watch smoke sift out from under the door. Everyone hops up and begins acting nervous, and then we hear,

"Who left the joint burning in the basement? Shit!"

"The futon mattress is on fire!" Calvin screams. "Someone throw me the fire extinguisher from the kitchen!"

I run to the kitchen, grab the red extinguisher, and run down the steps to throw it to my cousin. He puts out the blaze just in time, but a portion of the carpet is burned and the entire space is full of smoke and weed funk.

"Uncle Pete! I told you about smoking in bed. Your drunk, high ass almost burned down my house and killed my kids!" Calvin yells.

Uncle Pete fans smoke from around his face. "I didn't do it. Why am I always the one getting blamed? It's not my fault you didn't have no batteries in your smoke detector."

Calvin throws the fire extinguisher down on the floor. "You're going to pay me for this futon and a new rug. I'm not having that up in my crib. I knew I shouldn't have let you have no weed with the rest of us. Every time you drink you just can't hang—you get stupid as shit."

When I walk up the steps I'm embarrassed but I don't give Monica the pleasure of saying she told me so.

"All you niggas—out of my house before I start shooting, and you know I've got guns. I didn't stutter. I said get the fuck out of my house!" Calvin screams like a maniac.

"Man, Monica and I were about to roll. You know we didn't have nothing to do with that shit." I grab Monica's hand and pass through my family members. They've lined up across from each other, ready to start arguing.

When we reach the front door Calvin starts up again. "You niggas need to go back to D.C. and leave me alone. Get to stepping with them before you miss your ride. You can't stay here."

As I start the car I hear Monica sigh like she's full to the brim with disgust. By the time her cheeks puff out the car wheels are rolling. When I hear a gun shot, I see Calvin's arm sticking straight up in the air. He threatens to begin aiming at our two cousins and Uncle Pete. Maria is running toward the car screaming, "What about us? We're coming. Wait!"

I keep my head straight as I pass by her and pretend like I don't know her. After all that drama, there was nothing left to do. I knew I shouldn't have let Monica meet any of my family members. Now I've got to do some damage control. I'm not sure how I'll pull it off but I have a few minutes to figure the shit out before we head back home.

23

ALMOST AT THE END OF MY ROPE

Jalita

Only the determined are rewarded—so they say at least. Although posting my resume on Monster would make much more sense, I don't have PC access and there's no time for beggars to be choosers because time is obviously of the essence. Plus, dropping out of college twice won't increase my odds of finding a job that I won't want to complain about every five minutes. Especially since I'm not willing to put out to get it like before.

I looked up the address of a day labor place and oddly enough the guy who I share a bed with could use some extra money. After remembering that I'm a chick from the hood, I broke down and boldly started some conversation with this guy. At first he was evil as he could be, but finally softened up and explained he's got a record on his hands after serving time for something stupid, so he says. He claims he's unemployed by force, not by choice. It turns out that he *services* Ms. Dee when she gets cranky about his money being short, but at least he tries to do something with himself. He has a little rusty truck, and during these winter months he goes around moving furniture for people and hauling things to the dump between DC, MD, and VA for a reasonable price. I can't knock his hustle and I realize he's not as bad a guy as I'd stereotyped him to be.

After I pay him to drop me off at a day labor place near Patapsco Flea Market, I see a bunch of Hispanic men talking in Spanish, waiting for the doors to open. Closer to opening time a few women pull up in their cars and leave their engines running until a small Asian girl with jet black hair down to her ass turns the key to the front door and cuts on the fluorescent lights that brighten the dim office. One by one, people collect their assignments and leave. Me and one other girl are left. After I fill out the paper work and dodge a few details I'm told that I must go to some factory in Jessup, Maryland.

I pretend as though I'm leaving to get into my car but instead I hide on the other side of the wall and wait for the other girl to come out to see if I can bum a ride from her. Apparently we were going to the same location so I agree to pay her ten dollars each way in gas and we set out to go to a factory in Jessup for the day. When we got there it was dimly lit, depressing, noisy, and it smelled like hot plastic. We ask for the person we were told to look up upon arrival. After we find her she clocks us in, explains her strict rules, and immediately sends us over to the area where computer programs are being shrink wrapped in plastic.

Standing on my feet all day made me shake because my legs sometimes fall asleep, but somehow I manage to get through it. When lunchtime comes it seems like the longest thirty minutes of my entire life. Since I don't have any money yet I can't buy anything to eat. To take my mind off my weakness and growling belly I ask the supervisor to work in another area until break time is over. My pride made me lie—I tell her my stomach is upset and I can't hold down food. After I take several sips of water at the water fountain she is more than happy to help me violate workplace law, and puts me to work labeling the boxes that were ready to be sorted and counted for shipment. For eight hours I listen to the hum of factory noises, pass programs from hand to hand, and take turns boxing up the merchandise in neat piles of brown boxes. When the day comes to an end the supervisor with the dry leathery skin praises my efficiency and said she'd request that I come back to work for the rest of the week. At six dollars an hour the compliment wasn't all that grand, but at least it was nice to know she acknowledged my efficiency and ambition. People saying anything good to me is a rarity, so in a sense I should've been much more elated than I was.

After my temporary co-worker and I battle rush hour traffic and make our way back to the office, the Asian girl pays her for the day, and she leaves without telling me goodbye or anything that implies she appreciated the company during the car ride. When I open the door and flag her down remembering that I owe her twenty bucks she says loudly. "Hurry up and pay me. I have get out of here and pick up my kids from childcare."

The Asian girl looks at me with her exotic slanted eyes then calls over a white woman with a fried curly perm and crow's feet in the corner of her eyes. After she whispers something in her ear the white woman asks me, "Ms. Harrison, where is your car?" She gives me a false smile that makes me want to wring her neck because I know she doesn't mean it and is about to put my ass in a sling.

"It's in the lot across the street," I lie.

"Are you sure about that?"

I hold my ground and confidently say, "Yes, why wouldn't I be? Are you calling me a liar?"

"Well, it appears as though you checked the box that stated that you have your own transportation to get to and from work but you don't have a car."

"It may *appear* that way but I do have a car. I told you it's in the lot. If you must know, I had a flat on the way and turned into the lot where someone could change the tire for me. After a man changed the tire I didn't have time to move it. I didn't want to be late so I left it there."

"But you rode with Crystal. That's what I've heard."

"Like I said I didn't have time to get my car so I did ride with her. I never said I didn't."

"The sad thing is I got a glowing report from the supervisor at the factory and she was looking forward to you coming back in the morning, but company policy won't allow me to have you return. Here's your money for today. I wish I could help you but I can't. If you get transportation of your own come back and perhaps we can try again." The woman pushes the cash into my hand and gives me another plastic smile that makes me want to smack her crow's feet smooth.

"You know what?" I snap. "You employers are hard on the wrong people. Here's someone that wants to work and you won't let me. Later for you—I won't be back to beg for another minimum wage gig while you rack up a nice pension. The most stress you have in your life is probably sipping cocktails on your husband's boat, and figuring out how to give him better head. You don't have to live in the real world so why should I expect a wrinkled crow like you to understand?"

The woman is speechless and doesn't say a word back to me. I begin to walk out of the office but then turn back one time to look the Asian girl in the eye and let her know that I didn't appreciate her running her trap to get me booted. I give her the middle finger and then shove the door open. As soon as I do I hear attitude on the other side. "Will you hurry up? Damn! I told you I have to go. I get charged extra by the minute if I'm late picking up my kids."

"Here, now go ahead and drive like a rabid bat out of hell. Take twenty-five instead of twenty in case you get charged a few more dollars because of my ass. You and I both know you're in a rush to do something like suck a dick for a bag of groceries and a movie—I know your type. I've seen plenty of you in my day."

After the woman pulls off I feel tears build up in my eyes but refuse to break down. Instead, I walk to the other end of the red brick building. "Why is all of this happening to me? What have I done to deserve this?" I mumble. After I wipe my tears away and gather my faculties, I realize that I don't have enough to pay Ms. Dee for the night before or today. I feel a panic attack coming on but fight it off the best I can. In anger I kick a tin can across the parking lot and tell myself that I'm going to get my car. Fuck Kyle and his crazy ass wife! That's all I've got left, and he's done enough damage without holding that hostage too. But first I'll put some time on this GoPhone by dropping some bucks at the 7-11 in the shopping center across the street. Then I'll call Shawn to see if he can help me out by picking me up and dropping me off near where I need to be. As long as I don't go near Jackie I can justify trying to place one more call in distress. All I hope for is that Shawn answers his own damn cell phone this time.

$

After I purchase a Big bite hot dog from 7-11, top it with chili and cheese, and add time to my phone, I stall in the store to warm my fingers and toes. I'm walking out of the door eating my hot dog like it's my last meal, when I notice that I have three messages on my phone since I last used it. That is anything but usual. I play the first message.

"Jalita, it's New Year's Eve and this is Shawn's neighbor, Kendra. Shawn has been taken to Central Booking on Fayette and Gay in Baltimore. He asked me to leave you this message. Jackie and Shawn were fighting and I really can't tell you what he was charged with. It's 3:00 a.m. now, and if you get this message before 10:00 a.m. you can call me at 410-269-3243. I have his house keys. Also, he wants you to call the police because Jackie left with Myra. Shawn thinks she's with her brother, getting high. She's been seen nuttin' with him. Shawn says call the police to find her, and have them put Myra in protective custody. The little baby came home today and Jackie has him too. Shawn's really upset and worried because the baby's so young and he's a preemie. The other five kids are with their fathers so they're ok. Thanks."

The calm tone of her fluid voice tells me that she's most likely done this for Shawn before. I shake my head. I'm livid that Shawn fucked up by allowing an altercation with Jackie to screw up his probation. Although Jackie acts crazy I had no idea she had a drug problem or *seven* kids. In a way it explains more than I cared to find out. All I was looking for was a ride to D.C. I'm shaking and my stomach is turning. I long to get hold of a few anti-depressants and pop them in my mouth, but instead I swallow the last bite of my hot dog. Then I walk to a pay phone to call information and get the number for Central Booking since all of that special calling would burn up minutes and money on my prepaid cell phone. After I scribble it down, I dial 410-545-8080 on my prepaid and wait for someone to pick up so I can find out what happened to Shawn. No one does. Instead, I hear, "You have reached the customer service unit for the division of Pre-Trial and Detention Services. Our hours of operation have changed. Our new hours are 7:30 to 4:00 p.m."

There is a strong probability that Shawn has been released by now, and even if he hasn't I don't have money or a checking account to secure a bail bondsman to come to his rescue. My life is just as fucked up. As selfish as it sounds for me not to call around and track Shawn down, I don't have time or energy for the

Shawn vs. Jackie saga right now. In fact, I'm not going to listen to the other two messages because I'm pretty sure it's my cousin trying to find out where my ass has been.

I feel helpless because I know there's nothing I can do to help Shawn or the new little baby. Although I wish I were in the position to adopt two cousins I barely know, I'm not. Since I'm not I can't mentally prepare myself to see what I can do to look out for Shawn if he's still stuck at Central Booking. This is the craziest shit I've ever seen in my life. The baby manages to live, and has to come home to two parents that can't seem to stop the madness or go their separate ways. I say a prayer for my new little cousin and delete the rest of my messages of distress. If anyone had reason to have a nervous breakdown it should definitely be me, because once again I've been emotionally hit over the head by a fucking 2X4!

$

It begins to rain, then sleet, and before I know it I feel snow falling on my eyelashes when I reach Kyle's place. I don't see any car parked in front of his house and that's a good sign. I look both ways then ease over to his garage door to see if it will budge. Surprisingly it isn't locked and I'm able to raise it enough to give me an opportunity to enter. I'm not sure why it's open since if appears as though no one is home, but all I know is that Jalita just hit the jack pot. I feel my heart begin to pound as I nervously look around, crouching my way through the dark garage.

Once I tiptoe over to my vehicle I use my spare key to open the car. I grin when I realize that soon I'll be sitting in the driver's seat and won't have to go through any more drama because I don't have transportation at my fingertips. As I attempt to turn the key I hear a loud house alarm go off, then I hear barking dogs. "You're trespassing, young lady. What do you think you're doing?"

I nearly jump out of my skin when I hear Kyle's voice combined with the words "entry detected." A recorded man's voice repeats it again and again, like he's yelling it over a bullhorn. My heart begins racing and I feel frozen with fear. Apparently he was watching me the whole time. He turns on the light and confirms it's me.

I challenge him, pretending to be confident, still trying to make the car turn over. I yell over the noise. "This is my car and I'm removing it from your garage."

"You broke in here and the police are on their way," he says authoritatively. "I've already warned you about who I am and what I can do. You're stupid to draw attention to yourself."

"You stole my car!" I snap back. "Go ahead and report me if you'd like, but the car is registered in my name. You can't just hold my property in your possession like this." I continue trying to turn over the ignition, ignoring him. I have no idea why the car won't budge. I begin cussing when I realize Kyle must've done something to my car.

"I'm warning you. Get out of the car right now! I have a right to defend my home under the law." I don't budge. "Micah!" he yells. A dog appears and begins barking loudly. "I repeat, get out of the car! The wires have been switched around and I'll say you owe me for a towing bill if I call the police. If I sick these dogs on you while I call the police, you won't be very happy about that. All it takes is one command word." He smirks at me and then adds, "Remember, you're already in trouble. Have it your way. The police will side with me—I guarantee that." Another rabid acting dog appears and begins hopping up on the car door while barking and staring at me through the window.

Kyle jolts my memory about the pending trial and I decide that he's holding a hell of a trump card. I don't want any more media attention in my life. Shit. Unless I want to get torn to smithereens or get hassled by the cops, I have no choice but to comply with Kyle's commands. The hungry acting pit bull keeps barking ferociously and I begin to cuss again. I know he'll bite me or back me into a corner if I step out and attempt to raise the hood and see what the scoundrel did to the wires or something else. My chances of getting out of here with my ride have been shot. Weighing my limited options, I roll down the window. "You've got me. Now what?"

He commands the dogs to leave the garage. They circle his feet once, then leave, barking and drooling on the floor. Kyle walks over to my car, opens the door, and snatches me by my left arm. "I told you you'd come back. Now let's go in the house and talk about all of this. I have to answer the call center before the police show up at the door. After that I may or may not call the police on you. It depends on how well you convince me to forgive you for trying to break in here, and slapping my wife last time." He shoves me toward the open garage door and I nearly trip. Whether I like it or not I'm on my way to entering what is most likely the freakiest undercover house on the block and goodness knows what will happen next.

24

TRIPLE X SEX

Malik

It's getting late, Monica and I are both tired, and the roads are dark. As a result, it isn't hard to convince her to take a pit stop. When we pull into a popular motel chain I tell her to wait in the car while I pay for the room. Of course me telling her to do that had nothing to do with me being considerate. It was more or less me having to flirt with one of my many hos in order to get a free room that won't have mildew issues or loose tiles like the first one in D.C. I have to do some heavy mack-daddy flirting with her to convince her not to knock on the door or come looking for me later. I tell her that I'm with my elderly parents, coming back from a wedding in Virginia, and that she should respect my inability to lay the pipe right now. I promise to come back and service her when I'm alone and she goes for it. An eighty-dollar room bill is erased and I collect a room key, just like that.

Monica and I settle into the room and wash up. "Niggas will be niggas," I say. "I feel as though I need to apologize for my family showing out back there. They don't mean any harm though—that's just how they are."

"It is what it is. It's over now," Monica says, taking her clothes off.

After she sheds her clothes I walk up behind her and put my arms around her. "You wanna fuck?" I whisper, kissing her right ear. I let my hands fall across her breasts, then squeeze them.

To my surprise Monica doesn't give me any lip about being tired or not having a condom to cover my erect penis. She smiles seductively, turns to face me and replies, "Do you want me to get on my back or turn around? It's your choice. You brought sex up so you choose."

I run my fingers through her hair. "Neither one."

"Then what?" she asks, looking into my eyes.

"Look, little momma, it's time for something else," I say, gently reaching down and rubbing her clit.

"What are you thinking of?"

"I'll tell you." I pull my hand away. I'll lie on my back and you get on top of me."

Monica gives me a confused look. "I've ridden you before, Malik."

I laugh. "No, no, no. I mean let's have triple X-rated sex, girl. Put your pussy on my face while you suck my dick. You might need to visualize it to figure it out but I think you know what I mean."

"Give oral upside down? I've never done anything like that before, Malik."

"Monica, we're getting married and there's more to sex than the missionary position or something niggas do everyday. It's just us— it's ok. Let's do it. You'll be the first and the last to carry it like this. The intense stimulation will get you off, trust me. I want to have some marathon sex with my girl. Is there anything wrong with that?"

She hesitates a second, but then gets on top of me, looking over her shoulder and giving me the sexiest look I can ever recall her giving me. I spread her legs apart then begin playing with her butt cheeks. As soon as my tongue hits her wetness she moans. "Oh Shit! Malik. Baby. Shit. I like this!"

That's all Monica seems to be able to say as we have sex in the most intensely stimulating sexual position that ever existed: the 69. Although I normally fuck her face to face and lift her legs over my shoulder while looking into her eyes, after what my family pulled I felt like intertwining our bodies so we could both get sucked and licked at the same time. She crams my dick deep into her throat as I suck up the juice that is dripping down her cheeks and into my mouth.

After a while she begins to feel the groove of the erotic position and her hands begin to slowly stroke my balls. Monica really gets into it and gives me head that's good enough to pay for. She continues to moan, and begins to shake all over, her lips still moving up and down my penis. When I feel her level of arousal increase I begin to moan along with her. As we moan in unison I repetitively smack her on the ass.

Monica pushes her pussy into my mouth. "Don't stop big daddy. Don't stop! Right there, Malik. Right there!"

The pitch in her voice gets higher and higher and I feel my dick stiffen. By the time she repeats those words again, I feel her sweetness gush into my mouth, and I explode in her mouth before she has a chance to lift her head. We repeat this over and over again until Monica tires from leaning on her elbows and my tongue grows weary from the constant motion required to make my girl forget that I'm a moody broke baller, whose biggest asset is the ability to get her off and turn her into a certified nympho. If women can use sex as a weapon, so can men. And for the record, Monica came the most so I must've worked my magic tongue exceptionally well. Now I can be sure she'll sit with me in court next week and even help pay a lawyer to defend my silly ass. Just to keep her blinded I'll tell her that I'm going to pay to have her car fixed, but she'll soon find out that she's footing the bill for my use of her ride, too. You've got to talk and have good game to get over on people out on these streets. Lucky for me, I do.

25

THE BLACKMAIL EQUATION

Jalita

"You raped me, Kyle, and you've got some pretty big balls to make my life hell in light of what you did," I say, shaking my finger in his face. My voice sounds awkward because of my stuffy nose, but I mange to make the words clear.

"What?" Kyle says, crossing his legs calmly. He tilts his head and looks at me like I've made all this up. "You must be crazy, Ginger. How could you say such a thing? Surely you must have me confused with someone else. You keep saying that, and that's a dangerous accusation." He picks up a soft, pliable exercise ball for the hands and begins squeezing it. "I think it's time we get something straight once and for all. We partied, I passed out in my hotel room, and you went home. That's what went on and I can produce an alibi if necessary to corroborate those facts."

I have a coughing fit. My eyes feel puffy and my whole body aches. I pat my chest to catch my breath. "Are you serious? That's not the truth and you know it! I didn't consent to having sex with you, and I'm thinking that I need to turn you in to the police."

Kyle doesn't stop squeezing, the ball. "Like I said, that's what went on*, right?*" Then he adds, "Medical records helped Kobe clear his name and they can clear mine also if you insist that this little story of yours has merit."

"What are you saying?" I ask, scrunching my eyebrows.

Kyle places the ball in the middle of his desk. He leans over and looks directly at me. "Ginger, who knows who will be hearing the case with the Wes Montgomery scandal—the one that *you* are a part of. I can see to it that opposing counsel gets a hold of some interesting facts about your background—humiliate you before the American public, or at least anyone who cares to follow the trial on Court TV. Birth records perhaps? Something that shows you are related to the man you fucked. And if that isn't enough, I'll tell the police that you assaulted my wife—she'll go along with my story that you were chasing a married man because you're mentally unstable and became obsessed. Don't push me. You know I'm capable of all of this, and can add more hell to your life with no conscious. I suggest you do what I want or face the consequences. Like I said the first time you accused me of raping you, go ahead and call the police. You and I both know that you don't have the chance of a snowball in hell. Before you know it you'll be in more trouble for filing a false police report than I ever could be. You have no evidence or proof that I ever even touched you in this lifetime."

My eyes water and I wipe them. "You admitted to putting something in my drink, you fucking lunatic!"

Kyle picks up the exercise ball again and squeezes it. "What you drank is not my fault. You should blame whoever did it, not me. And when you find him I'm sure you'll feel that justice can be served. From what I'm hearing you should've gone to the hospital, gotten checked out, and let them prepare a rape kit. That's what any real victim would have done by most reasonable person's standards."

If I had my knife I'd cut Kyle's twisted ass and enjoy going to jail for it. Since I stopped carrying my knife all I can do is fume like a hot fire, once again wanting to kill the asshole with my bare hands. I consider picking up a glass lamp and busting his head open with it, but I'm slow to react because my cold has numbed my feistiness.

Kyle must be reading my mind because he grabs my wrists and whispers, "I notice you've been coughing a lot. What I say is that you need to get in bed and rest yourself instead of fighting this losing battle. If you run from me I'll find you and have you knocked off. No one will ever know who did it when you turn up in the woods amongst leaves and liquor bottles. Then do you know what happens? Do you?" He shakes my whole body with both hands, squeezing my shoulders. "If the officials bother to conduct an investigation and the sheriff department and medical examiner's office find out your identity, you'll be cremated if your family can't be located. Don't ask me how I know about what they do to unclaimed persons, Ginger. Don't be brave enough to ask."

I'm not brave enough to ask. His words give me chills and an eerie feeling overcomes me. I start shivering all over. I turn my head away from him, gulping hard.

"If I were you, I'd spare my life and take our secret to your grave," he whispers. "This is my last warning—snitch and you die. Now what's it going to be? It's your call, Ginger. Clyde made the right choice and I hope you will, too. I'm your in-house pimp now, he's history. I did you a favor, and you can't even see it that way—but in time you will. You're in the middle of a dangerous game. Make the wrong move and you lose."

Kyle's strong cologne breaks through the congestion of my stuffed nose, and it makes me sneeze across the room. My head begins to throb and as I turn to look at him Renee walks into the room. He quickly releases me from his grip like he was never touching me and mimicking a psycho killer who was delivering icy threats. "Renee," he says warmly. You'll be having a little company while I'm out of town. Our new friend that you like so much will be staying over. She's not feeling well so perhaps you can get her some soup and see to it that she stays in bed. She really needs some rest. You know there's a nasty bug going around. Hopefully you can help her head it off so we all don't catch it."

Renee looks at me. "I don't mind. It will give us a chance to get to know each other."

"It's settled then," Kyle says. "I'll be back after a quick trip to New York. The driver should be here any minute."

It took all I had to stay quiet when I saw Kyle mouth the words *remember what I told you* as I followed his wife up the steps and into a guest room. As crazy as it is to not only hold a conversation with your rapist, then set foot on his turf, I did it because after having the last conversation with Kyle I was clearly a hostage. It doesn't mean I'll play the game by his rules though. Right now I'll just submit to the blackmail equation and figure out my next move as I nurse this cold along. In the process I'll search my data bank for inspiration to hit this asshole where it hurts the most.

$

After Renee brings me chicken noodle soup, crackers, and ginger ale on a tray, she fluffs up two pillows and puts them behind my head. When I lay my head back my mind flashes through various scenes of my life—from childhood abandonment and my dead mother having her hospice nurse send me a letter explaining she never loved me, to trying to get with a baller that turned out to be my half sibling, to laying in a freaky household wearing a strange woman's ankle length off-white colored Vanity Fair gown. A tear falls from my eye as the craziness of it all sinks in.

"I'm a very intuitive person, Ginger," Renee says quietly. "There's a sadness in your spirit. Why are you so down?"

I wipe the tear from my eye. "Renee, I appreciate the soup but please don't get personal with me. Let's enjoy this silence—just don't go there. I'm not in the mood."

"I'm sorry if I came on strong when we first met," she says. "I'm just used to being dominant from training my husband to worship my black ass. I am capable of being tender to a female that I'm attracted to, so I hope you don't let my lifestyle prevent you from getting to know a nice woman who puts on a front to get what she wants from her old man. Please tell me what's the matter. It's just us women. Look, if you're honest with me, I can be honest with you. Ask me anything you want to know about myself. I don't want to appear as though I'm doing all of the talking."

"Okay. How long have you known Kyle?"

"Since I was twenty. We met at a political fundraiser. Kyle was twenty-nine. We were seated at the same table during dinner."

"How well do you know your husband?"

"Why do you ask?"

"I'm just wondering that's all. You said I could ask you anything so I am."

"Fairly well. We have a great relationship. I'm confident I know everything he does, and I do have love for him. Do you know he actually came home and told me that he met you and took you out and fooled around with you? I was okay with that because we've had an open relationship before. We've been to swinger parties together, picked people to seduce together, and have even hooked each other up for partner swaps. It takes a very special bond for jealously not to creep in and take over. With us, it never has. I know I have love and so does he. Most people deceive each other behind their mate's back whereas we share our urges out in the open. It really works for us and we're a happy couple. "

"I guess you've said it all, then." When Renee phrases what Kyle and I did as fool around I realize the bastard never even told her a part of the truth about us having sex. Even so I don't clue her in because I don't want to blow my cover or show my ace too early.

"We would much rather have a discreet intimate gathering with another woman or couple in our home because the women and men aren't always fine, and having to turn someone down at the parties can get awkward. This way cuts down on the stress of it during times we don't want to go there. Does the thought of seeing me or a room full of naked people turn you on?"

I take a sip of my soda and shake my head. "No, I'm not feeling it."

"You mean to tell me you don't think it would be fun to fuck someone new and watch your partner going at it with a stranger? That's what mostly every man's fantasy is about—their woman enjoying another woman or living out some erotic adventure. Think a little harder before you answer."

"Look, I've been there and done that. I'm not here for the reason you think. You said all I'd have to do is walk around nude and be a voyeur when you're fucking each other or some shit like that."

"A straight woman is a turn on. Once you take turns kissing us while you're being touched and stimulated, you'll be hooked. We're laid back, nice people. I have a feeling we'll all get along just fine. You seem like a nice young lady."

When I imagine Kyle's slimy hands touching me yet one more time I begin sobbing uncontrollably.

Renee leans backward and says, "Damn. What did I say? Did I upset you?"

I shake my head and don't verbally respond. After a while I tell her, "I've just got a lot on my mind."

"Look, maybe this isn't the best time to talk about all of this. Whatever it is will pass and when it does we can talk. How about if I slip in bed next to you and keep you warm?"

I continue crying and turn my back to Renee. As I continue to sob I feel her long arms wrap around me. For some reason I don't push her arms from my body or evict her from the bed. I cry because I feel guilty that I slept with another woman's husband, and because I let myself down when I was the one who was supposed to be turning my life around. I know I was raped but I feel some degree of guilt and regret for not coming out and saying "no." Although I know what the law states it makes the lines of definition seem so blurry, at least to me as the victim of a crime that was somewhat avoidable. At the same time I can't believe Kyle has caused me to second guess myself when he was the one that laced my drink with some chemical brew and took advantage of the after effect. Shit, I want to tell his wife the whole story but I can't trust her. I have no idea how she would react in light of her revealing that she thinks her husband would walk on water if it meant that doing so would prove his unfailing love for her gullible ass.

The funny thing is I felt she really cared about what I was feeling. I didn't feel a sexual vibe, only one of compassion and empathy. Something isn't right with her either. Although she spoke of Kyle as if he belonged high up on her pedestal, I know better than that. Some shit is foul and she's not the happiest woman as professed. Since that was the case I felt that I found the weakest link to destroy Kyle's life and free myself from this twisted mess: his lovely wife, Renee.

When I wipe my last tear I realize that Renee's no threat to me, it's that damn Kyle who I do believe would kill my ass without blinking twice. She's fronting about being the dominant sexaholic, but he's not. That man has another side that even Renee wouldn't want to see. She's the one missing the big picture. And for the record, my heart is heavy but not so heavy that I can't get a hold of my composure. Part of me letting Renee hold me like I need her comfort is an act to gain her trust. In time, I'll stab her in the back too. And when I do, I'll twist the knife around and around since she added fuel to the fire by causing me to slap her—giving Kyle more ammunition to blackmail me with. It's time to play this game by my rules. The fearless Jalita is back and ready to get this freaky party started.

26

THE COURT DATE

Malik

Our morning began with Monica cooking me a Southern breakfast and then washing the pile of dishes afterward. As part of her first phase of training for taking care of her man I explained that Southern women cook from scratch, clean without back talk, and keep the household running smoothly. Although she rolls her eyes when she does what she must to keep me around, the smell of freshly baked biscuits, smoked bacon, eggs, and grits fill my nostrils and makes me smile—until I take a bite of my scrambled eggs. "I don't eat eggshells, Monica," I complain.

When she answers, "Sorry, Malik," and scrambles fresh eggs for me I excuse her because the bags under her eyes tell me she's tired and still half asleep. After the sex I put on her, her bullshit tolerance level is much higher than usual. I'm shocked that she's singing and not complaining about someone in my family having the nerve to stick a joint in her pocket. She discovered it when we got home but didn't freak out. Instead, she mentioned it to me and said she'd secretly disposed of it. I had to do a double take. I would have never thought she'd keep her mouth shut after getting rid of the blunt that she was unknowingly transporting a couple hundred miles across state lines. But today I'm due to show up in court over that damn truck I returned. The dealership claims I didn't keep up on the payments—maybe I did, maybe I didn't. I'll never tell the truth about it. I hope the judge is a woman so I can turn on my charm. Hell, that always works, young, old, black, white, whatever. It doesn't matter. If they've got a pussy, I can sweet talk them and make a lie sound as a good as the truth. Since every woman has explored the thought of being fucked by a big black Mandingo type, I play into the stereotype that a strong, sexy, bald, and muscular man like me is hung like a horse, and can put it down under the sheets.

I lean my head back on the cloth car seat as Monica drives me to court in Rockville.

"I forgot to ask you something," she says out of the blue.

"What is it? I'm trying to rest."

"Who did you hire for this case?"

"My frat brother. The one you met."

"The coke head? You gave him a thousand dollars of my money! Malik, how could you?"

"You're always making something out of nothing, Monica. Here we go again," I complain.

"That's right, here we go again. I gave you that money to help pay for someone who was competent. He's probably too high to think straight. How could you rely on someone like him?"

"You don't know that."

"Oh come on, Malik! Your family members are potheads and your frat brother is a cokehead. Don't act like you don't you see the way he sniffs and twitches his nose and acts like he's bouncing of the walls. It's obvious that he needs to take a trip to detox or Cocaine Anonymous. Why are his eyeballs that red the first thing in the morning then? I don't mean once but every time we met him in his office. Last time you hired him he and his damn dilated pupils showed up when the judge had already called your case, remember? I don't like him and I think he's incompetent. Correction, I know he's incompetent. You use such poor judgment."

"He's my frat. He's looking out for a brother, Monica. Trust me—you don't worry about that. When you see me worry, you worry too. Other than that, everything is fine."

"I do worry about that when I gave you a thousand dollars of my money to buy vitamins and make a payment to him and here he comes walking in late. And we won't get started on how you wasted the rest of the money. He may be your frat brother but I guarantee that he doesn't give a shit about you as long as you fork over my money to him. I told you to budget that. You know how hard it was for me to make a grand?"

"What are you bitching about now? You switch so much I can't even follow what you're saying. Do you keep a running list of what to bitch over in order of your mood swings or something?"

"I don't know how much you spent on what. All I know is that you're doing a lot on my dime, including financing an eating out habit and bringing me long stem roses and a stuffed animal home. By the way, I've been meaning to ask you how in the hell can you spend *my* money to buy me a gift and expect me to be happy to receive it? I hear you told the florist about your contract and they expect you to come back and do all of this big business. Things you do get back to me, Malik. Why are you doing this shit in my hometown? You're going to ruin my reputation."

I roll my eyes and sigh loudly. "Not that again. I was trying to do something nice for you. Maybe I would have money if I wasn't using what people owe me to get your car fixed."

"And who is paying for this rental? Who is paying for the gas to get your big ass in front of the judge? Who will pay for parking? Me! Since I've met you I never get my hair done, I'm down to one pair of jeans, and I go around with an Aunt Jemima bandana scarf on my head because I don't have time to do it. I have them in all colors now to match what I wear. There's something wrong with that. I used to be fly when I met you. I dressed nice, kept my hair and nails done and always looked the part of a bad bitch. Now I'm always waiting on you. I know you're training but this shit is beyond ridiculous!"

"Monica, tell the truth. I told you get your nails and hair done."

"You did say that but you know saying it is bullshit. We can't afford it. Correction, *I* can't afford it. Taking care of your grown ass is expensive. You're always the one getting a manicure, pedicure and facial."

"A man needs that—especially one going in front of coaches, decision makers, and important people. It's about my image. You said so yourself, so stop twisting this shit all around to make me look bad," I say defensively.

"Let me tell you something brand new: Your ass should be concerned with your image when you jump into hot water. How about that?"

"I wouldn't be with you if I had my money, bitch! You're not the finest woman I've had! You're not even close!"

"Are you trying to tell me you don't appreciate what I've been doing for you? I know you didn't just say that crack, either."

"You heard what I said. I tell you what—"

"I dare you to say it, Malik."

"I can get any ho I want. I don't need you."

"Then why are you with me? I guess I'm just a convenience. They say that if you give someone a pair of shoes they'll walk away from you. Damn, I guess I should buy you some kicks so you can stay out of my life!"

"Don't bother—after I come out of court, it's over. Our relationship is a wrap!"

"Fine! I'd appreciate the favor! You're not the finest man I've dated either. You might have muscles and shit, but your attitude is so nasty that it makes you ugly as hell!"

"Whatever, Monica! I've got the touch, and you know and all these other bitches out here know it. I got the finest ho in D.C. chasing me right now. Fuck this. All this time I've spent with you, and I can't count the times I brought up marriage. I'm tired of kissing your ass. You'll have your wish—I don't care whose balls you suck, where you go, what you wear, how you feel, or none of that shit. Do what you want, Monica. All I ask is that you shut your mouth until we get to the court building and let me shut my eyes and finish meditating."

"Oh, so now you meditate? That's a laugh. As toxic and emotionally draining as you are you want to try to act like you're one with the universe—please! What's next, yoga?"

"What have I told you a thousand times about my blood pressure? Just shut up and drive. God, this bitch needs some Prozac!" I shut my eyes and mentally prepare for sitting my ass on a stand in front of a judge. Monica turns on the radio and ironically John Legend's hit single, *Used to Love U* begins to play. The bitch turns the volume up until the cheap speakers vibrate, just to work my nerves. It doesn't work though because John is singing everything I feel.

215

Andrea Blackstone

Although I couldn't admit it to Monica, I'm scared shitless. I spotted my probation officer talking to the truck company yet this woman hasn't said shit to me. I don't know what's going on but all I know is the scrawny blonde who I recall having bad coffee breathe is acting like she's on their side, not mine. I wouldn't even have this bitch nosing in my business, if my baby's momma hadn't reported me for giving her a reason to need four stitches above her right eye. Since the NFL has mandatory psychological evaluation for any player accused of a violent crime, I was subjected to a head examination, anger management, plus a legal watchdog. And people wonder why we prefer prostitutes to take care of business. Isn't it obvious? But now I've got a know it all on my hands. Monica's right— this shit has happened before although it didn't get this far. I try to take my mind off of my legal entanglement by listening to other people's problems that range from peeing in public to writing rubber checks.

My name is called after about five cases have been heard. I walk past the wooden benches and take a seat near the judge who's a white woman of about fifty years old. She has a chain hanging around her neck to hold her bifocals, and I feel her looking at me over the bridge of those coke bottles when I walk by. I hunch over in an effort to shrink my 6'2" frame and look less intimidating. This is one time I don't want to appear to be what I am, which is a big black man who looks like I fit the profile of someone who is guilty of everything society would say that I am. I don't know if I'm doing a good job of fronting or not but I did remember to wear my large twenty-four carat cross around my neck. I need all the help I can get—especially some divine intervention.

After the representatives for the truck company state their case and accuse me of not making the restitution payments, I feel my heartbeat pound just a little bit. I take a deep breath and hold it, trying my best to look calm.

"Did you send the payments in for the truck?" the judge asks, looking over at me.

As politely as I can I look her in the eye and humbly reply, "Your Honor, I did send the money when I was in Minnesota."

"In what form did you send it?"

"By money order, Your Honor. I purchased it from a United States Post Office in Minnesota and mailed it the same day."

"And on what street was the post office, Mr. Harrison?" she asks dryly.

"I'm sorry, Your Honor, I can't recall what the name of it was."

"Where's your proof of purchasing the money order? I would like to see it," the judge says, staring me directly in the face.

I hunch over a little more. "I lost it."

She turns away from me, grimaces, interlocks her fingers, and rests her elbows on her judge's bench. Then she clears her throat. "I don't believe you, Mr. Harrison."

"Your Honor, I mailed it. I don't know if it got lost in transition but I mailed it from Minnesota," I stress.

She shuffles some papers and silence falls over the courtroom. I grin slightly in an effort to look like a big, dumb, naïve dope but I don't think the judge is buying it.

She looks up and says, "In light of the facts that have been presented before me today I am ordering that Mr. Harrison be jailed for two weeks." I gasp. Then she adds, "He must also make restitution with interest to his debtor and will be on active probation for a period of two years. Bailiff, escort Mr. Harrison out of the courtroom. We'll take thirty minutes for a lunch break and resume at two o'clock." She bangs her gavel, then gets up and walks from the bench. When she disappears through wooden doors behind her seat and into her chambers, I feel my heart begin to race. I had no idea I could go to jail. I feel humiliated that I'm being handcuffed in front of Monica.

As I turn around so the two bailiffs can handcuff me, Monica runs up to the edge of the wooden wall that divides the seating area from where the cases are heard. Her voice shakes as she cries. "Oh my God! Where are you taking him? Malik! Malik! Where are you going?"

I continue looking straight ahead as I'm being lead out by two white men between five feet five and five seven. "Step back, ma'am. You're not authorized to come into this area."

I keep silent. I've gotten so close to Monica I don't have to look at her face to know she's crying and worried about the whole fiasco. As big as I am, I've never felt so small in all of my life—to have my girl go to pieces in front of people waiting for their turn to be heard. Shit, I guess whatever is whatever; it's done now and I can't take back not paying what I owed. Of all the dirt I've done this is the first time I've gone to jail for it.

27

CREEPING TO CREAM

Jalita

"Good morning," Renee tells me when I open my eyes. She has her legs crossed and is sitting across from me in a red wingback chair, nursing a cup of coffee.

"Hi," I answer sleepily. "How long have you been sitting here?"

She smiles. "Long enough to know that you have a thing for someone named Seth. You were calling his name over and over again."

"I was?" I ask with surprise.

Renee smirks. "Do you know a Seth?"

I try to sound blasé and reply, "Maybe so, maybe not. Ginger's personal life is not up for discussion."

"I rest my case. Just so you know it's just us again. Kyle called and he's stuck in New York because of the weather. They've already gotten five inches but I hope it doesn't break lose here today because I've got big plans. Did the Thera Flu I gave you in the wee hours help the congestion? Are you feeling better?"

"If you only knew—it's not just the cold."

"You know what you need? You need to learn how to let your hair down and be free. Having some fun would do you good."

"Fun is something that I'm not too well acquainted with these days. I told you I don't want to talk about it, Renee. I hope you understand."

"Well, if you want to keep things business, we'll keep it business. Your lesson for today is how to flip the script and play the game their way. That's my idea of fun and maybe you'll like it, too."

"Who says I need help in that department?"

"Look, I'm not talking about that weak time game you females run out in the street. You all think that if a man gives you a back rub and brings you flowers, you've got him trained and under control. My philosophy is the worse you treat a man the better he'll treat you. If you treat a bastard like a human being, he'll start smelling himself, trying to break bad. Then next thing you know you've got problems in your relationship and you get bulldozed. Bitchy women get what they want. Nice girls finish last, Ginger. My husband is scared to cross me because he knows I can get crazy." I look at Renee and am completely stunned at how wrapped up in this game she is.

"I'm hosting an on premises swinger party at a club today. During on premises events anything goes on the spot. There's no need to travel to a hotel room to hookup with a couple." I raise my eyebrows and grin while thinking of using this proposal to my advantage. "The whole reason I begged Kyle to find someone like you is because I'm stepping up the game with some wives in our swingers club. I hope I can trust you now because I'm about to tell and show you everything."

"You can trust me, Renee. I know you're horny as shit, and I'm doing my best to warm up to you and become your confidant. Hey, Kyle won't hear whatever from my lips," I lie.

"Good—I like the sound of that. Holding you last night was nice, something like good girlfriends who are close would do. Now you'd better hold on because I'm going to turn you out, Ginger. A woman has to be in the correct mental mindset before she has sex—men don't understand the art of seduction but I do. Now that the intimacy is over, it's time to get freaky with it and have a bad girl's bonding session. Men do it at titty bars and strip clubs, but I'll bring ours to us and have it served up on a platter. The club Kyle and I belong to is very exclusive. They adhere to guidelines provided by a national swing club association. Most of these clubs are for couples only. Membership requirements are strict and guest passes are few. Lately though some of the wives have been unhappy with the selection of beautiful people to sex, so I came up with an idea that's a secret amongst a handpicked population. Everyone involved tonight are hardcore swingers. We are sexual thrill-seekers who are open to doing anything with anyone, anywhere."

"I've never heard of anything like this but it sounds intriguing."

"There are more people in *the lifestyle* than you think. The thing is it's a hush-hush thing because everyone is at least middle class, some are upper class, and we all fear judgment or consequences if confidential membership information leaks out. None of the husbands and partners of the wives in my swinging club know about the theme night called *cream*. Tonight there's no committed couples only rule, and you don't have to bring someone of the opposite sex. The women can bring whomever they want to this event so long as he or she is very attractive, but each will be responsible for how her guest behaves. Everyone will be free to have sex at the event as opposed to hooking up and going home with a couple or paying for a hotel room. In fact, it will be encouraged. Bringing tickets, those not intending to have sex, will lead to a woman getting banned from any future adventures. Pre-registration and picture submissions were required to get on the list, so everyone who is grown and sexy is sure to have a nice time."

Although I'm thinking that swinging is a confusing thing because I thought it was some sort of way for couples to explore having sex without cheating on each other, I don't bring this point up to Renee. Instead, I comment, "I guess I can't come with you then, Renee. You don't have a picture of me."

She places her coffee cup down on a light tan coaster and explains, "Ginger, let me fill you in on something—*you're* part of the entertainment. Why don't you sleep a little longer because it's going to be a long night. I'll wake you up soon enough."

I don't know what Renee means by those three words but I'm not quite ready to ask. Renee and her horny friends may know exactly what they're in for tonight, but I don't. If I have a chance to get paid I won't slap Renee this time. I'll at least find out if doing what is requested of me is worth it first, even if I keep getting set up over and over again. But before the curtain falls on the scene I say, "Renee?"

"What is it?"

"Be careful what you ask for because you just may get it."

28

PLAYING DIRTY AFTER DARK

Malik

While I'm getting three hots and a cot at the Montgomery County jail, I learn that Wes has finally been officially declared missing after he didn't show up for another Blitzer's game. I also hear that two thousand twenty people have died in the tsunami disaster so far, and that the movie *Ray* received seven nominations for the NAACP Image Award. Although Wes was my flesh and blood I don't tell anyone when they remark that he and I favor a bit. Shit, I don't want to draw any attention to myself. I'll stay in the backdrop until someone spots what's left of my nasty, selfish twin. I'm hoping it won't take too long though. Had he not turned his back on me and helped his brother I wouldn't be in jail because this fucking truck would be paid for. I wouldn't be shitting out in the open where everyone can see me, nor would I have forged his name on insurance policy papers and staged what went down. But that's irrelevant now 'cause I'm not stressing. I have no guilt or regrets.

Although I hope my girl is smart enough to cover for me on the home front, I pass on calling Monica the whole week. I have a good reason. I don't want to blow my image by calling collect from jail on the chance that her brother or father answers the phone. Instead I call my homely standby—a woman who wants to have me but I'll never give her the time of day. Anything I need she'll handle it until I get out. I don't care if she has to walk, fly, or swim to do it as long as she gets things done. It's not my fault she doesn't have a car, it's hers—just see to it that I get it.

Jail wasn't but so bad because once I turned on my charm and everyone got wind of me going back to the NFL I had my own space, more helpings of food than I was supposed to get, and as many phone calls as the guards could sneak and let me make. It's more of a damn vacation than a punishment, now that I think of it. I have met some scary mothers in here, but even the guy who killed a little girl keeps trying to convince me that he's not a bad guy. I'm sort of like a hero or something. In fact, I only end up serving one week of time as opposed to two, but the probation issue still sticks.

At the end of my week I have someone drop me off at Monica's father's house with my son. I know that Monica can't deny me entry if a kid is in the mix, and figure I'll take full advantage of his rare visit. I had to hear his mother bitch for me not getting him more often, but I don't intend on going through that for at least another twelve months.

Monica answers the door but doesn't act happy to see me. Her eyes look like she's been crying a lot. After I get into the house I tell my son to sit down in the living room, turn on the TV for him, and dare him to move. I go up to Monica's room but my girl acts nervous and preoccupied like she's walking on eggshells with me.

"Aren't you going to speak to your nigga?"

"Why? You said we broke up. What are you doing here? I thought you'd be in jail for two weeks."

"I live here, Monica. What happened between you and I is a separate issue. Dad isn't going to kick me out. And as far as the other thing I got out early. You know me."

"It's not a good idea for you to be here if you left me. Is that your son that you told me about? If he belongs to you or anyone else, he shouldn't be in the middle of this either. What were you thinking of bringing a kid here?"

"Baby, you know I was just shooting off my mouth. I had this magazine in jail and I jacked off thinking about you because there was a girl in there that looked like you. I thought about that beautiful face of yours and those hairy legs. I'm sorry and I want to make up. C'mon, let's fuck and make up. I want another baby but I want to have one with you. My son needs to meet his stepmother because we're going to be a family." I touch her face and kiss her lips. She moves away from me and yanks her elbow away.

"I know you're mad but show big daddy those hairy legs, Monica." I reach down below her mini skirt and run my hands across her big legs. "Why in the fuck did you shave your legs? You know I like that!" I shout.

Monica pulls down her skirt and pulls her body away from me again. She crosses her arms and turns her back toward me. That's when I finally realize that her hair is done and she's sporting a nice green mini skirt and a tight lycra top. Her toes are painted pink and her feet look as smooth as a baby's bottom. Monica looks like she used to, and now I'm suspicious of her behavior.

"Some woman called me and said she wanted to warn me about you. She said she was paying for your cell phone and you didn't pay her for the bills. She's been calling everyone on the bill to warn them about what you've been doing around town," she says coolly.

"And you listened to that? Why didn't you hang up?"

"If that weren't true how did she get my number? She said she got it from her cell phone bill that you didn't pay, and I believe the woman. When will this stop? When will you stop asking people for favors?"

"Will you turn the fuck around?" I snap. Monica turns around and lowers her head like she's staring at her pink toenails, then looks away like she can't bear to look me in the eye. "I just got back here. Would you shut up? Shortie, I'm not trying to go here with you today. You won't let me touch you. You're acting funny and then you go and shave those sexy hairy legs. Something isn't right here and I want to get to the bottom of it."

"Malik, you've been to jail and you haven't changed. It doesn't sound like it taught you anything."

"Shut up! I swear you need Prozac for your ass! All you do is nag."

"Oh yeah, well me and my Prozac needing ass slept with someone," she blurts out, finally looking up at me.

"You slept with someone when I was in jail!"

"I'm not attracted to men behind bars. Who gets off on having a damn prison romance? I'm a college-educated woman, Malik. I

224

don't play that shit. I'm not your slave, maid, banker, or cook. I'm just a black woman who wants to be loved by a man, not a damned boy in a man's body! All you do is insult me. You told me to get with someone else—maybe I messed up, but I did it. Now you know."

"Wait, wait, wait. This doesn't make sense." I shake my head. "How could you do this to me—no, to us? This is the worst thing that ever happened to me except my grandmother dying. I never cheated on you, Monica. Never! Who was it? That nigga from the club? Who'd you fuck?"

Tears begin to form in Monica's eyes. She drops her arms. "I'm sorry Malik, but you made me do it."

"I was gone one week and you jump in bed with another man? You must've known him all along. My sister wouldn't even do that and she's a stripper!"

"How about why I did it? Does that count for anything? You didn't even call to tell me you were all right. None of this would have happened if you would've treated me right—we'd be married by now. I got tired of paying your bills, supplying you with Q-tips, toilet paper, soap, plane tickets, and whatever else. I wanted to be with a real man who can do more than sling his dick to divert my attention from what really matters. I was trying to get you out of my system." She wipes her tears with her right hand. Her whole face is red as a beet.

I turn my back to her, bend my right arm, and lean my head against the wall. I feel so weakened by Monica's low blow that I can barely stand. "I'm going to fuck you tonight then I don't ever want to see you again, you whore," I mumble. "I'm calling your mother and tell her what you did. Worried about me? Right. So worried you were getting dicked down behind my back."

Monica runs over to me and clings to the back of my body. "No, no. Don't do that!" she whines. "Don't call my mom!"

"Fuck me then. Just make love to me one last time so I can get over you. I don't want to talk, I don't want to debate. Monica, you really hurt me by doing this and you know it."

"If I were a bonafide whore like you said, I would've had all of the dollars to retrieve my car from the dealer! While your irresponsible ass was in jail a letter came stating that they were

225

about to auction it off because the check from the man whose ass you whipped for the plasma screen TV bounced. I thought you'd be smarter than to give the dealership a check from someone like him. I was mad after sitting in court with you and hearing people go to jail for rubber checks in addition to what you were there for. All you do is lie, lie, lie. That was two grand my dad had to pay! You can't imagine how I felt that you embarrassed me and almost caused me to lose my car. Now I owe him and had to sign an IOU to prove I wouldn't forget to do it. So obviously, you had it coming. I just wasn't happy anymore," she screams.

I lift my head from the wall. As I feel a tear drip down my warm cheek I walk across the room and say, "Oh, so this is about payback?"

"No it's not. I'm just letting you know I have feelings, too. I've brought a lot to the table to make this relationship work. For every time I come through for you, you let me down. I need someone I can depend on and you haven't proven that is you."

"If you wanted a way to hurt me, you did it. I had one day to get your raggedy piece of tin with four wheels out. You and your father overreacted about that," I comment, sitting on her bed.

"*Overreacted?* That shit goes on credit reports in addition to everything else." Monica points at me. "I hate you! You never acknowledge the part you play in these disasters of yours."

"The only disaster is my girl sleeping with someone else. Shut up! Get on the floor and open your legs. If you're going to carry yourself like a whore I'll treat you like one." I hop up off the bed and push her. "Stop crying. Shut up! She slept with someone. The bitch slept with someone. I can't believe it!"

I thrust myself inside of Monica. While I'm pounding my dick hard enough to make it painful, I ask questions about who she cheated on me with, and where this sucker lives. Monica slipped and told me—shortly thereafter we all were off to pay someone named Ted a visit in the infamous car that just made it back to sit in the driveway.

29

THE SECRET PASSION PALACE

Jalita

A line of people anxiously await their turn to present their membership card and ID, and to pay the thirty five dollar event fee to enter the swingers' party sponsored by Renee. From what I could gather their ages ranged from the twenties to the early fifties, although the bulk of the partygoers were about late thirties to early forties.

When Renee and I made out who was inside I immediately noticed a white woman wearing a short, see through gown and garter belt, whispering to the man sitting next to her. Minus one female that looked as if she'd been smacked with a frying pan in her posterior, mostly every woman my eyes could find looked sexually desirable, even if their shapes weren't perfect. The men wore dress slacks and sport shirts, but all the sisters, who were of various ethnicities, were adorned in sensuous outfits that ranged from skintight to trendy, and the outright seductive. I suddenly understood why Renee insisted that I wear a lace push up bra to accentuate my full breasts, and a g-string with a chained design in front and a cut in back that exposed my well-rounded cheeks. Renee wore a long zebra print robe, matching thong, and four inch heels with a small fake jewel woven into the knotted design in the middle of each shoe's elastic lace. The sleeves of her robe were trimmed in big black ostrich feathers, and the front is held shut by a tied bow. Her physique is proof that all black women aren't built to make babies and shake junk in our trunks, but she still looked like a sexy and classy host that would have an event for the grown and sexy.

As we walk around Renee explains that this adult playground consists of three levels and that each room is used for something different. Then she halts and drops me off at some seminar location where I learn the rules and what to expect of this experience.

After my briefing I am pulled further into the subliminal messages of the sexy environment. An assortment of colored aromatherapy candles release pleasant smells as people wander around in semi-darkness, mingling and introducing themselves in the living room area. Some sit in a place called the chill out zone and indulge in ice-breaking question games, while others circulate with flutes of champagne, Smirnoff, wine, fruity drinks, or other assorted spirits that they picked up from a full service cash bar.

A marble staircase leads to more theme rooms. I learned in *orientation* that the group room can be used for foreplay with other partners, to include oral sex, but never vaginal penetration. This type of setup is appropriate for newcomers who are exploring the swinger world but may not quite be ready for partner swapping or more than flirting with others. Either way, bowls full of condoms are placed in each room of the pleasure palace.

By eleven o'clock I can tell it won't be long before mostly everyone is ready to connect for no-strings fun. It's also obvious that the women are definitely not there to fulfill their husband's fantasies, but their own.

As the living rooms begin to empty Renee grows a switch in her narrow runway model hips. "Work that pole over there," she leans over to me and whispers. "I know you've got it in you. Spice up the party for me, Ginger. There will be something in it for you later if you do."

I look at the small wooden platform and step up on it with little trepidation. Swinging around the pole turns out to be fun since I've always loved to dance and show off my body. Each time I slowly bend my legs and push along with the centrifugal force. When I stop, I inch my way down from the top. I even caught on how to arch my back and grip the pole like a professional stripper. Stares began to increase and somewhere along the way someone walks up to the edge of the platform and touches my shoulder when my back is turned. When I face the man he smiles and gently leads

me toward a crowded dance floor where a slow song begins. I'm
sandwiched between him and an older woman, and they rub up
against my front and back. As slutty as it sounds I enjoy the
attention and warmth of the couple who are trying to claim me. In
the midst of it all the man's clothes come off. His muscular arms
are the color of Hershey's syrup. After the woman steps out of her
lavender bikinis, her date begins fondling my ass cheeks while she
gently strokes my womanhood. Renee observes me touching and
caressing them back and pushes her way through the crowd to
break up the anonymous encounter before they disappear with
me.

Although Renee told me to keep the good times flowing in the
room I can tell she feels a slight twinge of jealousy that I'm getting
so much attention. Now she feels the need to compete for my time
and make it known that I'm her guest. She grabs my wrists. "Have
you ever shared your body with another woman, Ginger?"

"No," I answer. I didn't want to explain that I had been licked
against my will once by another woman. I decide to leave Wes's
ploy to turn our arrangement into a threesome out.

"Then share it with me if you feel I can earn you."

As I follow her to the bar Renee's hips resume the sexy sway
that I'd observed earlier. She whispers something in the
bartender's ear while massaging my shoulders, stopping to apply
extra pressure in the middle where I'm slightly tense. Renee works
her way down my arms, kisses me on the neck, then softly says,
"Get up on the bar and lay down."

Without protesting I do what I'm told, laying flat on my back
and dropping my chin onto my folded arms. A cool feeling
overcomes me and I soon discover Renee swirling whip cream on
my breasts and stomach. Another woman hops up on the bar. A
man copies Renee, putting whip cream on the woman's buttocks,
working his way down her legs and slightly stroking her anus. The
woman that looked to be married with four kids faced me, as did
the good looking man. The freedom of being nude and watching
the stranger receive similar attention was incredibly erotic.

"I've been wanting to lick you from the day I laid eyes on you,"
Renee murmurs. "Now that I've made you into a human sundae

Andrea Blackstone

I'm going to—"she stops to flick her tongue across my stomach—
then continues, "get my wish."

Next I feel a row of tongues follow suit, and tingles shoot through
my body. I must admit that Renee's oral skills are definitely up to
par and I forget that the tongue that is delivering me such physical
bliss belongs to a woman. Soft moans escape my lips, and when I
tilt my head back slightly I notice several people watching us from
one of the observation cubby-holes that are above. After a while
longer I am dripping with excitement. I noticed that the other
woman on the bar being licked is now spread eagle, pushing her
pussy in her partner's mouth.

Renee grabs my hand and helps me regain my balance. After I
hop down from the bar I looked around for my clothes. "You can
get those later. Hold that other thought where you've got it and
come with me."

With my nipples standing at attention and moistness flowing
between my legs, Renee leads me to a room that is dimly lit by a
chandelier. Inside I observe two women tonguing each other with
a man underneath. They're lying on four queen-sized beds that are
pushed together to make one large orgy bed sitting smack dab in
the middle of the room. Next to them is a couple. The woman is
taking her partner's penis in her mouth and she looks sexy giving
him pleasure.

Renee and I stood near the edge of the bed. "Let's masturbate
together," I say.

I know that my suggestion arouses her when she quickly peels
off her robe and finds a spot for us on the large bed. She quickly
begins pleasuring herself, waiting for me to catch up with her. I lie
down next to her and stroke my clit. "Look at us in the mirrors.
We're surrounded by them."

Although Renee and I are busy creating a moaning rhythm
someone comes up behind me and begins sucking on my breasts.
As the reflection of a third woman catches my eye through the
mirror, Renee stops pleasuring herself and makes it known that
she doesn't like the intrusion. "It's time to go to a *private* room,"
she says with disgust in her voice. Then she jokes, "What do I
have to do, tie you to my bed frame at home, blindfold you, and
use you for my pleasure? Everyone here wants to seduce you."

230

As I follow Renee we pass a woman who is making a man suck on her stiletto heels. He's begging to have sex with her as if she's the only woman to screw at the event. We walk a few rooms away and enter a private exhibition room with a double bed and white sheets. Renee pushes me backward onto the bed and lies down on top of me, kissing my lips and using her tongue to tease my mouth. When she stops she asks, "May I go downtown now? I promise I'll be gentle with you."

Without wasting words, I gently tell her, "Get up, Renee."

Half-confused and half afraid that I might reject her Renee's face begins to lose its glow until I say, "You've done all the giving, how about receiving for a change?" Regaining control of the situation I carefully slide my tongue into her mouth and begin sensually moving my hips on top of her vagina.

Renee moans softly. "Don't think I haven't observed that your husband doesn't know how to treat a sophisticated woman like you. Don't worry about him though because Ginger is going to turn you out. You started this game by getting me to take your living arrangement seriously tonight, and I'm about to finish it." I slide down to her middle and lick her button a few times. "Kyle doesn't treat you right—I've noticed how he neglects you. We'll get his ass back for not being the husband he should be by giving you all of the pleasure you deserve. Won't we?" When Renee doesn't answer but continues to moan I grind my vagina into hers with intense pressure and repeat, "Won't we?"

Sexy sounds pour from the other side of the wall as Renee shakes from having an orgasm. "Yes! Yes! Yes—we will!" she screams.

With the passion in Renee's voice I know the ball is back in my court. Shit, now I know Kyle won't lay one damn hand on my body, and now the real party's about to get started. In addition to that I'm about to get paid for wrecking Kyle's marriage.

30

PAYBACK'S A BITCH

Malik

I am super pissed off that my girl Monica has the balls to screw someone else and tell me about it after supposedly feeling guilty. I drive fast and recklessly the whole way. When we get there I grab Monica by the arm, roll up to the nigga's step, and bang on his door nearly forgetting to throw the car into park. I tell my son to wait in the car while I begin to deliver a little payback to Monica.

A woman asks, "Yes, may help you?" She's wearing an oversized Million Man March T-shirt, a faded pair of black straight leg jeans, and a pair of bent up tennis shoes. She's holding a broom and I assume I interrupted her from sweeping.

"I want to speak to Ted. Where is he?"

"He's not here. Is this about a car repair? If it is he should be at the shop. Try there."

"The *shop*?" I say, flaring my nostrils, feeling my blood pressure rise.

"You know, over at the garage," she says as if I should know.

"Bitch, did I say I was here for that? My girl has something I'm sure you'd like to know. And I want to see what this motherfucker looks like, too!"

"I didn't know he was married," Monica rambles. Tears drop from her eyes when she sees children milling around in the background.

The woman places her free hand on her hip, rears back her string bean-like body and says, "My man slept with *you*?"

"I'm sorry. He never mentioned he was married. I swear to you. I didn't know!"

"Ted's married all right, with four kids and a dog. I should whip your skank ass, you yellow bitch!" she yells. She opens the screen door and starts to beat Monica with the broom.

I shove Monica out of the way and step in front of her. By this time she's sobbing loudly and never bothers to try to hit the woman back. All four of the children come to the door and stand behind their mother. Two look to be teenagers, one is pre-school age, and the last is still in pampers, drooling on the carpet.

"You need to let me whip Ted's ass for fooling my girl," I say, grabbing the broom. Then I snap the handle of it in half. I glare at Monica. "How do you cheat on me with a mechanic? A greasy, dirt under his nails son-of-a bitch like that, huh? Now you see for yourself that no man will ever love you like me. All they'll do is lie and fuck your brains out like a common whore. You don't know shit—you can't do shit right. You're nothing, Monica. I made you, and you've proven you can't make it on your own unless I think for you. You have no common sense to survive out here. Maybe now you can be thankful for who you've got, and maybe you can finally see that I'm not that bad after all! Now let's roll!" I'm so pissed I feel spit flying from my mouth as I speak.

I throw down the pieces from the broom. Monica doesn't say a word; she just continues to cry as her face reddens. She hangs her head low and follows me as the woman and her children throw insults her way as if Ted did no wrong, as if Monica forced him to have sex with her. As we approach the edge of their yard and fade into darkness I turn around and notice that his wife and the children have left the doorway. Through the screen door I see her picking up the phone, no doubt to ask Ted if he was creeping with a young redbone named Monica. I yank Monica by her coat collar and we take our last trip—Ted's place of employment. I was hell bent on slashing all of his tires and letting Monica know that cheating is a man's game, not a woman's.

When we arrive at the garage I don't see this Ted. I'm sure his punk-ass is hiding when I call his name around the shop building and bang on the front door. The lights are on, but no Ted ever shows his face. Since he isn't man enough to come out I park the truck across the street and find a pay phone to call 911 and report a fire at the coward's work address. I return to the car and call

Monica everything in the book but a child of God while we wait for the emergency vehicles to arrive. After they pull up to investigate the supposed blaze a man comes running out with a look of distress on his face. I know it's Ted, and plan to get even after the police car and fire truck pull off. When they leave I yank Monica by the collar and head toward Ted before he can hide inside of his shop.

As he tries to cross the street to get away I punch him in the back of the head and push him toward the privacy of a closed door. Once the three of us make it inside I say, "Since she wants to act like a whore, I'll treat her like one in front of you." I snatch my belt buckle open. "You tell this nigga that you're my bitch."

"I'm his bitch," Monica says, still crying."

"Tell your friend that this is the only dick you fuck and suck."

Monica's voice shakes and she repeats, "This is the only dick I fuck and suck."

"Drop to your knees and suck it right now. And look me in the eye when you do it!" Monica does what I tell her in between sniffling. "Shut up your damn noise!" When she gets quiet I tell her to stay on her knees but stop sucking me off. I shove my dick back in my pants just as it begins to harden. "This punk ass don't even defend you. Do you see that, Monica? I told you all you were to him was a fuck, but I'm the one that loves you. Stand the fuck up, girl!"

I swing toward Ted's head and knock him to the ground. As I beat him to a pulp Monica screams, "Stop! You're going to kill him! Stop it!"

"I told you I'm not to be played with. You keep putting me through this shit." When blood begins to pour from Ted's nose I kick him in the side. "Keep your mouth shut, you pussy. Now crawl home to your wife, four kids, and mangy dog."

Monica and I leave him struggling to crawl. He's hurt but not hardly dead. If I had my way I would've killed him, but then again Monica isn't worth causing me to go back to jail for a murder charge. Instead, after my tirade ends I call Monica's mother and my cousin in Winchester. I tell her mother how she cheated on me, and I tell my cousin if any bitches come looking for me down there to tell them I'm a single, free man. Then I call my frat and tell them the same thing. I awaken at least three of my sorority sisters and make dates with each one in Monica's face as she cries. I even go through my book bag looking for numbers and leave messages for return calls, including the waitress at the restaurant. No matter how you slice it all women are freaks and hos, and all men are players, retired players, someone's daddy creeping after dark, pimps, or hustlers. My son slipped out of the car and saw everything but I don't regret it. That's life and he may as well learn these streets like the back of his hand while he's good and young.

31

TWO DOUBLE LIVES

Jalita

As I lay the groundwork to turn Renee out at the event I ask her one question after the crowd begins to disband at the swingers' event. "Do you have a secret fantasy? Something you've been dreaming about doing but have never tried?" The response she gives me leads to three strippers trailing behind us back to Renee's house.

"Remember this is our little secret, Ginger," she says when she turns the car engine off.

I stroke Renee's face. "We slept together. Do you think I go around having sex with just anyone?"

"Of course not," she replies.

I drop my hand. "Don't ever question my loyalty to you ever again, Renee. I think we can make each other very happy. Now let's keep things light. You have three horny men waiting to get you off."

She laughs and prepares for the second round of her festivities. "Oh, I almost forgot. Here's a little something for you, Ginger, compliments of the club members." Renee hands me a stack of money. I don't want to be too obvious that I'm money hungry so I don't count it. She looks at me and smiles. "You earned every bit of the five-thousand dollars. You were great. I could really get used to this. Thank you for your loyalty and friendship."

When each of us make it inside of the house I'm thinking that I don't know what kind of libido the woman has because she still wants to get her freak on after hours and hours of cumming with me, even though it's pushing 3:00 a.m. She didn't infringe on anyone's territory by bringing the three strippers home because they were also paid entertainment and didn't come to the event with anyone in particular.

"There's something I've never done before that I may want to do," she tells them once we're all inside.

"What's that?" one of them asks.

Renee unfastens his belt, pushes him against the wall like an aggressive man, yanks on his pants, and starts sucking his penis like she's a sex-crazed maniac. The Latino man helps her to remove her clothes while the brother kisses her breasts and teases her nipples with flicks of the tongue.

"I want to finish things off by getting gang banged," she blurts out. "In all the years I've been swinging I've never had the pleasure. If you three men can't do that for me you need to leave right now. Now will you all be staying or going?"

Before I can blink the white stripper stretches Renee's arms over her head and the Latino and black one take turns moving between her thighs, licking on Renee like she's a human lollipop. Since Renee is paying them an additional thousand dollars a piece they're more than happy to help her with her little fantasy.

Renee's hormones start getting stirred up. "That's Ginger over there," she says. "You don't mind if my girlfriend watches do you?"

"We don't mind," says the white one, looking at me with heavy lust in his green eyes. He turns around and rubs Renee's clit. I watch her squirm and laugh like she's enjoying the foreplay.

I walk over the bed and stroke my breasts. "You know, the four of you are making me hot, too. Who knows where this could lead if we all had some wine. Renee, would you and your guests mind if we all loosened up a bit more?"

"You and me sharing dicks? I like the sound of that, Ginger—now you're talking. Go downstairs and you'll see the bar off of the dining area. Pour us some drinks and let's see if we can make that happen."

The black stripper begins to kiss Renee. I stuff my breasts back into my shirt and leave the room to go fix our drinks. Little do they know I'm taking a page from Kyle's book of fucking people up so their judgment is off. The only difference is I'm not doing it to fuck anyone, just to take a self-guided tour in my new temporary spot. While they sip on wine, I'll sip on something else. If Renee doesn't have any purple colored grape juice around I'll water down the color and say I made a mixed drink for myself. Otherwise, I'll come up with something similar.

When I return after making two trips, I say, "I could only bring two drinks at a time but I'll be right back." I wink and set down the two Mikasa flutes on coasters on the nightstand on the right hand side of the bed. My plan will be easier than I thought since they are so heavily colored that you can't see what's inside of them.

After I see that Renee has no grape juice in the house I take my time pouring a half a flute of Deer Park water, hoping the wine I poured is starting to sedate the sex fiends. When I walk into the bedroom I hear Renee moaning like the stranger is her husband.

"Now that everyone has some liquor, bottoms up everyone. Don't be shy. Grab a glass if you're empty handed."

Renee grabs her flute. "Let's make a toast." Each of the men picks up a flute. "To all the hot fucking we can handle while my husband is out of town," she says. They clink glasses, drink, and continue to flirt. After sipping the liquor, Renee adds, "Hey, gentleman. Let me give my husband a good wee early morning kiss. Keep it down but start licking on this." While Renee is getting serviced by a few of her paid *suitors* she dials a number on the phone and with slurred speech she says, "Yeah, Kyle. Mmmm. Guess what? That little hot girl you hooked me up with is licking the hell out of my pussy. I just wanted you to know that you chose well." After she hangs the phone up she says, "See, he don't have noooo idea I'm getting my shaved coochie licked and dicked by three strippers! I just held out on my husband for three years. Ginger inspired me to give it up to him and go back to swinging though, and now we've gone back to our rule to discuss and mutually agree on what we do, but shit, I do what I want to do whenever because I can. Two can play this game!"

The liquor sets in a bit more and the two men laugh with her. By this time Renee is sucking off the Latin stripper while the black one pounds her from behind, and the white one licks her clit from underneath. Then they change positions. "You're my kind of woman, baby," the black one says in a deep, booming voice. "You're fucking crazy!"

238

"No, I'm delicious and crazy," Renee corrects him with a laugh. "That's why I can handle so many dicks at once. If you haven't noticed, all my holes are full and I'm not even sweatin'!"

When she finishes her speech I notice that not one penis is wrapped up with a condom, so I suggest that I help my girl out and get her condoms for her. After she tells me where her stash is hidden I open the package and notice that the head of the condom is spiral shaped. I hand the first one to one man and open two more.

"Thanks, Ginger. The last thing I need is to get pregnant and have to explain why my baby didn't come out looking like my husband. You just don't know what you've been missing, Ginger. These InSpiral condoms are the bomb, and the others in the Pleasure Condom Sampler are off the hook too. Get in bed with us. C'mon, girlfriend, c'mon."

"In a little while, Renee. You wore me out at the event," I lie. "Have fun. You have my permission now." I kiss her on the lips and walk away.

When I see they're into their gangbang fest, and the conversation has progressed to talk of hot candle wax dripped on Renee's naked body, I roll my eyes and slip away to do a little fast browsing around the crib. I enter Renee's office and my heart begins to pound. I don't know what I'm going to do when I get online but I'll seize the opportunity to gain access while I can. An idea flashes through my mind and I have an epiphany: do a good quick search of the D.C. or Maryland sex offender registry and see if Kyle's mug pops up for my viewing pleasure. When I make it to the website I see a button to click for online registry listings. Just as I click it and begin to read about entering a zip code I hear Renee calling me.

"Ginger, baby. Come in here. Mmm. I want to train you how to enjoy taking two men at the same time. Ginger, don't be shy. Shit, bring me some Vaseline so I can get banged in the ass while being fucked in my mouth. I'm in that kind of mood and I want you to watch," she moans.

Trying to hurry, I mumble, "Shit, what's the zip code here?" Since I don't know it I hit a brick wall and I'm wasting time when I could be accessing information on the website. I am so close to investigating Kyle, but I can't risk Renee stumbling her horny ass around searching for me, and then giving a bad report to her psycho husband. I take a chance that she's not the type to look at the cookies in her computer log, turn the speaker volume back up, and walk back toward the bedroom. I figure I'll grab the dildo she showed me and help get her off so she can take her ass to bed, asleep in the arms of three well hung pieces of eye candy.

$

The next morning after Renee's gangbang extravaganza ceased, the alcoholic nymphos are knocked out like lights. They polished off one bottle of wine and one bottle of vodka, thanks to me. While they're all asleep I hear the phone ring in Kyle's office but not Renee's. This tells me they have separate lines, so I tip downstairs and listen as I hear someone leave a message.

"Good morning, this is Deborah with the law office of Forrester and Garrison. It's urgent that I speak with Bernard Williams, as soon as possible. My number is 1-800-303-0340. You'll need this reference number: 6851121. This matter is urgent. Please call me as soon as you receive this message. Thank you."

I look all around me and there's still no sign of movement from anyone upstairs so I call back and lie, saying I am the wife of Bernard Williams.

"Yes, what is your reference number please?" the woman asks.

"The reference number is 6851121."

"Bernard Williams?"

"I'm his wife and he's out of town. I'd like to confirm this message is for Bernard Williams and this isn't some sort of mistaken call that was meant for someone else."

"This message was intended for him, Mrs. Williams."

"May I ask what this is regarding?" I ask, trying to sound the part of the mature wife.

The woman sounds like a recording when she tells me, "This is an attempt to collect a debt. Any information obtained will be used for that purpose."

I cut her off. "Thank you—I'll give him the message. I guess he's at it overspending again. Wait until I get my hands on his ass."

I find it so interesting that Kyle has another ID and has some sort of scam in the mix that I am eager to solve this mystery and bust his balls open wide, even more than before. This may be the open door that I was searching for. If he's going to play dirty, so can *Ginger*. Next chance I have, I'll be back on the net doing some homework. Shit, as usual I've gotten sidetracked like I don't have anything better to do with my life than to crack this crazy code. But, for the time being, I'll do what I have to do.

A short time later I walk back upstairs to see if Renee and her part-time lovers are finished sleeping the liquor off.

"Good morning, Ginger. Turn on the TV, would you? Damn, what time is it? Shit, I have a hang over like you wouldn't believe. I don't remember too much of what happened when we got in."

I ignore her question about the time and turn on the TV. We find out that while the threesome was in full force, homeless men were encouraged to get off the grates in the city, people had been warned to bring their pets indoors, and now those who won't listen and stay off the streets are slipping and sliding all over the roads having serious accidents. Renee pushes herself to the edge of the bed, slips on a red silk robe, and looks out of the window. Her hair is matted in the back from sweating while she was fucking, and it looks like a dry rat's nest. She looks so funky that I bet she has some kicking morning breath.

"We have to get rid of these strippers. They can't stay here," she says nervously.

"Renee, they're snowed in. Kyle won't find out. If they're snowed in, he's snowed out. When they wake up have them bathe you and have some more fun. There's nothing moving, flying, or driving outside whether you like it or not. I'll keep an eye out on the weather but you need to stay calm. You pulled off that great event and it brought us closer together. Don't wreck the moment."

"Thanks, Ginger. You're right. I need to relax. You're so good for me."

"Go back to bed a while. When the time comes I'll cook breakfast and straighten up things to look like there hasn't been shit going on, Renee." I hug her and rub her shoulders up and down with reassurance. When I help her find her way to her pillow I notice she's stumbling.

Once I'm sure she's sleeping I'll get back to doing my dirt. Earlier this morning I snagged her credit card from her purse. Soon I'll sneak back into her office and use it to dig up some dirt on the *other* person's double life. I also grabbed her mini tape recorder and hid it under her bed. I'm not playing—Jalita's in this game for revenge.

$

I enter the computer room to sign on and dig up more details about Kyle. I turn the volume down and sign online again. After I'm connected I type in the words, investigate anyone. After I do I click on one of the top ranked websites, netdetective.com. My heart begins to thump as I type in Renee's credit card information to order an instant background check. While I'm waiting for the information to return I peek out of the door to make sure Renee is still soaking the filth from her skin and playing fantasy island games with the strippers. Since she is, I read the results. My eyes widen as I read the string of skeletons that hop out of Mr. Kyle's closet. My jaw drops open and I cover my mouth with my right hand as my eyes scan words like: three known aliases, embezzlement, and police officer relieved of duties. The kicker comes when the words *unsolved murder* falls under my eyeballs. Apparently Kyle's first wife was murdered and the police never solved the case.

I gulp hard and print the information that I can't believe I'm reading. I grab it from the printer, sign off, and then frantically search for a place to hide the document after bolting into the hallway. Something tells me to look to the left of a half bath and I follow my instincts. My legs begin to shake and my palms begin to sweat. I climb another staircase that spirals and leads me to a dark, lowly lit attic with light coming from around louvers. It's so dark I can barely see my hand in front of my face. I pull cobwebs from around my face and nearly scream when I feel the scratch of a small mouse's claws touch my skin as it runs across my bare foot. I gasp and cover my mouth to keep from screaming. I find an old broom and navigate around the area with the handle portion of it. When I find a long string hanging from the ceiling I uncover my mouth and pull it but discover that no bulb has been screwed into the ceiling. I curse softly and continue tipping around even though I am afraid and feel extra vulnerable because I can barely see. I keep poking around with the broom handle and finally knock over something that turns out to be a long flashlight. When I turn it on it illuminates a portion of the room.

I shine the flashlight around the room and stop at an old blue trunk lined in gold colored trim. I bend over and discover that an old brown rusty padlock is secured to the trunk. My heart begins to pound again as I look around for a tool to break the lock without making too much noise. In the far corner I find an old hacksaw with rusty teeth. I pick it up but decide to keep looking for something else because if I used it to cut the lock off the noise would carry. A couple of minutes later I find a bolt cutter in the corner, in a box of tools. It's so dusty I almost overlook it. I carry it over to the trunk, bend down, grit my teeth, and put pressure on it until the hook part of the lock snaps. I take a deep breath and open the trunk.

A musty stale odor fills my nose to the point where I can barely catch my breath. I fan the dust that flies under my nose. I begin to move things around and find a dusty hat to a cop uniform on top. I take it out and place it on the floor beside me. Next I see matching pants, a shirt, and large silver badge. I set them to the side too and continue looking inside. I open a black folder and see numerous yellowed articles. I pick one up, hold a flashlight near the paper, and read:

Whose Side Is He On?
By Heather McFarland
A narcotic officer on the payroll of the NYPD is currently under investigation for accepting money in exchange for favors to everyone from drug dealers to the Italian Mafia. An informant began the firestorm after reporting that the officer in question falsified evidence against a local drug dealer and stole a stack of cash from the dealer's apartment after an illegal raid. The informant added that he was also offered drugs to cover up for wrong doing

that he has been reporting to the police, including drawing attention to a possible false testimony and alleged corruption in which the officer helped to obtain a dismissal that helped to acquit a guilty defendant. The officer's name is being withheld, pending possible disciplinary action.

My heart beats so thunderously it feels as if it's going to leap out of my chest. I place the article in the pile of discoveries. I shine the light inside the trunk and see a brown folded blanket full of dust. I peel it back and find several stacks of money along with about six company checkbooks in prime condition. I'm surprised they are so well preserved because of the pungent odor, but they are. At first I wonder if the bills are counterfeit, but as I hold the flashlight closer to the faces of the presidents I can tell they are the real thing. Hastily I stack the items back in the trunk in the order that I found them. I shut the lid of the trunk, lay the busted lock inside of the circulate holes, turn the flashlight off, lay it down on the floor and run out of there, as quickly as possible. My head is spinning. I found out a little bit more than I wanted to know about Kyle. Now I've got to drum up a strategy that won't let on that I know a damn thing.

32

HANDLING MY BUSINESS

Malik

I stayed out all night and I don't regret it one bit. I called my baby's mother with a lie that I wanted to reconcile and make it work with her. She came flying over thinking she was going to pick up me and little Malik from my frat's house, but all I wanted was for her to come get our son so I could concentrate on how I was going to finish Monica off. My son was crying and begging to stay with me but I pushed him and his big-mouthed mother out of the door, then asked to borrow a sawed off shot gun from my frat brother—the one who picked me up from jail in the first place. I truly thought about shooting Monica and her fuck buddy, Ted, after everything replayed in my mind but I finally decided against it although my boy said if he were in my shoes, he'd get it done. I definitely can't afford any slip ups because of the Wes thing, so instead of letting my anger take over I end up shaving, showering, dressing, then going out to a club where the Lissen Band is playing.

After they close up shop for the night, I hang out in the VIP room where I watch my fellow ball players pick out hos for the bouncer to invite in. I laugh to myself when I notice sophisticated gold diggers with a well-organized plan invest in a bottle of $250 champagne to pretend like they aren't there to snag an athlete who is chilling after a home game. I need to cool my thoughts, and decide to get my head straight by taking my mind off my troubles. Getting laid by two best friends that are in the group of hos who ride back with me in the limo to one of my boy's spots for an "after party" is all good but I couldn't concentrate on busting a nut as usual. The best thing I got out of it is convincing the most gullible bitch that I called management of the club so her car wouldn't be towed, and that I would personally drop it off to her after she left work. Her girlfriend cosigns it and agrees to let her carpool with her until she gets her wheels back. I swear women think with their pussies, just like men think with their dicks. Had either of them even thought I was a "player" who they just didn't recognize from the roster, they would've told me to go to hell. I also confiscate Monica's new cell phone that I find out she's been hiding from me, and make all my calls without regard for her minutes, as I head toward her corner of the world. Now I'm standing on her father's step, smelling like a combination of pussy, liquor, and nightclub smoke.

Before my knuckles hit the front door to knock on it, Monica opens it. "Since you didn't show up last night after I left at least ten messages on *my* cell phone, I took the liberty of cleaning out your dresser drawer. Your shit is packed and sitting here at front door. Take it and be gone. You stink and it's obvious what you've been doing, although I'm not sure where and with whom."

I can't believe the bitch is putting me out after she fucked around but stranger things have happened, I guess. Monica begins placing my duffel bags and a few boxes on the step while saying, "You're living here rent free to train and now it seems like you're losing focus. I won't have you freeloading off me and my family anymore while you do what you want to do." When she lifts the last item and sets it in front of me she looks me in the eye and says, "You don't need to be here anymore—goodbye, Malik. All I want to know is when are you going to pay my father for the three hundred dollar phone bill that came in the mail yesterday?"

"Since I have permission to talk now, your highness, just tell him I'll mail him the money."

"I'm sure, just like you *mailed* a money order to the dealership," she snaps.

"Shut up you beady-eyed bitch! Don't start with me."

"Whose car is that?" Monica asks folding her arms.

"One of the girls I fucked last night."

"Move in with her then!" She slams the door and I can hear her stomping up the steps in the house I few seconds later I hear the door to her room slam. When I walk to the car carrying some of my things Monica opens her window. "Tell that bitch she can have you—good riddance!" She slams the window shut.

That ends my rent and job free fringe benefits compliments of the Jones family. But before I go that bitch needs to understand that I'll be back to collect the TV, stereo system, and water cooler I *gave* to her. She may have lost her shit but the replacement items only stay as long as I have a place to lay my head. Since I've got to go, it's all going, too.

One thing about me; I always know what to say, when to say it, and how to turn a spark into a flame. If I want to get something, or someone, I know how to make the pitch. I think about all of the free labor I get from Monica and how much shit she takes. I'm not ready to let her go. I'll be a little creative to work on keeping her around—dropping an online note that will make her talk to me even if she doesn't feel moved to untangle her folded arms.

I type in the subject line:
My aunt passed.
Malik.

Whenever Monica sees it she replies:
Please accept my heartfelt sympathies expressed in this e-card.
Take good care of yourself,
The X

How dare this bitch try to brush her shoulders off. Oh hell no, Monica!
Re: E-card
I really need to talk. Please call me.
Malik

When I hear Monica's voice I say, "I feel like shit, Monica. She's gone. Aunt Paula went on home to be with the Lord."

"What happened to her, Malik?"

"She had a heart attack and didn't make it. It's really that simple."

"I'm sorry to hear that but I never heard you mention she was sick," Monica says.

Andrea Blackstone

"It was a sudden kind of thing—you know how that can work. Tomorrow is promised to none of us, baby," I say, sounding sad.

"Was she in D.C.?"

"Yes."

"Why aren't you at the hospital?"

I ignore Monica's question. "Look, I know what you were thinking when I rolled out, but I was just testing you to see what you'd do and say. That wasn't a woman's car I was using—it was my boy's. Can you come see me? I'm hungry and I haven't eaten all day. You know Paula was like a mother to me. I'm so upset that I can't hold any food down. Plus my blood pressure is acting up. Monica, I need you. Can you please put our differences aside and accept that I still love you and you're my best friend? Monica, I really need to see you, even though you fucked around on me— that really hurt. Before my aunt passed she told me to make things right with you and that's what I'm going to do. I'm going to buckle down, get back on my training schedule, make my baby proud, and play some ball next season. After we get ours I'm going to get us shirts printed up that say: Kiss Malik and Monica's asses! That will get all of the haters who gave us a hard time. After we had that fight I went through all of our cards and notes to each other. A nigga has been hurting, girl. I've been looking at the ring I was saving for you and everything. I don't know what tomorrow is going to bring but I still hope you'll be my wife when it comes. My aunt thought so much of you—you know that."

Monica's voice softens up after my speech. "You hurt me too. I'm so sorry to hear the news. What can I do, Malik? I'll support you if I can."

"Bring me some food and just come hold me. I'm begging you to come be with me, and we both know that I don't roll like that so please get here as fast as you can. I'm just so upset. I've decided to stop fucking with my family just like you said. You were right about that. Them niggas are trifling as hell and I can't get back on top messing with them."

"Give me the address and I'll bring you some food, Malik."

An hour and a half passes and I know Monica must still be dick whipped because she fought rush hour traffic to make it to a dump with roaches crawling out of the sockets in Suitland just to come

248

comfort me. The only problem with the scenario is that I'm not grieving. As I kick chicken bones out of my way in the parking lot of a so-called apartment complex, I find myself arguing with the owner of a limo company. He seems to feel that I owe some female driver money for driving me around D.C. while I hung out at FUR nightclub, and then made my way to hang out with my big balling dawgs at Dream. When Monica pulls up I'm still arguing with him over the bill. "Go inside while I talk business about the limo arrangements."

She hugs me warmly and smiles. "Ok, baby but I need to know where you are staying, first."

"205. The door's open. I'll be in soon, baby. Get a glass of water or something." After Monica disappears inside the room, I turn my attention back to the bill matter. "I ain't paying that ho nothing more, man. She never told me it was extra to hang. The girl is lying about the whole thing."

"I want my money!" he yells. I'm not sure if he's packing so I move away from him as we argue. People drive by and shake their heads in disgust. The limo's taking up the small front area of the complex so they can't get by and have to park around the side or back of the building.

"When old girl came to pick me up, she came on to me and tried to suck my dick in the back seat. Since I didn't flirt back she got hot under the collar. You need to check your employee, and if you don't get the fuck out of here I'll call my crazy-ass cousin down the way to straighten you up! Don't call me about this shit no more. Ask your girl to tell the truth about the other night!"

I walk away and go into the apartment building. When I open the door I see Monica sitting on the floor since there's no furniture to sit on. The only other thing of notable size is a bucket in the center of the room that's catching the water that's dripping from the ceiling.

"Take off your coat, baby," I tell her.

"Malik, don't get mad. I need to ask you something," she says, picking her nails, not looking at me.

"What?"

"Whose place is this is, and why isn't there any furniture in it?"

"Oh, it's my sister's place. She's at work. She just moved in not long ago, and all she's got is bedroom things. You know how it is when you move into your first place."

"So, how are you holding up?" she asks.

"As well as can be expected but I'm crushed. This just caught me off guard, Monica."

"I know—I'm sorry." She twists up her face and adds, "I put your food in the refrigerator."

"Thanks." The last time I looked in the refrigerator a roach was crawling on an onion. I figure by her expression that Monica has either noticed the pest problem, or that there's nothing else in the fridge except a jar of tap water.

"I bought you a few groceries from Giant and left the bags in the kitchen. I couldn't put the things away because I don't know where everything goes."

"I appreciate it, and I appreciate you, little momma. You look good too. I don't know the last time I told you that."

"Just because we broke up doesn't mean I would see you hungry, Malik. I do care about you despite everything that's happened, but you and I are now on a platonic level."

"Would you just get in bed and hold me? Thanking me for the compliment wouldn't kill you, either," I say.

"Malik, us getting in bed together isn't the best idea."

"Are you fucking around on me again, Monica?" I ask defensively.

"No! Why do I always have to be guilty of that? Everything is always me and my man. Why, Malik?"

"Then if that's not the case, like I said, would you please do this for me? I just need that so much. It's not like I can ask any other woman but my baby. You don't have to do nothing but hold me and help me to calm my nerves—help me get some sleep for a few minutes."

"Ok, but all we're doing is lying down together."

I pull Monica by the hand and she gets up from the floor. As she walks in front of me I nearly salivate at the though of tapping that yellow ass again. Whether she realizes it or not, we're fucking. No real man would allow a woman to get in bed butt naked and just hold her. Get real, Monica. I've got a stiff dick and you've got a pussy.

After Monica and I undress I hold her. I begin whispering to her things about our past, our future, and how she's the only woman for me. In time, her legs open and I get my way. The whole time I worked my way in her head by reminding her about Ted and how she violated our bond by letting him touch her, let alone enjoy her body.

Forty minutes later I tell Monica, "Get some soap out of the hall closet. Take this towel with you. I've got to make some calls and see what time my family from down South is coming into Dulles."

"Ok," she says, wrapping the towel around her. Then I hear, "Whose condoms are these in the closet? The box is half used."

"First of all I'm sure my sister has a man, and second of all, my cousin brings his hos here when he comes from Winchester. Hurry up and take your shower before you get busted in your drawers by my sister. She'll be coming home from work soon. This is no time to be quizzing me down, girl. I keep telling you that I'll do the thinking for you."

While Monica is in the shower I make a few calls to arrange to "borrow" funds so that I can get my hair cut and do a few miscellaneous things. Before Monica can make it out of the shower I open the bathroom door. "I'll be back in a few minutes. I'm using the car to pick up my aunt and uncle from the airport."

"I want to go," Monica yells over the running water. "Wait for me—I'm almost finished in here, Malik. Don't you want to get cleaned up, anyway?"

"There's no time, little momma. I've got to roll."

"But, wait," she stutters. "My car. Malik!" By then it's too late because I've already snatched her car keys and made it halfway out of the door.

After I sit my ass in the barber's chair and get up, I head over to the other side of the salon to get my manicure. While the Vietnamese girl is soaking my nails in a pan of water my cell phone rings. I don't answer it but after a message is left I call my voicemail. "Malik, get back here right now! This bitch is up in my face talking about you're not her brother and she wants *me* to go wherever because her family is coming to visit and they can't know you live here. What in the hell is going on? Call me back because if she rolls her eyes at me one more time I'm going to smack every pea off her head!" I sigh and am pissed that my pampering time has been interrupted by two women bitching at each other. After I finish taking care of handling my business, I'll walk in the door and take care of them both.

Approximately three hours later I unlock the door with my key. "Monica. Come here," I call.

As soon as I say those words she comes flying out of the bedroom where I sleep, ranting and raving. "I told her I wasn't going nowhere. She knew I didn't have a way to leave here because you had my car. What was I supposed to do—stand outside in the hood? Who is this bitch, Malik? I thought you said it was your sister?"

I don't answer Monica's question. "Go sit in the car, it's running," I reply sternly. "Thieves target old cars like yours so get out there now. I'll talk to you when I come out." Once she's gone I deal with the other one. "Missy, get your ass out here!" She's a tall, homely looking woman with thick glasses and no style. By the time she stands before me, hanging her head low Monica is seated in her car. My temper flares at the thought of Missy double-crossing me since I signed for her to get in this dump, using my NFL credentials and part of my pension to do it. The deal was that if I ever needed a place to crash, I could. Now she wants to catch feelings for me after years of seeing me find them, fuck them, and dismiss them. I know that Monica is a threat to her because she knows that as rotten as I am I care about her more than any woman she's seen on my arm. When she opens her mouth to explain why she was rude to my girl I backhand her so hard that I know the sound of the slap can be heard beyond the apartment walls. Even so, I leave her in tears, holding the side of her face. I swing the front door open and get in the passenger's seat of Monica's car. By the way she's looking at me out of the corner of her eye I know that she heard me slap Missy but I don't give a shit. When she nervously asks me what happened I say, "Go out and make a left. I know you have money on you. You always do when you first get paid. I need sixty for a hotel room."

Monica's fear won't allow her to speak or deny it. I direct her to drive me to a motel near The Great American Cook Out near

252

Route one in Virginia. It's unlike Monica to keep her mouth shut for an entire car trip but she does. When will this naive bitch learn? As homely as Missy is I couldn't bring myself to fuck her, so I let her flirt just enough to have a place to stay for the night, and the next day I banged the short girl in the rental office who kept showing off her bow legs and nice smile. Obviously, my aunt didn't die. Shit, I saw her this morning. She was the one that advised me to get back with Monica in the first place and leave these no good hos alone. By the time my boo catches on, I'll be straight. Everybody does play the fool.

33

A MISSING PIECE OF THE PUZZLE

Wes

In our top news stories today, there could be a link between a series of local robberies and the missing Blitzer player, Wesley Antoine Montgomery. Police have reported that a twenty-four year old D.C. woman has been accused of robbing a bank and may also be linked to six other local bank robberies. Tawanda Jackson was arrested after handing a teller a note and escaping with an un-disclosed amount of money. After a tip given by a bank employee, the car with stolen license plates was spotted on the Baltimore Washington Parkway, headed toward Washington, D.C. When signaled to pull over by Maryland police Jackson led them on a high-speed chase, reaching speeds over eighty miles per hour, and lasting several minutes. After zigzagging in and out of traffic, the chase finally ended when Jackson broad-sided a tractor-trailer and spun out of control.

Credit cards and a wallet that are said to belong to the Blitzer's point guard were found after a search turned up an electronically controlled hidden compartment in the stolen vehicle. Heroin residue and three loaded firearms were also uncovered in the compartment. After further investigation, the passenger has been identified as Marvin Mathews, of New York City, New York. He is described as a member of a major drug trafficking organization in D.C. and New York. In 1997 he served time for drug trafficking, money laundering, and possession of firearms. Both Ms. Jackson and the driver of the other vehicle were taken to an area hospital. Ms. Jackson was released to police custody later that evening. The driver of the tractor-trailer is in serious condition at this time. More details will follow as they become available.

34

GETTING DOWN TO THE NITTY GRITTY

Jalita

Several days after the snowstorm subsides, Kyle sticks his key in the door, reminding me that my dealings with him aren't over. I tell myself that I'll try my best not to blow my cover about what I dug up unless the fucker touches me. Even if he invades my personal space, it's on. Over time, what he did to me replays in my mind like a bad nightmare. The other part of me that hopes to land him solid jail time knows that life can be a bitch and no one said it was fair. Since that's the case I have to suck this shit up as best as I can and continue to act shady for the cause.

Renee's phony ass walks over to Kyle. "I've missed you so much, baby. I hate it when you have to go away like this."

When she reaches out to embrace Kyle his face is expressionless. He picks up his suitcase and briefcase. "You and the girl get me two glasses of Jack Daniels on the rocks and bring them to my office. It's going to be a long night."

Renee follows him, a sad expression fixed on her face. "What's wrong? No kiss, no hugs? Didn't you miss me, Kyle?"

"Renee, I know you like to have things your way but let me be a man for once. Now do what I asked of you and get the drinks. I didn't have a good trip."

"But baby, if something happened I want to know about it," she presses.

"GET MY MOTHERFUCKING DRINKS!" he snaps. "Do you understand that?" With each word Renee flinches as if he's physically hitting her.

"Ginger, let's go," she says quietly. I follow Renee into the bar area and she pours two drinks, directing me to get tongs and an ice bowl. While we are at the bar we both hear the front door open but can't see who it is. Kyle's voice is low and his words are few. As the footsteps get louder I watch another layer of worry cover Renee's face. She and I walk toward Kyle's office and find a closed door with two arguing voices sounding off behind it.

When Renee eases the door open by pushing it with her elbow Kyle turns around. "Can't you ever learn to knock? And where are your damn clothes? Obviously, we have company. I know you have a thing for all types of men but you don't care who sees your shit, do you? Go put something on your ass and stay out of my office, Renee."

The white man paces back and forth around Kyle's office like he and Kyle were having a private, heated conversation. His face is red and he keeps running his right hand through his dark hair like it's a nervous habit. Every now and then I notice he mumbles, "Shit."

After Renee and I place the drinks on a side table near Kyle, we turn to leave. "Bitch, you know what coasters are for! Where are they? I want two coasters on this fucking table before I can think about—" Kyle catches himself then says, "Send the girl back with them. Just get out of my face. And one other thing—" he pauses. "I'll be sleeping on the couch tonight."

Surprisingly, Renee delivers no comebacks or protests. I'm amazed that Kyle is treating *Miss I've Got Him In Check* this way, and now I'm baffled that the script has been flipped back to the other side. We walk out, and I follow Renee to the kitchen. With tears in her eyes, Renee says to me, "You heard him, Ginger. She grabs the coasters from a kitchen drawer and looks at me as if I should deliver the coasters to Kyle's psycho ass.

When I get back to the door I hear Kyle say, "How could you let this happen?"

"It's not like I wanted it to happen," the stranger responds.

"Well do something."

"What can I do?"

"I don't know—you're the company accountant—figure it out."

"I can't control an audit. They want to look at the books," Jim explains nervously.

"I thought you had sense enough to have two sets. What kind of crooked accountant are you?"

"Kyle, you're sounding irrational now."

"No, I'm not. If they look at the books and see what's missing, it's my ass. I can't afford anyone snooping into my background."

"You have stability and experience running a telecommunications firm so who cares if they start digging? They won't find anything."

"Oh but they can find something, Jim. Maybe I don't have an M.B.A. Maybe a certain federal judge that ran for Congress put in a word for me so I'd keep quiet about some unethical fundraising issues."

"Look, I don' know what you got me mixed up in but I want out of it—today!"

"You can't back out now. You were embezzling money right along with me. If someone takes a fall it won't be who you think."

"I'm finished with this conversation," Jim says in a dismissive tone.

"Oh no you're not."

"Well, Kyle, I have something else to tell you."

"What is it now?"

"They've hired a forensic accountant. He's already snooping around and has looked at the books."

"Speak in plain English, Jim."

"The company is conducting a fraud investigation. They've already interviewed me and they will interview you too because you also had access to funds. I'm hoping for mediation and arbitration so I'm willing to turn in the money I didn't spend and try to strike a deal. I can't go to jail over this—I have a family to consider."

"You should've thought about that before you bought that real estate in the city. I told you to put that money away after you moved, but no—you went out buying your wife a fur, and throwing cash around town."

"And you don't think they're watching you at your bank when you're running back and forth to the safety deposit box after you write company checks to yourself and they clear? Come on, Kyle. I told you to slow down on—"

"You're mixed up on that one. I told you I was writing them to a guy I know who's a fence. I was giving him a fair cut to cash them."

"Same thing—the checks are numbered and are out of series from payroll. Don't think the people at the bank aren't talking about how often you come by to get into your deposit box. Why didn't you get a safe installed or something? They're already looking for proof, documents, and not long from now will be reporting on the findings."

"Look, this shit is going nowhere and I don't have time for it. All I know is that when they look for conflicting stories I better not find out that your white ass was singing like a bird. Just remember that you were giving your share of ideas when you heard about that secretary who was using erasable ink to rewrite the checks for cash after her boss signed off of them. If the truth be told, that's how you got involved with this scheme, remember? You didn't have a choice. You followed her lead and I busted you."

"You've written over five-hundred checks, Kyle. All of that is irrelevant now."

"And you have been working at the company for the last ten years. You're the company's *only* accountant who has never been out on a sick day, or taken a vacation in God knows when. Don't think that won't look suspicious. If this forensic accountant is any good he'll pick up on you not ever giving anyone a chance to see the books."

"Oh, so now you're turning on me, Kyle? Two million dollars later you're turning on your pal, Jim?"

"Obviously we've turned on each other, and this has become every man for himself. May the best man win, Jim," Kyle says, laughing.

"Yeah, my kid's college tuition and my nest egg are at stake. Plus I've got a two thousand dollar mortgage and my reputation as an accountant to uphold. You better believe that I don't feel sorry for you. Your gambling and credit card debts are typical of your kind. I should've known better than to trust one of you."

"Oh, so now this is a racial thing?" Kyle says sounding furious.

"No—I'll just dig up all the dirt I can to prove that I had nothing to do with this—that I've been upholding my ethical and moral standards of being entrusted with money."

" *What* did you say?"

"You heard me, Kyle. You're the one with the criminal background, not me. I knew what I was doing when I struck a deal with you. Does your wife know that her husband doesn't have an M.B.A.—that he earned his V.P. position by making a lie sound like the truth? How did you get around the background check by HR, Kyle? That's what I want to know, you lying thief. You never deserved the job in the first place. Someone qualified should've had it," Jim says with cockiness.

"Get out of my house!"

"Gladly but answer one thing for me before I go." I don't hear Kyle answer. Then his co-worker continues, "I've been curious about something. How's the swinging lifestyle these days? By my estimate, I think what you do at home or at some party by invitation only will be an interesting tidbit to add, especially since two very interesting tapes *fell* into my hands. Ask your promiscuous wife if she let three so-called strippers ejaculate in her ass without a condom after her secret event. They're all HIV positive, so I hear. Draw your own conclusions regarding how they ended up crossing paths with her and the rest of the swinging wives. Me, on the other hand, I'm an ordinary family man so don't waste your time looking for a kinky past on my part, because unlike you, I don't have one. And by the way, it wouldn't be a good idea to piss me off because I've already retained a criminal defense lawyer who happens to be one of the top fifty lawyers in D.C."

I hear Kyle call Jim a bastard, then footsteps moving toward me. I pull my ear from the door and just manage to run into the kitchen before I hear Jim storm out of the house. The door slams, then another set of hurried footsteps which I assume belong to Kyle follow behind him. The door opens and slams again. As I hear two car engines start and eight tires squeal I know that Kyle forgot all about the coasters. I just hope that no one will realize that I heard as much as I did.

35

BROKE BALLING

Malik

If there's such a thing as broke balling, I'm the gold digging pimp that invented it. Monica is running around with a damn red bandana on her head today, faded out and played out straight leg jeans that she bought from a thrift shop, and a pocket book that was in about four seasons ago. The strap on the damn thing looks like it's ready to rip and give up any minute. When she mentions needing to get her hair done I take out a pick and pick her hair straight out in all directions like bozo the clown. Her new growth is so out of control that about three inches of hair stand out from her scalp and the straight ends hang like they're dead. When she complains about needing new clothes I give her my college sweat suit and tell her to put it on. Although it's so big it's hanging off of her like she's not thick and about a buck sixty, I tell her, "Put my hat on." When she does I tell her, "Some of the finest women in the world dress like this. Now you look relaxed—you look good, momma."

Monica says, "I look worse, and I need my hair done," she says. She takes off my hat and replaces her red bandana, tying it behind her head.

"I tried to help you," I say when she steps back into her jeans.

I see a tear drop from Monica's eye because she can't afford to keep looking like the diva she used to be before I came into her life. In fact, making her look like a bum will help keep her under my thumb, and keep the fellas overlooking her. Part of this shit is my payback for her getting dick elsewhere. Besides, encouraging her to down play her looks and take care of me is doable because

I'm the one who will be making millions, not her. I routinely insist that she looks like she's got it going on because I need her to continue spending whatever money passes through her hands on me. Monica already put me up in a motel for a few days, and paid for my meals and movie habit while I stayed there. She tells me that there's no need of me relying on people while I'm trying to get back on my feet. I pretend to listen to the same things she's said fifty times, one thousand ways. It pays off because Monica drives me to a BB&T bank on 13th Street and digs down in her pocket so that I can have my own checking and savings account.

"Malik, you're going to have to manage your accounts properly because you'll need to prove you're an account holder for many reasons. No one will take you seriously without one. I'm sacrificing to set these up for you, so I hope you appreciate it. You have one hundred in each one. This means there's no more asking Monica to write checks for you, because you have your own checkbook. Since you overdrew my accounts I've had to cash my checks at one of the check cashing places. I can't even get an account until I clear things up with Bank of America."

"Not for long, little momma."

"Malik, please just be responsible would you? I keep telling you that I'm not made of money."

"I said, *ok.* I'll listen to you this time."

"The last thing I'm going to do is take you around to a few apartment buildings to check into having your own place. I see no reason why you can't get a short lease until you leave for Minnesota. A man needs his own spot, Malik. Living with women is unacceptable, including my family. I believe you can make it if you try, but you've got to start standing on your own two feet."

I remain silent as Monica pulls into the parking lot of a high-rise complex near the waterfront in South West. "I was going to live here when I was a provisional teacher but my income wasn't high enough because of my student loans. A few years ago it was a decent building with older tenants. Let's check it out, get a rental brochure, and see what rent is running."

We get out of the car and go into the building. A tall, redheaded freak smiles at me, and I know if she's the manager I'm in. Monica and I suddenly switch roles. After she starts me off trying to get things in place, I take the ball and run with it. I put on my baller look and strut over to the counter. I lean on it to show off my big guns and impress the woman.

She puts down a stack of papers, and starts cheesing like I'm her best friend. "May I help you?"

"I sure hope so. I'd like some assistance on this side of the counter." She walks around to the other side, and looks me in the eye. I notice her female co-workers are drooling at the sight of me.

I place my right arm on her back. "Can we take a walk, baby?"

"Sure! There's a room across the hall and we can talk there."

I follow the redhead into the room that was next to the entrance. It was equipped with a fax machine, a table, and small couch. Apparently, it was the business area for the residents. Even so the woman shuts the door for privacy. Then she says, "I'm Cynthia. It's a pleasure to meet you Mr. —"

"Montgomery. Call me Malik though," I answer.

I never acknowledge Monica. Instead I say, "I'm going to be up front with you. I'm in a little bit of a situation here. I'm going to be playing ball next season and I just need somewhere to chill out, train, and keep my mind straight. My girl here told me that this environment might be good for me, so I'm hoping there's something we can work out."

"How's your credit?"

"You know how ball players do—anything can happen in a split second. It's not the best right now. I'm going through something with my baby's mother. I've got a crib in Virginia but she's staying with my son there until she gets her house built. It's a long story, but all I'm trying to do is get back on my feet and forget the whole mess. My girl is trying to teach me how to get back to basics."

"Well when are you looking to move in?"

"As soon as possible. I've been spending all of my money at top hotels and eating out every night. My girl says that's got to stop. How much is a one-bedroom here?"

"Twelve hundred plus utilities."

"That's all?" I say perpetrating like I'm a big baller.

"I tell you what. Let me see what one-bedroom we have vacant. In the meantime, fill out this credit application and we can find out what we're working with here." Before the woman gets up I feel

Andrea Blackstone

her rub her foot in between my crotch. It makes me smile because
she's being so bold right in front of Monica, who's looking straight
ahead, unaware that we're both flirting with one another.

When she leaves I look to Monica for help filling it out,
spelling properly, and fixing it up enough to make Cynthia feel that
I'm worthy of a chance to live in the complex.

"Just fill out your company's information where it asks for
employment. You and your baby's mother own it together so put it
down. You say you're the CEO," Monica tells me. "Malik, you're
going to fuck this up. Let me print this for you because your
spelling is not going to win you any favor." Monica grabs the
packet and begins filling it out for me as we discuss what should go
where. Luckily this chick knows how to put ducks in a row because
I now see that Cynthia will need my banking information, and what
CEO of a computer company doesn't have a banking account?

After ten minutes the redhead ho returns with several papers.
"Mr. Harrison, your credit rating is the lowest there is."

When she sits down and begins looking at the figures and
blemishes on my financial life I tell her, "It's Malik. I warned you.
I'm not shocked. Like I said, this is what happens when you do the
wrong people favors. Unfortunately, it happens to ballers, rappers,
singers, and people in entertainment all of the time. I have money
I just can't get to it just yet. Like I said, it's a long story." I sigh and
shake my head a few times.

Cynthia looks me in the eye. "I have an idea—I'll be right back."
When she returns, she closes the door, sits, then looks at me and
whispers, "I'm not supposed to do this." She takes white out and
covers my poor credit rating score and doctors whatever information will make it look like I've got it going on enough to qualify
for a crib.

Monica turns to me. "She did you a favor, Malik. Don't blow it.
Mind your business, keep training, get on your feet, and move
forward. Remember, you're not here to socialize."

"I know, Monica. Thank you so much, Cynthia." I walk around
the table and kiss her on the cheek.

Cynthia starts cheesing after I kiss her freckled face. "My
children's father plays ball. I understand—don't worry about it. I
will need a check to verify the checking account though." Then she

264

whispers, "Don't worry about the deposit, just make sure you pay your rent on time every month and don't breathe a word about this."

As I hand her a check I smile back at her. She seems mesmerized by me and I'm sure she's imagining me twisting up her skinny pale legs like a pretzel. I don't care as long as I have a place to live. If she knocks on my door on the right day I may even make her fantasy come true.

"Welcome to the building. Let me get your keys and show you what your new home will look like. The unit you'll be moving into needs to be vacuumed, and I'll have a new refrigerator sent in for you. It should be ready for move in sometime tomorrow."

When Cynthia gets up Monica and I do too because people are starting to invade our private *meeting*—coming in to use the fax machine and sit on the small couch and gossip. After we walk up to the desk we see three brown children turn the corner and walk into the door behind the desk. It's obvious that Cynthia has slept with one or more black men at least three times, and now I understand why she was rubbing my crotch with her skinny foot— once you go black no woman can go back! Monica looks baffled but tries to appear unmoved. I know this is rather common so it doesn't faze me one bit. White woman love black men, especially when they're on a football or basketball roster. It happens every day, all around the country.

After Cynthia shows me the clubroom that can be rented out for special occasions, outdoor pool area, busted gym with old equipment, and the mailbox area, the three of us step into the elevator. Monica and I follow Cynthia when she gets off on the eight floor. "This is the model," she says. "It's where I bring my friend. He's a stripper at The Legend Night Club. Boy do we have some fun in this unit."

I know she's openly throwing me hints that she'd like to ride this big black dick, but I play along like I don't catch the vibe, just for Monica's sake. The more I think about it the more it sounds like something I may want to do just to show my appreciation for her white-out move.

$

Southern boys like big toys, and I'm a truck man. I lost one to the dealership but I gained a Lincoln Navigator by getting a bitch with good credit and a decent government job to sign for it on my behalf. She has a man now but I don't give a shit. If he finds out about it that's his problem, not mine. After that I talk the same ho into buying me a diamond earring, a few new pairs of tennis shoes, and I spring for the thongs. My last stop is to round up some new furniture for my crib. I promised a guy some season tickets and the next thing I know he's working some crooked deal to almost give me a black leather set complete with a loveseat, matching chair, and entertainment center. I pick a small dinette set, a bedroom suite, and I'm on my way to having my shit delivered in a few days.

I talk Monica into coming back to see me because I'm still grieving for my aunt, and talk as if I've turned over a new leaf. Actually I'm the same as I always was, just in a different mindset. Acting right leads Monica to bring me two armfuls of trinkets from the dollar store. She said she'd never buy me toilet paper and q-tips again but she does just that to get me started in my new place. She also pops by some discount place called Value City and picks up a few towels and a shower curtain. Then again, her doing that shit may have been due to me telling her that I was going downstairs to the sauna room and pool shower area for my daily washing because I didn't have a shower curtain. I wasn't bluffing though, because riding the elevator in nothing but a towel covering my privates and the shower shoes that Monica's father bought me a while back for camp, has become the talk of the building. Everyone wants to know who the half-naked, big black man is. Especially after gossip circulates that I played ball and am about to get my ass back on the field. All of the women are trying to stake their claim, giving me looks like they'd go as far as licking my balls to get a chance to get in my space. After I make my debut and let the women figure out where I live, my purpose has been served.

To keep Monica's big mouth shut after she puts up my shower curtain, unpacks my paper goods, sheets and trashcans, I decide to

266

take her to the movies and to get something to eat. All I have to pay for is the meal because I can go straight to the front of the movie line and get in for free mostly anytime I want. After we see a movie that sucks so bad I can't repeat the name, we're sitting in a Tex Mex restaurant, and I hear those eight familiar words, "Would you please sign this for my son?" Monica is silent. I pull my baseball hat down over my eyes and scribble something illegible. The woman thanks me and walks away from the table.

Monica puts down her fork. "How many times are you going to do that? Have you ever thought about getting a job in case you don't go back to football?"

"I'm getting my money back. I don't need a job," I snap.

"Yes you do, and I know of someone that can do a hell of a job on your resume. She's redoing mine."

"I don't need that done. I'm straight. Leave it alone, Monica."

"You're in denial, and you're not straight. You're getting too old to even play football, and who's to say what will happen next season."

"I don't need to hear this. You're always trying to stress me out. All you do is run your damn mouth, tear me down, and run up my damn blood pressure. I wish you'd shut up and eat your food!"

"You didn't used to treat me like this. What happened to the man who gave me hugs, saved all of the cards we gave each other, and used to bring me home stuffed animals? I couldn't wait for you to come home back then. I was the happiest woman in the world. Life sucked but I had you and it meant so much, Malik."

"Well that was before I found out how you are, and now I'm back to being me again—the nigga I was before I met you." Monica's cell phone that I'm using rings.

"Who's that?" she asks when I answer it.

I ignore Monica and continue talking. After I hang up I say, "One of my sorority sisters. We broke up—remember? You fucked around on me. I haven't forgotten about that, but I still haven't slept with anyone else. Don't get it twisted though, it's not because I don't have opportunity. Trust me, some fine hos are after big daddy."

"That's my phone. I'm here helping you to get yourself straight and that's all you can manage to say and think of? If you want those hos, go right ahead and be with them. You were scraping change for gas and food without me—remember? Where was she before your apartment, second truck, and contract?"

"I asked you to get married. You wouldn't."

"What in the hell did you expect me to say? I can't get married with you acting like this. You're half stepping. I'm the leader and you're the follower. And you go around telling people I'm your wife. I don't like that shit, Malik. Why can't you just grow up?"

$

Monica and I don't speak to each other from the time I pay the bill to the time we pull into a parking space in my new building lot. Before we make it to the elevator, I collect my mail. When the elevator opens I mumble, "Ain't this a bitch! How did someone get my address here? I just put in a change of address slip and mail's been forwarded that fast?" I continue to read the letter. "What? I didn't father no one's child when I was in New Orleans playing ball. Back child support, for what? These scandalous bitches!"

"Now you've got two baby mommas. Who will it be next? Someone in the building? How about the leasing manager who fudged the shit for you to get in here? I hope she can get along with the first chick that's still sprung over big daddy," Monica says sarcastically. "Don't think I didn't see her playing with your crotch. I know you think I'm stupid but I'm not, Malik," Monica adds.

"I didn't sleep with that freak. I don't even know her," I say, ignoring Monica's catty wisecrack. "Fuck—she was the one that slipped something in my drink and tried to insert the cum back up in herself out of the condom, after we fucked that night. I bet it's her. Damn that Cajun ho!" I say, balling up my left fist and punching the elevator door.

The elevator stops on my floor and Monica says, "Look, just stop making a mess of your life, just leave me out of it." We get out of the elevator and continue standing in front of the elevator while talking.

"After I had little Malik I found out I was sterile—she's a lying ho who's out to get me for child support for someone else's mistake!"

"Whatever," Monica says sarcastically. Then she adds, "If you really were sterile when you hit it, the issue of paternity for your son shouldn't take this long to resolve."

"Girl, you ain't nobody that I need to justify myself to. What 'chu and your wide hips coming to my apartment for? I don't even need you. You'll need me before I need you. Unplug my shit at your father's house too because I'm coming with a truck to get my TV, stereo, and water cooler. In fact I'm coming tonight so if you'll be at your man's house, tell someone I'm coming so that I can get the last of my shit and bring it to my new crib."

Just then the elevator door opens again. Monica rides back down cursing at me and I don't care. Shit, there's plenty I can get into, but somewhere along the way I better call this lawyer and see what's what. I don't care how this thing turns out. All I know is that Malik Harrison fathered one child, not two. If I have to pay to get out of this jam I won't be showing my face to one more baby's momma. If I keep repeating that I'm sterile maybe shooting blanks will come true. Damn, I fucked up!

36

TROUBLE IN PARADISE

Jalita

As promised, Kyle's been sleeping on the couch in his office but often complains about muscle pain and the crook in his neck when he awakens. If he's not shredding some sort of documents that probably verify that he's been in on the embezzling thing, he's relieving stress by jacking off to porn tapes with the door shut. Renee's been acting depressed, and if it's not that, she's indulging in screwing more and more men while her husband is at work. The last few times Renee has gotten ultra freaky, she's managed to throw countless Mimosas down her throat and demand that her company bring his wife or significant other for her enjoyment. After she gets off I've heard her throw things across the room and run couples out of her space explaining that she hates men and the trouble they bring to a woman's life. After they leave she turns to me for hugs and cuddling.

As crazy as Kyle is I don't know why she insists on testing his limits, but I'm just grateful that I escape threesomes by continuing to do the housework. I also save her the trouble of making breakfast and dinner for Kyle. Although I would love to poison his ass and get to the point of my revenge quick, fast, and in a hurry, I don't. Most of the time while Kyle is at work I snoop around his office. Usually his computer is password protected and his desk drawers are locked. Today he must've left in haste because a document that lists his credit card number is not completely shredded, and after I shake the mouse and the screen saver disappears, I notice the internet is still connected. Against my better judgment I click on the first email, assuming Renee will be blamed for accessing his online account, not me. I was snooping for corporate dirt and instead found a pile of some personal crap that I'm sure she would like to see if she wasn't knee deep in having an orgy fest as a way to compensate for her dried up marriage.

Married Man Looking For Hot Down Low Action

I'm a married black professional executive in a very prestigious position here in D.C. My wife has no idea I'm attracted to both men and women. I've been in the swinging lifestyle for some years but I'm ready to take things to another level, for my own personal reasons. I prefer a married boyfriend and someone that can teach me the ropes of living on the down low. Discretion is a must. I am open to exploring possibilities with a man who travels to the area a lot. I can never host, so your hotel room or home would be a perfect location for me. Race is unimportant so long as you're an attractive, consenting adult. I look forward to hearing from you soon but only if you are the type who is capable of making me late for work because what you're offering to a virgin bisexual man would be well worth it. I've grown tired of watching tapes and am ready to try the real thing. Your pic gets mine. NO LONG EMAIL EXCHANGE OR PHONE SEX DESIRED.

My jaw nearly drops to the floor as my eyes continue to follow more responses to the ad I just read.

Hi. I'm a straight guy looking for a generous man who wants to suck or get fucked by a young, large black dick. Yes, I can host in the Adams Morgan or Dupont Circle area today from 4:00 p.m. to 12:00 a.m. I hope you are serious about what you wrote in your ad because I'm horny and in need of an older man who can supply stability and cash to compensate me for my talents and discretion. I'm 6'3, 180 lbs, and nine hard inches long. I'm the jock type, work out at a local D.C. gym several times a week, 21, and am looking for someone good looking and lean to meet up with and screw or jack off with.

Based on my description, I think it should be obvious that I'm not used to doing something like responding to personal ads, but I am interested in giving it a try because I really need to save cash for my fiancée's engagement ring. I want you to know up front that I love her so there's only the possibility of being a fuck buddy to get you off whenever you want my services. Holla back at me if you want to know more about what I am looking for and why.

BTW, my girl says I am very talented using my mouth and give a great massage. Race is unimportant to me so long as you've got the $ and are HIV negative. I've attached a picture for your enjoyment. As you will see it's from the waist down. Focus on the middle and I don't think you'll be disappointed.

Your ad in men seeking men:
Greetings:

I'm a married, masculine, hairy, white bisexual man with baby blue eyes, and in pretty good shape. I would be interested in seeing what you like. I'm in town from Idaho, and am staying at a five star hotel in N.W. I'm looking for some safe, sane, and discrete, man on man play, in my hotel room—no strings attached.

I could be classified as extremely submissive, and attractive. When people see me, I appear to be very straight, but I do love to suck cock. I can relate to the first-time jitters but they will go away. The first time I got sucked off was when my college roommate and I got drunk after a frat party, and I've never forgotten how good that felt to me. At this point in my life I refuse to deny my feelings and what arouses me so I see no reason not to indulge.

Now back to the essentials: I don't have any diseases, I'm very clean, eager to please, love body contact, and discretion is an absolute must on my part too. I know this may be your first time but I can direct until you get the hang of how things can work between us. We can discuss more via email if you choose to reply. The champagne and room service is waiting. All I need is you and that black virgin ass of yours, as well as that thick cock that needs draining. I have good stamina and will not disappoint if things go well. If interested, let's not waste precious time.

Re: My ad in men seeking men

Hi there. I would like to meet you in your hotel room this evening. If you get this message please call my cell to confirm: 202-997-4122. Unless you reply immediately, I can't log on anymore today so this is the best way to reach me. If I don't hear from you I'll assume you are no longer available. Champagne might lead to me stripping, so watch out for promising me liquor. If you want to start out at a bar that's fine with me. Can I get a name next time? I'm Kyle, by the way. Maybe that will get us started.

Re: meeting tonight

Yes, Kyle, I can get together with you tonight. I'm glad you chose to respond to me. I've always wanted to experiment with a fit, well-hung black man, and have a particular interest in rimming, blowing, and then swallowing his big load all to the last drop. This all sounds very arousing and passionate. I can supply details regarding my location, a time when we can meet, and the particulars when we talk. My number is 208-334-2179, but I will try to call you too. If we miss each other and I don't answer it's because I'm still in a meeting on the Hill, so please leave a message for me, if you call. We can even exchange stories about our wives after we have our fun. If we click, I just may look forward to screwing you while looking at my wife's picture. I don't get to do this much but at the very least we can jerk each other off, sip on some champagne, spend some quality time, then get some shut eye. Anxiously awaiting that debut performance, as well. I have some toys that might inspire you to try something new. ☺ There's a bar in the hotel lobby so that's a perfect plan. Let's make it happen while there's still time.
Yours,
Chad (you got the name)

The next day when Kyle comes in, I watch as Renee tries to talk to him.

"Kyle, baby. Look, I know you're just getting in the door, and I know things have been crazy between us, but I want you to know I'm sorry about your co-worker, Jim. I just read in the paper about the awful fire that killed him and his whole family, early this morning. I don't care that you've been out all night. I just care about how my husband may be feeling. I can imagine the state of mind that you must be in since you two had an argument earlier this week. It reminded me that we shouldn't part angry. You never know what could happen."

"Nice speech, Renee. Tell it to someone who cares and might give a damn."

"Do they know how the fire started?" she asks, still trying to get him to talk.

"Do I look like a member of the arsonist squad?"

Renee spreads her arms open. "Come here. Give me a hug—I'm here for you. This has got to be devastating for you and your whole office."

Kyle sighs heavily. It was obvious that he didn't want to be bothered—at least to me. "It's been a long day, Renee. I just want to go to my office, settle my nerves, take a nap, and catch up on some work. Jim and I weren't friends, and I'll be just fine."

"Come up stairs, Kyle. Let me hold and caress you. We won't argue, I promise. Let's just enjoy one another. Whatever you need I want you to have it from me. I miss my husband."

"Not now, Renee, please. And don't ask me any questions. I just want to be left alone. Shit, what the hell does it take for you to leave me alone?"

"Why is everyone shutting me out around here? What's going on in this house? We used to be so happy, Kyle. How did this happen?"

"I can't do this with you right now, Renee. You're always so fucking emotional. My head is throbbing, I've been answering questions all day because investigators are coming around trying to find out about Jim, and I told you that I want to be left alone. The fire has been all I've heard about all day. If you must know I've been fantasizing about jacking off in the privacy of my own space."

"You don't want to make love to me? Fine—have it your way. I guess you're not attracted to me anymore."

"Renee. Please! Not now. If you want attention, go play with Ginger and see when the next swinging event is. I have more to do than have freaky sex. If you're bored find a way to keep yourself entertained. I've tried counseling, letting you dominate in the relationship, fuck who you want, and be what you need. What more can I do?"

274

"Well fuck you then! I tried to be nice. Don't count on that happening again anytime soon."

"I never do anymore. I never do. What do you think—our fucked up marriage is paradise for me? Send Ginger in with my drink before you do whatever it is you do with her because I've seen enough of your face for the night. At least she doesn't mind waiting on me when I come home from a hard day's work. It's more than I can say for my lazy wife who thinks the way to my heart is opening her legs for others in every possible position."

"Get off my back, Kyle. I'm the one who has tried so hard in this marriage."

"No, you're the one that's worked day and night to destroy it."

"I would've gone to counseling had I known you weren't happy. You never made that clear to me."

"Why should I? So you can bitch in my ear? By the way, I'm also no long interested in seeing your skinny ass parade around the house naked like you're from the African bush county or something. Would you please start wearing some clothes for a change? Ginger, you know the drill. Bring me a Jack with no ice, would you?"

Renee screams, "You better not touch her!" Her jealousy slips out but I ignore it.

When I carry the drink into Kyle's office I find him with his legs gapped open, a thin robe falling on both sides of his body, watching a porn video.

He turns to me and says, "That was thirty grand well spent." I gulp hard when I realize what Kyle is telling me. "Had I done it myself I may have done something careless like leave the gas can behind with my prints all over it. I paid to have it taken care of right and that just goes to prove to you that I'm not to be played with. Jim just wouldn't listen, Ginger. Now, unless you'd like to suck on this dick like it's your last chance to taste semen, go find my wife and listen to her bitch while I jack off. Since you two are so close why don't you tell her I know about the swinging event at the mansion. I think I'll stop there before I give away a little too much."

Kyle resumes stroking his penis with his right hand. He dips a finger in his drink with his left hand, then sucks off the moisture. I

Andrea Blackstone

don't know what's more shocking—finding out this maniac is on the down low, or hearing him admit that he had Jim and his family knocked off for a sum of money. Both scenarios make me want to call 911 but I know that escaping alive won't be that simple. I've got to work fast to cause a head on collision in Kyle and Renee's relationship. I feel it in my bones—the time to concoct a grand finale is officially up, and I better pull some good shit off like its never been done before.

37

BAD KARMA

Malik

Several weeks pass, and I haven't seen or heard from Monica. I know she's trying to wean herself away from me, but I can't let her get big ideas like removing her presence from my life. Although I insult her, abuse her trust, and treat her like shit, I can't afford for her to banish me, so I dial her father's home phone number and cross my fingers that she will answer it. When I hear her voice I sigh with relief. "Monica, I really need to ask you something. I don't want to fight. Are you listening, baby?" Silence falls but I know she hasn't hung up the phone. I continue, "I need your help—I'm in a bit of a jam."

"What for? The last time I saw you, you said I'll need you before you need me. That's why I cut off my cell phone that you were holding, because you don't need me. Now I don't have one to use myself. That's what I get for trying to help a selfish brother out."

I ignore her statement. "If I don't pay my rent I'll be kicked out of the apartment."

"I told you to budget your money, Malik," she says, sounding flustered. "You have way more to work with than I do, even with your frozen assets. What's your problem now?" she sighs.

I speak in a very soothing voice and say, "I know, but come on baby. I know you've got it. I'll pay you back tomorrow. I would help you if you were in this situation, regardless of if we were together or not. I told you that I'd always see to it that you were taken care of when I get mine. I mean it. My family ain't shit.

Everything you told me about people came true. Monica, I need your help—I really do."

"All I have for the whole month is three hundred dollars. I'm having a tough time finding a decent job and the market is so bad I'm considering getting on the list to substitute at any school on an as-needed basis. Someone called about a government job I applied for to tell me that I'm at the bottom of the list. Right now I've been doing odd jobs under the table so I can keep things going for myself. You don't even care about the sacrifices I made, Malik. Have you even been training since you've moved?"

"Of course I've been training. They've got a Gold's Gym down the street and a gym downstairs. I've been keeping up on my supplements. I'm ready for the show. I've just got to make it until it's time to roll out. And you know I'll help you get a good job. You can come with me to Minnesota and work there if you want. I talked to some people in the team's office and they already said they'd hook you up. I've got your back, Monica. Now please stop wasting time because I have to come up with this money."

"You said that mess before about hooking me up. Of all the people you know, you pick some woman who wants to fuck you to help me. Then I find out that you got some little ho a job when you knew I needed one. I'm not going out like that. If I can't trust you when my back is turned in Maryland, how can I trust you in Minnesota? You aren't my husband, not even my boyfriend. I can't follow you there now."

"Fine—you don't have to go but I'll help you here, okay. Bring your resume when you come and I'll make copies and give it to some people after you help me." Monica stays quiet, like she was thinking about what I said. That's when I put the finishing touches on hustling her. "Look, the sheriff put an eviction notice on my door. I didn't want to tell you but I got you a really nice ring and I don't want to have to pawn it. That's why I'm short. I was planning to make up to you and propose. I found out I'm getting my house back in a few weeks so we can move in there."

"How behind are you, Malik?"

"Two months."

"Two months!"

"I didn't pay for the month I moved in yet, and I have to catch up for this month, so if I don't pay both I'm behind again. That's how I'm behind two months."

"You need a job, Malik. You have connections, I don't."

"For your information I work at K-Mart. I was embarrassed to tell you, okay. One person from my old neighborhood saw me in there checking bags and now I'm sure everyone knows."

"Wait one minute—let me get this straight. You're a Mason, a member of the NFL, which also looks out for their retired players, you're a Greek—and you fucking can't do better than to work at Big K? I can't believe I'm hearing this, I really can't believe it. I don't understand you, Malik. You're riding on twenties working at K-mart? People do you all kinds of favors and you still can't get it together. I don't have all of those chances and I don't feel sorry for you. What in the hell goes through your mind sometimes? I just don't understand how you think."

"Every time I try to be nice to your psycho ass you start up on me. Well if you want to take it there I'll go there. I have two sets of naked pictures of you. Unless you want them all over the internet I suggest you look at things a little bit differently," I say in a hostile voice.

"You don't have pictures of me—you're bluffing," she says, contracting the words that leave her mouth. Monica sounds more than a little concerned.

"I saw you with them and went through the trash to get them. How could you be so stupid and leave something like that at the curb for pickup. Don't you know anyone could find something like that and blackmail you with them? Who took them of you, huh? One of those losers you used to date? Next time, burn them and dump the ashes!"

"How could you do this, Malik? I thought you loved me? I tore those up. I don't understand."

"You didn't tear all of them up, and the ones you did I pieced back together and made copies in case I ever needed to keep your hot ass in check. I have the negatives too. From the day I almost had to beat down that nigga at the club I knew you were a freak. Come get them—they're in my storage bin. I'll give them to you. Maybe your man will enjoy looking at them because I don't anymore. They're mine and I can do what I please with them including mail them to your mother's house. If she knew what a ho her daughter is, she'd be crushed. I don't mind being the one to help her see the light—it's about time she knows the truth! Since you threw your clothes off and took those pictures, pay for your mistake by getting off your ass and doing what I asked you to do. You've got one hour and ten minutes to get here and my clock is ticking. I'll be off work by then so pick me up in the parking lot at the one down the street from my apartment."

With that said, the line goes dead and I know I've hit a sensitive nerve in Monica. Unlike my old project chick, Diamond, Monica is the scary type. I know those two simple threats will motivate her to help me. Men know who they can fuck with and who they can't, but most women don't realize that we throw tests out there on a daily basis to see how far we can go. Monica just failed another one. That tells me I can abuse her until I get tired of it and she won't retaliate or refuse to take my shit. Since that's the case I walk toward the front of the store in K-Mart and continue to try to look important checking bags until the biggest push over I know shows up.

$

When Monica pulls up to help me on my rent run she's dressed in a sexy faux fur coat, matching boots, and believe it or not, her hair is done. I suddenly feel embarrassed that she sees that I went from sporting a mink when I met her, to not even having a real winter coat. I still can't believe that one of the hos I was with stole it and took off while I was asleep, but that's water under the bridge. Now I'm wearing a white shirt to blend in with the other K-Mart employee uniforms. It also bothers me that she knows I'm getting paid next to nothing to peek in bags and give people the green light to walk past me after paying for cheap shit. To cover up, I pile on a few lies about my boy asking me to fill in for someone to help him out in management. I don't even bother to greet Monica properly. I start talking to her like she's a taxi driver just wanting to know where I'm headed.

280

"Turn right at the light and get on the B/W Parkway. My Aunt Paula is putting in five hundred, my frat brother is putting up six, and if you put up three hundred all I'll need is a few hundred more. I can even go down the street to the bowling alley and beat some niggas out of that if I need to."

Monica looks over at me wearing confusion all over her face. "Malik, you told me Paula died."

"I have two aunts named Paula," I lie. "You didn't meet the other one. I mean the one you didn't meet died."

Monica shakes her head and says, "You are going to bother that old lady? Malik, you didn't pay her back before and that's not right. She cooks for you after she's been on her feet all day in the restaurant *and* pays your rent? She gets paid under the table, and doesn't even have a pension. I don't like the way you treat her. When's the last time you gave her a gift or a card? All you ever do is take from her, and she lives in a hole in the wall. The woman has mice in her place, doesn't have a shower, and her kitchen sink is damn near ready to fall off the wall. You won't even set her landlord straight and defend her. Not only that, but you misled me to believe she died, and now you spring on me that Paula is just fine. You don't play with people's lives like that. I swear I think you're a pathological liar."

"Bitch, give me my rent money before I do what I told you. I'm tired of your mouth." I stick my hand in Monica's purse, grab the money out of her wallet and dare her to say a word about it.

A tear falls from her eye. "Oh so you knew Monica would just come running to help you out of yet another jam, huh? All I am is a convenience for you—you don't love me and never did."

"No one has time for your shit, Monica. Get on the highway and pretend you can drive."

"How can you talk to me like that and I'm helping you keep a roof over your head?"

"You can ask my aunt if you don't believe me. I won't bite my tongue under any circumstances. I won't kiss your ass, Monica. If I had my money back I never would've been with you. In fact I've been with much better looking women than you who were glad to be with one of the most eligible bachelors in the metropolitan area or wherever the fuck I lay my head."

"You know what? You just don't respect me. After I help you get what you need, I'm out of your face."

"I'm sure you've got to be back to see your man. It's a wonder he even let you out of the house. Do you cheat on him like you cheated on me? You think you've fixed yourself up a little bit and now you can act like a stuck up bitch? You're still the beady-eyed bitch you always were and don't you forget it!"

$

Monica doesn't say a word to me as I collect all of my rent money so I can take it to the leasing office early in the morning. We pick up Paula and take her to an instant cash place on U Street. I wait in the car while Monica walks with her into the place. Monica holds her arm to make sure she doesn't fall because she rocks slightly from side to side and doesn't use a cane. Plus some shady nigga's are already eyeballing my aunt like they want to use one of the beer bottles they were slurping on to crack her over the head, knock her head off on the sidewalk, and snatch her purse. I know I should feel bad about having her get a cash loan against her upcoming paycheck but I don't because she's been like a mother to me. I wouldn't pay my own mother back so why should I pay Paula? When you love someone you help them. Women raise pimps and wonder why we're spoiled. Go figure.

After Monica and I drop Paula off I realize that my mouth will fuck up my chance to have her stay over at my crib, so I remember to talk to her softly and pretend as if I never insulted her earlier in the day.

"Thanks for helping me out, boo. I tell everyone my baby is such an angel. Look, I need to stop by the store."

"What do you need?" Monica asks.

"Just a few things."

"I'll wait in the car for you."

"No, I want you to go in with me." I reach over and grab her hand like I used to do when I first hooked up with her.

We walk into the grocery store, hand in hand, and I head for the isle where the candles are. I hold both of Monica's hands, look into her eyes and tell her, "Remember how you used to light candles while I took a bath? Then you'd dry me off and give me a massage when I was training—I miss that. Do you?"

"Yeah, I remember," Monica answers.

"Candlelight was so romantic, wasn't it little momma? I never realized it until now."

"You never said that before. I never knew you liked it that much, Malik."

"There are a lot of things I didn't say before, and there's a lot that you like that I like too. I don't know why I just never told you. Maybe it was because of all the stress I was under with my baby's momma shit—that's finally coming to an end soon. I should've known she wouldn't work out—she's not a light redbone. You know that's my preference."

"You can't say color has anything to do with it, Malik."

"Forget her. Do you think you'd be up to us lighting candles all over the apartment and having make-up sex for today?" I say, stroking Monica's hair, then moving my fingers toward her cheeks.

She replies, "Okay—get them, Malik, but all I'm here for is to help you and go home."

I move my hands from her face and pick up a pack of candles from the shelf. "Let's do that tonight. I want to light candles all over the apartment and we can have a romantic evening. We're missing romance, Monica. That's what went wrong. We stopped doing things to keep each other satisfied and interested."

Monica doesn't comment. I purchase the candles, a few drinks, and head back toward my apartment in her car. As soon as I open the door I keep it propped open with one of the bags, position the candles all around, and begin lighting them.

"I have to go to the bathroom, Malik. I'll be back." Monica kicks off her boots, sets down her purse, takes off her coat, and then walks toward the bathroom to the left.

"Here, take this. No cheating, Monica. This is supposed to be a candlelit evening."

Any other time the bitch would move slow as molasses but she quickly hits the light switch before I have time to light a candle and shove it in her hand, hiding the fact that my electricity has been cut off because I didn't pay the bill. I start cussing when I realize I blew my chances of hitting the pussy tonight. I can't invite any other woman over because it would be too embarrassing to go there.

As predicted she sticks her head out of the bathroom and tells me, "Did you know your lights aren't working. They can't be out in the building because they were on in the hall."

"I know about it, baby," I say.

"Don't tell me you didn't pay the bill, Malik. If that's the case you really are doing a piss poor job of—"

I cut her off and say, "I'll get them cut on tomorrow. I just forgot, that's all. I can't remember everything. Do you always remember everything—are you perfect?"

I light a candle and take it into the bathroom so Monica can see how to pee straight. Although I got busted, I got her over here and that's what counts the most. I'll fix it up by telling her how romantic it is to make love under candlelight and that's what they did back in the day. There's always a way to patch shit up if a woman is willing to be patient and listen to bull. The only thing left to hide is that I lost my truck already, and I went to jail behind a bullshit police report. My ex-girlfriend that signed for my truck stabbed me in the back and reported me as an unauthorized driver after her man got mad that she signed for me. Plus, I was a little behind on the payment. I'm waiting for the court date to come up about that. I paid my frat brother another thousand to stop puffing weed long enough to represent me in front of a new judge who I'm sure will drop this case. Everyone at the dealership knew me and my name was wrapped up in some of the extras that I paid for. So for Monica's information I'm not riding on twenties working at Big K—I just work at Big K until further notice—or to help me get over until it's my time to live off of Wes's insurance policy pay out. And if living in my house is still off limits, I hope my stingy ass brother left me his phat crib, too. Yeah, baby, yeah, a player could work with all of that. Lady luck, come to big daddy. Right after you get here I could stand to pack a bag and lie on the beaches of Copacabana in Brazil.

38

PAYING BACK WHAT YOU OWE

Jalita

I spent most of the day letting Renee cry in my arms, pouring her heart out to me while under the influence of 80% proof Southern Comfort. Although I've managed to speed up the demise of Kyle and Renee's marriage, which is already shaky, things have gotten really out of hand. Somehow, she came to the conclusion that Kyle is more attracted to me than her and feels as though her days as wifey are numbered. The whole thing makes no sense because at first Renee was bragging about collecting jewelry from Tiffany's while fucking everyone but her man. Now she's jealous because Kyle has finally backed off and apparently accepted that she likes to lay there like a wet noodle with him individually, but throws her legs open when she's swinging or getting in tune with her switch hitting bisexual side. Trying to use reverse psychology on Renee isn't easy, but somehow before she gets sloppy drunk she agrees to pay more attention to Kyle by being a warmer wife who doesn't rely on sex to show her interest in him. According to my advice, she needs me to remind her of how to please him—that involves a bit of ego stroking and spoiling, not implants, nose surgery, or adding more sexual partners at swinging events. I recommend that she skip the next scheduled event and take a chill pill, but never reveal that Kyle knows about the party she threw.

Renee makes a hair and nail appointment at a day spa, plans to come home and cook for Kyle, and then tell him he can have his space as long as he needs it. And when he's ready to talk she'll be there to listen. After at least a solid week of TLC she's planning to

Andrea Blackstone

announce that she's booked a vacation for them in Aruba. Sure, I have my own selfish agenda at stake but Renee is not the victim, I am. She can leave freely anytime and I'm in this house about to go stir crazy. As soon as Kyle comes in from working half a day, Renee leaves in preparation to woo her man, and I get busy setting up a "mix-up" to foil her ultimate plan before she has a fighting chance. Along the way, I hear someone else enter the back door of Kyle's office but don't catch a glimpse of who it is. I don't want to know in light of what I learned the last time I eavesdropped. Instead I lock the guest bedroom door and barricade myself in it until I hear Renee come home.

Less than an hour after leaving the house, Renee comes flying in the house like a herd of wild animals. Her hair is sitting all over her head like she stuck her finger in a light socket, snot is dripping down to the edge of her lip, and her eyes are fireball red.

She screams, "Kyle. Get out here now! What the fuck? Kyle, come here right now!" The black salon cape is still affixed to her neck. She walks through the house yelling for her husband and checks his usual sitting spots, including his office.

When she hits the top of the steps I hear her open her bedroom door. "What the fuck!" she exclaims. Then I hear Kyle's voice which is uncharacteristically calm and nice. In fact, he sounds as if Renee is in charge of his feelings again and this leaves me scratching my head.

"Calm down," Kyle says.

When I hear those words I peer into their bedroom and see Kyle bent over with his pants around his ankles positioned like he'd just been going to town on a man's butt hole.

As I gasp at the sight, Renee smacks Kyle across the face then shoves him. Kyle falls on top of his lover who scurries away and bolts around the corner with his erection still sticking out. I notice that Kyle's wearing tight, black latex briefs, with an opening to allow his penis to hang out, but covers his pubic hair, and made like a G-string in the back—but no condom.

"I hate you, you undercover cock sucker!" Renee says, half-crying. "How could you do this to me? If I had a knife in my hand, I'd stab your ass!" she says, taking her purse and beginning to beat

286

him with it. Change, bits of tissue, makeup, and money fall out as Kyle shields his face with his hands.

"I don't know what's wrong with you. Stop hitting me. Are you crazy?"

"Oh, so you're denying you're a cock sucker? You deny you suck dick? You deny what you've been doing behind my back, and are bold enough to lie and say that I didn't see a man run into our bathroom? I'm going to find his ass and prove it's so, Mister!"

Kyle backs away from his wife, still shielding his face. "You're the best thing that ever came into my life and I have never done any more than swing *with* your permission. Whatever has brought this on is a mistake. This is what *we* do. What's the problem, Renee?"

She rips the plastic cape from her neck, throws it down and yells, "I thought I knew you but I don't. Who would ever think that you of all people would turn out to be a down low brother? Where is he? Where is that home wrecker?" She begins crying hysterically and walking around looking for the man.

From out of nowhere the man reappears. "I'm right here, that's where. I was minding my business eating Thai food and he came to me, I didn't come to him. He never said he was married so don't get it twisted, girlfriend. I don't *like* sloppy seconds."

Kyle pulls up his pants and says, "Down low brother? What are you talking about—I'm a swinger, we're swingers. Swinging couples experiment sexually. You can't have this just your way, Renee. You made the sexual rules between us and you know what? They melted down to one gigantic rule: You do what you want to do and I fuck whom I want to. You never saved any indulgences for me, so why should I save them for you? Our marriage is shot and we both know it, so don't go blaming some horny single gay guy. So what if gay male sex is prohibited in the club. I'm in my own home and I pay the mortgage here."

Pointing to the man who hasn't bothered to get dressed yet, she says, "*Him,* the big beautiful bouquet of flowers you sent to the hair salon—that you *mistakenly* sent, that's what. My stylist read the card you sent to me instead of some man you've been messing around with, in front of the whole shop. And you know what it said Kyle, you know what it said? Since you don't want to confess I'll fucking remind you."

In a fit of anger Renee yanks a wrinkled small note from a crevice in her purse. She unfolds it, then reads the words scribbled upon it.

"What can I say—I know it may seem a bit forward to send you flowers on your job, but I really enjoyed the hotel meeting the other night and I wanted to do something extra special for you. When you come to town again, look me up. Next time, the bubbly is on me. You're right, our wives are prudes that need to learn how to give blow jobs correctly. You blew my mind!
Hit me up,
K.L "chocolate drop"

Then she repeats again and again, "Chad. THAT READS CHAD, YOU GAY MOTHERFUCKER! I CAN READ BETWEEN THE LINES! YOU'VE BEEN HAVING AFFAIRS WITH MEN. HOW LONG HAS THIS BEEN GOING ON?"

The black man says, "When you get your life straight, call me." He reaches over, picks up his clothes and adds, "Girlfriend looks tore up!" Renee tries to kick him in the nuts but misses. Then the man tells her, "Don't hate on me because I can do it better than you can. God was on your side because you missed." He walks out of the bedroom laughing at Renee like he enjoyed hearing of her public humiliation.

Kyle tries to play if off and laughs nervously. "I didn't send that and I don't know a Chad. It's a mix-up, you fool. I hate the cackling hens at that beauty shop you go to, but why would I go this far to give them something to talk about?"

"You think it's funny? You want to take me for an idiot? Well on the way back home I called the credit card company, and yes that charge for those flowers was made from your account. Nice try, you buttfucker!" Her hand shakes as she shoves the paper back in her purse. "I'll tell you what. You tell *Chad* and the flaming fag that just left here, that said your wife looks tore up, they can have their chocolate drop all to themselves. I'm leaving you and I never want to see you again, Kyle. You've hurt me. You've really, really hurt me. I thought our relationship was so strong. I never thought you would've done something this deceitful in a million years. You've tried everything but telling the truth. Do it, Kyle. If you were man enough to send the person flowers and a card you should be man enough to tell me why he and anyone else is worth it."

Kyle turns on his wife and bitterly snaps, "Go ahead and leave then. If you must know Chad *and* the brother suck much better dick than you. Instead of acting like an irate bitch you should be taking notes on how to treat a man. Chad started stroking me with baby oil and the next thing I know I was I sucking his toes, had my tongue in his pink ass, and he put his cock right up my tight asshole after I came in his mouth. I only stayed with you this long because your family has a little something, and I was waiting for one of your parents to die since I knew they'd leave their only child everything. You wanted to hear it so I'm telling you just like it was and I don't regret a damn minute of the best sexual experience I ever had. I've had a miserable life with you although I tried to give love. You did what you wanted to do with all of those bisexual women, single men, and married couples while denying me the right to have my wife's body to myself at least some time in three years. After waiting and waiting I turned the tables when I found out that you were swinging behind my back. You're the one that started me in the lifestyle, and you of all people have no right complaining because I took it to the next level by cutting you out of some of the action. All you wanted to do was control me and I got sick of that annoying shit! I have feelings too, and somehow a stranger in a hotel room was the one that reminded me of that while helping me to cope with being married to you."

Renee rambles, "What about our son? How could you do this to our family, Kyle? How could you let another man turn you into a faggot? You don't know where he's been. If he would do this with you he'd do it with anyone. Have you thought of all of that? I need to get checked out to make sure I don't have some sort of disease! Tania found out her husband was on the down low. Wait a minute—you're friends with him. Fishing trips, golf, trips—have you and Charles ever—"

Kyle places his hands on his hips and says, "I said it was my first time. Fuck you and *your* son! If I catch something it was well worth it to me. Are you aware that those strippers at your *event* are rumored to all be HIV positive? They were plants, Renee. Now our business could leak out and wreck everything I've built."

"First of all I never had any secret event," she lies. "And what does our son have to do with this?"

"While we're clearing the air, I know Dante isn't mine. For the last ten years I raised him as my own but I've got news for you—I also know about the condom that broke at one of the swingers' parties that you went to with someone else. He's a bastard child all because his momma was a sneaky whore, and your best friend has a big mouth and told me all about it! Why do you think I convinced you to send him to a military academy? I couldn't stand to look at him every day and be reminded that he isn't mine. It's been a long time coming since I figured out how to get back at you in a big way so I've enjoyed this moment. When your son grows up, tell him the truth, and don't forget to blame yourself when you do it! And by the way, I know that you fucked a room full of men when I was in New York. You forgot to hang up the phone all the way on the receiver. I heard you all laughing at me, so take your blame for that too! Like I said, you're a whore and that's why I've had the phone lines tapped to check up on my darling wife, who supposedly missed her workaholic husband so much."

"Even if any of that is true—a man, Kyle? Why a man? You used to fantasize about me being with a woman, but you and a man?"

"You never let me fuck you up the ass and I'm supposed to be your husband, Renee. All you ever told me is it was too painful or it didn't turn you on. I had great practice on Chad—he broke my cherry and now I guess I can't get enough of not having to beg. I see why my brothers are turning to their own. Women are impossible to please, especially ones like you who are complicated histrionics. Thank God my episode of sexual exploration got me off. I can't wait to do it again."

Renee lunges at Kyle and let's out a scream of frustration. As she moves toward him she adds, "If I had a gun I'd blow out every window in this damn house, then shoot you! I hate you! I feel so humiliated. All I wanted was love, a family, a good man. Instead, I got a man who is willing to take it up the ass!"

Kyle storms up the steps and shortly after when he returns I hear, "Someone's been in my footlocker! Renee!" He returns brandishing a revolver. Renee hides behind me, shielding herself.

"Protect me, Ginger!"

"Did you see any of this?" Kyle screams. He pulls his wife her by the arm.

Being in the middle of this lover's war is making my head spin.

"No! I don't know what you're talking about, Kyle. I don't. Where'd you get that? Put that down!"

Before I know it things get out of hand. Kyle and his wife begin wrestling. They knock over a crystal vase in the foyer, and Kyle pushes Renee into the steps. He repeats that he's not gay or even bisexual and had the affair with Chad and the anonymous lover to relieve his unhappiness and frustration. When he continues swinging the gun around, Renee takes her high heel and puts a long gash in his forehead.

With blood dripping from his head, Kyle says, "Bitch, you know about my past, don't you?" He shoves the gun inside of her mouth then pushes her backward. As she falls to the floor he says, "The card, the flowers sent to the salon, breaking the lock, my missing viagra prescription. You did this to make me look bad! You want to destroy me. You hate me. You don't love me. I knew I couldn't trust you. I should've followed my instincts."

Renee continues shaking her head no. When he takes the barrel out of her mouth, she says, "No, Kyle. It wasn't me. Don't shoot. I didn't mean to hit you. This is all getting out of hand. Baby, please, just calm down. There's no need for all of this."

Renee continues to push backward with her feet on the marble tiled squares until she sits in the pile of broken, jagged glass. Kyle blocks the front door, grabs me by the arm and holds the gun to my head. He asks, "Is that true? Did you do this?"

I lie and say, "No! I don't know what you're talking about—really."

"I love her," Renee screams. "Don't hurt her, Kyle. Please!"

Kyle looks confused like he doesn't know whom to believe. Then he yells, "I'm taking you both, and the three of us are going to have a real soul-stirring talk. One of you did this, I know it. Now both of you will pay. But first you're going to listen to me. Up the stairs, get up. Move, you whores!"

Kyle pushes Renee first and I follow behind her. Blood oozes down her leg where she cut herself on glass. When we reach the top of the steps Kyle screams, "In the attic. Hurry up!" He pushes me and I bump into Renee as she turns the curved staircase. After we walk toward the middle of the dark room he says, "Here. Now sit."

Apparently I didn't find another string that was in the attic when I was snooping because Kyle yanks one in a different spot and everything is illuminated. He pulls a light beech wood crate under him and positions himself about six inches from Renee and me.

Blood drips down Kyle's face but he doesn't wipe it. A deranged look covers his face as he shouts, "Slide the footlocker over here, Renee. Move!" Then he adds, "And you, hand on your head, making a triangle out of your elbows. You drop them, you die."

Kyle points the gun toward me and I do what I'm told. Then we both watch Renee struggle to pull the footlocker over near Kyle. When she does, I watch sweat form on her nose and her hair falls in her eyes.

"That's the most work you've done around here in years, Renee. So you are useful after all. Sit your ass down and put your hands on your head like hers. Hurry the fuck up!"

After Renee does what she's told Kyle rummages through the contents of the footlocker and pulls out handcuffs. He walks toward us. "If either one of you try any funny shit, you both die. Renee and I look at each other and nonverbally agree to allow Kyle to join our right arms together.

Kyle returns to the crate and sits on it. "Neither of you know what it's like to work hard and have everything snatched from under your feet. So you try to build a new life. Your first wife just nags and nags and you're trying to take it like a man—a strong black man. But she just keeps on complaining about what you can't give her. She wants five-thousand dollars to remodel the kitchen yet the heating bill was five-hundred dollars that month. She doesn't want to take a second job so all the shit falls on you, because you're the man, and society says the leader of the household is supposed to make things work and provide for the family. So you know all of that and carry around the burden in your mind. You make a measly $18,000 a year working in a liquor store. You're young. You bag shit for the local lushes, mop at the end of the night, stock the shelves and do it all while the China man makes a killing because he's the owner of the place in the hood. You get hip to that so what you do, what you do is—you study and make your dream of becoming a police officer come true. You get on the force of the NYPD—now you're somebody society respects. Now you've got the power," Kyle screams, beating his chest with his hands. When he stops, I watch sweat break out on his forehead. He continues, "There's a brand way to look at your life because people don't push you around. You're a black man with the ability to arrest, shoot, convict and kill. All of this is addictive and gives you a rush. You come home on time dinner's not made. You make a half way decent salary but your wife still is set on complaining. Moving from the hood to a one-bedroom house is not enough. The bitch ain't never had shit and was raised on layaway plans, but now she wants her nails done every week. She wants to drive the latest car, and she wants to live the life of a drug dealer's girl. But she doesn't see she has it good. So she pushes and pushes and complains and complains until you start thinking— what if we could have a two bedroom house, what if I could afford to pay off more bills, what if I could keep her looking sexy so she'd give up that pussy when I hit the door, what if, what if, what if? This is the eternal question that every good guy gone bad asks himself. Is it really worth it? So you're here caught in between a rock and a hard place and then the opportunities start to pour in after you get to know the streets. The first payoff scares the shit out of you, but the second and third becomes a habit that allows life to be lived on a better pay scale."

He walks over to Renee and caresses her face with a crazed look in his eyes. He continues, "Your wife is happier, you're happier, but everyday you go to work with that burning feeling in your stomach because you know that you're now a dirty cop. Still you think the good outweighs the secret you keep. You take the pay offs, you cut deals with drug dealers, pimps, and criminals.

The memory of being poor when no one cared won't allow you to stay true to your profession, plus you know there are more just like you who are getting paid to lie at trial, and do all sorts of slimy things to get ahead."

He withdraws his hand and walks back toward the crate, then sits down. "Everything seems like it's going well. You're expecting your first child. You and your wife are picking out names and discussing how he or she will dress and where he'll go to school. Then tragedy strikes. Boom," Kyle says, jumping up suddenly, balling up his fists, looking around like he's startled. He begins walking slowly around the crate. "One day someone runs your wife off the road but the police come looking for you because you're the spouse. Your own turn on you, and act like you would kill her and the baby in her stomach. Now you're mad. Now it seems like there's no way out of unfair things, being cheated seems a way of life a black man faces year in and year out. Damn, here you go again. Word on the street is that it was no accident. Someone rotting in jail was mad because a dirty cop couldn't help him get from behind those bars and turned down the offer of cash, drugs, and whatever he could bargain. As a result, the one thing that money couldn't buy was taken from that cop and that cop was me." Kyle spits on the floor, then sits down on the crate. I gulp and feel my heart begin to pound.

Kyle continues, "Fast forward to your second marriage. Suppose hustling is a way of life but your wife doesn't understand that ten years on the force has led you to play dirty for a profit. She gets wind of some rumors after a reporter prints a story told by a crab in the basket junkie and so-called informant. He is capable of breaking up your whole family and tries to shame you in the city, in a profession that you love. Your punk-ass wife takes your children, packs them up in a car, and says they won't be back if you don't turn in the money she finds wrapped up in cellophane and packed in a flat packing box under the bed. Instead of letting her and your children leave, you kiss her lips and swear you'll turn in the money or quit the force—whichever way you can get away from playing cops and robbers the safest. She kisses you back, tells you she's taking the children to her mother's around the corner, undress and go to bed, shuts your bedroom door and makes love to you because you are her king, her hero, her black man that's going to do the right thing. You tell her you want to have sex in a motel room where the both of you can let loose without the neighbors knowing all your business. She laughs and agrees to make a thirty-minute drive. She's proud of that but you have her fooled. You decide that a pillow over her face will muffle the sound of your wife fighting for her life. That's what you're willing to do for the love of money. It's not that you want to do it; it's that you have to. As you sit in the bar wondering if the hit man has killed your wife, you think survival of the fittest is best, and continue sipping on a foamy beer. Do you feel bad that you set her up to look like she was having an affair with a lover? No. After your name is cleared you pretend you're so distraught that you can't raise your own kids, so her parents raise them. You're sure they'll be taken care of. So what? And just to be sure that the hit man can't blackmail you, you use some of your money stash to get plastic surgery, change your features, and create a new face, then you steal a new identity to match."

Kyle pauses, staring off into space as if we're not even there. Then he continues. "And now we get up to the present. You meet a woman and she's tall, sexy, funny, and fine. You also find out she's from a family with a little something, and since you love money it inspires you to propose. After a few dates you didn't think would lead anywhere, you can't tell her the truth—can't confess that you're not the V.P. of a prestigious company, you don't have an M.B.A. from Wharton, and you're nothing more than a dirty cop in street clothes. Hell, you didn't even earn a B.A. or B.S. although you are a master of talking bullshit. After marrying wife number three you wear a suit to work, hire limos, ride in first class, and live in a five-bedroom home in a community that anyone would envy. Now you've got the Italian marble, the gardener, household help, four-car garage, and you are the man. From the hood to the boardroom, people respect you. Blacks, whites, Asians, Indians, just everyone. Now you finally really love a woman and she switches up when you have the good life at your fingertips. You think you found the girl next door type but *she* doesn't want to have sex with you." Kyle gives Renee a mean look

Andrea Blackstone

as he talks through his teeth. He continues, "She prefers to let you swing and partner swap."

Kyle finally wipes some of the blood from his forehead. He walks over to Renee and me, smearing blood on both of our faces while saying, "This is animalistic, it brings out the suppressed dirty cop, that bad boy, that man addicted to playing dirty and enjoying the adrenalin rush because swinging too has few rules, and the silence of what goes on in private. Now you both play with fire. Either way both of you get burned because the vicious cycle that created that secret past is revived. Everything is turned upside down when your urges take over, sexual, monetary, emotional—all of them." He walks over to the crate and sits down on it again. He adds, "So you get an idea that there's a way to make more than your six-figure salary. Shit, you can become a millionaire and never have to work again if you and the accountant get together and start embezzling from the dick head that's in charge only because he's the boss's son-in-law. The company is insured so big shit. In time, you strike a deal and the dirty cop syndrome is at work within. But this time it's out of control sexually too. You use your pretend power to rape a young girl, force her to stay in your home, and dare her to escape unless she is willing to face your wrath. She knows you're a murderer but your own wife doesn't."

Kyle smirks. "So here I am, painted into a corner for a third time with someone named Ginger, I mean Jalita, and my lovely wife Renee who will soon follow in the footsteps of Mrs. #1 and #2. Don't feel alone Renee because you both will pay for this knowledge tonight. I didn't tell either of you all of this to repeat, but just want you to know by putting all my cards on the table so you wouldn't have to guess who I was. Now you know it's way more than a down low brother who got busted in his wife's bed. You didn't know me, Renee. Who knows, maybe I'm a psychopath, maybe I have multiple personalities—or maybe it was a combination of my unresolved shit and yours. Maybe you didn't care who I was as long as I married you, because in your mind you wanted at least one child with a man that had my image. Surprise Renee, you chose wrong. I'm a crazy motherfucker!" Kyle screams while beating the gun against his chest and looking up at the ceiling.

296

When his head returns to the normal position, Kyle begins to laugh like he's mad, putting on his police hat, then the rest of his dusty uniform. As soon as he places his gun in his holster he orders us to get up, explaining that we're about to take a car ride toward the Woodrow Wilson Bridge. After he sends us on a permanent vacation he's going to escape to the islands with his money and make a new life there. But out of nowhere someone dressed in all black and a facemask with the eyes cut out, snatches Kyle around the neck as we walk down the steps. Kyle struggles to get loose from the stranger's hold and begins sliding down the steps. I try to run but that damn Renee that I'm handcuffed to is too slow for her own good. No wonder she was sleeping with a psychopath and didn't know it. The woman has a lot to learn about survival, for sure.

When we finally make it into the foyer we see five other masked people. Some are armed with semi-automatic guns, but a few are holding twenty-two calibers. When one of them realizes Renee and I are bound together he says, "Someone find a key—quick. Move, move, move!"

The person returns with the bolt cutters and free Renee and I. When the cuffs hit the floor, we hear, "Run! Both of you, run!"

Renee screams, "My husband—Kyle! Kyle! What will you do to him?" I can't believe she's stressing over a cheating lunatic and doesn't choose to run. Another masked man covers her mouth with gloves to quiet her then shoots her in the head, but I don't hear any noise and figure a silencer is the reason. Blood flies across the room and I gulp hard. As I'm running I look to the left and witness another masked man shoot Kyle in the chest several times. Once again, shots don't ring out, but the sight is no less gruesome.

Kyle stumbles and falls as blood oozes from the front of him but I don't tarry and get caught up in staring at any of this. I finally escape and smell the crispness of fresh air. As I run onto the lawn the hair on my arms isn't enough to keep me warm and goose bumps begin to form. My heart beats so hard that I feel as if it could leap out of my chest. I spot a running car and the driver nods his head and motions for me to run toward him. Although I'm not sure if it's a good or bad decision, I find myself seated next

Andrea Blackstone

to a stranger dressed in black as I listen to the hum of an old blue Chevy Nova, and then listen to car tires squeal. We whip around corners and finally speed toward an open highway.

39

LOVE DON'T LIVE HERE ANYMORE

Malik

If you owe someone money, and it happens to be a woman, mixing sex and payment is an easy thing if a man knows how to work it. All you have to do is say just enough to give the appearance of a desire to dig into your wallet and a woman will be at your front door with bells on before you can say "thanks for the loan." Bitches don't let debts slide as much as men do. When we get stung by a debtor, we get stung once, at the most twice, and then vow never to go down that road with the cheapskate ever again. A woman in love, like Monica, will show up even if it doesn't make sense. Shit, if your ex man or part-time booty call owes you and hasn't coughed up the money in the stated time period, accept you ain't getting shit back, ladies. If you don't, you're about to get used—again.

I'm about to prove to myself that love is blind by stringing Monica along, telling her to come back over to my apartment so I can repay her some of the money I owe. When it's all said and done I'll have everything I need for my Super Bowl Party, plus whatever I'm in the mood for if I want to get it from her.

"Monica, I went to the bank and I have some money for you. Come and get it while I have it because I know you can use it. I don't have all day so you need to let me know if your man will let you swing by my place," I say when she answers her cell phone.

"Malik, I told you about greeting me that way. You have no manners. I'm always supposed to drop everything and come running to you."

Andrea Blackstone

"I'm not trying to start with you today. All I was trying to do was pay you back what I owe and I'm wrong for doing that, too."

"Oh, so now you want to pay me back. Just say you want to pay me back something because I'm sure it's not everything you owe me."

"Do you want me to put it in the mail?"

"No—I'll never get it. When you say you'll put something in the mail all that means is you aren't going to do anything. Plus, you can't put cash in the mail and I don't trust a check coming from you."

"If that's how you feel I suggest you catch me while I'm home then. Get over here and stop bitching and moaning. You don't have a job so drop what you're doing."

"I'm on my way, Malik but I have nothing to say to you. All I want to do is get my money and get the hell out of your space. Better yet, why can't you bring it to me? I'm tired of coming to you, and you owe me in the first place. Why should I burn my gas to pick up what you owe?"

"My truck's in the shop."

"But it's brand new, and it's not even time for it to be serviced."

"Let it go, okay. You're always running your damn mouth, trying to analyze everything."

"Like I said, all I want is to just permanently wrap up our dealings with each other, as soon as possible."

"Aren't you listening—I just told you my truck is in the shop. I promise you that if you'd get your ass on over here, the next time I go to church I'll be dancing in the isle knowing that I don't have to ever see your crazy ass again. The feeling is mutual, Monica. Now fire up that tin can on wheels and get your ass over to my place before I give your money to one of my bitches that respect big daddy," I lie.

$

"Where's my money?" Monica asks as soon as I open the apartment door.

300

"You'll get it after you take me a few places," I say as she walks in.

"Do you or don't you have my damn money, Malik? I'm not up for games," she says, looking me up and down like I'm due for some sort of inspection. She notices that I've begun to grow a beard, wear a diamond in my ear, and also that my apartment is hooked up better than the model we were shown when I first moved in.

"Let's go to D.C. to pick up my aunt. I called her and she's home from work now."

"Here you go again, making other people's schedules for them. I just want my money. I'm not trying to get mixed up in riding you here or there. You've got friends and a list of women who you say would love to cart your linebacker ass around. Why don't you call on one of them, Malik? And I hope you're not borrowing money from Paula to pay me. How does that go, rob Peter to pay Paul?" Monica comments, crossing her arms.

"Very funny. If you want your money I suggest you stop prolonging this. I said let's go."

Monica nearly throws a hizzy fit as she follows me out of the door. She has no choice if she thinks it will help her get whatever I owe her back, if even a ten dollar bill.

When we make it to my aunt's place I knock on her door. I even put my eye close to the peephole to see if I can see what's going on behind the door. "You're trifling," Monica says. "What do you expect her to do? Run because your ass wants a favor?"

With that single comment, an argument begins. By the time Paula opens the door I'd just finished telling Monica something crude, but I forget about insulting her when I notice that my aunt is still dressed in her work uniform after she opens the door.

"Come on, Paula. Let's go. You should be ready," I complain.

"Oh, hold your horses. I'm coming. Hi, Monica, it's nice to see you again," she says with a slow Southern drawl and warm smile.

"I'm glad to see you're looking well. Malik led me to believe you weren't feeling your best, not so long ago."

I feel my cheeks swell and puff because I know Monica is on the verge of telling Paula I lied about her dying. When I look at

301

her cross-eyed she grins at me as if to say, *you're a shady motherfucker and I'm going to expose you to your sweet old, aunt.*

Paula replies, "Oh, I can't complain so much. It's the same old thing when you get to be my age. You fall apart all at once not some at a time."

"You do very well for yourself. In fact you set a wonderful example and work ethic for your nephew but he doesn't value the lesson he sees," Monica continues.

I feel like punching Monica in the mouth but instead I mumble under my breath that she can suck my dick. Paula rocks side to side, moving slowly but surely on her tired feet. After she locks the door we walk down three flights of stairs, passing pungent odors of piss, weed, and funk in each hallway.

When we reach the sidewalk I say, "I'll drive." Monica will never make it through D.C. traffic and we don't have all day. "I need the keys, Monica," I say when she takes her time passing them to me.

She hands them to me and helps my aunt into the back seat after I unlock the car. Then we drive from store to store looking for perfect cuts of meat for ribs, tender green beans, and whatever else I order my aunt to cook for my Super Bowl party guests. By the time we reach the sixth store it's about 11:00 p.m. I inform Paula that I'll pick up the trays of food in the early afternoon. I don't care that she'll be up all night cooking without having a chance to wiggle her toes and relax, or watch TV on the couch, because good Southern women aim to please—even senior citizen ones.

$

"Relax, you're right where you need to be," I tell Monica as she sits on the side of the bed facing the balcony.

"I want my money, and I want to go home and sleep in my own bed. I've waited all day and now you're dragging this out some more."

"Oh, is your man going to be mad if you're missing?" I joke.

"I don't have a man!" she turns around and snaps. "Will you stop saying that, Malik?"

"Then stop stalling—take off your clothes and stay the night. You know we have to pick up the food for the party from Paula as soon as she's done cooking. What are you afraid of? I don't want to fuck you," I lie.

Monica ignores my comment. "No, *you* have to pick up the food from Paula. I don't have to do shit for your greedy friends that are going to stuff their faces like pigs. Where are they when you need help with something? I keep asking you that like a broken record. If it were up to me I'd serve them hot dogs, sauerkraut and tell them to bring their own beer. I can't stand those leeches—they make me sick."

"Why do you do this every time I see you?"

"Do what?" she snaps.

"This."

"And what's *this?*"

"Act like a bitch and run up my blood pressure."

"I don't. You just get on my nerves when you play games. You never seem to be able to do what you say," she says, stretching her legs out on the bed.

"You know what you need, Monica?"

"What would that be?" she says, rubbing her temples.

"A good fuck." When I do she stops rubbing her temples and lifts her head. I continue, "I know you. Whenever you need some dick you start mouthing off and acting grouchy. Come here and sit on this," I tell her exposing my big black dick to arouse her.

She looks at it cautiously like she's not sure whether she should devour it or push it away. I don't let go of the moment she's vulnerable. "I need the same thing. Tell me you don't want this anymore," I say. "I miss fucking you. Our breakup is hard on me too. Outside of Paula, you're really all I've got when you think about it. Just because I don't admit you're right about a lot of things you tell me doesn't mean it's not true. I know those motherfuckers just want to be around me again because I'm going to back to play ball." Monica is silent.

I slowly move closer to her and stop at the edge of her thighs. After I position myself in her personal space, I open my mouth and start licking and sucking on her reddish brown nipples. When they become long and hard she says, "Get off me, Malik! Stop doing that!"

"Not until you open your legs," I tell her, continuing to suck her nipples. Then I press her breasts together, sucking both of her nipples at the same time.

In a sultry whine, Monica blurts out, "I wish I could just detach your dick from your body and take it home for my enjoyment. The only thing you're good for is getting me off. I hate what you do to me, Malik. You always get your way and I can't stand you for it." She lays her head on the pillow, sighs heavily, then presses her thighs together.

"I miss this juicy pussy. Please, let's fuck and get some stress off, baby," I say, pushing her legs apart to thrust myself inside of her. Although I'm half-asking for her permission to fuck I don't wait for her reply. After I feel Monica's tight pussy fit around my dick firmly I can tell she hasn't had sex in a long while. "I'm sorry for acting wrong. Let me make it up to you and eat your pussy."

"No, I don't want you doing that," she says, pushing my shoulders away from her like she wants me to stop making love to her.

I look at her. "Why, is that someone else's job now?"

"No—that's not it," she answers.

"Stop resisting me—open those pretty motherfucking big yellow legs wide and let me lick on your clit." When I part Monica's legs I bury my face in between them. When she arches her back I know that she won't tell me to stop now. "You miss this don't you? Answer me, little momma."

"Yes, Malik I miss this," she says, moaning softly. Her breathing is relaxed.

After I lick her and nibble on her clit a long while I feel her legs begin to quiver. Monica is obviously on the edge of having an orgasm so I take that as a cue to raise my head and look into her light brown eyes. "Do you still love me?"

"Yes, I still love you. I've never loved anyone more—that's why I've been so supportive of you," she explains in between struggling to regain her composure.

"Then suck my titty—then I'm going to fuck you good."

304

After Monica licks and sucks my nipples, I push her backward and go to work. When the headboard begins smacking against the wall Monica moans so loud I know the neighbors upstairs and downstairs can hear her teetering on the edge of multiple orgasms. After we have sex for hours, I assume Monica belongs to me again and start talking about her ring, marriage, what we should do with our future, and even find myself believing that I can be a family man that could appreciate a woman like this.

"Go ahead and use the bathroom first," I tell Monica when we're done. I pour two glasses of Gatorade and bring them into the room.

When I pass by the bathroom door Monica asks, "Whose hair is this on the bathroom floor? Most of my perm has grown out. This is long permed hair—mine is curly."

"It's your hair. I don't know what you're talking about," I say, sitting on the side of the bed nude, sipping my Gatorade.

"I'm sure it's not mine," she yells through the crack of the door.

I take another sip of my drink. "Who inspects hair on the bathroom floor? You've got mental problems. I keep telling you that. Now quit it, you're making my blood pressure go up, and I'm trying to have some fun and host a Super Bowl Party."

When Monica walks into the room after showering she says, "You should be getting ready to run your ass up and down that field, not having a party. When you were at my dad's house you were supposed to be working on your cardio training and had the nerve to ask him why he passed you by in the car when you were running from the gas station. When's the last time you trained hard, Malik? You can't be lazy at a time like this."

"I keep telling you I've been in the NFL before. I know what I'm doing. Drink your Gatorade and take your crazy ass to sleep. I'm going to take a shower—maybe I can get some peace and quiet in the bathroom."

Monica sighs loudly and turns her back toward me again. She pulls the cover over her head, mumbling that she's mad at herself for giving up the pussy to the same old motherfucker who tells her the same lies in different ways. The only difference is they come from a different angle when they land in her ears.

$

"How are you going to have a Super Bowl Party when you didn't pay your cable bill? You can't get reception without it, Malik."

"I'll get it on by game time," I tell Monica. She had no business trying to look at the morning news anyway—nosey ass.

"Yeah right. I can't wait to see you pull this one off. Eight hundred million people are hyped to watch the game. Why will your people be any different? You've bled me dry, I can't help you."

"I didn't ask you for anything. I'll make a call to the cable company then we can pick up the food. It should be ready by then. I told you when I worry then you worry."

I know my guests will be impressed by my football helmet and the NFL gear that's on my curio shelf. Little do they know I only played one game in the last two years, or that the coach from the arena ball team has been calling since then for me to return his equipment. Even so, it makes a good impression so I leave it there. Not only that but I've also decided that if Monica hounds me about my progress one more time today, I'm going to tell her that I told the Vikings coach that I don't feel ready for football, and that I'll decline to show up for mini-camp. Although it doesn't take a rocket scientist to realize the whole contract thing was a lie, and my best days of playing football are behind me, Monica still doesn't get it. Now, I'm questioning if keeping her around until my cash stash is up to par is worth sacrificing my sanity.

Monica pulls up the car to the main apartment entrance while I get a shopping cart to load up the party food and take it upstairs to my place. I have at least twelve trays of soul food and I'm thinking my aunt had better done her best cooking it all, because I'm not one to eat what I don't like.

Although I have no business paying anyone to clean my apartment I miss having a maid and pay one of the Hispanic housekeepers that tend to the building to clean my bathroom and vacuum the rug. I could've done a better job myself, and I put Monica up to tell him that I'm not pleased with his work since she's bilingual. I know her ass didn't tell him to do the job over but

I leave good enough alone and put the finishing touches on preparing for the Eagles versus the Patriots.

When the guests start arriving I assign Monica to door duty. She's ok with making herself useful because I can tell she's bored. The first guest that arrives is someone who frequently gives me rides, free of charge. He's the only for real dude I know in the building. He limps because he has one artificial leg, but he gets around well just the same. He walks in tossing a football in the air, toting a large foam finger like fans haul into stadiums, ready to sink into the leather chair and watch some football. The other guests trail in and flow into the small crowd that gathers in the living room. The last guest is a porn actress with size triple F tits, or whatever size those deformed things are.

Monica's eyebrows form a deep line when the woman ignores speaking to her and isn't courteous when she hands her a plate like a good hostess would. Instead the woman flings her dried out blonde wig in Monica's face and brags about all the dick she's fucked as she nestles between her so-called agents. I know she fucks them whenever the freak fever hits her. Somehow I let it slip that she gave me her card and wanted me to be one of her bodyguards too. She gave me a picture of her sitting on a motorcycle, damn near naked. I put it in a frame and keep it out of sight while Monica visits, but she found the picture and questioned me down about it. The best I could do was lie and say my friend with the limp likes her and that she was asked to the party for his enjoyment, not mine. Monica tells me she can't believe I'd have a trashy whore in my home. I proudly brag that this *actress* is well acquainted with a rapper whose name I can't mention here, but the outcome is that she isn't impressed. In fact she replies that she knows celebrities too, so what in the hell is so impressive about that?

I don't know how I manage to fool a room full of black people that we don't have to watch the thirty-ninth Super Bowl in Jacksonville to have a nice time. I keep suggesting that they eat and drink. Monica sits on a barstool in the corner and watches. She shakes her head when I throw out a quick lie about the line to buy TVs being too long today because everyone wanted to get one for the big game, so I didn't have enough time to set up my flat panel

TV. Now if it were me I would've tried a remote or offered to hook the shit up but no one went there. One of them even went downstairs to the clubroom to check the score and reported back to the rest of us what it was—dumb fuckers!

After everyone disperses I clean up, throw away trash, then relax on the sofa. As soon as I start talking on the phone to one of my boys I hear, "Malik, where's my money? You promised to pay me back. I'll leave after I get my money. You run me all over town and aren't even going to pay me back after I waited this long? Look at all the things I bought you from the day you moved in. Look at this flower arrangement. You promised to pay me back for that. One hundred dollars worth of silk flowers and my time to make the shit look nice, and come to find out it was to impress some niggas at a party in your apartment. Who paid your water bill for you so you could wash your dirty, stinky tail? And who helped you pay your rent every time you called with a hard-luck story? This is how you treat the girl who's been there through the drama that you should've saved for your momma? You make me sick! I don't know why I continue to do this to myself. I guess I deserve it for being so stupid!"

I continue talking on the phone to one of my boys, ignoring Monica. She walks over to the flower arrangement she made me for the Super Bowl Party and throws it onto the floor. Then she takes one of my golf clubs out of the bag and lets it fall, making a clanking noise that gets my attention and makes me to notice what she's doing. I jump up from the sofa. "Go, bitch! Git to gittin'! Get out now before I call the police on your ass. There's a cop right upstairs and I've already told her about you. Do you want me to call her? She doesn't mind coming down here to deal with you. Get the fuck out!"

"I helped you get this place and now you're going to throw me out? You would have me drive on the road at this hour?"

"You should've thought of that before you started up with your mouth. Shut up—I'm on the phone. Damn!"

Monica continues pestering me. "But, Malik it's 3:00 a.m. I'm tired—I don't feel like an hour's drive back home."

"But Malik, nothing. Go see your man! Wake him up and do whatever you want with him. I don't want you, Monica. You're making my blood pressure go up."

"I don't have a man!" she yells.

"Excuse me a minute," I say to my boy. "Let me call you back after I take care of this bitch over here." I hang up the phone, pick up the golf club she threw on the floor and walk toward her with it while holding it high in the air.

Panic covers Monica's face and she runs into the bedroom screaming, "Don't hit me. Don't hit me! No, don't hit me, Malik! I'm sorry. I didn't mean it. Please!"

I stand over her as she shakes, cries, and pleads, holding the club over her head. "I'm going to call your mother and let her hear you get your ass beat, bitch. What's wrong with you touching my golf clubs, huh?"

"I didn't mean it. Don't hit me!" she screams, balling up into a fetal position on the bed, crying.

I swing the golf club over her head, somehow missing her just as I envision whacking her with it with no mercy. I begin cussing and calling her names, then walk into the other room, still holding the golf club.

"This is my motherfucking house, and I am the king of this castle. Anybody doesn't like how I run it can get the fuck out, starting with you, Monica," I yell.

In a fit of anger, I feel my heartbeat pound and turn on the big screen television. I can't enjoy whatever it is that I am supposed to be watching and get up, placing my golf club in its case. After a few moments I walk into the bedroom. Monica is under the covers, sniffing like a little wimp and shaking.

"Look what you almost made me do. You know how strong I am. If I would've finished swinging it I would've hurt you."

Monica keeps her back turned toward me and I know I've scared her more than ever before. In the morning, when the sun rises, my eyelids open and I listen to her put on her clothes. Apparently she knows I'm awake because she tells me, "I only put up with this and yesterday because I really needed my money back. I don't even have food, Malik. In fact I have barely enough gas to make it home. I'm having a hard time and a lot of that is due to believing that you'd never use me like this."

"I let you sleep here last night so get your things and get the fuck out. I'm not playing with you, Monica. Get to stepping. You've got five minutes to get dressed."

"It won't take me but two," she snaps.

Before I know it the front door of the apartment slams. I feel blank and Monica's words don't make me feel guilty for one second. As soon as she leaves I call the cop from a few floors up and to offer to fuck her brains out, and see if she'd be willing to cook me a thank-you breakfast. When I do she's the one that asks me if I've heard the news that my twin Wes's body was found in icy water in the Potomac River. Although I should feel the pressure of tears building up I don't shed a single one. My lottery ticket just came through—insurance money here I come! I managed to keep up the payments by putting aside some do not spend loot for shit like this in a safe at my house, when no one was home . Now that I almost don't need Monica, I can kick her to the curb in the very near future. Time for my insurance payout, and that bitch is broke as a bad joke. Like I said, she'll need me before I need her 'cause love won't live hear no mo'—as soon as I make my first real bank deposit in the account she started for me!

40

Jalita

"Shit! What just happened? Who are you?" I mumble, looking over at the masked man.

"It's ok. I'm not going to hurt you. Baby girl, it's me—Clyde."

"*Clyde?*" I say, holding my chest and struggling to catch my breath. The man pulls off his mask and I see the familiar face from Ms. Geraldine's apartment building. I sigh aloud with relief, still holding my chest. "How did you know where I was? Why did you storm in Kyle's place like that? Why did those men murder him and—"

He cuts me off. "I didn't know you were in there. Why did he have you handcuffed to his wife?"

"Clyde, you don't know, do you?"

"Don't know what?"

"So you didn't set me up," I mumble with confusion.

"Set you up how?"

"That dude Kyle is crazy. He took me to the party I was supposed to get paid to attend with him and he came on to me sexually, talking some weird shit about taking me home for some freaky swinger shit. After that he raped me and told me he'd kill me if I called the police or left his house. He and his wife Renee are freaks and get off on some bizarre sexual trips. A lot broke loose—he snapped after his wife busted him in bed with a dude. I was plotting to get my revenge when you happened to show up with your peoples."

"Baby girl—he raped you?"

"Yes Clyde, he did," I answer, dropping my head in shame.

"Oh hell no! I'm so sorry. Shit like this has never gone down on my time."

"He implied he'd scared you because he's not to be messed with. It turns out he's a dirty cop who's murdered several people."

"I'm still hustling, just elsewhere. The neighborhood got hot with cops after some boys were shot on the basketball court and I didn't want no one snooping around too close to my operation. I hunted Kyle down because he owes me for some other business dealings in addition to your little gig. Don't worry, he got what he deserved. I called him and gave him a friendly warning that his drug deadline was up—either pay or be sprayed. That motherfucker, he raped you!" Clyde bangs on the steering wheel. "Tell me, I want to know everything that happened to you. And don't leave shit out no matter how hard it is to talk about it. In the meantime I'm taking you to get checked out. Don't worry about nothing because I have a hook up there."

I fill in all of the blanks of my abbreviated version and tell Clyde everything that happened from the time I left his old apartment—the whole story, although I was nervous that he could be so calm after playing a part in a double murder.

When we drive up to a hospital in South East, I lift my head and begin to panic. As my heart pounds, I tell Clyde, "I don't want to report this. My nerves are shot and I've got a trial coming up. This is all too much. I don't want to be implicated in whatever you just did back there."

"That had nothing to do with you. I want to make sure you're physically ok. You've got to do this. My boys got it all covered. My hands weren't in it and the guns will be handled properly. I'll stay with you the whole time if you want me to. You don't have to tell anyone anything besides when you were raped and what happened. Get the checkup and don't do all of the rape kit prepping. It's your right, baby girl."

"I just don't want to subject myself to all of the questions in light of how it went down."

"That makes sense, and I feel you on that. All I'm saying is that you need to get checked out. Don't be walking around here after a nigga did something like that not knowing if he gave you something or if you're pregnant or something. I just have to be totally blunt."

"Ok, Clyde—I guess you're right."

"You may want to have babies running around some day and find yourself a good man to love and make them with. You've got to come correct for that future of possibilities."

"Me? Never. I'd take my last ten bucks to Vegas and bet that will never happen. Relationships never work out for me. I'm pretty much alone in life."

"Hey, you never know what could change."

"Before we go in there, I have to ask you something."

"What's up?"

"The *business* that you and Kyle had going on is really none of my concern but did you have to kill him and his woman?"

"What do you care about a motherfucker who took you against your will and did all of that other shit? The law don't care about a black woman getting raped by a nigga or any other race of man. They ain't going to do nothing. A sick, twisted dude like Kyle needed to pay the stiffest penalty—otherwise he'd be out there doing that same shit to someone else. Do you think two less murders are going to change anything?"

"Yes, it starts one person at a time. I'm not down with spraying bullets. Look, I had to shoot someone once and he died. I don't feel good about it even though it was self-defense. I just wish you hadn't beefed like that. I had dirt on him—you didn't have to go there. I wanted to see him suffer and get some time behind bars. As far as your money, he had it right under your nose if you would've taken the time to look and listen."

"What?" Clyde looks at me, flips open his cell phone, presses one button then says, "Stop the plan! Don't argue with me. We're going to switch some things up. Make sure all of the curtains are closed and move quietly in case some nosey neighbor is watching or listening. Two of you do some snooping in his office and see if you can find any financial documents, and also get up to that attic and carry that whole footlocker down. Close it and don't touch anything. Grab that and get out of there. Ring the phone when you're finished. Don't talk, just ring it. I have a little run to make. Oh, and there's a car that didn't belong to our dear friend—it's in his garage but dogs may be around somewhere so be careful. Check the wires under the hood and make him hand over the keys to it. If you can start it, drive it back to the crib. Hurry." After Clyde informs his crew of the revised plan he hangs up the cell phone and says, "Satisfied?"

I don't answer him, and a tear drops from my eye, thinking of Renee. The most she deserved was a chipped tooth or broken nose, but not death. I wish that twit would've run. Damn!

"We better get a move on it. Oh shit! We can't take you in there like that," Clyde says, looking at the handcuff dangling from my wrist.

"Now what?" I ask.

"I've got to take you somewhere and we'll come back."

"Where are we going now?"

"To get a hacksaw."

"Yeah, right—I knew that. Of course we need a hacksaw," I comment with frustration, throwing up the arm that's making me look like a runaway prisoner. Tears begin to flow down my face. I'd just worked up the courage to get checked out and now it has to be put off once more. I begin bouncing my knee, craving one of my antidepressants. I can't tell Clyde how scared I am and try to appear tough, but somehow he sees through my tough girl act. Man, whatever happened to Negroes settling shit with their fists?

"Umm. I don't know what I should say right now so I'll just put it to you like this. Look baby girl, my sister was raped before. She was hit in the head with a lead pipe. Some asshole dragged her in an alley and did what he wanted to do on a street in Baltimore. No means no, whether it's in an alley, in a crib, or in a hotel room. I've been through this and it's not an easy thing. The police never found the guy and my sister hasn't been the same since. Now wipe your face, baby girl, because I really want you to heal over this shit and move the hell on past it. It can ruin a woman if she lets it and I hope you won't let it. Not all men would do a woman this way so don't fool yourself into believing that's true. Together, we're going to straighten everything out, but you've got to be strong and hold it together for me. Okay?"

In a barely audible tone, I respond, "Okay."

By the time we stop talking Clyde pulls up into a Home Depot Lot in New Carrollton, in search of a hacksaw. I slouch down in the seat wishing I could disappear from off the face of the earth but I can't. This is the kind of shit that kills you or makes you stronger. I make a choice to try my best to get through this mess and become stronger than I was before I got wrapped up in all of this new trouble.

$

Hours later it's nearly sunrise. A woman from a rape crisis program held my hand as I was examined. I was relieved to find out that I wasn't pregnant by Kyle, and didn't catch some of the typical STDs, but I'll have to wait on the HIV test results.

Over and over they asked, "Who did this to you? Don't you want to tell?"

Although I felt as if they felt sorry for the degradation I described, I tired from the pressure and that made the tears flow harder and longer. It was my right to refuse providing details but the sympathetic white women kept telling me fifty different ways that I'm upset but need to consider this very important decision. I didn't break under the pressure so all they could do was allow me to get up from the hospital bed, return my clothes, wish me well, and then give me a number to a rape crisis hotline if I ever felt the need to vent or receive anonymous emotional support.

By the time Clyde and I make it back to his place the previously masked men are sitting around drinking and looking at TV. I spot a few bullet proof vests lying on the couch.

"Don't bother baby girl," he tells them. "I'll fill you in on what happened to her. She needs to rest."

As I hang my head low, clutching my elbows through my coat, they stare at me like they know that I've been raped, abused, and that my emotions are swirling wildly around my head. I shut the door to Clyde's bedroom and lock it, longing for an antidepressant or a sleeping pill to calm me down and make me forget that I'm at my weakest when I'm alone in my own space. Now I can stop fronting, cry my eyes out, and prepare for phase two.

I drop my coat in a corner, then let my jeans fall to my calves as I shake from too many thoughts invading my mind at once. Out of paranoia, I walk toward the door to check the lock for a second time. That's when I hear them talking on the other side of the wall.

"Open the chest. Let's see what we've got."

"Damn! There must be several hundred grand in here."

Another voice says, "Who cares about what he did to that bitch. She ain't one of our sisters. Let's split the money and call it even. She might even be lying, Clyde. I bet she was trying to get up in his pocket and didn't tell you what she did to bring it on. You know the first thing bitches do is cry rape when shit goes sour. It happened to me when Shareese got mad at me for screwing her little sister." He laughs then adds, "I bet if we threw some big bills out on the floor and popped a CD in the player she'd be popping her coochie like a pro, making us drool because she knows we're soldiers making that street paper. Didn't she believe that video producer line you threw, making her ass jiggle for you and shit, acting like she was in Nelly's *Tip Drill* video?"

Clyde replies, "You've got a point. She looked like she was telling the truth though. I can usually look in people's eyes and tell if they're lying. The girl had handcuffs on and shit. Plus that dude was parading around in an old police uniform. It was some bizarre shit going down."

A deep, serious voice speaks up. "Yo, Clyde—I think you need to check yourself. That could've been due to some kinky game—you don't know 'cause I done some creative shit myself. He laughs. "And let's say it wasn't like that, what's her name got out of there because of you. She's not your girl so you need to squash those thoughts. These streets don't love nobody unless you've got peoples and family, and that bitch seen us do too much. I say we act like we're going to cut her in on some of the money but knock her off before we get to New York and set up shop somewhere else. We can be on I 95 in a heartbeat and don't have to look back. I can't believe you sent her in a room with ten bags of coke under the mattress. Are you crazy? What if she does us dirty? You know bitches ain't no good. If there's a choice between a dollar and their loyalty, you know how that turns out. Let's be real about it—she'd probably suck dick for a McDonald's Value Meal. We can't do business with no pussy, so man up and look at the big picture. Is your conscience getting to you or something? You know your grandmother found a reason to kick that girl out illegally when you came into town. Did you tell her you're Geraldine's grandson? No. It's bad enough your dumb ass took her to the hospital. That was a very stupid move. Now let's get back to business."

"What's in there—three hundred grand or so?" Clyde asks. We found it because of her, and if she realizes what we've got she'll expect a cut. Ya'll are right—fuck that ho. It's not like I forced her to take the gig, or like I'm some pimp answering the phone to keep her out on the block. I got a single mother and a college girl short on the rent who let me post their pictures up on my website, hoping that some dude will pay for *companionship* by major credit card or pay pal. I'm the one taking a chance of not getting busted 'cause no matter what you tell these horny jackass men, one of them will always slip and insist on trying to discuss sexual services over the phone instead of keeping shit discreet. Come to think of it, it's time to roll out on that account alone. I'll set up shop in New York and find some professional escorts who won't complain next time. Give me a little credit, dawg—I ain't paying her shit, not even the cash I took from Kyle for the girl's "escort" services."

With those words I feel my heart sink. My ears and face grow hot knowing that Clyde dumped this whole mess in my lap after his boys put a few suggestions in his weak mind—and that he'd acted as if Ms. Geraldine had rented him my apartment out of the blue. I dress, slide on my shoes, and check the lock on the door again, struggling to keep from screaming. I forget how cheap I feel, pretend my nerves are made of steel, and look under the mattress. I find drugs in bags and a pile of money that was probably the result of one of Clyde's boys trying to get a little extra, before it all got counted. I gulp hard and decide that I better take what I can because I ain't getting shit but a bullet in my ass if I don't try to escape tonight. As my heart pounds I think fast and notice that one sheet covers the bed and a few more are stacked in a corner. With shaking hands I collect five of them and tie them in knots. Next, I tie one end around the leg of the bed, quietly raise the window, and throw the other end out of the window.

I spot a backpack in the corner, throw the contents on the bed, and then stuff the money inside of it. After I slide on my coat and

Andrea Blackstone

situate the backpack I breathe deeply and scale down the side of the two-story apartment building on my homemade rope. When I hit the bottom I shoot to my car remembering Clyde didn't hand over my key. I see Ms. Geraldine's light turn on and I begin cussing to myself. I better fill in the blank fast or her devil seed of a grandson and his homies will take care of my ass before sunrise.

41

THE DIRT BAG

Malik

Although I almost knocked Monica's head off the last time I saw her, that's irrelevant. Why? Because she had no business pressuring me about money I owed her. Winning the heart of a woman is simple if a man knows what's he's doing. I've always told her that if she wants to play "the game" she better know the rules. She has yet to understand that I make up my own rules to my own game. I've tried phone contact and now it's time to resort to a new email address. Monica has managed to block the last three email addresses that I've emailed her from but today my message will get through to her because I'll make up yet another one. When I'm finished making my point I'll leave her alone, but right now I'm not finished. And since the game isn't over I'll keep some shit going by typing a simple two-lined email. That's just enough to get under her skin. There's some room left for manipulating her yet so I'm going to put more pressure on her until she agrees to start seeing me again.

Subj: Re: are you at home?
Date: 2/12/05   Pacific Standard Time
From: aballer@verizon.net (Malik Harrison)
To: Words4victory@aol.com

240-460-1121, my new number, whenever you come back home...I was at your home tonight just to see if you were home...like I thought

Andrea Blackstone

Subj: Re: are you at home?
Date: 2/13 /05   Pacific Standard Time
From: Words4victory@aol.com
To:aballer@verizon.net (Malik Harrison)

Ok. Thanks for stopping by.
Bighead.

Subj: Re: are you at home?
Date: 2/13 / 05   Pacific Standard Time
From: aballer@verizon.net (Malik Harrison)
To: Words4victory@aol.com

   this is it, you have until the end of today to deside if you want us
are not...dispite who your fucking now, and I know you are stilll
fucking someone, if you don't give me a answer today, he, he, she
thim can have you it will be all over and I will begain doing what I
can do...if I am wrong about you fuckin someone you have to
understand your past......but I promises you monica on my
GRANDMOTHER grave...I will cut you completely losee today,
I need no talk if you do not step up today it will be all gone, I don't
want to hear about I this or I that I need to no its yea or nea, all
you have to do is call me240-460-1121, and say yea are nea...thats
all I will listen to, no talk...so like I said once before if you want to
get rid off me just say nea and am gone, now if I do not hear from
you thin I will take it as nea...this is all I want to hear, this is my last
note, unless I hear yea...and if that's the case I wish you and your
family the best...I promise this is my last e-mail, so please don't test
me, if I don't here from you today thin tomm I will be doing what
your doing now still are done to me, I will be fuckin someone eles
on valentine's day just to spell it out..now you can get all cought up
in what I just spelled out if you like but thas your decissipn, but I
will not read any long message, so its eather y or n...so the clock on
I'll waite to hear or not...have a blessed day...

Subj: Re: are you at home?
Date: 2/13/05 Pacific Standard Time
From: Words4victory@aol.com
To: aballer@verizon.net (Malik Harrison)

If I didn't reply the first time, don't you think there's a reason?
I've received all of your nasty phone messages, my dad told me
someone hangs up when he answers, and I'm sick of your juvenile
delinquent shit. You must have way too much time on your hands.
Stay out of my life, would you. If I'm so terrible and such a whore,
just be gone. Leave me alone, Malik. If you continue to harass me
I'll contact the police and begin procedures to bring charges. I'm
also keeping this email for my records.
Monica

Subj: Re: FUCK YOU
Date: 2/14/05 Pacific Standard Time
From: aballer@verizon.net (Malik Harrison)
To: Words4victory@aol.com

Breng it on bitch. I am not scerd of you. Go back to yearn man
house. I got me someone new. She coming over tonite.

After a mild email war, Monica calls me and that's what I
wanted all along.
"Malik, who cares about this stuff. I need to ask you something
important. I found a job I want to apply for that was listed on the
Player's Association website. Ms. Moran made it clear that I need to list
you as a reference to verify all of the business work I've done for
you. I tried to avoid using you for a reference by telling her I can
no longer contact you, but she said I should've asked you for a
letter of reference. The conversation was on its way to getting ugly
because I didn't want to put your name out there and explain my
personal involvement. Malik, I need to finish my new resume
today so I can fax it to them before the job is taken. Would you
please serve as a reference so I can apply for this?"

I laugh then reply, "Ask your man unless you want to do a favor for me on Valentine's Day. You know what I want—that's why you called in time."

"What are you implying? I'm no hooker," she says.

"Hey, well. Never mind then," I tell her.

"Malik, remember what you told me about having my back, no matter what happens between us?"

"I don't owe you shit, Monica. I asked to marry me even after you fucked around on me and you wouldn't. I forgave you and still wanted you back."

"I gave up everything I had to help you and you can't even allow me to tell the truth on my resume?" Monica complains.

"I've always told you that you did no more than anyone else did for me. Others have been much more. Crystal used to cook for me before she went to work and rode the bus so I could have the car. *That* was a good woman."

"So you're not going to help me then? I'm working for free these days and you still won't even help me?" Monica asks.

"I don't care that you've been having to volunteer at the Endowment for the Humanities, or that you eat toast for lunch while you're there because you don't get paid. I got all of those silly messages, Monica. You're not telling me what I want to hear so I won't tell you what you want to hear! I know the lady at Player's Association and people in the government who have hiring authority but I'll never put you on. Maybe this will teach you a lesson or two. Look at the bright side though, you'll be able to pinch less fat after your mandatory diet is over with. Missing some meals will force your greedy ass to slim down. You're too thick anyway."

Monica's voice escalates. "Wait a minute here, you ungrateful piece of shit—don't come at me sideways with an earful of insults when you screwed up my resume and you owe me money. People want to know what I've been doing and I can't tell them because I need you as a reference. Now I've got a gap in my resume in a who-you-know town."

"Oh, so now I'm a piece of shit. All right, Monica. Let me tell you one motherfucking thing. If you won't be with me anymore

I'm going to move on this year and find my wife. Your man knows people. I'm sure he'll help you, bitch!"

She screams in the receiver, "I don't have a man! I don't know why I feel the need to keep telling you that!"

"Right, just listen at you. I tell you what—go eat some toast and starve for all I care. You ain't got shit going on and never will. I know shot callers and I'll fix it so you'll never get a job in this town again!"

I can hear Monica beginning to cry and she screams into the phone, "I hate you, Malik! And by the way your emails are so hard to understand it's like reading a foreign language! Give Hooked on Phonics a try because it might do your ass some good!"

After Monica hits her insult limit, I hang up on her. At least we're communicating and the ball is in my court. On that note I can call my aunt and put in my dinner order for this evening. It's too bad Monica is becoming more resistant to being trained. If she weren't she'd be eating a nutritious dinner—with me.

$

The next day I walk to the mailbox in my building to check my mail. I find a green package slip in it and hold it, wondering who sent me something that couldn't fit into my box.

I walk over to the front desk and flirt with one of the leasing agents. I wave the slip in my hand. "I think there's something here for me. How are you doing today?" When she playfully snatches it I wink at her and laugh. She tries to make her ass look bigger than what it is by arching her back more than normal as she switches hard to the other side of the counter.

After she bends over, grabs something and sets it on the counter she asks, "When are you going to ask me out?"

"As soon as you start giving me props and special treatment," I answer.

"How do I do that?" she asks, looking confused.

I pick up the box and put it under my right arm. "Baby, you'll figure it out if you're smart." I turn away and step onto the elevator, laughing.

After turning the key and unlocking my door, I notice the package is from Monica. I assume that it's a few trinkets that I left behind and unwrap the package. Underneath the paper is a plain white box, and in it is a plastic tube with a piece of paper is inside of it. I open it and find a certificate informing me that I'm a "dirt bag." I feel my blood pressure begin to boil when I realize that Monica didn't make up the certificate herself. She ordered it from some type of company that delivers hate mail. After I throw it down and cuss her out I find potting soil that's included, sitting in a bag that's labeled with the two words that will earn her a phone call I know she won't want me to make.

I dial Monica's number and begin cussing her out before I even hear her voice on the line. In a sweet voice she interrupts me. "Malik, watch your blood pressure. Little Momma has no idea what's wrong with you—calm those nerves down, baby."

"I know there's got to be a full moon tonight because you came out of your bat cave to fuck with me!" I shout. "I know you did this and I don't find it funny, bitch! Who the fuck do you think you is? I'm going to ring your neck. I should've knocked your head off the last time I saw you!"

She laughs. "Thank goodness for senddirtbag.com. I feel my money was well spent. I had to scrape up my pennies to send you that special message but it was worth it because how I feel was summed up for me. Now since you can't talk about what I want to talk about, which is fixing my resume properly, I've got to go. I'm job hunting, Mr. Dirt Bag!" Monica slams the phone down in my ear.

Next, I dial her mother's number and explode as soon as she says hello, in the sweetest voice imaginable. "Do you know what your daughter did to me? She sent me dirt in the mail. You think she's so innocent—do you Miss Monica's momma? Well, I have naked pictures of your daughter. Then I lie on Monica and say, "Did you know she's gay? She sleeps with men and women so that makes her gay to me. She fucks around so much she's on the pill. Did you know she's doing that without protection? She goes to clubs in Baltimore and D.C. picking up strange men and women. She's wild I tell you. By the way, she also had a relationship with a white man." When Monica's mother remains quiet I add, "I just wanted you to know who she really is because your daughter has got you fooled. In fact I'll be mailing you some nice pictures of your daughter."

I slam the phone down on her mother and don't think twice about yelling my character complaints in her ear. Since Monica called me a dirt bag I may as well behave like one. After that I leave Monica harassing messages, explaining that I scanned all of the photos, including ones she didn't know I took of her with my camera phone. I called her again when I had female fuck company. I put my fuck buddy's ear up to the receiver and told her to laugh at Monica.

"After I dick this bitch down I'm posting your shit all over the net and forwarding it to all my frat. You're done!"

In between crying, Monica screams, "I wish a bus would hit you the next time you step off the curb. I hate you, Malik!"

I laugh. "You can't beat me at this war because Malik will win. I'm sure your mother will let you know when her present arrives!" I slam down the receiver. After that I make good on everything I said I'd do. I also wonder why the woman I'm with is laughing when she should've run away realizing I'd do the same vindictive shit to her.

42

PUTTING MYSELF OUT THERE

Jalita

Thank God I left an emergency key under the car in one of those magnetic cases, and that I refreshed my failing memory just in the nick of time. Clyde and company realize that I'm missing after that damned Miss Geraldine walks outside and tries to start some shit with me, and then starts yelling for him. I take off over the hill realizing that I could hide temporarily but those *boys* will be looking for my ass in this car. Realizing that, I drive to Philly in a frenzy, snatch the plates off of my Toyota, and abandon the car on a side road. I salvage what belongings I can, find my way to a wig shop, and finally to Filbert Street to leave the rest of the driving to Greyhound, my old standby. Although I have no idea how much money I'm toting around from what I took from underneath Clyde's mattress, I peel off a bill from one of the money stacks to pay a cab to take me to the Greyhound Station. I consider hiding the money in a bus locker when the bus dumps me back in Baltimore.

After adding some time to my GoPhone in case I need to chat with anyone, I purchase and pull a long auburn wig on top of my head, then place cheap shades on my eyes to cover them as I wait in the station for my bus. I pay my nineteen dollars to make my way out of the city of Brotherly Love and sit on the bus doing something I said I'd never do again in life: smell farts and ride along with crazy people who couldn't afford the train or plane. As my luck would have it I'm seated next to a big fat old man who smells like a bear that has been hibernating a good year. He periodically takes nips out of a shortie liquor bottle like he has a professional drinking habit. Then he feels motivated to show me a torn wallet full of photos of his grandchildren who all looked like troll dolls. I can't take a cat nap or move one inch for fear that he or some other loser will try to get their hands on my dead presidents, so I clutch the book bag, holding it in my lap the entire trip.

If that wasn't enough, upon pulling into O'Donnell Street in Charm City, I'm told that mostly all of the lockers at Greyhound have been removed because of September 11th and bomb threats. Cussing to myself over this matter, I see no other solution than to call Shawn and Jackie and find out if I can crash there until I figure out the next part of my plan. As much as I hate to do it, I use reverse psychology, put on my sweetest I can-get-anything-I-want voice, speak to Jackie and persuade her, telling her that I can help her with the new baby and Myra, as opposed to her drug-addicted brother playing part-time daddy. I shudder to think of what I'll be dodging when Jackie starts throwing shit, and I wonder what I'm getting myself into. Shawn will be at work while I pretend I can hang with his bipolar wife who may be on drugs herself. Oddly enough I never bring up Shawn's call of distress when he got locked up, but neither does he. Jackie agrees to allow me to set foot on their front step so long as I supply my own food and help her daily with the preemie and her little spitaholic, Myra. Not wanting to put my dysfunctional family in danger, I make my way to their place with my knapsack full of booty, and vow that I won't stay longer than reasonably necessary—*unless* the cash in my stash turns out to be all one-dollar bills.

$

I haven't been in Shawn and Jackie's spot for a whole half hour and they've already had at least three arguments that span from Shawn farting in the bed all night, to Jackie's inability to discipline her daughter Myra, to some sort of confusion over Jackie being taken to child support court by a greedy ex who shares some children with her. Go figure. I never knew they could garnish a woman's income tax return and sock it to her for child support even when the daddy is making a decent buck. Ha! I try to tune out the bickering sessions but they're hard to ignore since I'm forced to put away my groceries and take a front seat to the Jackie and Shawn show.

"You hair looks like bullhorns sticking out like that. Why don't you go comb it, Jackie?" Shawn says.

"Well maybe I would if you'd do something. I don't have any time for myself with these kids because you're trying to make me into some house nigga. I'd rather go back to the field, massa."

"Oh, I see you're out to show off now because you think you have an audience. My cousin is here to help, and I'm cooking a ham right now. You always focus on the negative."

"Well you wouldn't be doing that if you didn't burn the crab cakes. Ask her if she'd like to eat that. Look at that shit," Jackie says showing me the pile of burned crab cakes on a plate. "Twenty-one dollar back fin lump down the drain, and *I* paid for it. Why are you putting pineapple on that, Shawn? It's a ham, not a dessert. It looks like you're about to fuck something up again."

"Would you like to cook it then, since you're the master chef?" Shawn snaps.

"How can I cook when I'm trying to open the baby's formula and put it in a bottle, genius?"

"We're lucky to have any milk left thanks to your brother. He stole half a case of the baby's milk and sold it in the street so he could buy more drugs. That milk is expensive. I can't afford to keep replacing it. Why don't you say something to your sticky finger brother about that?"

"Who says he stole it? My brother don't steal? Why's it got to be like that?" Jackie says like she's offended.

"He stole half of everything in here—that's why we don't have shit now. Pretty soon our house will echo. Are you going to deny that he was the one who stole that family's funeral shirts when the whole block was walking around with shirts on for a person they didn't even know?"

"My brother would never do something that low. You probably stole it and accused him of it," Jackie says, placing her hand on her hip.

"I have a job and I don't need to steal. I work hard every day."

"You could've fooled me because you never bring home any money to me."

Shawn stabs the ham with a huge fork, twists up his face and says, "What do you think I pay the bills with—my imagination? Just get out of my face, Jackie. I'll bring you your plate when the food's ready. You're just mad because one of your baby daddies is sucking every dime out of our household. Take this nasty attitude of yours to his ear. He's just mad because you talked him into having a vasectomy when you were with him and then you went on to spit out four more babies."

"I ain't got nothing to say to that clown. If I wanted to talk to or about him on the regular, I'd still be with the man. Don't be repeating what his ex-girlfriend told me about him worshiping his penis. You can't hold water." Jackie changes the subject. "Don't be picking off my plate either. You've got your own food—it's marked and in the refrigerator on your shelf."

"I'll pick on whatever I please. Do you hear your son crying? Go pick him up instead of irritating my ass like a damn hemorrhoid!"

"I can't move that fast, Shawn—I just had baby. I'm not healed yet, remember? Oh no, that's right, you don't remember because you're already humping on me at night trying to make another one—I'm not supposed to have sex yet. Thank God he didn't come out with toes stacked on top of each other like yours. I'm getting my tubes tied, that's for sure. All you men are worthless. Every last one of you!"

"I'll take the baby his bottle," I interject, looking for a reason to escape this mess.

"Do you know how to feed a baby?" Jackie asks.

"Yes, Jackie, I do."

"Well go on and feed him then. Your cousin don't do shit around here. My feet are swollen and I have to take a piss."

"The baby will be fine," I tell her. Then I add, "I can help you comb and brush your hair if you want me too. I'm sure I can make it look nice."

Jackie comments, "She can't be your relative, Shawn, because she acts like a damn human being and knows how to respect my house."

"Your so-called friends in the hood expected your stuff to be sitting in the street by now yet you still tote around their kids in a car I'm insuring. Now who doesn't respect whose house?"

I shake my head as I walk up to the baby's room. When I look down in his crib he's crying and moving his tiny legs and arms up and down. "Shhh. It's ok. Cousin Jalita is here. Don't cry little one," I say gently.

I place my hand behind his head and lift the little bugger with strong lungs from his crib as my wig hair brushes my shoulders. My baby cousin is so adorable—his tiny face makes me smile as I sit in the rocking chair and feed him his milk. Jackie and Shawn continue to bicker but I kiss the baby on the forehead and wish him peace. I see I'm not the only one who has it rough and I feel for the kid. Since I had to put myself out there and set foot in this house I may as well try to do some good. Once the little one begins to count sheep I'll lock the upstairs bathroom door and count my loot.

Twelve thousand five hundred fifty dollars. That's a long way from the measly dollar I won in scratch off! I pace back and forth in the small bathroom, my heart pounding with disbelief at the fact that one of Clyde's boys, who tried to hide this loot for himself, is missing nearly twenty thousand smackeroos. I pile the money up in the middle of the floor and begin running my hands through it, stuffing wads in my bra, switching and sticking my booty out, walking around with my hand on my hip, and even alternating between doing the booty call and the monkey. I was having so much fun fantasizing about how I could work with the cash and get some things done that I forgot that some hustlers may have put an ABP out on me in Charm City. Even so, I continued my celebration until the door opens and I'm busted having a fiesta in my drawers.

"Oooh. Where'd you get all that money? I'm gonna tell mommy and Mr. Shawn," Myra says. That little girl must know some trick to open the bathroom door, because I know I locked it.

I feel sweat begin to pour down my face as I push her out of the bathroom. "It's monopoly money," I tell her. "Now go in your room and Cousin Jalita will tell you a nice bedtime story. If you tell mommy and Mr. Shawn I'm not coming to play with you."

I gulp hard when I hear, "Mommy, Cousin Jalita has a big pile of money for your bills. I want a new bike. Can I have a new bike?"

I cuss to myself and scoop up every bill from off the floor. I run into Myra and the baby's room, stuffing the cash back into my book bag then hiding it under the bed. By the time Jackie appears I'm sitting on the bed, brushing my wig and whistling.

"I saw it, Mommy. She had money!" Myra tells her.

"The baby just went to sleep. We don't want to wake him up. I say. I'm just fixing up my wig here, I'll be ready to do your hair in a minute if you want," I say.

"Myra, I done told you about making up shit! You had me walk down here to see her brushing a wig? Go to bed!"

"But Mom, I saw it! I did. I did," she insists.

"Go to bed. You never want to go to bed. Get in there right now."

"I'll put her to bed, Jackie," I offer.

Jackie leaves without saying a word more. My first thought is to wring my little cousin's neck, but since I didn't get busted I tuck her in. When she asks about her bedtime story I grab a daily paper that is laying on the bed, just for spite.

"My favorite book is on my dresser. Read that one over there," she says.

"You'll like this story better," I reply. "Now listen up kid before your momma comes back with a belt. I won't be able to save you then."

Myra's face lengthens like a sad puppy. I flip through pages of the paper and decide to make her listen to the driest story I can find. That'll teach her little ass to mind her business! At this point I'm not really reading the news stories but more or less looking at the pictures and headlines. Just as I'm about to choose one about stocks and bonds, I see Seth's face with a story to follow. I read each line as my heart beats rapidly. I feel a hunger to learn all that I can about his new career and happenings. After reading about his ups and downs to make it as a rising new author, my eye falls upon his contact information at the end of the article. Apparently he'll be in the area for some signings at Karibu Books in Bowie Town Center, in addition to Borders and Reprint Books in L'Enfant Plaza. Without thinking I walk over to Myra's computer and hope that I don't need a password to sign on.

Andrea Blackstone

"Hey, what about my story?" she complains. "What are you doing? You didn't ask to use my 'puter!"

I go back over and grab her by the collar on her pajamas. "If you want that shiny new bike, you better lie down and shut up, Myra. You got it?"

She grins and then answers, "Yes."

When I realized that I'm still holding Myra's collar I catch myself and release her clothing from my grip.

I'm able to log onto the net, and without thinking I become obsessed with saying something—anything at all to Seth. Who would ever believe a girl who always had the perfect comeback line for everything would have to search for her words, hoping that she doesn't embarrass herself by delivering jumbled thoughts—but that's how I feel as I type a message. My leg bounces up and down with nervousness the entire time I type.

My Dearest Seth,

I guess you and Brenda have been wondering where I've been. I thought about it, and out of love and appreciation for you both I decided to email this letter to the email address provided at the end of an article where I read about you. I did try to call you once but I received a message stating that you were away. I won't go into detail but let's just say that drama has chased me down once again. I have no idea why I ever thought that I could fight this whole world all alone. I can't. The streets don't love me, and if you let the people that walk them promise you the moon and stars, they'll burn you out, use you up, or play games then throw you away like you're trash. In the end you wind up empty handed. I'm hip to the whole game now. Maybe these are the end of times because this place just seems to be a breeding ground for hatred and hard times. I mean, look at the world. There are things like black on black crime, racism, the Tsunami disaster, new diseases, and we've got homeless people sleeping underbridges, right in Washington, D.C. I'm venting a bit but I don't want you to feel as though I'm up to my old tricks.

Enough about me though. I always did have a habit of being self-absorbed, but that annoying quality is nearly gone! I almost shudder to think that I was that loud big mouth who thought she had it going on because she had a big butt, tight jeans, a Coach bag, and a baller that she was sexing to maintain the whole destructive habit. I was a fool but no one could stop me. Perhaps I was a little comical at times, but I was a very big fool (I still have a big butt though...smile). It's hard to believe that I've mellowed out so much in not even a year. Maybe it's the antidepressants (oops). Should I erase that part? Hell no, I still am not totally into not saying what's on my mind.

Well anywho, congratulations with moving up in the publishing world. I picked up a paper and was happy to learn that you'll soon be coming out with your third book, and that your second *did* make it to the New York Times Best Sellers List after all. When I read of your success I smiled and I haven't done that in months, to be quite honest. I know your mother is so proud of her son. I know that so many people only want to read street life these days but maybe they'll feel the need to be inspired, too. In everything there's a balance. I know I would love to get my hands on a good inspirational book because I know enough about the streets firsthand. I could use a lesson in something else.

I wanted you to know how hard I've been trying to rise above my flaws, not that it matters at this point. Please tell Brenda what I said, and that I didn't want to feel as though I was mooching since she was giving me free counseling sessions. I'm sure she could use the hour's time for someone who is insured and can pay her fairly. Who enjoys working for free? I know I don't. When I'm able to sit in that chair because I can afford it, I'll be back to stress her out with some new issues! Not that you'd want to ever call me, but if I've got time on my prepaid I can receive messages. I'm sure you remember those days. I teased you enough about them and now it's my turn. I better end things here.

Keep doing big things,
The one and only Jalita
443 994-3216

$

After ten minutes my cell phone rings. My breathing stops for a moment, and I'm praying that it's not that sicko Clyde or one of his thugged out boys. I debate whether to answer it because I don't recognize the number that's sprawled across the blue screen.

"Hello," I say cautiously.

"How's my girl—the one and only Jalita?"

I smile when I hear Seth's voice. My mood lifts and I forget my troubles for a moment. "It's good to hear from you. I didn't expect you to call me though," I answer.

"Why wouldn't I? My emails are forwarded to my cell phone when I'm traveling. When I saw your number I couldn't wait to say hello."

"That was nice of you, Seth."

"So what's this about you not doing so well these days? Brenda did mention that she hasn't seen you and she's been very concerned."

"Please tell her I apologize for that. I just got swept up in some things."

"Swept up in what?"

"It really isn't worth getting in to. I know you have a signing tomorrow and I'm not going to hold you on the phone," I say. I want to talk to him for as long as I can, but I knew my prepaid time will run low if I talk much longer.

"That's sweet of you. Jalita?"

"What's up?"

"I don't know if you have plans tomorrow, but after my signings I'd love to swing by and take you to dinner. I hope I don't sound too forward but you know how I am."

"Dinner?" I repeat, stunned that he asked me.

"Yes. You know, just have a friendly bite to eat between friends. I would love to catch up with you. And don't worry about my ex-wife. The annulment is straight, over and done with. I'm a free man."

"Sure, Seth," I say without thinking.

"Great. Well where should I pick you up?"

"I can meet you somewhere. That way you don't have to inconvenience yourself," I lie. I don't want Seth to pick me up at Shawn and Jackie's for obvious reasons.

"Don't be silly. If we're going to become friends we can't start off this way. Now where do I come pick you up?"

"Ok, I'll tell you. But when you come, excuse what you may see."

Seth chuckles and says, "I'm sure whatever I see will be fine. I tell you what. Why don't you leave me a time after seven and the address on my voicemail. I see the events coordinator for the store coming to greet me."

"All right then. I will."

"Don't forget. I look forward to seeing you."

"You too, Seth. Goodbye."

When I hang up the cell phone I realize that my ass is supposed to be in hiding. Oops. It takes a fool to learn. Now I'm about to really put myself out there. Money makes some crazy but so does my crush. Hmmph, I hope I won't have to choose between the two!

43

THE LAST TALL MOUNTAIN OF BULLSHIT

Malik
Two months later...

I love hotels, especially suites that are as large as small apartments. When you come from the hood no one waits on you, not even when you're just learning to talk and walk. When I was a young kid wearing pajamas with the feet in them and still drinking milk out of the bottle, I remember opening the refrigerator to make my own bottle. I'd spill milk all over the counter every time. Even so I'd pull up a chair, stand on it, and try to pour some vitamin D for myself because my mother wasn't interested in doing it and I was hungry.

After I got older and found my ass in college people took care of me. Women did my home work, my laundry, fed and sexed me. I really got used to being served because I was on the football team. I didn't get drafted to go to the NFL, but fell into it by an accident. My big mouth landed me a contract after I saw some so-called pro players practicing. They really couldn't hit hard or keep the plays straight. "Is that the best ya'll can do?" I yelled out. "I can do better than that." The next thing I know I'm signing an injury waiver and the coach is asking me to show them what I got. I did, and knocked a cornbread fed looking motherfucker flat on his back. That's how I ended up playing in the National Football League. It also taught me that money and power equals respect. But sometimes when you get a little taste of all that, it's easier to trick people into waiting on you because you get tired of doing the work to keep that position at the top. It's easier to call Monica and tell her I injured my rotator cuff during practice, and may have to have emergency surgery, than it is to tell her the truth and admit that I fucked up again—that I don't have enough money to pay my hotel bill. So I won't give it to her straight up, with no chaser. Instead, I'll force Miss Monica to forgive me for trying to sabotage her good image with her mother.

I know a nervous woman's knock when I hear one, and that one belongs to you-know-who. When I hear the succession of several quick taps on the door I know that my "victim" has arrived. I stumble out of bed and kick the soda cans, pizza boxes, and dirty underwear out of the way. I open the door with a fifth of whiskey in my hand. Somehow, Monica looks fly. I'm shocked because her short haircut looks sexy. She's sporting gray stiletto boots, a matching handbag, and a black leather coat. When she takes her coat off and walks in I watch her hips move. I can tell that she's wearing thongs under her tight bell-bottom jeans, and even her skin looks radiant and smooth.

"Malik, what happened?" Monica asks, taking a seat on the edge of the bed.

"My shoulder hurts."

"Which one?"

"The same one that I hurt before."

"First of all, it's a mess in here. And you're drinking now?" she asks, looking at the liquor bottle I dropped on the bed, and the empty ones scattered all over the room.

"Naw, little momma. My cousins were here. You know how those fools do. I'm stranded here until they bring back my house keys and my wallet. I dropped it in their car. I need to get around, go to the bank and do some shit, but I need to pay my bill first. No maid's been in here today because I hung a do not disturb sign on the door."

"I can drop you off on my way out if you want me to, since you're not feeling well," Monica offers.

"I wouldn't want to hold you up. I'll be gone all day. You have any money? I want to pay my bill. I can pay you back first thing tomorrow. You can have my ring as collateral."

"Forget that!" she says, shaking her head. "You've got rotten fruit in your fruit bowl. Aren't those fruit flies bothering you? They're everywhere. You act like you don't even see this mess,"

Monica says, swatting flies. Then she adds, "You've got pizza crusts on your table and pizza boxes in your bathroom. You need to pay the maid to clean this shit up. Malik, what's going on? I think you're drunk. You stink like a skunk, too. When's the last time you had shower and shave?"

"I'm not drunk," I lie, trying not to slur my speech.

"It appears that way."

"I'm just sipping some liquor."

"If you're on a roster you have no business sipping nothing, let alone at ten o'clock in the morning. Your body makes you money. You just told me you weren't drinking. You need to be treating it like a temple but enough of that—what you do is your business now. I can't stay long because I've got a life of my own, so I won't be putting up with this much longer anyway. Turn over so I can rub your shoulder."

When Monica puts her soft fingertips on my skin I feel my dick get stiff. I miss the way she'd rub me tenderly and spoil me with her special treatment.

After kneading and lightly poking around on my shoulder that I did actually hurt back in the day she says, "Turn over."

I slip off my shorts first, and then lie on my back and begin playing with myself.

"Malik, I'm here to help you with your injury. What are you doing?"

"Let's fuck," I reply. "I want to fuck you, Monica. Get in bed with me."

Monica stops massaging me. "I can't do that," she answers.

"Yes you can. Let's fuck, little momma. Don't you want some of this? Big daddy misses you. If you won't fuck me, how about you jack me off then?"

Monica jumps up. "Oh hell no! So you got me here to try and pull the okie doke on Monica, huh? Get me to scream your name to hook me in your web? You're not sick. In fact, I bet you just finished partying. That's what this looks like. I didn't come here to fuck you, I came here because I thought you were sick and injured but you're not. Here you go again, playing games. This time I'm time enough for you. You said to get me a man and I'm finally in that frame of mind to think on it. Although D.C. is a who-you-know town, lady luck shined on me and I got put on to a real job. I'm finally making decent money and can afford to keep my hair done, my bills paid on time, eat what I want to eat within reason, and hang out with my girls if we want to do our thing on some weekend."

"You still have that dirty, raggedy car?" I ask, in between drinking liquor.

"Oh no, dear. I bought me a little used BMW that's straight. The heads do turn when I drive it, not that I need anyone to cosign that I look good in it. I'm getting an apartment of my own, and I'm going to fix up my crib like a classy little joint while I stack my paper and save money to invest. Who fucking knows, I may even use the skills I learned from putting up with you, along with my sports knowledge, and start helping out some real ballers who need a smart person with a good work ethic on their team. Go ahead with your plan of faking it until you say you're going to make it, but in my book life goes on and I've got to get mine now. Life is too damn short to throw it away on diversions like you."

I wipe the droplets of Jack Daniels from around my mouth with the back of my arm and drop the bottle of liquor on the floor. "Your family is your safety net. You'll never grow up because they treat you like a baby. I bet your mother gave you the down payment for your first apartment."

"Now I'm not trying to sound picky about your choice of words or anything, but I've got to correct you on something. Don't hate just because they treat me like I'm loved and your folks treat you like a chump, with the exception of one person. We may not have the perfect set-up in my family but we all care about each other. Hakim and my dad had to go ahead and let me make my mistakes with you so I'd understand who I am, what I need, and what I don't want out of life and a partner that I choose to live it with. On the other hand, my mom told me she'd pay me to *stay away* from you, so technically she was glad to give me the down payment as a house warming gift. Because she has good manners she tolerated you, but your own soror wanted you kicked to the curb as well as all of my friends. No one liked you for me, Malik—no one. And that's pretty bad considering I know so many people. And they

339

didn't get to see even half of the shit you pulled on me because I hid it from them."

"I don't care about your family anyway, Monica. Your whole family is crazy! And you can tell your friends I don't like them either. Those stuck up girlfriends of yours don't have nobody and they just wanted you to be alone like them. If I was so bad why'd you stay with me? I was good to you and you know it. Tell the truth and shame the devil when you write your life's story about our relationship."

Monica shakes her head. "I may have appeared to be dumb, but I stayed with you so long because the weeding out process is hard. I felt I'd always be alone if I had to continue weeding men out, starting all over again. I had poor self-esteem because I'd failed at some things, and after all of the work I put in with you I was hoping to be around to enjoy some of the benefit. I didn't realize I was lowering my standards, but now that's not an option, even if it means being alone. You could've had anything you wanted with me if you didn't take your blessing of love for granted. We would be married today if you weren't so busy using me and making me feel it was necessary to run to another man's arms for a little tenderness and affection while I was still connected to you. I'm not saying I was perfect. I'll even come clean a little bit and admit I was wrong in some ways, but you don't want to clean up your act and become a better man. What you'd like to do is continue playing the role by making 4:00 a.m. booty calls, trying to give the image of someone who can floss, going around town like you've got it going on, trying to bamboozle everyone who will pay you attention. Why don't you tell them you don't intend on doing anything? Little do they know some other woman paid for your ice, down to the damn cubic zirconia earring, and you can't afford to pop bottles of champagne like you pretend. You'll stiff the club owner for that bill, I'm sure. Those poor suckers in the club, on the streets, and in your hood, wherever that is these days, just don't know! I can't judge though because you got me once."

"I'll tell you what I got, I got my money back. My house in Virginia, my place on the Inner Harbor in Baltimore, *and* an apartment," I brag. "I have a Hummer parked right outside. I'm living large again. Did I tell you I was on the practice squad? Look on the website for the—"

"Why? I think you're lying about the little gig, but even if you aren't, after all of this work, you have the audacity to brag that you're on a practice squad? How much could you net at the end of the year, like 40 grand? You're beating up your body and risking paralysis for forty-thousand dollars when you could've made millions? That's just enough to still put the black under your eyes to prepare for every game, and *appear* as though you're going to do something. Has it ever crossed your mind that the coach may never call you to get up off of that bench? How are you going to pay child support for two babies with that? Why don't you just get a job and grow up because you blew your best shot and you can't get it back."

"I wouldn't be on the roster if the coach didn't think I had enough juice to contribute or help the team win. It's not that I *couldn't* go to Minnesota. I told the coach I'm *not* coming to Minnesota because you said you wouldn't come live with me there."

"That's bullshit! You don't give up a two million dollar contract over that. Jeff Theisman was picked up on the streets and took weeks off to play in the Super Bowl. He was in shape, they needed him, and he took his chance and didn't run scared. Terrell Owens played with a broken ankle, so what in the hell are you waiting for?"

"I gave up my contract because I love you. Now are you going to help me again? I need you. I can make us money if I get support. I bet he had support and that's why he could get out there and do it."

"You're lying through your teeth, and I don't have time to waste my life away while you continue clinging to your NFL dream, using me as a scapegoat every time you fuck up. It's not that kind of party—the free ride with Monica is over. You wimped out because you were scared you'd get cut, or felt that you just couldn't do it."

"I'm getting signed, and I'm getting another contract as soon as there's room on the team where I'm on the practice squad for."

"Malik, after all of the rot you've done I'm not even mad at you anymore, because being angry over what happened between us

Andrea Blackstone

would be counterproductive for me and my sanity. With that said, the next time you call I won't be there. Keep this little one hundred dollar bill, and take your cab to wherever so you can scam as many people as you need to pay for this suite. I won't need the money back because I'm coming up and one day this will be nothing but chump change, my friend. When I found you I was paying your room tab, and now that I'm rolling out I'm leaving you the same damn way. Please note that this is your last *gift,* and I consider it my charity donation for the year. My days of taking care of a man have finally ended. And I promise I won't find your same type in a different body. I'll be more careful next time by paying attention to all of the loser alert indicators."

"I'd be playing right now if I didn't get injured. I'll be at the show next year," I ramble. "You wait and see, Monica. I'm still the man—you're the loser! I'm one of the most eligible bachelors in the D.C. Metropolitan area."

"In whose book? If you really believe the words that are coming out of your mouth then you missed your calling, boy. That's right. I called you boy because you're definitely a boy in a man's body. Well anyway, man-boy, you should've been an actor, not a football player. Maybe you should try taking your act to the big screen. Now that would make you some loot. Obviously you don't have the juice to be in the show, as you call it. Malik, you're too lazy to even run and do your cardio training. I watched you—you don't want to work for anything, not even a once in a lifetime opportunity that some boys dream of for their whole life. If I were you I'd take a few non-credit classes and improve your English skills. I'm not trying to put you down, but you have two degrees and can't even spell or talk properly in front of the kind of people who would take notice. That's what happens when your college professors accept home cooked pies to boost your grades. I was wrong to be your walking dictionary and life coach. You're so used to people doing for you that you don't even want to try to do for yourself. This is why everyone assumes athletes are so stupid— you're a perfect example. And I'm not calling any names, but a certain elder in *your* family needs to tell you to get off her titty and work out your own damn scrapes and the problems you create. I know she's got to be tired of you sucking on it by now!"

342

"How could you disrespect my family like that? You think you're funny? You think you're fine. You aint all that with your fake ass hair."

"Uh—I don't have a man just yet, but if I keep my head on straight I don't think I'll have a problem attracting one. The question is will I want to keep him when I get him and will he want to keep me? I had two boyfriends who were a hell of a lot better than you—one was my right hand, and one was my left *until* I bought some new toys from a Passion Party that require heavy duty batteries and the flip of an on and off switch. I'd rather get off with a factory-made dick than to even consider fucking you again in this lifetime. The good thing is those toys don't talk back, they just do the job. I won't settle for a no-good sorry ass like you again so long as I have breath in my body. If I have to be alone, even that will be an improvement. And as far as my hair I paid for it and have the receipt to prove that it's all mine! If the women in Hollywood can sport wigs and weaves, so can Monica."

"Go see your man! I know you're late! I told your mother about you, Monica—you look like a hooker and you act like one too."

"Anyone who wouldn't have respect enough for my mother by calling her to demean me has got to go. Are you crazy? I'm my mother's flesh and blood. Did you think she'd love me any less if any of the lies you told me were true? And as far as the pictures, go ahead and make more copies if you want. You're just mad because I fixed myself up the way I was when you slithered your way into my life. What goes around comes around. I'm not scared of you anymore."

The liquor begins to go to my head and I feel my speech begin to slur. "No one is ever gonna love you, you beady-eyed bitch. I told you that. All you'll ever be is a ho!"

Monica walks over to the heavy curtains and opens them, letting daylight in the room. I squint and say, "Daylight—shit! You know I have a hang over. What are you doing?"

I watch her sit down in a puffy claw foot chair, cross her legs and fold her arms. When I see that Monica isn't going to stop the bright light from pouring into the room I bend my arms to shield my face from the glow.

Then I hear, "Let me drop some knowledge on your right quick, baby boy. I really feel sorry for you because you need help. All you'll ever be is a washed up broke baller with a drinking problem that's as bad as your attitude *unless* you admit to yourself that you're fucked up. I don't care what color you are, where you've been, what kind of car you drive, how tall or short you are, somehow, we've all been short-changed in life. Babies who raise babies—someone gets short changed. Drug-addicted parents—someone gets short-changed. Murder—the victim and the family get short-changed. War—fallen soldiers get short-changed. Domestic violence—the victim gets short-changed. In divorce, at least one party gets short-changed. The unemployed, uninsured, underfed, homeless, those who have been discriminated against, cheated, robbed, lied on, or diagnosed with some serious illness. The list of challenges are too long to complete, Malik. The point is that some of us have been hurt and never heal—those are the ones like you, stuck in the past, making excuses of why you can't move on and get it together—but others like me acknowledge that hurt, and fight to get where we need to be while we have time left. No one can do this work for you. I can't, Malik. No one can do it for me either. All I know is that my days of crying over spilled milk and complaining about the ways I've been short-changed are over. A part of me will always care about you, but I can't let you weigh me down. And to be quite frank with you I thought you were a soldier. I thought you were someone who wanted to prove that adversity can build strength and really make me appreciate how hard it was to get to see that rainbow. You used to tell me you've got to go through the rain in order to appreciate the sunshine and all of these clichés that sounded good. The thing is you didn't show me that you believed them. I see you, Malik. You're a wounded person who doesn't' know which way to turn because you've been through some shit and feel short-changed. That's why you think it gives you a license to lie and manipulate. If the truth be known, you're the one with low self-esteem, and tearing down someone else makes you feel stronger, but it doesn't make you stronger. The best thing I can tell you is to stop fucking everything in a skirt before you catch something and pass it on to someone who may love you despite your trifling, hideous ways. Wrap it up and don't make any more babies because you've got a long way to go and a short time to get there. I pray to the Lord above that I won't have to pay for my short-term stupidity, when I didn't care whether I lived or died. I was in a terrible funk when we met, but now I'm awake, so I better get tested and stay away from you. The only good thing about seeing you today is that I can finally let you go without wanting to look back. This little meeting has been really cleansing for me. In fact, I feel like a new damn woman right about now. Oops, I think I slipped and grew a backbone! Who ever would have thought this day would come? And why am I here arguing with someone who smells like his drawers has shit stained skid marks in them, and appears to either be an undercover alcoholic, or is on his way to walking down that road? I have to get some rest so I can get up for work in the morning. I am no longer your keeper, homeboy!"

When she stands up I try to point at her and yell but I can't hold up my arm. Each time I raise it I lose my equilibrium. All I can do is continue lifting my arm, yelling at her. "Your brother Hakim tried to tell me to leave your ass alone—that's why he didn't want to introduce me to you. I don't need this."

Man, she done lost her mind if she thinks she can teach me anything about life. I told the girl to stand up for herself with people, and she goes and uses what I taught her on me—crazy bitch! I let my arm fall. Monica puts on her coat and turns to walk away.

As she shuts the door she laughs. "Phony asshole available for immediate pick-up, buyer haul at her own risk. So long, you drunk, dirty sucker. Have a nice life with the person whose bra and panties were stuffed under my car seat!"

"Had you cleaned your filthy car earlier you would've known I screwed some bitch in it," I manage to bellow out. My head falls backward. Within my liquor binge I get so drunk that I don't notice that Monica left me the money to pay my hotel bill. When checkout time comes I fall asleep and pretend that I'll see her again although I know that's the last time she'll ever give me the time of day. When I awaken I'll patch myself up and lie to the world that I've still got it going on like I used to. After that I'll see who I can scam to get up money for the tax bill on my house. The

Andrea Blackstone

notice was listed in the paper. If I think hard enough there will be someone, because a sucker in a skirt is a dime a dozen.

44

THE BREAKING POINT

Jalita

The date with Seth yesterday went so well that he invited me to attend church with him. It was a church where he'd donated five thousand dollars after hearing about a minister wanting a used van for outreach work, and shortly following the blessing of his publishing deal. Fearing that I could still run into Clyde and his crew, I convinced him to be adventurous and visit a church he hadn't been to in a while. He agreed to visit a nondenominational church in Northern Virginia instead, and we blabbed and blabbed about a thousand subjects until we yawned and were forced to part because sunrise was approaching. He told me to be ready to be picked up at 8:00 a.m. so we could make it to the early morning service. It was very embarrassing to open the door and subject Seth to Shawn and Jackie's antics when we finally parted, but he's the one that insisted on keeping things real by picking me up at the door and dropping me off in the same place. So he surely got two eyeballs full when he witnessed my dysfunctional family doing what they do best—acting a fool.

When I returned at 4:00 a.m., Jackie and Shawn were still performing as if it were 2:00 in the afternoon. This particular blow out was over Shawn using the toilet plunger to unstop the bathroom sink. The only productive thing that came out of it is that I was awake to change the baby, and Jackie was up so I could ask if she had an old dress that I could borrow for church. She threw me several, telling me that I could keep them, because thanks to Shawn it would be a long time before her figure returned and she could wear dresses that didn't look like a muumuu.

On Sunday morning Seth and I made it to church on time. I was a bit nervous because I'd never formally visited the house of the Lord. I recall my brother Wes and his girl Tomi playing with God last year, but I had no real reference point since I spent so much time moving from foster family to foster family growing up. The main thing I noticed when Seth and I sat down was the diversity within the congregation, and the fact that so many of the people were friendly. Although there was a fair share of African-American members, there were also several different races present. That made me feel good since I'm biracial and Seth is multiracial. Although I refer to myself as black and the world may see me that way, I'm not all black. I'm proud to be black but I don't hate others of various races either. With as many people that have hopped the race fences in the world, from slavery up until now, racism has become a very ridiculous concept. I'm a prime example because I'm brown and don't look biracial, yet I am. You never know who you're looking at, that's for sure. Most of us are mixed with something, so celebrating diversity is a good thing that people should truly do more often.

After everyone takes a seat an organ begins to play. Seth hands me a program and I study the format of the church service. Although I have a short attention span I find the sermon interesting. Seth grabbing my hand and holding it doesn't hurt either. I can't believe he put the moves on me in church.

"Hallelujah praise the Lord, everybody. Let the church say amen," the minister says, standing in the pulpit.

I lean over to Seth. "What am I supposed to say?"

"Just follow along and relax. You'll see," he whispers.

"Amen," Seth says late. I miss the cue because I was running my mouth.

"It feels so good to be blessed. If you feel blessed, turn to your neighbor, nod your head and say, I feel blessed," the minister says.

"I feel blessed," I say to Seth. He says the same to me. We smile and I feel Seth tighten his grip on my hand.

"You know, when I was preparing the sermon for today something led me to do things a bit differently. I said—self, what is God trying to tell me? Then something hit me in my spirit. God said to tell His people that we all have crosses to bear, but He won't put more on you than you can take. Let the church say amen."

"Amen," I reply.

"Now let's go to church. If you feel like dancing, I want you to dance. If you feel like shouting, I want you to shout. If the spirit hits you I want you to praise His Holy name. Now some of you were up in the club last night, I know you were because I used to be doing the same thing. I was out there drinking, smoking, and getting high, but God touched me, church. I know that if you can get your dance on in the club, you can get your dance on for the Lord. Tell the truth and say amen. Let's keep it real, some of us still have a little ways of the world left in us, don't we now?"

"Yes we do," someone shouts.

"You were the only one brave enough to admit it," the minister says. Everyone laughs and looks at the person.

"Today we have a very special guest who is going to sing a selection for us. Maybe you all have heard of it—does anyone here know *We Shall Behold Him?*" Heads nod, including Seth's. I'm impressed that Seth is in tune with his spiritual self and looking around I notice that even the young people feel that God is cool to acknowledge. My senses are open and I take in all of the sights and sounds as the service progresses.

The minister continues, "Now I met this young man when I was pumping my gas. I heard him humming and humming. Then he started singing. I looked around and thought I was hearing things but I wasn't. And he can talk more than me, church. Well it turned out that he's an up-and-coming gospel singer. Mike Blackstone, would you come out here. I'm not going to say one word. All I'm going to say is just sing brother, sing."

A deep baritone voice sounds and I feel tingles move through my body. Between the words of the song and the gifted singer's talent I feel captivated. People in the congregation begin waving their hands, some stand, and others shake their head and say, "sing it," over and over again.

I feel as though I've drifted off into another land. As I sit there I realize my mistakes, my pains, and my joys. Something breaks and tears begin to flow down my face. I can't seem to stop them. I think of all of the rejection I've suffered, what Kyle did to me, and the pile of money I hid in a can and buried in Shawn and Jackie's back yard. I couldn't risk leaving it in the house for Jackie's dope fiend brother to find, nor could I take it with me and risk Seth questioning me. I remembered Grandma Beverly telling me they used to do that back in the day, so I went old school on hiding my little secret. Seth looks over at me and pushes several Kleenex in my hands. I sit there in tears and reconsider my new rot. Originally, I was going to spend every dime of what Kyle most likely collected from drugs or cashed in after stealing corporate money. But for the first time in too long I consider my desire to connect with a higher being and my consciousness—the root of my growth and potential as a human being. Thus far, nothing has filled that void.

"Let it out, Jalita," Seth whispers. "You're in the house of the Lord. It's ok."

When Mike finishes the song people stand and clap. The minister makes him promise to sing another number before he leaves and he does.

Then the minister says, "I'm doing this all out of order but after that soul-stirring selection I just have to ask. Are there any among us who'd like to accept Christ as their personal Savior today? The doors of the church are open. Come to the front and receive Him if you feel led to confess your sins and make the change of a lifetime."

Before I realize what I'm doing I feel my feet moving toward the preacher. I tap Seth to let me out of the aisle as I dab my eyes and prepare to accept God as my personal Savior. On that day I found my spirit and accepted God into my life. I've finally realized what it takes to survive through life—a higher being that will never let you down. Now I've got to walk the talk but I'm not sure how.

$

When we park in front of Shawn and Jackie's place Seth says, "Jalita, I don't know what to say. I'm proud of what you did for yourself today."

"Seth, I've tried everything else so I figure I may as well try God."

"I hear you. I've been there myself."

"Well, thanks for everything. You've been a really great support," I tell him, opening the car door.

"Jalita, don't go yet," he says, looking at me intensely.

"Why?"

"Well, don't take this the wrong way." I shut the door. "Look at the way Jackie's brother is in the street doing pushups. My guess is that he's on crack. I hear your cousin and his wife arguing before you can even reach steps. How are you ever going to rise above anything if you spend the bulk of your time around those with dysfunctional lifestyles?"

"I know it's pretty jacked up, but this set-up is all I've got. I don't have anywhere else to go right now, Seth. In a perfect world I wouldn't have to be here, but inner city life is where I'm from. I swear I won't let it drive me to drink even if I feel like going there. This is what I'm comfortable with because it's all I know."

"Jalita—well, never mind," he says, looking away.

"What, Seth? Remember our keeping it real rule? Look at me," I tell him.

He turns. "Right, well you've got me, and I don't want to leave you."

"What are you saying? Are you trying to tell me something, Seth? If you are, spill it brother."

"I care about you and I'd be lying if I said it was just as a friend, Jalita."

"Really?" I'm stunned by Seth's words.

"Yes, really," he says. I don't know how you feel, but I've had the time of my life in two days. I've never felt this way. I really was feeling rotten before I saw you. I haven't been myself lately," Seth explains.

"Me too, Seth. I feel you," I tell him, rubbing his arm through his coat, wishing that I could pawn this hideous wig off on Jackie.

"Why don't you come hang out with me for a while?"

"I can't do that, Seth."

"Why can't you? It's not even safe for you to be here, Jalita. People get shot up on the block over here. This street stays in the paper and on the news."

"I'd be imposing, and I know the streets well enough to dodge bullets reasonably well."

Seth scrunches up his eyebrows. "How could you be imposing if I offered?"

"I just would, that's all. I've got to pay my way in this world. I don't look for hand-outs anymore."

"Jalita, I know you've changed. If I thought you were still that scheming, feisty, gold digger I wouldn't have asked you out to begin with. I already know."

"I'm going through so much—I don't even have a job. I'm just tore up," I confess, sighing heavily.

"So what? I'll help you find one or get a plan. You said it in the email, Jalita—no one can do life all alone. You're human and so am I."

"You don't need me weighing you down. You're doing so well. The books, your career, look at the nice car you have now. You traded in old Betsy for a nice Mercedes. You're handling your business and now it's time for you to reap your rewards."

"Who cares about those material things? Right now I'm talking about us, and we're much more important. Now let me decide what I need and what I don't. There are some things that have occurred on my end that aren't common knowledge. You just don't know." Seth shakes his head somberly. "Please, I could use the company. If you trust me, give it a chance. If we don't get along you can come back here. This is the best thing to do. I'm not hitting on you like that—I'm not trying to trap you into sexing me or anything. I don't want to hurt you. All I want to do is help you out and find out what made you break down and cry like that in church. I know that pain. Something heavy is really testing you."

"You're right, Seth. I'm very preoccupied over something."

Seth sighs. "Well I have those cries, too."

"Why?" I ask, concerned for him.

"I can't tell you that unless we agree to remain open and honest. We'll both have to become vulnerable to each other first."

"Ok, Seth. Let's try it all. But just so we don't jump the gun I won't move my things just yet or tell Jackie and Shawn we had this conversation. I won't burn my bridge with them."

"Deal," he says, looking me in the eyes.

"Jackie's expecting me to braid her hair because I promised I would when I came back. I also have a few things that I have to take care of."

"That's fine. I'll call you and we'll meet up this afternoon, ok?"

"That sounds good."

"And one more thing, Jalita."

"What is it now, Seth?"

"There's something I've been wanting to give you for a long time."

"Another book?"

"Not quite," he says. "I'd like to give you this." He leans toward me and kisses me on the cheek. After he releases me I feel dazed, and am stunned that I feel like a giddy teenager. I smile and say goodbye when I see Jackie opening the front door, shaking a comb at me through the storm glass window. If it were anyone but bad-luck-having me I'd swear that life wasn't going to suck like a great big lemon forever. At least I can ride the crest of today's wave while it lasts.

45

UNPLUGGED

Wes

My funeral service has been the talk of the town, and the home going ceremony is packed beyond capacity. Some people are sitting in the pews, while others are standing and lining the walls or sitting in folding chairs. Looking down and observing this whole scene, it seems as though everyone from the media, all of the local celebrities, fellow athletes, groupies, and on-lookers from every state around the globe have shown up. Even the drug dealers, iced out in their jewels and expensive rides got curious and blew through. Look at the elders leaning on thick canes and sporting large hats as they ease into the church. Thugs removed their hoodies and baseball hats to pay their respects. I can't say I'm too surprised though, I was considered a pretty cool cat in many urban areas.

People on all levels of society worshiped me like I was some bronze god. Some did it for the money they made off of my ballin' skills, others because I could afford to drink Cristal straight from the bottle like it was water at night clubs around the country, and ones impressed by fashion gave me props because I could dress in ill furs when it was time to show off in the lime light. Then of course the dealers are all about me because I used to make a big contribution to their drug enterprise every time I hosted one of my famous parties—supplying my guests with what they needed to have a good time. There's only a select few that cared about me before I started making all this money—before it all went to my head.

The list of those that showed to pay their respects for the right reasons is a short one—a few teachers and coaches who inspired me to reach my full potential with no ulterior motive. The rest of the population made the trip just to see who and what they could see. It will give them something to gossip over because they just aren't ready to let go of the legend of Wes Montgomery.

Since I didn't really have any close family there was no need for both a private and public service. People are still walking, driving, being dropped off in cabs, and are also being chauffeured to get into this crowed church. There are so many of them packed liked sardines I bet it feels like a furnace from all the warm bodies. Instead of being a quiet solemn setting, people are chattering and babies are screaming as if competing to see who can yell the loudest. Someone needs to shut them up—this is about me, not them.

Dominique and Marquita are getting up from the front row of the family section now that it's time to view my body. At least those two are quiet like they give a damn that my life was cut short. Despite having been dead for such a long time, the undertaker had managed to preserve my body well enough for an open casket, but my face was mangled from the gunshot wound. The hold up was a combination of my having been missing for so long, and the fact that no one had come forward to handle the arrangements. Marquita finally stepped up to the plate, despite the angry words we'd exchanged in our last conversation.

Dominique walks up to my casket, looking beautiful in a pale lavender dress and patent leather shoes. She's holding her mother's hand and carrying her favorite stuffed animal in the other. She rubs her eyes and says, "I love you Daddy, but I don't know why you didn't love me back."

"Your father loved you, Dominique. Don't say that. He just didn't know how to show it, and you really didn't get to a chance to know him very well. He can still hear you so be careful with your words," Marquita says.

"Is he in Heaven, Mommy?" Dominique asks, rubbing her eyes, already feeling sadness overcome her.

"Yes, he's in Heaven. If you can bear to do it, look at him for the last time, honey. They'll be closing the casket soon."

Although I look less than up to par, Dominique stares at me, and I wish for the millionth time that I'd been a better father to her. How could I have been such a fool and ostracize a sweet little girl like her?

"But how will he breathe if they shut the casket, Mommy? You tell me not to cover my head with things because it could make me stop breathing."

"Honey, he'll be fine. He's with the angels now and he doesn't have to breathe anymore. You're just looking at his shell. Your daddy is above." Marquita brushes Dominique's face, then looks down at me. "Goodbye, Wes. I'm sorry this is how it ended." She wipes a tear from her left eye, and then they walk away.

Damn, Marquita—I'm sorry how this ended too. Baby, if only I realized so much, way back when.

A woman taps Marquita on the back. I'm not sure who she is, but half of her teeth are missing, her hair is so thin you can see her scalp, her cheeks are sunken in, and she is dressed in a summer black peasant skirt and a mismatched blazer with one gold button missing. "Did you know my son?" she asks.

That's my mother! What is that bitch doing here?

Marquita looks her up and down. Her eyes pause on the dirty, black, bent up shoes.

"Did you say your *son?*" Marquita asks.

"Yes," she says with a pungent odor of cheap beer coming off of her breath.

"We had a child together, ma'am," Marquita replies.

"I'm Vikki, his mother. Unfortunately the last time I saw my son was when he was a young boy. This is all my fault." Then my so-called mother reaches into the casket and holds my face with her hands. An usher dressed in white rushes over and mumbles something in her ear, pulling her away from my body.

"Oh, Looord. My baby! My baby! Look at you!" she wails. "What have I done? I should've been there for you. I should've been a mother. And now you're gone. Oooh Lord, what have I done? Wesley, momma is sorry!"

She's a liar! Did she come to my rescue me when her pimp tried to drown me in the tub that night? Hell no!

Malik runs to the front of the church. "Vikki?"

"Malik! My other baby!" she exclaims.

"You're making a scene. Stop it! Get away from the casket before I take you outside and whip your ass," my twin says.

If I could rise up and slap his ass silly, I would. He has some nerve pulling our mother's card, escorting Vikki to the back of the church and out of the door.

"You have some nerve showing up here. Look at you—drugs have eaten you alive."

"Son, I've tried to get clean. It's not easy. You don't know what I went through just to get here to this funeral. Don't talk to me like that."

"You ruined our lives, Vikki—you're just another bitch to me. Do you think I care how or why you crawled out of your hole to show up after all of these years? I don't miss you and I never will. When dad left, you did what you wanted to do and didn't look back, so why are you here now? You didn't want us. You turned your back on your own small children who needed you."

"I'm not Vikki, I'm your mother, boy! And I tried to contact Wes. He wouldn't answer my letters when I wrote him. I was hoping to find out where you were too. I always wanted the both of you. Things happened. You just don't understand what was going on at the time."

"You're Vikki to me, and don't you forget it. Don't shame Wes like this. Why don't you just leave? I bet you asked him for money. Is that what you wanted, his *money*? Did you just want to ride on his coattail because of his fame? That's what it sounds like to me. I bet that's why he didn't answer your letters."

"I'm not going anywhere. I have a right to be here. I slid him out of my birth canal—and you too."

"You haven't changed one bit. You're still the same selfish junkie ho you were when daddy left. I don't want to talk to you anymore. I could care less if you live or die after how you treated us." Malik waves his hand in disgust and turns to walk back inside the church.

A reporter walks over to Vikki with a microphone and shoves it her way. "We're here with slain superstar Wes Montgomery's mother. Ma'am, how do you feel about this terrible tragedy?"

"Please respect that I'm mourning—this is not a good time." Vikki pulls out a cigarette, lights it up, and turns her back to the camera. Her hand is shaking so I figure that she must be feeling edgy from a much-needed high— apparently her body is beginning to crave one of the many drugs she uses. She takes a few deep drags but extinguishes the cigarette quickly. My best guess is that nicotine doesn't satisfy her craving. As she twists the cigarette butt into the concrete on the church steps, a man passes by dressed well from head to toe. Before she realizes what she's saying, the words are out of her mouth. "I'll suck your dick for five dollars."

I can't believe she embarrassed me like that. I know she has issues but now she's smearing my name by insulting one of my guests. I don't recognize him—but still.

His hand touches the door of the church. When he hears her words he releases it but doesn't turn around. "What did you say to me?" he asks.

"I'll suck your dick for five dollars," Vikki repeats in a low voice.

The man slowly turns around. He recognizes Vikki and she recognizes him. The young lady that is holding onto his arm is about twenty-two years old, and he is well into his fifties. Todd, Vikki's lost ex-husband who abandoned his family because he couldn't stop womanizing, all of those years ago, looks at his former wife with a face of stone.

He touches the young woman's arm and reaches for the door again. "Even junkies loved my son, baby—he was so well liked by everyone. Wes was such a good kid. We were very close." Todd? That's my pops that's looking at my mother like he doesn't know her? I wish he'd turn his ass around and walk into the church. Maybe I am fortunate that I don't have to deal with my dysfunctional family anymore.

Oh, so now Vikki is finally realizing how far down she's gone, and how low she's stooped on the steps of the house of the Lord. She leaves the steps and begins to walk down the road toward the highway crying the most soul-stirring tears of guilt—the kind of tears that I know will never dry.

"I'm sorry I allowed you to endure sexual abuse, just to get a hit, among other things, Wes. I did so much shit to you and Malik, and now I can't make my wrongs right. Son, I never should've allowed what your father did pull me down into the gutter and wreck my life—wreck you and your brother's life. That's how it all started—the drug use and prostitution, I mean. I was forced into a corner and didn't know which way to turn, so I turned to tricking because my ego needed a little dose of the glamorous life with pimps and drug dealers with loot. If it's any consolation, none of it turned out to be so glamorous, after all. I contracted herpes for starters. After that came hepatitis from using dirty needles, and now I have full blown AIDS. I can't stop turning tricks for drugs—I'm still doing it. I live in a halfway house wishing I could turn back the hands of time, get to know my grandchildren, hug my two sons lovingly, and celebrate holidays with the twin boys that once loved me, but I can't. These days, my heart doesn't sing, all it does is ache with emptiness and darkness. Now that it's too late, I wish I'd never stepped into sin city when I was a young, pretty woman who didn't understand the responsibility of motherhood. What am I telling you all of this for? You can't hear me."

Oh yes I can mom—I mean Vikki. If I could answer I'd tell you that you deserve all of this heartache, and more. I hope you roast in hell when you kick the bucket. This shit should've happened to you, not me. Thanks for screwing up my life—your sob story means nothing to me because I know it's all hot fucking air.

$

"Hello everyone. I'm standing here before you because I would like to say a few words on behalf of the dearly departed. I know what I'm about to say is not the forum to do so, and that what I'm going to do will be quite unusual, but please pardon my actions. I feel as though there is no other effective way to proceed at this time as I'd like to clear Wes's name and let the entire community know the truth surrounding his death."

Does Marquita really know what happened to me—what's she doing? Her words captured everyone's attention. Whatever she's got to say has them hanging on to the edge of their seats. Just spill it, Marquita.

"Malik Montgomery, Wes's twin brother, received a distress call from Wes and didn't assist him. As a result he was killed by his captors—he did not die of a drug overdose, as was reported.

The police have done a full investigation and in collaboration with federal investigators, have broken up a major drug and gang ring. The offenders have been charged with murder and I'm sure you'll hear full details about the bust. Also, during the investigation the police discovered that Malik took out a large insurance policy on him, forging Wes's signature to get it."

Marquita takes a deep breath and continues, "The next part that I learned is what floored me." Marquita points to the front row where Malik is sitting, pretending to be shocked and hurt by her words. "That man over there, the one that I'm pointing to with the fake tears trickling out of his eyes, cut a deal with a stripper whose boyfriend was in the gang I spoke of. They conspired to kill Wes, and Malik agreed to pay her and her affiliates a portion of the insurance money. Wes was stuck with drug needles, roughed up, robbed and then shot in the back of the head. These facts came to light after she cut a deal to reduce the charges. Malik is a murderer! I am the mother of Wes's child, and this man—" Marquita's voice rises as she glares with hostility at Malik. "This man is trying to take away what should go to my child. As gruesome as it was, I insisted on having an open casket funeral so everyone can see how ruthless you can be. Malik, you're done— your goose is cooked. That's all I wish to say at this time."

Oh shit! Marquita is leaving the pulpit as tongues wag and mouths whisper. All heads turn toward the first row where Malik is sitting just a few feet from my casket. News cameras swing toward him as if expecting him to deny every word Marquita uttered. She busted Malik, then left the pulpit smooth as butter—that's good enough for his ass!

While all of this is going on a woman in the back rises to her feet. "No, I'm Wes's baby's momma. He put me up in an apartment and visited me on the regular. This is his son, Khalil. He and I are here to pay our respects to his father." She looks around the church. "Stand up, boy." The small boy stands up next to his mother and hugs her around her legs. "I may as well clear the air at this time. Wes never publicly recognized our child, and the only reason I didn't make a big deal out of it was because I didn't want to be humiliated by the media."

"I sympathize," said another woman who stood up in the middle of the church. "I have one on the way." She rubs her stomach, showing the round protrusion to the congregation. "My child is just as much his as any of yours. I just had a sonogram—it's a girl. This is my lawyer sitting next to me."

And just like that, the entire funeral service becomes chaotic as arguments begin to brew and boil over. I can't believe how many women that swore they'd keep their mouths shut for life over our dealings chose to speak up—greedy gold digging groupies! I guess a monthly check to shut up wasn't enough after all.

Money, the thing that is supposed to make life better, not only led to my demise, but has also managed to wreak havoc on the day when I should be resting in peace. As the scene unfolds below me, I can't help but wish that things had ended differently, just as Marquita said. I regret that I never sent her that letter that expressed my true feelings, all of those years ago—the one that said "Big Hugs and Big Kisses," with all the x's and o's drawn all over the bottom of the page. She would've liked that.

More importantly the letter held the words that told the story that I never told anyone—about the unresolved issues from my childhood and my fear of intimacy due to the sexual abuse and parental abandonment. It would have given her the clue that something wasn't quite right with me. I can remember the words of the letter as if I'd just written it.

—*I'm already more attached to you than I planned. If you work with me to nurture, build, and fortify our existing relationship there will be no boundaries in what can happen between us. You were there for me when I needed a friend the most, and now you are carrying my child. Marquita, I can't describe how much I miss you. I'm lying in bed, wishing and hoping that you could be at my side. I know this sounds crazy but I can't be weak and falling in love while I'm trying to make it into the NBA. I want you and my basketball career, but I can't have you at the same time as I'm reaching for it. I know you're good for me but maybe I'm just not ready to admit you're the one. If anything should ever happen to me please tell our child that daddy wasn't the best at communicating how he feels because he simply didn't know how. I've never told anyone this, but I was sexually abused by a man and that experience seemed to change everything. I just want you to know that my not coming back had nothing to do with you, but rather with me not being able to face myself. In a perfect world my mother would've been half of the mother you'll be to the baby, but it's not a perfect world. I don't think I'll ever be who I really am because I just can't seem to conquer this whole thing. Do me a favor and be both the mother and father to the baby because I doubt I'll ever be able to do my part. But if someday that should change maybe, just maybe, I'll have you as my wife. Since I can't be a part of the solution I'll stay away from you both because I'd be wrong to do a half-ass job in owning up to my responsibilities. I've seen that too much in the hood and I'd rather leave you and the baby everything in my will. When I'm gone you two will be well taken care of. I hope that counts for something although I know it's hardly enough. Set up a foundation for underprivileged kids or do something to give back to the hip-hop generation. I love my people and I love all people. Marquita, I know this is all hypothetical, and I may be dumping a lot in your lap, but I know you have a permanent interest in me, and I have one in you and my child. I trust you in life, and if fate calls me, even in death. I'm not saying that I want my time to be cut short but in case it is, do me proud, momma. Wes.*

46

COME AS YOU ARE

Jalita

Seth insisted that I give myself some TLC, and he insisted on paying for it. Something told me he hated the cheap ghetto wig I was sporting with a passion. The part in the scalp wasn't even my natural color but he let me keep my dignity and never asked me what was up with the do. For starters he told me he had some business to take care of and that while he was on the Eastern Shore I'd get my hair done at a shop called Envisions. Although I was uneasy at being dropped off amongst women in a salon their topics of conversation made me chuckle, and I enjoyed myself as Ericka combed through my naturally curly hair. Since it had grown out quite a bit and it was hard for me to handle I asked her to perm it. She agreed to do so under one condition—that I take care of it like I should. I promised and said goodbye to my thick curly hair. Although it was my trademark I just didn't have time to fight the tangles as it lengthened and gained extreme fullness. By the time the hairdresser was finished making me over I looked so different without the wig I retired it to the trashcan and hoped for the best. When Seth picked me up he couldn't speak. He told me I looked liked a movie star and all of the ladies laughed. One of Ericka's clients came from under the hooded dryer just to get a good look at Seth and she gave me the thumbs up on the sly. He paid my bill, asked her to pick out some products to help me keep my wig up and we rolled out, saying goodbye to Ericka, Theresa, and Lani.

Now that my hair is hanging smooth and tamed, just below my shoulders, and I'm wearing a dress that Seth picked out for me from wherever he disappeared to, he and I are sitting in some elegant restaurant called Maestro in McClean, Viginia. I'm not sure why he's taken me way out here since we've already traveled a lot today, but I don't say anything and act appreciative. All he tells me is, "I've already ordered dessert because I hear it's so good."

When the waiter brings it to the table it's strewn with rose petals and looks too beautiful to eat. I'm confused because Seth may have eaten dinner but I didn't. I'm not sure why he felt that skipping an entrée was a good thing but I leave the old Jalita out of this and patiently wait to see where this is all going. Seth watches me try to cut the dessert with my fork but it won't budge. At this point I'm hot because my mouth is watering and I'll take a mouth full of sugar over air.

Out of the blue, Seth's words become as gentle as kisses in the rain. "Let's talk, Jalita," he says softly. "After we talk I'll feed it to you." He pauses, looking deeply into my eyes. "Love is a fragile thing," he begins. "All it takes is one wrong word, one wrong interpretation, one episode of not being able to forgive and it's gone forever. Somehow I've been able to look back and find the first time I saw you in my mind, the first time you touched my spirit. When I saw your face again it reminded me that I need you to love me. What you did to me last year was wrong. You tried to tear me down when I was the struggling Seth who didn't have two dimes to rub together. Even so, I'm not perfect either and I can finally see who you really are and where you were back then. You're stronger than you think and so am I." Seth pauses again, taking a moment to let me try and process what he just said. Unfortunately, I have no clue what the brother is getting at.

He continues, "Love changes things, and what I've discovered is that it's a destination of choice that all begins with self-love. I thought I couldn't forgive you for the way you treated me, but God showed me it's not my place to put limits on you, and your place if you really are changing for the better. Now that you've accepted God into your life you've found the missing piece of the puzzle. I hadn't lost hope that you would, but then again I was wondering if you could humble yourself and get on your knees to do it."

I sit there, listening to Seth's words, wanting to ask him what it all means, but I'm hypnotized by the tenderness of his voice.

"There are some things that I'm ready to share with you now, and at this point maybe you will be able to understand why I could read you so well in the beginning. When I was growing up the house I lived in was so cold I had to wear gloves inside during the winter. I had tacks in my shoes to hold the soles together, and I had to wear my father's clothes even though he was four sizes bigger than I was. Kids used to laugh at me because I had to wrap a belt around my waist to try to hold up the pants. When I was eleven I shined shoes, bagged groceries, and worked in a bar to help my mother pay the bills. I also paid for my own school clothes. I had one day off a week and what I was paid was very little since I was working illegally. It took me years not to care about what people said. I avoided people for so long because I was hurt. So I know all about hard times and rejection. Trust me, I do.

I am doing well financially and spiritually, but not emotionally. Just before the holiday, my mother passed away from a rare form of cancer called multiple myeloma. She was diagnosed with this the very day my first book came out and I had to make a choice to quit or keep things moving. Luckily I was able to take care of mom and jumpstart my book career. The only consolation is that before mom died she was able to see the seed she planted begin to grow. She was around when I got into my first book store, first distributor, and first radio interview. In fact, I couldn't have done any of this without her help.

While people were in the mall shopping for gifts, I was hunting for mom's funeral dress and jewelry. No one was close enough to me to go with me. That was hard and it hurt. Jalita, she was my best friend, and I can't believe she's gone. I know you told me you also lost your mother to cancer so maybe this will make sense, just a little. I still talk to my mom every day, and I choose to remember her before she changed. The day before she passed, I almost couldn't bear to look at her hooked up to an oxygen machine. She was so weak that all she could do was squeeze my hand to let me know she knew I was with her. I promised her that I would do my best in life and would continue working on my goals. We shared some private hurts that I won't get into, but from that hurt I've learned something.

Andrea Blackstone

I've been the glue that held things together for so many people for so long but now it's my turn to live. I really don't care what people think of me—if they like me or they don't, if they approve or disapprove of the way I run my life. In running my life my way I realize that my mother's love was what carried me through to this point. She is still with me in spirit, but she always wanted me to bond with someone who could respect and cherish me. Sadly, she didn't get to see me have children, or live to see me complete my second book, but I know she is watching, and I remember what she told me.

We often talked about you and she'd say, 'Seth, someone will get her too. She's young. Give her time if you think there's something there worth waiting for.' I think this was her way of telling me that as strong as I am I'm not an island and I shouldn't let go of the thought of you if my heart isn't ready to let go of you—despite my annulment with my former wife, and having a sour-first attempt at marriage. As scared as I am to become vulnerable again, because love does require a beautiful side of vulnerability, I may as well be the one to try and step up to the plate. Don't think I'm doing this because I'm grieving and I'm confused or lonely because I'll grieve for her until I join her someday—it's not about that."

When Seth pauses I say, "I'm so sorry for your loss, Seth. Really I am."

"Thank you, Jalita. After all this talking I've done, I need to ask you something."

"What is it?"

"Do you love me?"

"Yes, I love you Seth. Despite my past actions I can admit that now."

Seth slides the saucer across the table, gets on his knees, then takes hold of what I'd been trying to cut with a fork. Apparently it's a ring-bearing dessert, not an edible one. My jaw drops open when Seth takes the ring in his hand and asks, "Jalita La Shay Harrison, will you marry me?"

My heart beats so hard I feel like it's going to jump out of my chest. I stare at the engagement ring and stutter, "Wha, wha, what did you say? There's so much you don't know about me, Seth.

366

You don't know what you're saying. This is crazy. We've only seen each other this year just a few times. My life is a mess—there are still so many problems that I haven't worked out for myself. You have no idea what I'm in the middle of right now, and truthfully speaking, I don't have anything to offer you."

"I don't have false expectations—I'm well aware that you're that morning flower that still is waiting to bloom. Some people have long engagements and it works out but just because they do, it doesn't mean love at first sight doesn't have its place. I pray, follow my heart, and don't lie about what I find within it. You know I'm big on faith and I don't care what people think. If you could imagine us being a team, enlarge your vision. I don't want to be a middle-aged man looking back wishing that I wasn't a professional bachelor who only has one-night stands and trips out to a club or sports bar to look forward to. Friends nor anyone else can fill this void that I have. There's nothing out there in those streets I want. I need a queen I can put on the throne and show how love is supposed to be. I've done a lot of growing to get to this point and now I'm ready to be a husband to a woman I know has *plenty* to offer me if we're both wanting the same things."

"You really mean all of those things you just said, Seth?"

"I do and I'm willing to prove that I want to be there for you through thick and thin."

Before I can rethink everything I blurt out, "Yes, Seth. I'll marry you!"

My hand shakes so badly I can barely keep it still enough for Seth to slide the beautiful white diamond ring on the fourth finger of my left hand. To my surprise it's a perfect fit. Before I can think straight I grab his face and stick my tongue deep inside his mouth. He picks me up like I'm feather light and spins me around the room. The entire restaurant claps and congratulates us. After he puts me down I notice people wiping their eyes and smiling like they can really see how in love we are.

"Maestro is known for being a place to pop the question," he says. "I was hoping you didn't know that because I didn't want you to see it coming. I can be creative when I sit behind a PC but sometimes things like this sort of have me confused about what to do."

"You did a great job," I tell him. "I'll never forget this day. Of all the people in the world I never would've dreamed I would end up with you. Seth, you don't give up when you really want something, do you?"

"No, I never do. And somehow I always manage to earn exactly what I want. Right now, what I really want is you."

47

WHAT COMES AROUND GOES AROUND

Malik
Two months later...

As I'm sitting up with my elbows dug into my legs I'm thinking about that damn Marquita. Had it not been for Wes's baby momma, who I never knew existed in the first place, my celebrity status as an NFL player would have been renewed. Just after the insurance company investigated my claim for Wes's death, and I collected a death certificate from the funeral director, my number came up and I was supposed to return to playing ball—for real this time. I was ready and in shape. I signed on the line to fly out to a team on the West Coast, and the next thing I know I'm standing before a judge in shackles, facing conspiracy to commit murder and insurance fraud. I was accused of forging Wes's name on the insurance policy to have an insurable interest—whatever.

To add insult to injury, that negative press from the church fiasco put too many people on my tail. People started sending letters, got a hold of my new phone number, and started calling. Some even dug up my new email address and started demanding repayment for what was supposed to be free merchandise, so-called loans, and all sorts of unpaid shit that were really gifts. Plus, I thought I'd be enjoying getting my house back, with its peaceful wooded view, and ten-thousand square feet of living space; I should've been soaking in the Jacuzzi by now. Instead, some bastard bought my 1.85 million dollar mansion for eight thousand five hundred and fifty seven dollars—the cost of property taxes for the year! As soon as my baby's momma's house was built she moved into her new house, near Six Flags, and the fuckers on my legal team couldn't really explain how this fell through the cracks—they just told me it did. I was in the midst of initiating a malpractice suit over this when phase two of this drama began. The stupid bitch from the garage strip club decides to play dirty and tell all about our deal so she could get less time for the role she played in Wes's murder—not to mention some other things she was balled up in. It turns out her gang was the subject of an FBI investigation, and one of the so-called enforcers was really an undercover informant. But what kind of informant commits all types of fraud while working for the government? Man, the witness isn't even credible! I've been set up! There's no justice for black men. This is a prime example of racial discrimination. OJ is the cause of this—thanks for nothing, Orange Juice!

After my hearing I leave the courthouse through a back tunnel so I don't have to speak with reporters, but it really doesn't do much good. The Federal Bureau of Prisons didn't agree with the judge that I should be sent to a dormitory-like prison where white-collar criminals usually serve, so my jail to prison transition will begin in the morning. I'm not looking forward to serving ten years there. It can't be worse than here though. My first cellmate stabbed himself with a ball point pen to earn a few days in the hospital so he could enjoy a T.V. that works. I say if you're going to do something that drastic at least wait until it's time for air conditioning and desperation has really set in.

The first time I went to jail, it was nothing like this though. Here, knuckleheads get down and dirty in a heartbeat. I'm chained and led around with people who had hoped to get rehabilitated but those hopes dried up, and instead of being rehabilitated, they've turned into madmen. But who can blame them? Most people on the outside think that we have all kinds of privileges—we don't. Even dignity is denied. We can go to the yard, a twenty-five by twelve foot area with twenty foot walls, for one and a half hours a day. But when we do there's a video camera keeping an eye on us, and the only thing to do is walk around in circles because we don't have a basketball or anything to make it worth our time being there. Word is that where I'm going I'll start work at 7:30 and be paid fifteen cents an hour. I'll at least save up and buy a radio to listen to—I hope.

There was a waiting list to have a job but my celebrity status helped to pull a few strings, even if it doesn't seem like it. In a sense I guess that's good news. We've had no running water for three days and our toilets are full of shit. Me personally, I've been relieving myself in a bag that breakfast is served in to lessen the pile up, and my shit goes out with the trash. So much for chicken breasts and the food that I'm used to. Thanks to hell on earth I've lost forty pounds because I don't have money to order chips and Granola bars from the canteen. I refuse to eat green bologna, moldy white bread, and rotten oranges that are collected from neighborhood refuse clean-up campaigns. After finding a dead rat in my stew and hair in my potatoes, I claimed I was a vegetarian and am now at least able to get veggie burgers in place of the so-called-meat.

I'm still one bad, tough man though. Neither jail, nor prison will break my spirit. I won't be serving much of my sentence because I got wind of who I need to get next to, no pun intended. The case manager that's in charge of a supervised pretrial release program just may take a bribe I've stewed up in exchange for writing a favorable report. I'll work on the little whore as soon as I confirm she knows all of the people I'm told she does.

Ten years? Shit! I want to close my eyes and lay on the thin mattress of the single bunk but I feel the cock roaches walk on my body and begin to scratch myself before settling down. I don't sleep much, but I got tired of running my mouth to my new cellmate and have decided to cut him off since I'll be leaving anyway. He always asks me questions about NFL life, how it was fucking all of those women, and shit I used to get away with. It's getting old now because there's nothing I can get out of bragging to a man like him. It serves no purpose and everything I do is calculated. I tune out the creepy crawlers for the night and turn to lay down.

"I never liked you anyway, so this will be easy for me," he says.

"Man, have you lost your mind? Who are you talking to?" I ask him. He doesn't respond but suddenly I feel a bed sheet tied around my neck so tight I can barely breathe.

"Your little tie here is threaded through the drainage hole in the bunk," he whispers. "Call it a noose if you'd like. You've yapped and yapped and yapped like a bitch, now I'm going to make you into one and tell you all about me. You move and you'll hang yourself. It's all up to you 'cause I'm about to play hardball. If I were you I'd bend over and give it to me sunny side up."

I feel his penis enter my rectum. My eyes tear up as my butt hole feels an unfamiliar pressure. Within seconds my world changes and I've just been made a jailhouse bride. Why, I don't know, but I didn't see this one coming. After Butch removes his penis he quietly laughs in my ear. I can feel blood trickle down my legs and now I am officially a broken man.

"That was for Tameka Smith. Remember her? Well she's my cousin. The one you beat when you were playing ball in New Orleans. You got away with it. My favorite cousin was lying in a hospital bed with black eyes, a collapsed lung, and broken ribs because of you. The 911 tapes didn't do a thing to help her case because of who you were. You were able to concoct some phony alibi and turn everything around. Yeah, I remember. Butch has a memory like an elephant, and when I heard you were here I sent a message in a sandwich to someone that owed me a favor. We didn't end up cellmates by accident, and the correctional officers can't protect you from everything. They have no idea that a scumbag like you has an enemy inside of these walls. Well, surprise. Here I am and I've been waiting for this night ever since you started bragging, talking about your past—screwing over women, one of which was my eighteen-year-old cousin. Why didn't you just let her walk away? No, you couldn't do that after what she'd been told. I'm sure you recall her frantically yelling in the phone saying that someone wearing a wedding ring came down on her job starting shit and claiming you set up a life with Tameka on the side. When she showed up at the house you beat her within an inch of her life for asking if you were really married with two children, or if the anonymous woman was just one of the many shady whores you cheated with. Tameka was paralyzed from the neck down after she crashed her car trying to get away from you. She was driving to the hospital to get medical help—and what do you care? What do you care that she's disfigured for life and is confined to a motorized wheelchair? Well *I* care—I didn't believe in fairytales, until now. You won't be going to your next stop tomorrow. When sunrise comes and the correctional officer shines the flashlight on your face he'll find out that you committed suicide. You see, no one will suspect me of a thing. You'll be the eighth inmate this year that took this route and all I've got to say is you finally got your celebrity status, *overnight.*"

Just as I'm struggling to tell him I didn't mean to hurt his cousin, and to give her my deepest apologies, I feel a strong push forward and instantly, I begin to choke. My air supply is cut off and I begin to gag and shuffle my feet on the bunk. I try to stand but I can't manage to gain footing since I'm nearly on all fours. With no thoughts of real regret for any wrong I've done in life, I take my last breath—and that is the end of my story.

48

LIVING IT UP

Jalita
Two months later...

"Hi cuz. It's Jackie."

"Hi. What's up Jackie?"

"I just called to thank you for sending Myra that nice pink bike. She loves it, Jalita. And guess what else?"

"What?"

"Shawn took her out for a little ride around the block a few times. You know, with the training wheels attached so she can get used to having a real bike that doesn't require batteries. I was doing my usual thing, complaining at the back door off from the kitchen. I was yelling at Shawn because I noticed I was losing my little backyard to crab grass. All of the sudden Shawn let the bike go when he was putting it up and stumped his foot. When he did, his foot sunk down in the mud because it had been raining a few days before. He started hopping all around the yard and when he stopped he found a spot where he said he felt something under the dirt. Girl, he found a can with almost twenty thousand dollars in it!"

"For real? Now that's some news!"

"Yeah, twenty thousand dollars worth of news! Ain't that some shit? I invited some people over from the block to celebrate and have a party. We're having steak, fish, crab cakes, macaroni, collards, Tang, and Kool Aid! I feel like I'm going to bust, I've eaten so much. Myra, sweetie, don't try to pick up the baby. You could drop him, now stop. Yeah, so anyway, in the morning we're paying ahead on our mortgage. Shawn told me to catch up on my child support, and your newest cousin is getting a brand new crib because we're turning our room into a nursery and we're taking the kid's room. That boy Shawn, I mean my *husband*, can knock my gizzard over and go all night long as far as I'm concerned! What did I do to deserve his love?"

"Spare me the details, now—"

Jackie ignores my request. "I don't mind being in a small space by him because I love me some Shawn. Shawn, did I tell you how much I love you, baby! You're all right, boo—sweet like lemonade. Fine, too. I could put you on a stick and eat you up. I'm the luckiest woman in the world. Come on, let's shut this party down and make another baby."

I hear Shawn in the background. "Drop it like it's hot!" he says. I roll my eyes and shake my head over the pair.

Jackie tells me, "I've got to go—womanly duties call. Come visit soon, Jalita. Bye! Oh wait, Myra's tugging on my shirt. She's begging to say something. Hurry up, Myra."

In a sweet, angelic voice, Myra says, "Hi, Cousin Jalita. Thanks for the new bike, and thanks for helping us pay our bills with that money I saw you with last time you—"

"Shhh," I whisper into the phone. "That's our secret, Myra. Remember the bike?"

"Okay, okay," she says, half annoyed. "I don't spit on Mr. Shawn anymore because mommy says that's not so nice," she adds. "Uncle is in rehab and he's not allowed over here 'til he gets out and stops stealing from our house. Uh, I gotta go."

"Bye, Myra."

"Peace out!" she replies.

I know Shawn's little Brady Bunch won't get along forever but at least it's a start. I knew someone in that household would sniff out the money I left behind and thank goodness it wasn't the family crack head—the poor souls have been struggling so long. If only it could be like this every day for Shawn and his crew. I know that's wishful thinking. Besides, I have to get my butt in gear and prepare to tend to some unfinished business in my *husband's* life.

$

"It's ok, baby. I'm with you—you can do this. I'm right by your side," I tell Seth, holding his hand firmly.

"I haven't been to my mom's gravesite since the funeral. Man, I don't want to do this."

"Baby, I'm your wife and I want to meet my mother-in-law. Tell me where to stop the car."

"Right here, Jalita. Stop here." We get out of the car at a gravesite in Davidsonville, Maryland, and walk up a muddy hill where fresh graves are.

"Let's see. I think it's here. Yes, there's mom."

"Where's her headstone?"

"I haven't picked one out yet."

"Seth, I'm going to support you through this and you're going to make it."

"Thank you."

"Now go ahead—talk to her."

As tears stream down his face, I hear his voice begin to waiver. "Well, Mom. This is my wife, Jalita. I got her. She's a piece of work but this is my baby. We eloped in Vegas. That was her idea, not mine. At first I was set on having a ceremony and then I thought about it. Dad passed all of those years ago and now you. I'm sorry you didn't get to see it."

"Mrs. Culligan, I love your son. I understand I'm wearing a lovely ring that once belonged to you, and I'm truly honored. I will cherish the privilege always. I'm not a perfect girl, and I even tried to give it back after I started thinking about my past, but your son insisted that I keep it, and that you'd want me to have it. Instead of returning it he slid it back on my finger while telling me that it's a new day. Umm, let's see. I'm finding out that I love cooking for him, keeping the house straight, and letting him know that he's as tone deaf as I am when he calls himself singing R&B love songs in my ear. Seth often stays up until 2:00 a.m. writing, and every time I hear him open his office door in the wee hours of the morning, he quietly crawls into bed with me and I put my head on his chest. We fall asleep together like we've been bonded for long time. I hope me wiping his tears right now feels as good as the comfort I experience when he dries my tears during the night. For Seth tying loose ends involved coming here and introducing me to you, spiritually speaking. I've looked through a tall stack of photo albums, one by one, and Seth pointed out who was who. You were—I mean you are such a beautiful lady, inside and out. Thank you for raising such a fine man. What can I say—Seth is a blessing. He is the total package and I know how he got that way. I'm going to take as good care of him as he takes of me. It was a pleasure meeting you, *Mom*."

I hug Seth as tears continue to stream down his face. I rub my hands up and down his back and look at him tenderly. "I meant every word, baby. I'm going to give you back everything you deserve. I made the promise of fidelity and I'm going to live by it. You believed in me when I didn't believe in myself and now you've got a fan for life." I kiss my husband's lips. He kisses mine in return, then I tell him it's time to go. When we get in the car I hand Kleenex to Seth. "She's in a better place," I say.

"You're right. It's time to pick out a headstone for her. Thank you for helping me get the closure I needed to face this fear, Jalita."

To lighten the mood, I say, "Stop thanking me. When you find out all about my smart mouth you'll find out that I can't quickly change all of my ways."

"Somehow, I believe that. You're cussing less though."

"You noticed?"

"That's an understatement. I thought I was going to have to wash your mouth out with soap for a while there."

"All jokes aside, Seth. We should do something. I want to do something about your mother."

"What do you mean?"

"I never stopped to think that a man like you ever could feel hurt and wounded, but I've learned that men have feelings just like women do, and no one can beat the world, not even a strong man like you. Some situation will bring you to your knees and when it does all you can do is process the pain and prepare to stand again. You know I lost Kate, the woman who gave me up, to cancer. I see that so many people are affected by this disease. When you told me all about multiple myeloma and what it was like when your mom went through it I was thinking about this. I think you should publish an inspirational book or something to pay tribute to your mother and increase cancer awareness. You could make it different, give it a nice flavor—really hook it up and make this a personal mission. There's nothing stopping you. You self-published before you got picked up by a major publisher. If you don't get any bites, we can get it done."

"See, that's why I married you. I've been thinking of starting my own small publishing company—one that will deal with all things inspirational, from urban to non-fiction."

"It's about time I use my wit for something good. Great minds think alike."

"You've been scheduling my signings, maintaining my website, doing some other things to keep me on track, and I know you know this book business is no joke. I want you to be my editor, the one who accepts book submissions. Are you with me, baby?"

"All the way. I don't mind earning my keep. One thing though—"

"Hold on, baby. That's my cell." Seth puts his cell phone up to his ear. "Hello. Oh, hi Stacey. No, I can't go out to dinner. The last time we talked I told you I was getting married. So what, you say? One second. I'm going through a tunnel." Seth hands me the phone and says, "Would you do the honors?"

"Hello, Ms. Stacey. Jalita here. I'm pleased to inform your purposefully deaf butt that Seth is taken, and is now officially off the market. If you'd like to swing by and have dinner with my husband and I though that can be arranged, you dirty little bitch. Now what time will you be arriving, since you're hell bent on seeing my man again? Let's work out a time to make sure to save us all the embarrassment of you hearing me ride his magic stick like a cowgirl. When he smacks my ass, it shakes like jelly, and that really makes me scream his name. You know how newlyweds act, I'm sure." The line goes dead. We both laugh.

As tears of laughter come to my eyes, I begin halfway weaving down the country road. "Why'd you do that, Seth?"

In between Seth's fit of laughter, he answers, "Because you're rubbing off on me and I want the world to know that I'm proud to

378

be in love with my wife. Watch the Mercedes though, baby. I just paid for the thing."

"I've got skills. Calm down, baby boy. I can drive better than you can."

"When we get home, I hope you do prove what kind of skills you have. And I told you about cussing, girl. You can't go off on the phone like that when someone pisses you off if you're working."

"Look, I still have my cussing habit until God decides to take away my desire to indulge in expletives. She is a dirty little bitch. I was just telling the truth." I pause. "Now wait a minute—if I'm your employee now, I can sue you for sexual harassment," I say playfully.

"My money is our money, so go ahead and sue me baby," Seth says, squeezing my breasts through my coat, then kissing me several times on the neck.

"First I couldn't get you to do anything until we got married, and now I can't keep your hands off of me, you big fat freak! You've kept me up every night since," I joke.

"We're stuck with each other, so get used to me turning you out."

As I smile I think, who would've ever though that Seth and I would find our way back to each other and live life together? I was the one who said I'd give him some time the day pigs fly better than birds, and now I'm here thanking God for His grace and mercy while sending true love back my way. In love, I found hope, and in hope I found a reason to look forward to a future with the man of my dreams who already has begun to prove he loves me for better or worse.

Tomi still has to face a judge and I'm now the star witness since Wes was killed. I don't want to show up and go back down that road but Seth says I better have my face in the place or I'll be subpoenaed to testify. He'll be sitting in the courtroom, so I guess I'll be okay as long as the defense doesn't dig up my biggest skeleton regarding my blood relation to Wes. If they do maybe I'll revisit the old person I used to be and remind them that they know they've copped a feel on a cousin or distant relative when they had too much to drink at a family reunion. Don't get me started on people perpetrating. I do feel bad that Wes's life ended early and violently. I skipped the funeral because it truly would've short-circuited my nerves. I caught a clip of it on the boob tube and it was a certifiable hot mess. People are fighting over money before his estate is completely sorted out. Damn, the man's body isn't even cold yet. Have they no shame?

It wasn't fair for me not to share my latest drama with Seth, as far as my sexual experiences with Renee and Kyle. After coming clean about the rape and the lifestyle I got caught up in, Seth accompanied me to pick up my AIDS test results since there was no way for the tech at the hospital to get in touch with me. Thank God, the results were negative and this bit of news enabled me to fully desire to marry Seth and move forward with starting a new life with him. Since a full six months haven't passed, I will have to be retested in a few months. Until then, I will force Seth to use condoms, when he makes love to me, just in case. His willingness to possibly wed an HIV positive woman more than proved his love for me. He repeats how strong his faith is and insists that another clean test will soon prove that I'm healthy.

After that part was partially resolved, I discovered that I was afraid to stay in Baltimore and risk Clyde and the crew breaking up my chance to start life fresh. I went in the money and bought two tickets to Vegas and presented them to Seth when he got home that evening. I didn't explain why I wanted to elope but somehow he went with the flow and didn't interrupt with logic. We got married in Vegas and honeymooned there.

As far as Clyde, when I was in Vegas, to my surprise, I heard, "The government seized two homes, four SUVs, and illegal contraband from a New York resident that had ties to Maryland. Clyde Simmons and two members of his organization were shot in a raid that took place at Simmons' car dealership front. He was pronounced dead at the scene and the other man that was shot is not expected to survive." I turned off the television and shook my head, although I felt some bit of relief. Greedy Clyde will no longer be on my heels, and I'm sure his boys won't be after me now. I feel freedom in my choice to give my life over to God just in the nick of time, and I now enjoy living a clean lifestyle. When I heard the coast was clear, without explanation I told my husband that we could return to Baltimore. We ended up finding a spot about an hour from there where we could get a fresh start and Seth could write in peace. I won't tell you where because it's not a crime for me not to tell everything!

I don't know how or why, but in the end, a big-mouthed drama queen like me got my man and that's what matters the most. For once I'm not scheming to get mine, and I find myself wanting to help Seth and pull my weight instead of sticking out my hand seven days a week. I never thought I'd mellow out this much but I have. Hmmph, when you die you can't take money with you, but you can take love and that's what I've got to replace my mother's legacy of abandoning me in a welfare office. I'm living proof that anything is possible if you've got the faith that God can turn it all around. When I realized that, the layers of toxic buildup that had accumulated over the years was gone. Yesterday is something we have no control over, but tomorrow's a new day. And I've got a funny feeling that what God has for you, *no one* can take away.

Dear Readers,

Thank you for your support. I truly hope that you enjoyed the end of the gold digging saga and you had as much fun taking the journey with me as I did writing it. If you haven't read *Schemin'* yet, find a copy and check out part one of this story.☺ Some have already told me that Shawn and Jackie have enough drama for their own book. If you like them, let me know. I just may have my reasons for asking (wink). If you enjoyed this book, please spread the word and encourage other readers to give it a shot by purchasing their own copy, too. Hopefully, you enjoyed the messages inserted within the drama.

Ladies, I hope that happiness finds you and it remains always in your life. If you need some extra tips regarding which types of men that should be banned from your life, visit the website and look for the Loser Alert. There is much truth to be found in a joke. On a more positive note, you can take a trip to my cyber spot to learn more about my cover model and how you can manage to have his likeness hanging on your wall, or even framed! If you know someone in need of resources to become more committed to self-improvement and self-love, you can also find a partial list of a starting point, including real letters that were sent to me.

Gentlemen, we all know that there are some Seth Culligans out there, and if you are one, thank you for giving single ladies hope.

Finally, I value my readership and those interested in my current and future endeavors. You may also visit my website to keep abreast of new happenings, participate in the forum, or just swing by and sign my guest book. If you'd like to send me comments or questions, you may email or write to me at the appropriate address listed below.

In all things be blessed,
Andrea Blackstone

Dream Weaver Press
P.O. Box 3402
Annapolis, MD 21403
dreamweaverpress@aol.com

ABOUT THE AUTHOR

Andrea Blackstone was born in Long Island, New York, and moved to Annapolis, Maryland, at the age of two. She majored in English and minored in Spanish at Morgan State University. While attending Morgan, she received many recommendations to consider a career in writing and was the recipient of the Zora Neale Hurston Scholarship Award.

After a two-year stint in law school, she later changed her career path. While recovering from an illness, she earned an M.A. from St. John's College in Annapolis, Maryland, ahead of schedule and with honors. Afterward, Andrea became frustrated with her inability to find an entry-level job in her field and considered returning to law school.

Andrea found that she was happiest using her research and writing skills. Jotting down notes on restaurant napkins and scraps of paper became a habit she couldn't shake. One day she pondered over her predicament and emptied the contents of a box. In the box she found an old photograph of she and the late Alex Haley looking over her writing, taken during the eighties when Andrea was a shy high school student. She was reminded that her uncle complimented her work and offered encouraging words that Andrea should continue writing. Andrea felt that finding the keepsake was a sign that she should make an effort to do what her heart was telling her would bring her contentment. In 2003, she created Dream Weaver Press, in an attempt to realize her dream. Andrea's long-term goal is to use the written word to entertain while encouraging others to reach their maximum potential by overcoming obstacles to live a balanced, blissful life.

To date, Andrea has made various appearances and participated in many community service efforts. *Schemin': Confessions of a Gold Digger* was her first self-published novel. She is currently working on an inspirational book, in the memory of her late mother, and has also begun offering consulting services to those who dream of getting their words into print.

ORDER FORM

You may order *Short Changed* at www.dreamweaverpress.net, or use the form below.

Although you may order an autographed copy of *Schemin'* from the website listed above, please be advised that you may order a copy at a 20% discount from www.writersandpoets.com.

Our titles:

Schemin': Confessions of a Gold Digger- ISBN 0-746847-0-8 ($15.00)
Short Changed- ISBN 0-9746847-1-6 ($15.75)

Please mail money orders to:

Dream Weaver Press
ATTN: Andrea Blackstone
P.O. Box 3402
Annapolis, MD 21403

Please send me ____ copies of *Short Changed* @ $15.75 each. (Please add $2.00 for shipping and handling. No cash, checks, or C.O.D.s) Maryland residents, please add $.75 to allow for state sales tax.

Recipient's address:
Name _____

Address _____

City _____   State _____

Zip _____

Phone _____

Feel lifted. Get inspired. Capture your purpose.

Look out for our next title, which will be an inspirational book like none other. It will pick you up anytime you need to feel lifted. A portion of the proceeds of each book sold will be donated toward cancer research of multiple myeloma.